MW01381162

UFO

Steve Hanson vs the Flying Saucer

MATT ANDRUS

Book 1 of The Unexplained, Explained

All rights reserved, including without limitation the right to reproduce this book or any portion thereof in any form or by any means, whether electronic or mechanical, now known or hereinafter invented, without the express written permission of the author, except for the use of brief quotations in a book review.

This is a work of fiction. Names, characters, places, events, and incidents either are the product of the author's imagination or are used fictitiously. Any resemblance to actual persons, living or dead, businesses, companies, events, or locales is entirely coincidental.

Copyright © 2020 by Matt Andrus

Cover Art & Design by Jeff Brown Graphics
ISBN: 9798684949760

For Mom and Dad,
With Love

Steve Hanson vs the Flying Saucer

Book 1 of The Unexplained, Explained

"At the moment of attack, how will we, on an instant basis, distinguish hardware from phantom?"

Excerpt from CIA memorandum warning of the dangers of mass hysteria, dated August 19, 1952, in response to the UFO scare of Washington DC one month earlier.

During the summer of 1947, two short newspaper stories changed how we look at the universe-

East Oregonian, Pendleton, OR, June 25

Impossible! Maybe, But Seein' is Believin', Says Flier

Kenneth Arnold, with the fire control at Boise and who was flying in southern Washington yesterday afternoon in search of a missing marine plane, stopped here en route to Boise today with an unusual story-which he doesn't expect people to believe but which he declared was true.

He said he sighted nine saucer-like aircraft flying in formation at 3 p.m. yesterday, extremely bright-as if they were nickel plated-and flying at an immense rate of speed. He estimated they were at an altitude between 9,500 and 10,000 feet and clocked them from Mt. Rainier to Mt. Adams, arriving at the amazing speed of about 1200 miles an hour.

"It seemed impossible," he said, "but there it is-I must believe my eyes."

Copyright *East Oregonian,* used with permission

* * *

Press Release, Roswell Army Air Field, NM, July 8

The many rumors regarding the flying disc became a reality yesterday when the intelligence office of the 509th Bomb group of the Eighth Air Force, Roswell Army Air Field, was fortunate enough to gain possession of a disc through the cooperation of one of the local ranchers and the sheriff's office of Chaves County.

The flying object landed on a ranch near Roswell sometime last week. Not having phone facilities, the rancher stored the disc until such time as he was able to contact the sheriff's office, who in turn notified Maj. Jesse A. Marcel of the 509th Bomb Group Intelligence Office. Action was immediately taken and the disc was picked up at the rancher's home. It was inspected at the Roswell Army Air Field and subsequently loaned by Major Marcel to higher headquarters.

-and we are still feeling their influence to this day.

Part One

FLAP

Chapter 1

Portland, Oregon, Wednesday, 9:32 p.m. PDT
Present Day

"Trick . . . or treat?" Hanson said as the door opened, hoping his attempt at humor wouldn't fall flat.

A woman with a fake candle stood in front of him. It had a piece of plastic balanced on a wire that wobbled above a yellow LED, simulating a flickering flame. It cast weird shadows that danced across her face.

"It does feel like Halloween," she admitted, the corners of her mouth turning up into the barest hint of a smile.

Hanson took the smile as a small win, relieved that this moment wasn't a social misstep that he would remember for the rest of his life. He stepped into the darkened foyer.

"Sorry, I couldn't help myself," Hanson said. "It is spooky in here."

A huge man lurched out of the nearby shadows and into the woman's feeble light.

"Most haunted houses are," Calderone replied with satisfaction.

Hanson frowned at the self-declared ghost hunter now crowding him. Hanson had his doubts about spirits haunting the place, though the house looked the part. The home was two stories high with gables, exaggerated brackets, and even a tower topped with a cupola. Hanson guessed that during the day the place was beautiful with its new paint job. But now, at night, it looked like the setting for the old *Dark Shadows* soap opera.

The woman, a petite blonde, was holding the candle in her left hand, so she extended her right.

"Steve Hanson? Thank you for coming over. I'm Lily Garber."

Her hand was cold and clammy, even though the house was still warm from the previous hot August afternoon. Hanson felt uneasy also, as if some unseen presence was nearby. The hairs on his arms were standing up a bit, propped up by goosebumps.

Haunted or not, he had been hoping for that.

"Honey, who's this guy?"

A man was nearby in the living room, holding another fake candle. He was near the same age as the woman, so Hanson guessed he was her husband, Jake Garber. Though while she appeared nervous, his face was pale, as if he had just seen a ghost.

Cool.

"He's a skeptic, a non-believer," Calderone answered for everyone.

"I reached out to him this morning and asked him to come over," Lily added, looking at her husband and Calderone. "You have your expert, and I have mine."

Hanson winced at that. An expert was overstating things. He was an IT support employee at the head office of the local supermarket chain, Cosgroves. His skeptical blog, *The Unexplained, Explained*, was a hobby.

"He has a website, like me. Though it doesn't have much of an audience," Calderone sneered.

Hanson didn't argue the point. Calderone's blog, *The Unknown*, had a following that was ten times that of his. At sixty years of age, the ghost hunter was a decade older than Hanson. His beard and hair were snow-white. Hanson wondered if Calderone flaunted that as proof that he had seen a ghost sometime in his past.

Hanson had only seen head and shoulder photos of the ghost hunter. It surprised him that Joel Calderone was 6'4" and a three hundred pound giant, though he carried most of that weight around his waist.

Hanson was almost a half a foot shorter and had a slimmer physique. His dark hair was still thick and full, though it had a touch of grey. Bright green eyes, a clean-cut face, and a boyish grin made Hanson look like someone in his mid-forties.

Hanson walked over to Jake, holding out his hand to him.

"Your wife contacted me through my website's email," Hanson said. "She told me that you were having Calderone coming over to exorcise a ghost in your place. She asked me to join you and give my opinion."

Jake's hand was trembling. Something was terrifying him, but he also looked relieved that Hanson was present.

Safety in numbers.

"Lily doesn't believe in ghosts. She says it's all in my head," Jake said.

Hanson already knew this. In her email, Lily had laid out her alarm over her husband contacting a ghost hunter.

"I'm guessing it's more than that," Hanson said. "We'll know in a few minutes. When did it all start?"

Jake was eager to tell his story. "We moved in last December, but the hauntings began a month ago."

"We had no issues through the winter and spring," Lily continued. "But in July, Jake started seeing . . . them."

"Ghosts, phantoms, whatever you want to call them," Jake continued, glancing up the stairway. "They were following me. I'd sometimes catch them out of the corner of my eye. But whenever I turned toward them, they would dart away."

"Where did you see them most often?" Calderone asked.

"Upstairs, in the master bedroom," Jake answered. "And also in the basement."

"That makes sense," Calderone said, typing into his phone.

"Why's that," Lily asked.

"This place's background," Calderone answered. "It's posted on some haunted house websites. This building was constructed in 1905 by a shipping magnate, Vince McGowan. In 1911, authorities discovered him hanging upstairs in the master bedroom. Blood covered the sheets of the master bed and his four-year-old daughter's bed. The authorities never found the bodies of the wife and child. The theory is that McGowan sealed up the corpses in the building's foundations. That's why you see your spirits both upstairs and in the basement."

"I realize that Irvington district homes have long histories," Jake muttered. "But I wish we knew that before buying this place."

"What do we do now?" Lily asked, looking at Hanson.

"We take a look upstairs," Hanson answered. "Though we're not splitting up *Scooby-Doo* style," he added with a grin to reassure her.

He brought out a small but powerful penlight. Hanson held it out as he started up the stairs, half expecting them to creak. They didn't. The Garbers followed, and Calderone brought up the rear with his phone in hand.

It was dark upstairs also.

"Was turning off the lights your idea, Calderone?"

"Darkness is the medium to best experience ghosts, Hanson," Calderone answered, wheezing a bit as he climbed the stairs.

Hanson shook his head. A switch was nearby; he should reach over and flip the lights on.

But he didn't.

Calderone was only partly right about him. In his articles, he came across as a cynic of the paranormal. But back when he was younger, he used to believe it all. A part of him still did. If this was a real haunting, he wanted to experience it for himself.

They made the landing. There were several doors they could choose.

"The kid's rooms are on the right and left. The master bedroom is that door in the back," Lily said.

"Are the kids here asleep?" Hanson whispered.

"No, they are at my sister's place," Jake answered. "They've been there for a week."

"Do they see the ghosts?" Calderone asked.

"The kids and my wife 'feel' their presence sometimes, but only I see them," Jake answered, frustration in his voice.

They entered the master bedroom.

The hairs on Hanson's arms stood even straighter, and he felt a slight sense of foreboding. He focused the tight beam of his penlight into the room's corners, trying to chase away the shadows that clung there.

Calderone stepped forward. He was holding up his cell phone, and its screen glowed with a fluctuating bar graph.

"What's that?" Jake asked.

"I have a ghost hunting app," Calderone proclaimed. "It's on EMF mode, looking for electromagnetic pulses that ghosts put out. Even though we have everything turned off, it's picking up a signal."

Hanson listened with interest. For once, Calderone was on to something.

"There, do you see it?" Jake shrieked out, whirling towards a direction that Hanson's light wasn't pointed.

"What is it?" Calderone yelled, waving his phone.

"In the corner, I could see it better this time. A man was hanging by his neck from the ceiling," Jake whispered.

"It's okay, sweetheart," Lily said. She put a reassuring arm around her husband, though she was also pale.

Concern filled Hanson. Calderone's ghost story had the Garbers more terrified than he had realized. He needed to end this.

"Quick, we need to go down to the basement."

Everyone's eyes were wide with fear as they followed him down the stairs. On the main floor, they made their way to a kitchen with gleaming stainless steel appliances. Jake pointed to a narrow door in the back. Since no one else did, Hanson moved forward and opened it.

Old wooden steps descended into the darkness. The hairs on the back of Hanson's neck stood on end, as if some palpable evil lurked at the bottom.

Though he had been expecting it, the intense feeling of fear still surprised him. Not wanting to lessen the experience, Hanson ignored the light switch and plunged down the stairs with his flashlight held out.

What he saw surprised him. While the upstairs was modern, little had been done to improve the basement over the years. The floor was earthen, the walls stone and mortar. Massive, low- hanging beams held up the ceiling.

Stacked plastic crates dominated the room. Set against the north wall were a new furnace and fuse box. The air was cooler here. And though Hanson could see vents scattered across the room, the room still retained the smell of a freshly dug pit.

The Garbers were standing close to each other, both looking over their shoulders.

"Did they ever find out why he killed his family?" Jake asked, his voice quavering.

"Rumor had it that Captain McGowan came back from Peru with several shrunken heads," Calderone answered. Sweat was on his forehead, and he held his phone up in the air. "Even with their lips pinned shut, they still whispered to him, goading him to commit the worst crime imaginable. He hid the bodies down here."

Goosebumps again rose on Hanson's arms. It was now easy to see how the hidden body idea started. The mortared walls had an Edgar Allen Poe feel to them.

"But where—" Calderone mused, holding his phone up to his face.

"There," Jake shrieked, pointing behind them to the west. "I saw the mother and child. They passed into that wall."

"We need to get out of here," Lily wailed.

Calderone brought forth a cross from his backpack and called up a different screen on his phone.

"I'm going to perform an exorcism; this app has the words," he yelled. But he was shaking from fear also, and his phone slipped from his sweaty hands. With a crack, it fell to the ground and went dark. The ghost hunter dropped down on all fours to pick it up.

The Garbers moaned in terror.

Fear gripped Hanson also. He could now sense things moving about the edges of the room, reaching for him. When he turned toward them with his light, the phantoms would disappear back into the shadows.

"Calderone, you need to stop it with the ghost stories," Hanson shouted. "You're scaring the crap out of everybody." Hanson bumped into and toppled a trio of stacked plastic crates as he stumbled toward the fuse box. It had a master switch, a red-handled lever on the right side.

"What are you doing?" Calderone screamed from the floor.

"Exorcising these ghosts myself, once and for all," Hanson yelled back as he grasped the lever.

He pulled it down.

Chapter 2

The relief was instantaneous.

"The ghosts, they're gone," Jake said, panting as he looked around the room. "What happened?"

"I turned off the reason we were seeing ghosts," Hanson explained as he walked back to the center of the room. He held out a hand to help Calderone off the floor.

Everyone was looking at him with puzzlement on their faces.

"It's your attic fan," Hanson explained. "It was generating infrasound."

"Infrasound—what's that?" Lily asked.

"Sound beneath human hearing range," Hanson continued. He was at the west wall now, which had a vent near the floor. "Our hearing range is around 20Hz to 20,000Hz. Though we can't hear it, sound just below 20Hz causes unease and anxiety in people, some more than others. That's how animals sense an impending earthquake. They hear infrasound rumbling from deep in the ground before the earth shakes."

"But I saw them," Jake said.

"That's because what we have here is rare," Hanson said, speaking faster with excitement. He was examining a wire that ran along a beam and continued into the west wall. "Sound at 19Hz interacts with our eyeballs, causing them to vibrate. This leads to some people seeing grey blobs in the corner of their vision, and they think they see ghosts."

"But," Jake faltered a bit. "I swear it looked like a body was hanging in our bedroom a few minutes ago."

"The power of suggestion," Hanson said. "The mind sees what it expects to see. Calderone had you all worked up. In your stressed-out state, you filled in the gaps on your own."

"So you knew it was infrasound all along?" Lily asked.

"I suspected at first. Then I was almost sure when you told me this all started when the weather warmed up. Your attic fan must be on its own circuit with a thermostat. And I'm guessing it's toward the back of the house, above the master bedroom."

"That doesn't explain the basement ghosts," Calderone challenged.

"The Garbers' attic fan is a more elaborate setup," Hanson said, pointing to the vent near the floor. "There's a second fan right here that pulls up basement air to the attic to keep it even cooler in the summer. I'm guessing the fans are old, and nearing the end of their recommended life span. Generating infrasound must be a recent thing, a result of them wearing down."

They all went back upstairs, where it was still dark.

"Thank God there aren't any ghosts," Jake said. "Though I don't know what to do about the McGowan family buried in our basement."

"Don't worry about that either," Hanson said, scowling at Calderone. The ghost hunter was looking sheepish. "I knew of the McGowan story myself, so I went to the library and looked up news-paper articles from 1911 to confirm it. Vince McGowan didn't kill his family; he sold the place and relocated to San Francisco. There was a news story lamenting the loss of his business. From what I can tell, the McGowan murder-suicide story didn't start making the rounds until the 1970s. That's around the time when *The Amityville Horror* movie came out. Your home looks old and unique also, helping in keeping the haunted rumor alive."

Lily was looking around the kitchen. "Well, if we want to save the food in the fridge, I guess we have to turn the power back on."

"But not those fans, we'll keep them flipped off," Jake said. "Tomorrow, I'm calling contractors to swap them out."

"Mr. Hanson, thank you," Lily said, shaking his hand. "Is there anything we can do for you?"

"No. But Calderone can, since he's aware of my website. He knows how I always end my articles," Hanson said, turning toward the ghost hunter. Hanson made a show of clearing his throat before he spoke. "There are no such things as ghosts; it was infrasound, and that's . . . ."

"The unexplained, explained," Calderone finished, glaring at him.

* * *

Hanson let out a deep sigh as he pulled away from the Garber house, glad that it was over. Though he had lain to rest the Garbers' spirits, Hanson still had his ghosts to deal with.

Anxiety. It was a persistent pall that hung over him. Leaving his home was a challenge. When Lily Garber had contacted him, his first reaction was to decline her request for help.

But the chance for experiencing a haunting, real or not, was too good to pass up. Most of Hanson's blog was of him refuting information on the web. Experiencing something first hand didn't happen very often.

So, as usual, Hanson had quantified the upcoming gathering. It was going to be just the Garbers, and Calderone, who he knew of by reputation. On his social scale, it would be on the same level as that heart-racing moment when rehearsing what to say for roll call.

Here. Present. Check. Yes.

He could deal with that.

So Hanson put on his game face and showed up. That was the most challenging moment of this evening. Not the exploring of the haunted bedroom or basement.

It was knocking on the Garbers' front door.

Hanson turned the corner into his neighborhood. He was a few minutes away from home and on familiar streets. Good. He was feeling drained and needed to recharge.

He frowned and gripped the steering wheel tighter. He was looking at the negative side of things. Concentrate on the positives. No social faux pas that he would remember for the rest of his life had occurred, and his theories had prevailed.

Focusing on that, he hummed the theme song from *Ghostbusters* as he pulled onto his street.

He stopped his humming when he pulled up to his house. Parked in front of it was a dark SUV with a man sitting in the driver's seat. Another man was at his front door, ringing his door-bell. Hanson's cats, a Russian blue and a tabby, were gazing at the stranger from the front window.

Hanson parked in his driveway and stepped out of his van.

"Computer, lock doors."

The van's doors thumped in response. Hanson had most functions on the vehicle voice-activated.

The person at his door was staring at him. He was a Black man, and he was wearing a tailored suit with a dark blue tie. He stood a little taller than Hanson, and he was more solidly built. His hair was cut short and neatly trimmed, and his gaze was piercing. It felt like his eyes could strip away anyone's secrets. Intimidated, Hanson found himself looking away.

Bingo and Sebastian were now standing and leaning against the window. Their excited cries penetrated the glass as they looked toward Hanson.

"Steve Hanson?" the man asked, glancing at the cats.

"Yes," Hanson answered, now forcing himself to look back at the stranger at his door. "And you are?"

The man held up a bi-fold wallet. It contained a badge and an ID card.

"I'm Special Agent Daniel Fisher, of the FBI," he answered. "And I need your help."

Chapter 3

"I've been trying to reach you on your cell for the past few hours," Fisher added.

Hanson's hand went to his phone in his front pocket. He had it turned off, not wanting it to ring while searching for the restless dead.

"Sorry, Agent Fisher," Hanson said as he tried to switch his phone back on. Pressured by the FBI agent's intense stare, he fumbled with the buttons.

"The matter is urgent," Fisher said, frowning.

Flustered, Hanson looked toward his front door. All he needed was an excuse and a quick exit, and he would be out of this situation.

But his nerves conquered him. While meeting a few strangers was low on the anxious meter, people of authority buried the needle in the red. It had been a problem all his life—babysitters, teachers, drill sergeants, or the police. There was a reason Hanson drove under the speed limit. It wasn't only to be safe. He couldn't stand the thought of the police pulling him over.

So he gave Special Agent Dan Fisher of the FBI the only answer he was capable of giving.

"What do you need me to do?"

* * *

A half-hour later found Hanson in a helicopter. It had been waiting in a nearby high school football field. The FBI agent driving the SUV had dropped off him and Fisher.

Hanson looked out the window as they lifted off. Since he was still in familiar territory, he could pick out his house. He stared at it until it faded from view.

Fisher had only given him a few moments to feed the cats and put on some hiking boots and his dark blue fall jacket. It was going to be cooler where they were going.

Though where they were going and why was still a mystery. Fisher had told Hanson that he wanted him to have an open mind when he arrived.

It was only Hanson, Fisher, and the pilot in the helicopter. Everyone wore a headset, and Agent Fisher and the pilot were talking shop. From what he overheard, Hanson guessed that Fisher was based in the FBI field office near the airport. The FBI pilot had flown up from California to lend aid to the investigation.

For the moment, they were ignoring Hanson. That suited him. He stared out of his window at the city lights. They were going north, and soon the dark ribbon of the Columbia River passed below them. After a few minutes, the views of Vancouver receded also.

A waxing moon had already risen, but it wasn't enough to illuminate the forested landscape. Hanson looked ahead at the next landmark under the night sky.

The glowing summit of Mount St. Helens.

The volcano had shaken itself awake a few months ago, and steam had risen from the glacier covering the crater's floor. Then several lava domes appeared, one to the north and one to the south.

The heat from this new activity caused the small glacier to break apart and slide down slope. That event revealed a fissure-laced crater, in the depths of which magma could be seen. Earthquakes occurred with regularity, and the Toutle River reached dangerous levels from the snow melt.

The Pacific Northwest took notice. After lessons learned from the 1980 eruption, officials activated emergency plans. Hospital patients in Eastern Washington relocated to the Puget Sound area and Oregon. Military bases shuffled war planes to protect their engines from the destructive ash. Airlines were diverting commercial flights from Portland and Seattle. The precautions had a sense of urgency because the United States Geological Survey's spokesperson for their Volcano Hazards Program, a volcanologist visiting from Iceland, Kristofer Steinsson, had recently made a bold announcement.

The USGS team knew when, to the day, Mount St. Helens was going to erupt.

Tuesday of next week.

Six days from now.

The nation had responded with disbelief. Steinsson, experienced with his own country's volcanoes, explained to the public. The mountain's past four decades were well-known and documented. Modern observation equipment dotted its slopes and crater. A powerful computer was crunching the numbers and running simulations. Mount St. Helens was the most studied volcano of all time, and it now had the best minds of volcanology focused on it.

"To your left," the pilot announced.

Hanson pressed against his window. The helicopter was nearing the mountain. Below him, he could see glowing red fissures in the crater. Hanson snapped a few photographs from his cell phone, wishing he had brought a better camera. This was something one didn't see every day. Six miles north, he could make out the parking lot of the Johnston Observatory. Though closed, the volcano tourist center still had power running to exterior lights.

Hanson switched to his Mount St. Helens app. The USGS had

designed it. With it, users could call up monitoring cameras, seismographs, and lava dome size increases to the centimeter. It even had animations of the magma chamber. Computers updated it by the minute. So far, it was proving to be the most popular new app of the year.

It had an oversized countdown timer on its front page. Hanson looked at it to reassure himself.

Six days.

"There, to our right," Fisher said into his mic, pointing for the pilot. "Make for those two lights."

The helicopter banked toward them. Mount St. Helens receded a bit, though not far enough for Hanson's peace of mind. They were landing on a dry river-bed that was lit by two sets of portable lights powered by diesel generators. Parked on a nearby road were several SUVs.

They were somewhere on the mountain's eastern shoulder.

So Hanson knew why he was here.

* * *

"Did someone shoot Bigfoot?" Hanson asked.

He and Fisher were now bouncing along a rutted Forest Service road. Only the SUV's headlights illuminated their way.

Fisher glanced at him. "What makes you say that?"

"Have you ever visited Mount St. Helens before?"

"Last year," Fisher answered. "My wife and I took the trip to the Johnston Observatory."

"Didn't you ever wonder about all the signs advertising Sasquatch souvenirs? Or that huge Bigfoot statue on the drive up the mountain?"

Fisher shrugged. "I posed for a photograph next to it. I figured that's something you would see in any forested recreational area."

"It means more here. We're on the eastern slope of the mountain.

This area is the location of our region's most famous Bigfoot encounter. Ever hear of it?"

"Enlighten me."

"We're near Ape Canyon. Back in July of 1924, five prospectors spent their nights in a roughly built cabin to guard their claim."

"And what, they saw Bigfoot?" Fisher asked, disbelief in his voice.

"It was more than that. They killed one. During their stay they felt that something was watching. At some points they even caught glimpses of large, shaggy figures shadowing them. One of these encounters came to a head when they shot a creature at the edge of a cliff. It tumbled into a steep gorge and the stream below swept it away.

"Thinking it was over, the miners retired for the evening. But as they prepared for bed, they heard strange whistles and calls. It scared them, but the noise soon abated, and the men fell asleep. They woke up later when something began pounding against the cabin's wall.

"Then the assault began in earnest. The men would later tell reporters that a half-dozen tall, hairy ape-like men laid siege to the cabin. They hurled rocks against it, and their massive bodies crashed into the door. The miners heard them on the roof. The frightened men emptied their guns into the dark. That would deter the creatures for a bit, but they maintained the attack all night long."

"How did it end?"

"The ape-men—"

"Now hold on," Fisher said, holding up his hand. "You keep using the term ape-men. Why not Sasquatch, or Bigfoot?"

"Because this happened in 1924. The terms Sasquatch and Bigfoot weren't in use yet."

Fisher looked interested at that.

"At dawn, the ape-men retreated. The miners packed up and also bugged out of there, and told their fantastic story to reporters."

"But, unfortunately, since the stream washed away the one they had shot, they had no body, no proof."

"Correct."

"Do you believe that story?"

Hanson took a moment to answer. He used to consider it gospel.

"No."

Hanson looked forward. They were approaching another cluster of lights illuminating parked vehicles. Besides the FBI, Hanson picked out several SUVs from the Sheriff's Department and Fish and Wildlife. There were even two trucks from the United States Geological Survey. One of them had yellow tape around it.

Fisher came to a stop. "Remember, I'm going to need you to keep an open mind. If anyone asks, you're with me."

They stepped out, and Hanson zipped up his jacket. He looked west toward the mountain, once again trying to gauge its activity. Bigfoot or not, it still commanded his attention.

There was another patch of light about fifty yards up a tree-covered slope. Both men broke out their flashlights and made their way toward it.

About halfway there, they came upon a small area roped off by more yellow police tape. It protected four long patches of white on the ground. Hanson shone his light on them.

"Jesus Christ."

They were plaster casts of footprints, still drying in the night air. Left by each one were small, numbered markers. Hanson guessed each print was about twenty inches long.

"First time?" Fisher asked.

"Yeah," Hanson answered. "I've seen pictures, video, but nothing like this." He dragged his phone from his pocket.

Fisher put a hand on his arm. "I'm going to ask you to take no photographs," Fisher commanded. "What you are going to see next is sensitive."

Authority figure. Anxiety. Hanson nodded and put the phone away.

They walked the final twenty-five yards and broke into the next clearing. Hanson's heart was beating fast, and he tried to prepare himself mentally. Bigfoot! Years of skepticism proven wrong. Though there was a part of him that was sad. Judging by the activity, this was more than a movie clip. The poor creature must be dead.

The area was well lit, and Hanson saw the real reason why everyone was all worked up.

The clearing was about thirty feet in diameter, anchored on its west side by a large pine tree.

Impaled to the tree was a man.

Something had violently forced the victim against a broken branch. The jagged point of the limb stuck out about a foot from the victim's chest. His feet dangled six inches off the ground. Hanson couldn't see the man's face, only the top of his head since it hung down with the chin against the chest.

Law enforcement personnel and forensic technicians crowded the area. Dogs bayed in the distance, and diesel generators maintained a constant hum. Mixed with the generator's exhaust was a musky, foul animal odor. Hanson and Fisher made their way forward. Plaster casts littered the ground, and Hanson took care where he stepped. Two of the large prints were right in front of the corpse.

A woman who Hanson guessed to be the medical examiner was standing on a stepladder near the body. She turned and looked at Fisher, and he nodded to her. She dismounted and moved the ladder so the two men could get in closer and look up into the dead man's face. Hanson recognized it.

Kristofer Steinsson.

Now Hanson understood the gravity of the situation. Something had killed the USGS's spokesperson in the shadow of the volcano he had announced would erupt within the week.

And the prime suspect was Bigfoot.

Chapter 4

Hanson stepped away from the corpse. He had seen death before, in Kuwait, but a man impaled on a tree was the most gruesome thing he had ever experienced.

"When did they find the body?" Hanson asked.

"Around 14:00 hours," Fisher answered. "Steinsson was out here this morning checking up on a seismometer, a personal setup he had created. When he didn't check in, a coworker came out to look for him and found this."

"Who was the first to respond?"

"A few game wardens," Fisher said. "They were closest. Sheriff Hart arrived a short while later."

Hanson glanced over to where Fisher was looking. A short, wiry man in a sheriff's uniform was talking on his radio, looking toward the path Fisher and Hanson had used.

"How did you get involved?"

"We don't have an *X-Files* department, if that's what you're getting at," Fishier answered, glaring. "Steinsson was a big deal in Iceland, and even had political connections. Reykjavik has been in contact with the White House. Even though this is Hart's case, the

President herself wants the FBI to help, and bring a quick resolution to this case."

Hanson wasn't surprised by that. President Hayes had taken a keen interest in the volcano when it began to stir. Her office had screwed up with its handling of a hurricane making landfall in Florida last year. And though a vaccine had been found, last year's COVID pandemic had worked against her also. She was hoping to make up ground in opinion polls with a strong response to Mount St. Helens.

"I get the FBI being here, then, but we're north of the Columbia. How is it Oregon agents are leading the charge?" Hanson asked.

"Proximity," Fisher answered. "Vancouver has a few resident agents, but Portland is home to a large regional office, a state-of-the-art facility completed less than a decade ago."

Fisher was turning his head as he talked, his eyes picking out the people he was referencing.

"We're in Skamania County," he continued. "An area whose population is low enough that death investigations are done by a county prosecutor acting as a coroner. I called in the Clark County medical examiner instead. I also brought in an FBI Evidence Response Team."

That explained the crowded meadow. Hanson gazed around the perimeter. Deputies stood guard with rifles, eyes wide, as if they expected Bigfoot to pop out of the brush at any moment. Dogs strained against leashes held by the game wardens tasked with tracking Bigfoot. The dogs looked reluctant to leave the clearing.

The forensics team was busy with the crime scene itself, and the medical examiner was still tending to the body. The area was a hive of activity.

Except for one woman.

She was sitting on a log on the north side of the clearing. She wore a light blue jacket with an ID badge clipped to it. She had long, straight dark hair and a deep tan, and looked to be in her mid-forties. Her lips were full, and her eyes were almond-shaped. Hanson liked the way her hair framed her face, and he paused to stare at her a bit. She turned his way and looked straight back at him.

Caught, Hanson's face reddened, and he looked away, pretending that he was listening to Fisher talking.

"As you can guess, this thing is a jurisdictional nightmare. Hart doesn't want us here, and the Wildlife guys are wondering if it should be their case since they think Bigfoot is an animal."

Hanson shook his head. That was nuts, but he wasn't surprised. Due to the Ape Canyon attack a century ago, Bigfoot lore was prevalent in the area. It wouldn't take much to convince anyone that worked on this mountain that Bigfoot had something to do with the day's events.

Hanson returned his gaze to the geologist's corpse.

"It's been ten hours since someone discovered Steinsson. Why hasn't anyone taken him down?"

"Several reasons," Fisher answered. "As you know, the Governor issued an evacuation notice in the volcano's immediate area. We're in that 'Red Zone' right now, and we shouldn't be here. So we're taking our time, making sure we don't miss anything. Because in a few days, a thick layer of ash will cover this clearing. None of us will have the luxury of returning to the scene of the crime."

Again, Hanson cast an apprehensive glance up at the faint red glow from the crater above them.

Fisher was looking at the path on the clearing's east side. "The other reason is that we were waiting for him."

A mountain of a man stepped into the light, looking to be around six-and-a-half feet tall. He had a full beard and mustache. If he hadn't been wearing glasses, Hanson would have thought he looked like Grizzly Adams.

"His name is Kevin Nesbitt; he's a local cryptozoologist," Fisher continued. "Though I'm still not sure how one becomes a cryptozoologist."

"There are no governing bodies handing out degrees," Hanson answered. "All you have to do is self-proclaim yourself an expert on cryptids; animals that people claim to exist, but that are not proven to exist."

"Sheriff Hart told me he knew him and was going to send for him," Fisher said. "I looked Nesbitt up. He even had a television series, *The Search for Bigfoot*. Things looked to be getting out of hand. It felt like everyone knew each other around here, and I was getting outnumbered—"

"So you looked up skeptics, and you found me," Hanson finished. Like Lily Garber, Fisher had gone searching for an expert of his own.

"It was either get you or watch twelve episodes of *The Search for Bigfoot* to get myself up to speed. It was going to take Nesbitt around three hours to get here. I made a helicopter run to Portland to look for you."

"You're lucky that you did. I've seen the show—well, fast-forwarded through it. The bulk of the series is Nesbitt pouring plaster into footprints and reminiscing about an encounter two decades ago. Episode nine is exciting, though. Nesbitt finds a supposed pile of Bigfoot feces near Mount Shasta."

Fisher's cheeks bulged as he blew out a breath of air, relieved that he didn't have to binge-watch the series.

Nearby, Nesbitt's eyes and mouth were wide open with awe.

He stepped into the clearing, studying the footprints on the ground. He smelled the air and cocked an ear toward the whimpering dogs. He gazed at the body on the tree for a moment. He then turned toward Sheriff Hart.

"Jim, this had to be a misunderstanding," he said, pointing at the corpse.

That statement surprised Hanson. Was this guy going to see the situation for the fraud it was?

"Bigfoot is a creature that avoids contact with humans," Nesbitt continued. "This geologist must have done something terrible to provoke him."

Jesus, thought Hanson, shaking his head.

"Kevin, I need you to calm down a moment," Hart said, stepping toward his friend. "For now, treat this area as a normal crime scene. Tell us what you see."

Nesbitt pointed at the ground. "Look at these prints, not only for their size but their gait. Bigfoot puts one foot in front of the other when he walks, as if balancing on a tightrope."

Hanson looked down. It was true. Most of the prints were in a straight line, even the ones approaching the tree.

"But then, he meets up with our victim here," Nesbitt continued, waving his arms. Hanson could tell Nesbitt was in his element now, and he was relishing his moment on stage. "Was this guy somehow threatening him? Whatever it was, Bigfoot must have grabbed him by his sides . . ." Nesbitt paused to mime the action. He held out his hands as if grabbing something and thrusted violently forward. "And pinned him to this tree."

Hanson glanced at the woman sitting on the log. She winced as Nesbitt described the murder.

Nesbitt turned toward Sheriff Hart again. "Were there any hairs found on this man's clothes?"

"Yes," the sheriff answered.

"And how about on the bark of any of these trees, or the branches of nearby bushes?" Nesbitt continued, gesturing around him. "Bigfoots have a wide build. They usually brushes up against something."

"We've found some of that also," Hart answered. "Large clumps. The FBI's lab is going to analyze it."

"Good. And forget about those dogs," Nesbitt said. "Bigfoot gives off an off-putting stench, much like their cousins, the Skunk Apes of Florida. So they aren't going to be of much—"

"Please."

Surprised, the men turned around.

The woman had approached them. Up close, Hanson could see she was almost as tall as he was.

"Please, you can't believe that some sort of creature did this," she continued.

Nesbitt faltered a bit. "I'm sorry, but who are you?"

Fisher stepped forward. "This is Doctor Makani Bateman of the USGS. She is over here from Hawaii, helping out the Mount St. Helens team. She's the one who discovered the body."

"Kris was a good friend," Bateman continued, looking at Nesbitt. "And I can't believe that some mythological monster did this to him."

"Bigfoot, or Sasquatch, as it was earlier known, is more than a myth, Doctor," Nesbitt stated. "His existence has been orally handed down for centuries by the indigenous people of the entire North American continent. Explorers have detected him ever since they arrived. A hundred years ago, local miners battled them only a few miles from here. Decades later, William Roe saw a female Sasquatch up close. Ever since, there have been thousands of sightings.

"Large footprints were found in Northern California in the fifties. And now, there are hundreds of plaster casts like these." Nesbitt pointed to the ground around him. "And in 1967, Roger Patterson filmed one."

Bateman was shaking her head. "I've heard that footage was a hoax."

"No one has proved that," Nesbitt countered. "Every professional imaginable has studied that film. Zoologists, biologists, film experts, special effect wizards, and costume designers. For everyone who says it's a hoax, there's someone who says it's real."

"But—" she began.

"I'm sorry for your friend, Doctor; I truly am," Nesbitt said. "But, more than fifty years later, the Patterson film still holds up. Sasquatch, or Bigfoot as we call him here in the states, is real, and set in stone."

Nesbitt turned away to look for more signs of Bigfoot. Bateman remained quiet. Hanson could tell she was distraught about something more than the murder itself. If word got out that the FBI even entertained the idea Steinsson died at the hands of Bigfoot, then everything about her friend's life would be a joke. Hanson could picture social media blowing up tomorrow with humorous memes.

Steinsson's legacy would be boiled down to a tragic but laughable moment. Remembered forever by the unforgiving internet.

It was in Hanson's nature to remain quiet, to disappear into the background of any given social situation. But the look of distress on her face got the best of him, so he stepped forward.

"Actually, Nesbitt, you're wrong," Hanson said.

Chapter 5

"This is Steve Hanson, I asked him to join us," Fisher explained.

"Is he part of your forensics team?" Sheriff Hart asked. He was looking at Hanson's chest for an ID badge.

Nesbitt spoke up. "He's a blogger. His website is *The Unexplained, Explained.*"

"You follow my blog?" Hanson asked, surprised.

"I glanced at it. I did a search on my name one day. I found that you mentioned me on your website," Nesbitt answered, his eyes narrowing.

Hanson could understand the Bigfoot hunter's attitude. The article had been critical of him.

"Well, since the rest of you haven't been to my website, I will explain the real history of Bigfoot, or Sasquatch," Hanson said. He took a slow breath to steady himself. Nesbitt might like an audience, but Hanson didn't. The situation was a bit overwhelming.

"Sasquatch being a part of Native American lore across the entire continent for the past several centuries isn't true. There was nothing named Sasquatch in their stories.

"But they did have tales of creatures of the wilds. And in some regions, these creatures were violent, fierce giants that hunted and ate humans. Most cultures have these same stories. Europe had hags that drowned children if they strolled too close to the water's edge. Further north, Norway had trolls that lurked in the forests. These were scary tales told to children so that they wouldn't wander off and do something stupid on their own, like playing on the edge of a fast moving river, or getting lost in the woods. We still come up with these cautionary stories to this day, only we call them urban legends. And our monsters are maniacs with hooks in place of hands, making sure teenagers don't go too far in the back of their cars."

"What about this area?" Fisher asked.

"Around here were creatures known as the *Skookum*," Hanson answered. "Fur-covered giants that were dangerous and cannibalistic. They laired on the peak of Mount St. Helens."

Everyone looked up at the glowing red crater.

"One of the earliest modern encounters with these supposed creatures was a century ago. The miners that clashed with them called them 'hairy devils'. Another label was the 'Ape-men of Ape Canyon'. Similar to Bigfoot as we know it, but different. The miners described them as having large, upward pointing triangular ears."

"Where did the word Sasquatch originate from?" Bateman asked.

While Nesbitt and Sheriff Hart looked annoyed, she was leaning in, interest on her face. It emboldened Hanson.

"A hundred years ago, up in British Columbia, a school teacher and Indian agent named J. W. Burns was hearing stories of giant, hairy men from the First Nation people he was living with, the Sts 'Ailes. He coined a word for them, Sasquatch, an anglicization of the local name for the creatures."

"So Sasquatch is an English term?" Hart asked, looking to Nesbitt. The Bigfoot hunter remained quiet.

"And that's not all," Hanson continued. "On April 1st, 1929, Burns's findings were printed in a magazine article. His many interviews of the Sts'Ailes interacting with Sasquatch revealed that it wasn't a creature they were dealing with, but 'wild men'. Men that were unnaturally tall and hairy, but still men. They spoke the local language and lived in remote areas. There's even a story of a female Sasquatch encounter. She was tall and strong, but not covered in thick hair. After Burns's article came out, everyone's idea of Sasquatch was that of wild men that kept to themselves in Western Canada."

"Then how did Sasquatch become the creature depicted in movies and beef jerky commercials?" Fisher asked.

"For that, we return to British Columbia, but now in the late 1950s. A highway worker named William Roe sent out a written statement to cryptozoologists. He had an encounter in which he spotted a creature in a remote clearing. Ducking behind a bush, he observed the thing at length.

"What he described is what we are all now familiar with. A giant and bestial humanoid covered in hair. The shoulders were broad, and the neck thick and short. It had a sloped forehead, and the hands hung to the knees. And it walked upright with a strange, 'heel down first' gait. Roe also noticed that the creature had breasts. It was a female. But he made no mention of the feet. Even now, 'Bigfoot' as a term didn't exist."

"Roe must have been famous and sought after when that came out," Fisher said.

"He wasn't," Hanson said. "Roe was never interviewed."

"So you're telling me Sasquatch as we know it comes second-hand from a letter from a man that we know little about?" Fisher asked incredulously.

Everyone looked at Nesbitt. He shrugged.

"It wasn't a letter. It was an affidavit," Nesbitt grumbled.

Nearby, the medical examiner team was approaching Steinsson's body. Two of them were standing on each side of the corpse, ready to lift him off of the branch. A third was at the feet. A gurney was nearby to receive the body.

Witnessing the transfer would be a troublesome sight for a friend of the victim. Hanson moved a few steps over, forcing Doctor

Bateman to turn her back to the crime scene. Hanson continued with his lecture to hold her attention.

"A year later, in Northern California, the story of Sasquatch evolved even more. The highway near Bluff Creek was being repaired. One morning, workers found large humanlike footprints around the area. Newspapers came up with a name for the creature that made them. While Canada had its Sasquatch, America now had Bigfoot."

"Where were all these tracks coming from?" Fisher asked.

"Raymond Wallace owned the construction company," Hanson answered. "In 2002, after Wallace passed away, the world received the whole story. His family came forward and presented to the media a set of large, plywood 'shoes' cut in the shape of feet. They said that Wallace was a jokester and that the footprints were a hoax, his idea of a prank."

"Maybe the later ones," Nesbitt interrupted. "But not the first prints. They don't match the plywood feet."

"The family also said that there were several sets of fake feet," Hanson countered, rolling his eyes. "But I won't let you muddy up the issue any longer. Let's move on to the centerpiece of this story, the Patterson film."

"Talking about that won't do you any good, Hanson," Nesbitt said, a smile back on his face. "As I said before, many experts have studied the footage. It still stands."

"You're right about the many experts part. It's up there with the Zapruder film of the Kennedy assassination, so I won't add to that. Instead, I will focus on the circumstances."

Hanson brought out his phone to call up the film. His eyebrows knit with confusion when he saw no bars on the screen.

"No signal up here," he said.

"We have a hotspot from a satellite set up," Fisher said, gesturing to a nearby forensic tech. Fisher borrowed the man's tablet. Soon, he had the Bigfoot film called up from the web. Everyone gathered around to watch it.

It was a good distraction. Hanson glanced at the tree. People were placing Steinsson on the gurney; his chin still rested on his chest.

Fisher started the video.

For Hanson, it was a familiar sequence, a grainy film of a dry river-bed where fallen timber littered the ground.

Then Bigfoot entered the scene, stage left.

It strolled forward across the landscape. After about fifty feet, it looked over its right shoulder, as if assessing the cameraman. It then continued in the distance, disappearing behind a stand of timber.

The video ended.

Hanson addressed Bateman.

"What do you know about this film?"

"I first saw it on a television special when I was a child," she answered. "I always thought they filmed it somewhere in California. I took it as a guy riding horseback while filming animals and nature. Then something spooks the horse, and things get jumbly. The cameraman then focuses on this creature shuffling away from him. It all happens so fast."

"That's what most people think, for they don't have any context. Let me give you some background.

"This is Bluff Creek, the same area that Wallace left his foot-prints, though it's nine years later, 1967.

"The man behind this film is Roger Patterson. And before he shot this footage, Bigfoot was his obsession.

"In 1966, Patterson self-published a book, *Do Abominable Snowmen of America Really Exist?* Later on, he began working on securing money for a docudrama he wanted to film. It was to be about a group of miners and the creatures that attacked them."

"Patterson was making a film based on Ape Canyon?" Sheriff Hart asked as he turned to look eastward.

"Yes. He was well-acquainted with the story; it takes up a large part in his book. Patterson rented a camera in May and did some filming for his movie. His friends, Bob Gimlin and Bob Heironimus, helped him in doing this.

"But money was running out, and investors were becoming scarcer. So Patterson, with his rented camera, announced in mid-October that he and Gimlin were riding out to film a real Bigfoot in the wild.

"They succeeded. The first part is exploring the woods on horseback. The latter half, the Bigfoot sequence, lasts for about a minute."

"So he filmed an alleged real Bigfoot while he was making a Bigfoot movie," Fisher said. He was playing the video again.

"I'll let you in on something else. Back when Roe was spying on his Sasquatch, she detected him. Startled, she stood up and walked away, looking back over her right shoulder as she retreated."

"So, except for the fact that Roe's Sasquatch is female, the two encounters are identical," Bateman said.

Nesbitt and Sheriff Hart were exchanging guilty glances and shifting from foot to foot.

"Agent Fisher, look up Bigfoot, frame 352," Hanson prodded.

Fisher typed it in. A photograph of Bigfoot, a still from the footage itself, appeared. It showed Bigfoot mid-stride, arms swinging, looking over its shoulder.

Everyone recognized it. It was the creature's most iconic image, gracing beer bottles, posters, decals, and bumper stickers.

"Look closer," Hanson said.

"Bigfoot has breasts!" Bateman exclaimed.

"All this time, all those advertisements. I thought this Bigfoot was a male," Fisher added.

"Patterson nicknamed her Patty," Hanson said. "He never hid that fact, but now, fifty years later, it's mostly forgotten with the general public. I've read the affidavit, since it is reprinted in Patterson's book. Roe's story is the basis for Patterson's film."

"Why does no one knows this?" Bateman asked.

"It's out there on the web for anyone to see, and published in books critical of Bigfoot," Hanson explained. "But most of us experience Bigfoot through sensational documentaries, and they usually omit these facts."

"Because they're not important," Nesbitt said.

Nesbitt was grasping now. Hanson ignored him.

"And now, the final nail in the Bigfoot coffin. Who was wearing that suit? Remember Heironimus, Patterson's friend that was helping him film the docudrama? He came forward as the guy in the ape costume. He even went on television connected to a lie detector to explain it all. Case closed."

"He was bitter. Patterson hadn't paid him for his part in the movie, Hanson," Nesbitt snarled. "And until someone comes up with a costume, Bigfoot will always be real."

Nesbitt stormed off. He stopped at the edge of the clearing to talk to a deputy stationed there. The two looked like they knew each other.

Sheriff Hart moved off also. "I guess I should look into wrapping up this crime scene," he grumbled.

Fisher turned toward Bateman.

"You've been here for almost twelve hours, Doctor," Fisher said. "May I have one of my agents drive you and your truck home?"

Though she was trying to hide it, Bateman's fatigue showed through her sagging shoulders.

"I accept your offer, Agent Fisher," she answered. "I would have left sooner, but when I heard that the sheriff was bringing an expert in, I stayed. Kris was a friend. I didn't want this Bigfoot business to get out of hand."

She turned toward Hanson. This close, he felt a thrill along his spine as her dark eyes locked onto him. "Though I would have been out of my depth with Nesbitt. I realize that we haven't stopped the Bigfoot rumor completely. But I do think we at least averted the terrible scandal that could have risen out of this. So thank you, Steve." She took a moment to look back at the gurney that Steinsson was on. Someone had covered him with a sheet. "Thank you for everything," she added. Hanson realized she was well aware of his earlier manipulations.

She turned away, following an FBI agent that led her back down the path.

"She's right," Fisher said. "You stopped this thing from becoming a real zoo around here. It's almost midnight; let me get someone to get you back to the helicopter."

Startled that it was so late, Hanson brought out his phone. The clock on it read 11:59. He switched it to the Mount St. Helens' app.

The six changed to a five.

Again, he looked upward. Getting off the mountain was a good idea.

Nearby, Fisher was staring at Nesbitt.

"Though I have to admit, the idea of Bigfoot being real and the only suspect would have made solving this case easier," he mused.

"Well, I'm no detective, but I have a guess about what happened here," Hanson said. "This 'Red Zone' thing caused the authorities to evacuate nearby businesses and remove families from their homes. A lot of people are taking a financial hit because of USGS's prediction. And we're all still recovering from the COVID lockdown."

"So you're thinking that someone from one of the groups protesting the evacuation could be behind this?" Fisher asked.

"That's my feeling," Hanson answered. "People are riled up. I'm thinking some of these protesters found out Steinsson was nearby and took out their frustrations on him. They added the Bigfoot stuff because nothing says 'don't mess with Mount St. Helens' more than that."

"You think so?" Fisher said. He didn't refute Hanson, but he sounded unconvinced.

Hanson held up his hands as his FBI agent led him away. "Hey, as I said, I'm no detective, but I'm sure this whole thing is local."

Chapter 6

St. Petersburg, Russia, Thursday 7:45 p.m. Moscow Standard Time

"What do you mean by 'Bigfoot is trending?'" General Tonkov asked.

Filip Gontarev thought about his answer. He had forgotten that Tonkov, while fluent with English, was not quite up to date with internet jargon.

"It means it's gaining in popularity," Gontarev explained. "Despite the FBI trying to keep a lid on things, there were a lot of people present at the site. Word has leaked out, and people are eating it up online."

The older man, who had been looking over Gontarev's shoulder, straightened up, smiling. He was wearing a military uniform, and medals decorated most of his chest.

"Good. We were expecting that," he said.

Gontarev breathed a sigh of relief. No one wanted to disappoint Tonkov. The General, who Gontarev guessed to be in his mid-seventies, was a long-standing member of the Main Directorate of the

Russian General Chief of Staff. Gontarev knew that Western media still called it the GRU, but no one said that to Tonkov's face. No one wanted to make the news because they fell out of a tenth floor window.

A third man wearing an expensive suit was also in the room. "Does that mean we're still on schedule?" Chernov asked.

Tonkov brought out his phone and called up an app. Gontarev could see a large '5' dominating the screen.

"As long as the American volcano acts as anticipated," Tonkov answered. He looked up at Gontarev. "Please, continue with your report on the American's social media sites, *tovarisch*."

Gontarev shifted in his seat. The other two men were standing in his office, located in a building in the Olgino district of St. Petersburg. Six large screens mounted on the wall displayed American news programs. Outside of his office door, nearly a hundred Russians sat at their computers in a large room. They spent their day logged into American social media accounts.

They were the 'Trolls of Olgino,' one of Russia's online influence brigades. Everyone in the building had hundreds of accounts, where they would post images, memes, and comments. The trolls could deploy internet bots to down-vote American comments they wanted to bury. Or upvote opinions they wanted to promote. They also secretly controlled millions of American computers with malware so subtle that their owners didn't know they were hacked. At the right moment, these 'zombie' computers could be used to spread Russian propaganda at overwhelming levels.

Their job was to fan the flames of American discontent, to widen the divide amongst its factions. The trolls' reach was long, and they held sway over the opinions of a vast swath of Americans.

Gontarev dealt with Moscow on a regular basis, as his marching orders were issued from there. What was unusual was having the head of the GRU's Second Directorate, the man in charge of Russian assets in America, actually standing in his office.

The other man was out of place also. Gontarev knew him by reputation.

Yaropolk Chernov. Or, as the web called him, Siberia. He was Russia's most infamous hacker.

American intelligence speculated (correctly) that he was part of the Russian cyberespionage team Strontium. Gontarev had heard that Chernov's main task was to penetrate the White House and Pentagon firewalls with zero-day hacks, exploits that no one except the hacker was even aware of. Gontarev could only guess as to why Russia's elite hacker was here now.

Chernov was young like Gontarev, both men being in their thirties. But while the troll was short and stout and wearing a knock off t-shirt with Baby Yoda on it, the hacker was tall and gaunt and dressed in an immaculate dark suit with a red tie. Strontium paid its staff well. Or Chernov hacked bank accounts for himself on the side.

Gontarev continued his report in English. As hackers dealing with the West on a constant basis, he and Chernov found it easier to use the language. Only Tonkov's accent betrayed that the three men were Russian.

The troll pointed to the computer screen on his desk. It had a large, colorful graph displayed.

"On the news, local law enforcement and the FBI are stating that they are working a simple murder case," Gontarev said, shuddering a bit. The man who had ordered the geologist's death was standing right next to him. Gontarev had always felt a little detached from the ramifications of his job. But now, the consequences of his actions felt all too real.

"But, as we had hoped, the Bigfoot story caught on the internet overnight. A blogger and TV star named Nesbitt had obtained some video images from the crime scene. He posted them on his website, and the networks couldn't ignore it. They mentioned the theory as an aside. Things snowballed from there."

Gontarev pointed at another chart. "Now it seems like everyone in the United States is coming forward with Bigfoot stories of their own. I've never seen such an explosion of interest in the paranormal like this."

The old general leaned forward again, appearing pleased as he studied the screen.

"I have," he said.

"The only problem I see to our campaign is a blogger named Steve Hanson, who lives near our Bigfoot crime scene. He was there, and his articles oppose the story we are spinning. If you want me to, my crew can work on discrediting him," Gontarev said.

"Yes, but use only legitimate accounts, and the bots sparingly," Tonkov said. "We don't want the Americans to suspect our involvement. They might increase their security at their Cascades Volcano Observatory office."

"Steinsson was close to figuring your man Terrington out," Chernov said, stepping forward. "Are you sure your other assets are safe?"

"The rest of my team is in place, and their cover is secure," Tonkov assured them. "Projects Rod and Front Door are still a go."

Gontarev had learned of the two secret projects a few weeks ago when the USGS had announced the imminent eruption of the American volcano. He wasn't aware of all the details, but he knew that somehow the volcano increased the chances of success for both.

Five days from now.

Chernov didn't sound convinced.

"I've been in contact with Terrington," Chernov said. "An FBI agent named Fisher has already been around, conducting interviews."

"Yes, but since he is unfamiliar with the USGS, and with our crime scene muddled up, I'm sure he's distracted and not asking the right questions," Tonkov responded.

"True, but Terrington noticed that a colleague is starting to poke around also, like Steinsson did. She might know the right questions."

Tonkov looked concerned at this.

"That is an issue. Who is this woman?"

Chernov brought up his phone to read off the name.

"Doctor Makani Bateman. I could hack her accounts if you want me to. Find out what she's looking into."

"*Nyet.* I know you two think computers are the answer to everything, but we must minimize our electronic footprint," the old man said. "I admit we need intelligence on her. But we must use some of our own spies, and we cannot risk Terrington." Tonkov turned to Gontarev.

"Pull up a map of the volcano."

Gontarev did so. Soon, an image of America's Pacific Northwest region appeared, centered on Mount St. Helens.

"Move the map a bit north," the General commanded.

Gontarev manipulated his mouse. A region a bit east of Mount Rainier was now on the screen. There was a strange square patch noted on it.

"What's that?" Chernov asked.

"It's a National Radio Quiet Zone," Tonkov explained. "Wayne Kesler, a capitalistic billionaire, has his SETI radio dish located there."

"How does that help us?" the hacker asked.

"Kesler is part of the equation, Chernov, and he is throwing a party there tomorrow night," Tonkov revealed.

Gontarev raised an eyebrow. Tonkov had a lot of plates spinning on this operation.

"Two of my assets will also be at that party," Tonkov continued. "And they have some influence on Kesler. I will have Doctor Bateman invited to the gala. There, we will find out how much of a threat she is."

"As long as there isn't another murder to bring attention to—" Chernov began.

The old man leaned in on the hacker. "People have disappeared all around the world under my direction, Chernov," Tonkov growled. "And no one is the wiser. So don't tell me how to do my job. I've already looked into Hanson's blog. We can't have a knowledgeable skeptic like him entrenched with the FBI, so I'm having him eliminated. And if Bateman is also a threat, then her death will be another opportunity to confuse the Americans even more."

Chernov blanched at that.

Tonkov turned to Gontarev. The troll felt a bit of sweat trickling down his back under the GRU General's stare.

"Does your team have their script?" Tonkov asked.

"They do," Gontarev stammered. When the time came, his trolls were to unleash an unprecedented information dump on the United States' primary social media sites. "Though what you want us to post seems so unbelievable. Are you sure the Americans will fall for it?"

"You would think not," Tonkov snorted. "With all this information at our beck and call, one would think this is an age of enlightenment. Of science and reason."

Tonkov pointed at one of the screens. It was displaying a news segment from Olympia, Washington. Enraged protesters were marching on the capitol building's steps. Gontarev could read some of the signs.

My Home and My Life

Only God Knows When A Volcano Erupts, Not Man

"But no, it's more of an age of confusion," Tonkov continued. "The Americans, some of them still believe the world is flat. And others argue against vaccinations. Vaccinations! I'm old enough to remember polio and the iron lungs."

Someone ran forward and waved his sign in front of the camera.

BLM!! Bigfoot Lives Matter!

The old general shook his head.

"What you are going to promote in the next four days may seem absurd. But trust me, with these Americans, we're already halfway there."

Chapter 7

Portland, Friday, 4:18 p.m. PDT

"I hate flying saucers," Tolmany said, relinquishing the controls as his spaceship exploded.

"Flying saucers always win," Hanson acknowledged as he took over the buttons.

The two men were standing in a retro arcade room and restaurant in downtown Portland. The place was a din of synthesized explosions, screeching tires, and gunfire. On a balcony above, pinball machines pinged and rattled.

Tolmany was playing a round of *Asteroids* with his longtime friend. He had met Hanson three decades ago in a *Dungeons & Dragons* group. They shared the same interests, and they still role-played with pen and paper, or met here as much as life allowed.

Tolmany took a drink from his beer at a nearby table and returned to the video game cabinet. Hanson was flying his delta-shaped spaceship through an asteroid field. The game's speakers maintained the sound of a heart beating at an accelerated pace.

"Any updates from your trip up the mountain?" he asked. Hanson had sent out an email to the few friends that he had, detailing his excursion up Mount St. Helens.

"The FBI agent who took me up there called me an hour ago," Hanson answered, his eyes focused on the screen. "He's upset that the Bigfoot theory still has some traction. He asked me how my website's numbers were."

"And how are they?"

"Higher than normal, but I'm getting a lot of negative commentary, and Nesbitt's site is crushing me in views," Hanson answered. "I updated my Bigfoot posts and moved them to my front page, but Nesbitt has some footprint images up. I can't compete against that."

In the game, asteroids were closing on Hanson's position. Robert watched his friend take a moment to raise his left hand to shift the sleeve on his red t-shirt. Doing so exposed a tattoo on his right shoulder, which he then rubbed.

The tattoo was in the rough sphere shape of a twenty-sided die from *Dungeons & Dragons*. The polyhedron was blue, and each triangular face had a digit inscribed in yellow. The number '20' was front and center. The tattoo represented a natural twenty, which in gaming circles always meant success.

It was Hanson's good luck charm. Every time he touched it, he always succeeded in what he was doing with his right arm.

Hanson snapped off a staccato shot of three missiles from his ship. Asteroids exploded and broke up into smaller pieces. Hanson darted his ship into the clearing he had created, skirting by flying debris.

"Never tell me the odds," Hanson shouted.

Tolmany groaned. Hanson always said that when they played this game.

And now he was winning. Tolmany brought up another subject to pull Hanson's attention from the screen.

"Have you heard from the Vulcan?" he asked.

"No," Hanson answered, his brows knitting in concentration. "And stop trying to distract me."

"Come on, Steve, she's a vulcanologist," Tolmany prodded. "That makes her a Vulcan. It sounded like she appreciated what you did for her friend. You should at least give her a call and see how she's doing."

"I will, maybe later."

Tolmany sighed. For Hanson, that answer meant no. Tolmany couldn't keep a worried look off of his face as he watched Hanson continue with the game. Hanson had always been withdrawn, and lately, it had become more difficult to get him to leave his house for any sort of social gathering. For Hanson, playing video games on a Friday night in an actual arcade was daring.

"Steve, it's been three years since you've been out on a date," Tolmany said. "Spock and Uhura are together in those new movies. That means even Spock is getting more than you do, and he used to have sex on six-year intervals."

"Seven-year intervals," Hanson corrected. "And anyway, they call themselves volcanologists, not vulcanologists. I least I think they do. You should look it up."

Tolmany started reaching for his phone but stopped when someone spoke up behind both men.

"We prefer volcanologist."

Tolmany turned. Hanson must also have, for he could hear Hanson's spaceship collide with an asteroid on the game's speakers.

The woman that Hanson had described was standing behind them. Hanson was right— she was beautiful. It was hot outside, so she was wearing shorts with a blue t-shirt that had an image of Mount St. Helen's crater on it. Printed below was the phrase *Where Were You When Mount St. Helens Erupted?*

He held out his hand. "Dr. Bateman? It's nice to meet you. I'm Dr. Robert Tolmany. Steve has told me a little bit about running into you on the mountain. I'm sorry about your colleague. My condolences."

"Thank you, Dr. Tolmany," she said, smiling, though he could still see the grief in her eyes. "But please, both of you can just call me Makani."

"As long as you stick to Robert for me," he said. Behind him, Hanson was still silent. He could guess why. Hanson never revealed his nerdiness to the women he met until he was well acquainted with them. Being exposed like this must be mortifying for him.

"Steve here is indulging my habit of playing these old video games from our youth," Tolmany said, pointing over his shoulder. He rubbed his bald head. "Back when I had hair," he added.

Spaceships still exploded on the unattended machine. "I'm going to get myself a beer. Can I get you one?"

"No thanks, I'm only in town for a short while."

"Okay. I'll be right back."

Tolmany turned around. Hanson was still standing there like a deer caught in headlights. He crowded around Hanson, forcing him into the space he made next to Makani. It was the best set up he could do for his friend. He hoped Hanson didn't blow it.

* * *

"Was I interrupting something?" Makani asked, looking at the game cabinet. Asteroids were smashing Hanson's ships. Flying saucers also attacked from random corners of the screen.

Hanson smiled, relaxing a bit. "Nah, I was winning anyway," he answered, immediately regretting what he said. It didn't sound right, bragging right off the bat. He focused on her instead, observing that she still looked troubled by her friend's death. "But, how are you doing?" he added.

"Better," she answered. "We had a small ceremony for Kris yesterday. The authorities are holding onto his body for a while longer, so I don't think he'll be able to return home to his family until next week."

"With that and the volcano, you guys must be busy."

"We are, but we learned some lessons from the Kilauea eruption back in 2018. That crisis ran my crew and I to the point of exhaustion. Here we have a cooperative of geologists from all around the world. That is allowing us all to catch a break here and there."

"So, you're from Hawaii."

"Born and raised. My mom's Hawaiian. Dad was from California, and we lived on the big island. Volcanoes have always dominated my life. I knew that I wanted to be a geologist ever since I was six."

Hanson could guess that working around volcanoes was a dangerous and exciting career. He couldn't believe that someone so interesting was taking the time to talk to him.

"How did you know I was here?"

"Agent Fisher told me," Makani answered, holding up a business card. "He was at the Cascades Volcano Observatory offices in Vancouver yesterday conducting interviews, and he left me this card. I called him a half-hour ago for information on how to contact you. He said he had talked to you here. I was already in town shopping, so I hopped over."

"Why did you want to see me?"

She glanced away. Now she was acting shy about something.

"This morning I received an invitation to that gala at Wayne Kesler's SETI site, the KET Observatory."

"That party for his billionaire investors? The one up north in the radio-quiet zone?" Hanson exclaimed, his eyebrows shooting up. The event was news-worthy, barely eclipsed by the volcano. A gathering of wealthy entrepreneurs at Kesler's tourist attraction. He was making an announcement to his investors, and the press wasn't allowed.

"Yes. Since Mount St. Helens is close by, Kesler wants me there to give a presentation to calm everyone's fears."

"The volcano is erupting in a few days. Will your bosses let you attend it?"

"They're pushing me to go. My supervisors are hoping that Kesler's wealthy friends might consider donating to the USGS."

"You're lucky. The Kesler Extraterrestrial Telescope Observatory is his pet SETI, or search for extraterrestrial intelligence, project. I would love to see the Galaxy Dish, the radio telescope that they have there."

"Would you like to be my date tomorrow?" she blurted out.

Stunned by her invitation, Hanson's mouth moved wordlessly.

Beer in hand, Tolmany joined them.

"A date this Saturday night," he said, clapping Hanson on the shoulder. "It's a good thing he's free. Hanson told me his only plans for this weekend were giving his cats a bath." Tolmany turned back to the game. It was still running through their inventory of space-ships. "Oh look, it's my turn," he added as he started pushing buttons.

His friend's distraction helped Hanson recover from his shock. He grinned at her.

"I would love to," he said, cringing a bit, though, when he said 'love.' Was that too strong of a word?

"Good," she said. For her part, she had that look of relief on her face of someone going out on a limb and having it work out okay.

"Here's a copy of the invitation for tomorrow night," she added, handing it over to him. She had written her phone number on the bottom of it. Hanson brought out his phone and dialed it.

Her phone rang, and she took a moment to tag his name to his number.

"Well, I need a new dress," she said, turning away. "Thanks again, Steve, for everything." She looked over Hanson's shoulder and waved. "Nice meeting you, Robert. Aloha."

"Aloha," both men responded. Hanson watched her leave, her long hair swaying back and forth against the small of her back.

"You were right, she's gorgeous," Tolmany said. Behind them, ships exploding came through the speakers again.

"She's into you, you know," he added.

"You think so?" Hanson replied, his voice laced with doubt.

Tolmany was pushing on his back now, toward the door. "I know so. Come on. We need to buy you something to wear. That Millennium Falcon shirt is not going to cut it."

Chapter 8

Portland, Friday, 9:41 p.m. PDT

The header on the flyer stapled to the nearby utility pole read 'National Night Out'. Trent Foster recalled it was an event where people left the comforts of their home and mingled with their neighbors. Sometimes the police would send officers out so that everyone could meet them and learn some home safety tips.

It always occurred on the first Tuesday of August, which had been three nights ago. He felt fortunate that he had missed it, as he was here to break into an unoccupied home. Doing that in the middle of an anti-crime street party would have been awkward. Even with his training as a Russian sleeper agent, he would have had a difficult time blending in.

His birth name was Stanislav Lukin, and his home was originally Omsk. His childhood had been hard, and he had joined the military still in his teens. A standout, interested parties had recruited him into the special-purpose military unit of the main military intelligence service. Spetsnaz GRU.

He obtained a new identity and paperwork a decade ago. Moscow placed him with a helicopter company out of Ohio, its staff comprised of other Russian moles.

Secure in America's heartland, Foster had participated in several missions ferrying Russian spies across the Canadian border when needed. Not sure of how long they would be staying in the states, the agents settled in for the long haul.

Then the American volcano reawakened, and his crew received new orders. They were to relocate to the Pacific Northwest. In the 1980 eruption, helicopters had been critical for search and rescue efforts. His company was the perfect cover. By bidding low, Pacific Northwest Emergency agencies had hired them. Now Cardinal Air flew out of a rented area at the Portland Airport.

Foster stepped out of the truck, a hat pulled low over his face. The sun had set a half-hour ago, but there was still a bright glow to the west. The street was empty of traffic and no one was sitting on their porch. He quickly ducked into the driveway of a Craftsman style house.

The home of Steve Hanson.

A deck covered the entire front of the house. Two cats watched him from a window. That jibed with the information he had received from the Strontium group a short while ago. This Hanson guy didn't have any dogs, which would be helpful.

He made his way to the backyard. Tall rhododendron bushes gave the area privacy. A light above the back door, connected to a motion sensor, snapped on.

Since he had light, Foster slipped on some dark latex gloves and bent over to pick the back door's lock. Strontium had determined that Hanson had no security system in place.

He found himself in the kitchen. He kept the lights off and used a small flashlight to get around. The two cats, a striped tabby and a Russian blue, had made their way to him. They were hungry and wound around his feet. Foster took a moment to pet the Russian blue before he looked around.

The kitchen table looked unused. He noticed the salt and pepper shakers on the counter, along with a plate yellowed with egg yolk. Hanson had divorced a few years back. Foster guessed that he ate most of his meals standing over the kitchen sink.

The living room was a mix of old and new mismatched furniture. There was a huge television connected to a gaming console. On the wall, large prints displayed images of Mount Hood, or of the Oregon coast. On a desk were two framed photographs. One showed a black and white image of a couple, the other a colorful print of a girl.

Hanson's parents and daughter. He recalled the dossier Strontium had put together. The father, a Marine veteran, had passed away when Hanson was six. Hanson was a former Marine also, having followed in his late father's steps when he graduated high school. He had spent some time overseas, participating in the Battle for Kuwait Airport during Desert Storm.

The daughter, Elanor, was still in her teens. According to her social media sites, she was in Astoria, visiting her grandmother.

That was a break. Having her here tonight would have complicated things.

He made his way down a hall to what he thought would be a downstairs bedroom.

Instead, he found a study. It had a desk with a laptop computer resting on it. Bookcases covered two of the walls, and the final side had sliding doors for the closet.

Most of the shelves had books. Foster pointed his flashlight at them. It was weird crap, like *Ripley's Believe it or Not*, *Chariots of the Gods*, *Communion*, and the entire *Time Life: Mysteries of the Unknown* volume set.

The rest of the shelves had colorful statues of comic book heroes, model spaceships, or sci-fi replica weapons. Leaning against a corner was a realistic-looking short sword and wizard staff.

Foster snorted to himself. The guy was a real nerd. But for some reason, Moscow thought he was a threat to their plans.

He shone his light on the wall behind the computer.

Note cards covered it, arranged in a grid-like pattern. Simple images were on each card, and most had the red prohibition circle slash symbol over them.

He recognized most of them. Familiar illustrations of The Loch Ness Monster, the Pyramids, and Crystal Skulls stood out. He even picked out Bigfoot.

Foster smiled. He had spent the other day promoting the creature's existence. He and his crew had bypassed road-blocks and snuck onto the mountain to find one of the cameras the USGS had posted around the volcano. Foster had donned a Bigfoot costume and taken a stroll in front of one of them, making sure to keep his distance and within the shadows of a tree line. The plan was to do it again in front of a second camera but Tonkov had called. The general had received some last minute intelligence that a geologist from Iceland was going to be a problem. Tonkov ordered him to kill Steinsson.

A call to Tonkov's mole at the CVO revealed that Steinsson would soon be on the mountain. Foster quickly came up with a plan. Changing brief video appearances to a full on murder by cryptid was an opportunity he couldn't pass up.

There was a card next to the Bigfoot one. It had a simple flying saucer depicted on it. It wasn't crossed out, but it did have a question mark over it.

Gazing at the two cards next to each other, Foster could see why Moscow thought that Hanson could be a problem.

Next to him, the two cats snapped to attention, looking to the room's door. Then they bolted out of the room.

Hanson was home.

Foster went to the closet. Boxes for the science fiction toys filled half of it. He squeezed himself in, knocking over a large and heavy statuette on the floor. It was a figurine of a heavily muscled comic book super-hero, a green-colored swamp man. Foster wasn't sure if the character was from Marvel or DC. Didn't matter; swamp guy was standing next to a rotted stump, so the figure also had a large, heavy base. He reached down and picked it up, feeling its heft.

Perfect.

He left the door open a crack so that he could spy out.

Hanson entered the house. Lights turned on. The cats once again took up their hungry cries.

Foster listened in disbelief as Hanson began singing to the cats.

And kitty has hungry eyes . . . .

A can of cat food made the cracking-open noise.

That glow at the smell of fries.

A pause as Hanson scooped out the cat food.

B-I-N-G-O!

And Bingo was her name-o!

Hanson walked into the study, humming the *Bingo* song as he snapped on a light. Foster watched as he sat at the desk, his back to him. Hanson powered on the laptop.

Foster held his breath, not making a sound as he spied on Hanson. He was curious if Hanson was in the midst of anything that could jeopardize the mission.

It didn't look like it. The first site Hanson went to was an article about first dates.

Foster shook his head. The guy lived the life of a loser.

And he was going to die a loser.

Foster wasn't here to recon.

He was here to kill Hanson.

As a member of Spetsnaz, Foster had done it before, his most recent being the geologist. He had run him through with a sharpened pole, and then hung him on a tree. While doing it, he made sure that the foot shaped paddles strapped to his feet left clear prints.

Besides promoting Moscow's paranormal agenda, it helped to confuse the FBI.

Again he felt the heft of the statue in his hands.

It was to be the same here. Mislead the authorities. Foster had a gun, but he didn't want the police to think that someone connected to the protests came here to kill Hanson. That would spoil the support the protesters were now enjoying. He had to make it look like a crime of opportunity.

A would-be robber, caught in the act and grabbing the closest thing at hand.

At his computer, Hanson switched to *YouTube* and turned up the volume on his speakers. His cats joined him, one on the desk itself and one on a nearby shelf. On the screen, images of the actors Martin Landau and Barbara Bain appeared as Hanson started playing the music from an old television series. Foster could see the show's masthead on the screen, *Space:1999,* season one.

From his desk Hanson grabbed a toy spaceship and leaned back in his chair, studying it.

Foster smiled. The operatic music was loud. It covered the sound of him opening the closet door.

Foster stepped into the room and raised his weapon above his head.

Chapter 9

"I have a date," Hanson told his cats. "Polo or Axe Body—"

Next to him, Bingo looked away from Hanson and focused on something over his right shoulder. On the shelf, Sebastian arched his back, puffing up to twice his size and hissing.

Hanson instinctively turned his head, catching movement out of the corner of his eye. With a yelp, he rocked back in his chair and pushed back from the desk with his legs.

Something whiffed by his head and grazed his shoulder as a man went crashing by him to his right. The attacker had put so much force into his swing that he fell forward, knocking over the printer and various sci-fi weapon replicas off a shelf.

Chaos erupted.

Hanson tumbled out of his tipping chair, rolling into the room's back corner. The cats jumped from their perches, screeching in surprise and clawing their way over the intruder's arms and back as they fled the room. The would-be attacker howled in pain. In the background music was still blasting.

"What the hell?" Hanson gasped from the ground.

A burglar was in his house. He was wearing jeans with a dark long-sleeved shirt. A black baseball cap covered his longish blonde hair. One of Hanson's larger superhero statues was clutched in his gloved hand.

The burglar stood up and spun toward Hanson, raising his makeshift weapon.

Hanson hurled the spaceship model he was still holding. It wasn't plastic, like from a kit, but made of die-cast metal. The *Space:1999* Eagle had some mass to it, and it bounced off the blondie's head with a satisfying thunk.

The man yelled in pain again, pausing for a fraction of a second out of surprise.

Hanson used that moment to jump up and grab his nearby replica of Gandalf the White's staff from the *Lord of the Rings* movies.

Recovered, the other man rushed him.

"You . . . shall not . . . get away with this," Hanson yelled, bringing the staff down on the intruder's hand. Blondie grunted as the statue fell to the ground and bounced off the carpet.

Hanson brought up the staff, clipping his attacker's chin, forcing him a step back. He raised it for another blow, but it caught on the ceiling. The room was too small for the six-foot-long weapon.

Now it was the intruder's turn to take advantage. His hand went to his back and he pulled out a dark, snub-nosed revolver.

His adrenaline pumping, Hanson choked up on his staff and brought it down on the assailant's right hand again. The gun fell to the ground.

Hanson went for another swing. The staff struck the bookcase behind him, breaking in half.

He dropped one of the pieces and charged, relying on his Marine hand-to-hand combat training, a hybrid form of fighting designed to be easily learned and remembered. It didn't have any exotic moves or flashy techniques. It simply got the job done. Hanson closed in on his opponent, figuring he could club the would-be burglar over the head.

Blondie surprised him by stepping into his attack, casually

deflecting Hanson's swing as he landed a blow to his gut. This close to one another, Hanson caught a whiff of grease and motor oil from the guy. With his own gasp of pain, Hanson dropped his broken staff and fell back into the corner again.

Blondie bent to the ground, trying to locate his gun in the clutter of knickknacks scattered across the floor.

As he rolled off his side Hanson's hand fell on the hilt of his *The Hobbit* replica of Bilbo's sword. He sprung up with the weapon as he sought to close the distance again before his attacker found his gun.

Hanson's heart sank though as Blondie raised up his weapon in triumph, pulling the trigger as he did so. Hanson winced in anticipation of piercing bullets.

Nothing happened.

Confused, the intruder held up the gun to study it.

It wasn't the revolver. It was the Han Solo DL-44 Blaster replica that Hanson owned. Blondie's gun was somewhere in a mess of sci-fi weaponry, everything from the *Star Trek* Type Two Phaser, the *Aliens* Pulse Rifle, and the Sandman Pistol from *Logan's Run*.

Hanson held up his sword in front of him, yelling out in his excitement.

"This is Sting! You've seen it before!"

With a look of disbelief and confusion, the intruder paused for a moment.

Then he dashed out the door.

Hanson didn't follow. He didn't want to engage this guy again if he could help it. He took a moment to locate the prowler's gun and pick it up. In the next room, he heard a door crash against a wall as it was flung open.

Hanson gave the gun a look over. It was a small revolver with a shrouded hammer. Hanson frowned. The weapon was designed to be hidden and easily drawn. Holding the revolver up, he entered his living room. The front door was ajar, and the cats were out of sight. Wary of an ambush, he stepped out onto his front porch and looked up and down his street.

A truck was pulling away halfway up the block. It was too far away for Hanson to read the plates, but he got the make, color, and model. Hanson went back inside, searching the house until he found the cats safe in the kitchen. Both were licking their paws as if nothing had happened. He returned to his desk to turn off the loud music. He set the gun down and pulled his phone out to dial 911.

He stopped, his thumb hovering over the last digit of the emergency number.

As usual, his anxious mind went over the possible consequences of his next action. He could guess the outcome here. News crews with cameras on his front lawn, all working to come up with the catchiest headline.

Homeowner chases off burglar with Lord of the Rings toys!

It would be a circus.

Hanson knew he had to report that a burglar capable of violence was running loose. But no one needed to know all the details. He spent a few moments cleaning up his study. He replaced everything to their shelves and powered down his computer. The broken staff and revolver he took down to his basement to stash away. Hanson grabbed a baseball bat on the way back up and leaned it in a corner of his living room. The statue he placed in the middle of the floor.

Hanson felt guilty about changing the crime scene. He consoled himself with the thought that though he changed the narrative, the end result would be the same.

He called the police.

Two police officers showed up within minutes. They introduced themselves as Officers Kosel and Tietz. Kosel was a lean guy in his forties, his brown hair cut short. Tietz was a little shorter and younger, her thick black hair in a pony-tail.

Hanson showed them the house, explaining that he had returned home from tuxedo shopping and dinner with his friend. After he fed his cats, he caught an intruder who was trying to sneak out of his study with one of his statues.

"He tried to hit me with it," Hanson said, "But he missed. I grabbed my baseball bat . . ." Hanson pointed to the corner. "And chased him out the door."

"What did he look like?" Kosul asked.

Hanson described him, including the latex gloves. He didn't want the police dusting his house for prints.

Kosul's eyes rested on the statue.

"So the guy was trying to steal the toy—"

"Collectible," Hanson interjected.

"Collectible," Kosul noted. "When you interrupted him."

"Yeah," Hanson answered.

Tietz spoke up. "Do you have a lot of these toys—"

"Collectibles—"

"Lying about the house?" she finished.

"Yes, and they're worth money," Hanson said, trying to impress them. "That one is rare, as only a few replicas were made. It's worth almost a thousand dollars. Not everyone has a statue of—"

"Let's see the rest," Kosul said.

Hanson led them into his study. They both took some time looking it over, and Hanson's card-covered wall caught their attention.

"So did Bigfoot—" Kosul began.

"No," Hanson answered tersely.

His partner was at the window.

"Do you keep the curtains open in this room?" Tietz asked.

"Yes. To let my cats look outside."

"That's most likely how the burglar knew you had all these expensive toys," Kosul said. "He must have cased out this house. We talked about this last Tuesday right outside your home during National Night Out. Weren't you there for that?"

"No," Hanson answered. He didn't elaborate that going to such a gathering would have been last on his list of things to do. He didn't even know his neighbor's names.

Shaking his head, Kosul launched into a speech about household security. Hanson could only bite his lip as he continued, feeling the heat on his face as it reddened. There were few things he hated worse than a condescending lecture.

As they let themselves out, they promised to patrol the neighborhood to see if they could find the truck Hanson had described. Hanson watched them go. As they were getting into their patrol car, Tietz laughed at something Kosul said. The phrase, 'it's a collectible,' barely reached Hanson's ears.

He put the statue back in the closet, making sure it didn't have any nicks. He then secured the deadbolts on his doors and turned off the lights. The cats followed him upstairs. When he finished washing up and entered his bedroom, Sebastian and Bingo were already curled up on the top cover.

Hanson petted both of them as he crawled into bed.

"Thanks for the save."

He turned off the lights and reflected on the encounter. Something about it had bothered him since it happened.

The intruder knew how to fight, and he was willing to kill. Was there something more to it besides a simple burglary?

Hanson couldn't shake that thought. That's why he had held onto the gun. Agent Fisher needed to see it. Hanson planned on getting it to him the first chance he got. Let the FBI handle it.

Satisfied with that, he turned his thoughts to how the cops had lectured him earlier. He relived the moment over and over, each time trying to come up with a better counterpoint to every point the police made. A half-hour later, when he finally won the imaginary argument raging in his head, he fell asleep.

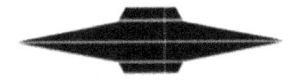

Chapter 10

FBI Field Office, Portland, Saturday, 11:48 a.m. PDT

"And remember, no one is to give any interviews, or contribute to any social media sites," Fisher ordered.

The two agents nodded as they turned to leave his office. Outside the window, an airline jet was making its approach to the nearby Portland Airport. A television hung on the wall opposite the desk, a muted carpet cleaner infomercial playing on it. Fisher had it tuned to the channel in anticipation of the local news broadcast. Out in the hall, Fisher could hear one of the retreating agents whistle the haunting theme music from *The X-Files* as they left.

Fisher dropped the report that Agents Stillwell and Catling had delivered on his desk. He took a moment to pinch his nose between his eyes in frustration.

I don't need this.

The case was proving more difficult to handle than he had imagined. Video had hit the web last night. The CVO had several cameras pointed at the volcano and running 24/7 for their app. Several Bigfoot enthusiasts had thought there was a chance to catch Bigfoot on the move. They were successful. A closer look at the archived video from one of the camera feeds revealed a vague image of a large, hairy creature moving in the shadows of a line of trees. Nesbitt announced online that he was going to put together a *YouTube* video as soon as possible to dissect the creature's every step.

That, and the murder, were creating a Bigfoot mania on social media sites. Everyone was sharing stories and theories online. And now television stations were rerunning whatever series and specials on Bigfoot they had access to.

It also didn't help that the national news sites had sent their star anchors to Portland for the week preceding the eruption. Even the morning news programs hosts were in town, setting up location shots that included Mount St. Helens. The network's presence brought greater public scrutiny to Steinsson's death, and to Bigfoot.

At least the evening news was still being straight with the story and treating it as an unusual murder. They were also covering the evacuation and business closure protests, and news anchors were hinting at a possible connection, as Hanson had theorized. Last night's broadcast focused on people gathered in front of the Cascade Volcano Observatory, an office building in Vancouver where Steinsson had been working the last few months. Someone with a sign that read *Let Our People Go Home* had explained to the reporter that they were a grass-roots organization. Locals concerned about their way of life.

The anchor had ended the segment with screenshots from websites spurring on the protests, and he had speculated that this was the true driving force behind the dissent, and possibly the murder. He then used a term for false grassroots movements. Astroturfing. Though so far no one in the media had any idea who it was. They were covering their tracks well, and even the FBI couldn't determine who was behind it. Best guess was a powerful business interest opposed to the President's policies.

The morning shows were focusing on the Bigfoot angle and were running polls. Sixteen percent of Americans believed in the cryptid.

Fisher wondered if that number would grow if the public caught wind of the report on his desk. He sat down and reopened the folder.

The lab in the building had finished their DNA analysis of the hair samples from the murder scene.

They were from a primate.

Agents Stillwell and Catling were wide-eyed when they had dropped the report off. Fisher wondered if they were slipping into the believer column—if they weren't there already.

He hoped their next assignment would fix that. They were on their way to the Oregon Zoo, located in Portland's west hills area. Once there, they were to look for any signs of suspicious activity around the zoo's primate exhibits.

Because though the DNA result from the lab was problematic on the face of it, it also was a blessing in disguise. And it played into Fisher's biggest advantage in this case.

He knew it wasn't Bigfoot.

And that meant someone was going through a lot of complicated nonsense to convince others that it was.

And the more complicated, the more chances for his suspect to make a mistake. Fisher had several circumstances to choose from.

The primate hair had to come from somewhere. Was anything out of place at the zoo?

Someone had spread pungent oil in the clearing, emulating Bigfoot's reputed stink. It also neutralized the dogs. Fisher suspected a scent spray that hunters used to mask their scent. He was looking into that.

Nesbitt had told everyone that he was going over the Bigfoot video with a fine-tooth comb. So was the FBI. Whoever was in that suit was most likely the murder suspect. Maybe something could be gleaned from the images.

The cause of death played into Fisher's favor. The medical examiner had determined that the murderer had bludgeoned Steinsson on the head. While it didn't kill him, it most likely incapacitated him.

A sharpened stake, or pole, had then been driven into his back and out his chest while he was prone. The ME determined this because there was soil in the wound. The dirt had got in there when the stake was pulled back out.

Then the killer hung Steinsson on a branch like a wrench on a peg board—a gruesome endeavor that required the murderer to spend a lot of time and effort to pull off. Was any evidence left on the body? The lab was still examining what they had gathered.

Steinsson being from Iceland also helped. He had arrived only recently and had spent most of his time at the CVO. That limited the number of people he had interacted with here in the states. Fisher's suspect pool from that standpoint was small, finite, and easy to deal with.

On his side of things, anyway. Sheriff Hart's story was the opposite. He had a mountain, both literally and figuratively, of suspects. And his job was now more difficult since most of his manpower was now spent trying to keep home owners and protesters out of the Red Zone. He also had volcano thrill-seekers and Bigfoot enthusiasts trying to sneak onto Mount St. Helens, the latter hoping to save the beloved creature. If the killer was someone who lived on the mountain, as Hanson had thought, then this case might never be solved.

His phone rang. Fisher looked at the ID on the screen.

Speak of the devil.

Fisher hit 'accept' on his phone and reclined back in his chair.

"Hanson, what can I do for you?"

"Agent Fisher? Hey, thanks for answering. Um, there's something I need to talk to you about."

Hanson sounded uncertain, unsure of how to proceed. It didn't surprise Fisher. He already had Hanson pegged as someone who didn't know how to deal with other people very well.

"Is it about your website?" Fisher prompted.

"That? No. Things are still the same; Nesbitt's site is overwhelming mine with his new Bigfoot video. Whoever's in that costume knew what he was doing when he set that up," Hanson answered. Fisher heard him take a deep breath. "Someone broke into my house last night."

"Are you okay?" Fisher asked, his chair creaking as he leaned forward, elbows back on his desk.

"Yes," Hanson answered. "It was a burglar. He was after my collectibles. They're worth quite a bit of money."

"You're talking about what? Baseball trading cards? Stamps? Vinyl records?"

The phone was quiet for a moment.

"My comic book superhero statue collection," Hanson answered sheepishly.

Fisher was not surprised. He should have guessed that.

"What happened? Did he run when you discovered him?"

"No, that's why I'm calling you. The intruder attacked me."

Hanson described the confrontation to Fisher.

"He drew a gun on you? What did the police do about that?" Fisher asked.

Hanson was even more hesitant.

"I didn't tell them. I still have it. I wanted to give it over to you and the FBI."

Fisher stood up, ready to give a searing lecture to Hanson about withholding evidence.

But the folder on his desk caught his eye.

Everything about this case so far was unusual. And now, someone had attacked Hanson.

Coincidence? Fisher didn't believe in coincidences in murder investigations. Was the attack on Hanson related to Steinsson's death? If so, then it was another opportunity for the murderer to make a mistake.

Fisher wanted that gun.

"You did the right thing," Fisher said. "Bring the gun here. I also want you to give our sketch artist a description of your assailant."

"Can I do that tomorrow morning? I left the gun in a safe at home, and I'm at work right now. When I'm done, I'm driving straight to the Vancouver Airport with Makani. She has an invitation to Kesler's party at the KET Observatory. I'm her date."

Hanson stressed that last part, saying it like he was announcing he was running for the Senate.

Again Fisher almost launched into a speech about working with the authorities. Once more, he thought about it.

In the middle of all this, Makani Bateman, a friend of the murder victim, had received a last-minute invite to the region's most exclusive event? Fisher sat back down at his desk, the thought he had earlier again running through his head.

No coincidences.

"Then come to the FBI field office first thing tomorrow," Fisher said. "You go on ahead to that party. But Hanson—"

"Yeah?"

"Keep your eyes and ears open."

"You feel there's something wrong with this, don't you?"

"I do."

Fisher could sense that Hanson felt the same way about Makani being invited to Kesler's party. Guilt washed over Fisher. There was now a possibility of danger for the two of them.

But he needed to know what this Kesler connection was all about. On his end, he would contact Jacobs, the Special Agent in Charge for Portland, to inform him that he was including the billionaire in the investigation. Someone powerful was directing the protesters. Could it be Kesler?

He wanted eyes at that party, and Hanson was his best option. Fisher took some consolation from having read the file he already had on Hanson. Hanson was a former Marine, having served in Desert Storm. He even had received a medal for something he did during the Battle for Kuwait Airport. If any trouble should arise, he would know how to handle himself.

"Watch out for yourself over there."

"I will. See you tomorrow."

Fisher put down his phone. On the television, the local noon-hour news was starting up. The lead story was not the volcano, but Bigfoot. The recent video of the cryptid moving near the USGS camera was being played. That was followed by the 1967 Bigfoot footage.

Fisher sighed. He needed to wrap up this investigation soon.

Out in the hall, someone walked by, whistling.

Real soon.

Chapter 11

Pearson Field, Vancouver, Washington, Saturday 6:38 p.m. PDT

"Well, the clothes do make the man," Makani said approvingly. "Thanks," Hanson responded, focusing on his face not turning red. It was the most flattering thing a woman had said to him in a long time.

"And you look stunning," he added.

She was wearing a simple floor-length black gown. Its open back style framed her cascading dark hair against her tan skin, and the neckline hinted at her cleavage. From a delicate gold necklace an oval-shaped fire opal depended. It blazed when it caught the light of the low-lying sun.

Hanson was wearing his new tuxedo since the invitation advertised the party as a black-tie affair. It had taken him a while, with an online video running on his television, to master the bow tie that came with it.

They were standing near a single-engine plane on a small airfield in Vancouver. The air was comfortable and still as the sun lowered.

She smiled her appreciation as he helped her into the Kesler Swift.

It was one of their host's own planes. Wayne Kesler had come from a family that had close ties to the aerospace industry in Seattle. They had branched off to make their own brand of luxury corporate jets and planes. Kesler Incorporated even had some large military contracts. He also had investments in most everything that sprung from the Puget Sound area. On the list of Washington's richest men, Kesler was third behind Bezos and Gates.

The Swift was the Roll Royce of single-engine airplanes, and a perfect fit for the short runway. Kesler had arranged for the pick up here since Pearson was located only a few minutes from the Cascade Volcano Observatory building and convenient for Makani. Though commercial airlines weren't flying in the Pacific Northwest at the moment, private planes were free to do so. The official government ban on all flights wasn't due to be implemented until Monday evening.

The cabin had room for six, plus the pilot. Makani sat in one of the rear leather seats, facing forward while Hanson sat across from her. There was a small table between them. A bottle of expensive champagne, in a silver ice bucket, sat atop it.

"This is a new experience for me," Makani said.

"Same here," Hanson admitted. He nudged the ice bucket. It held fast, magnetized to the table.

The pilot, a young man dressed in a blue jacket with gold wings pinned to his chest, leaned in.

"Seat belts, please."

He went through his pre-flight routine and prepared for takeoff. As the plane raced down the runway, a look of concern crossed Makani's face, and she leaned over to address the pilot.

"Shouldn't you be flying the plane?" she asked.

Hanson turned around and felt some alarm also. The pilot was looking back at them, his hands up in the air, a smile on his face.

"This is a Kesler. It practically flies itself."

The pilot was right. The Swift took to the air and banked north. Once again, Hanson watched the Columbia River fade in the distance from the air.

"Champagne?" he asked as he reached for the bottle.

"When in Rome," she answered. After some searching, she came up with two fluted crystal glasses.

Hanson popped the cork, careful as he did so. He didn't want it spraying everywhere. When he was confident he had avoided the embarrassing scenario, he poured.

They lifted their glasses together.

What should they toast to? Hanson wanted to say, *to a wonderful night,* but would she think that as all he was thinking of sex? Which was close to the truth, with her sitting across from him in that dress. He went with something bland, but safe.

"To our host," he said, taking a sip.

He put the glass in a holder designed to keep it stable. On his pants legs, he noticed cat hairs. He pulled out a small lint roller from an inner pocket and began running it over his suit.

"Cats?" she asked.

"Yeah, two of them," Hanson answered. "Bingo and Sebastian. They shed, but they keep me company at home."

"Any family?"

"I went through a divorce a few years back," Hanson answered. "I have a daughter, Elanor. She's a teenager now. You?"

"I'm divorced also. Twin boys," she replied, her eyes distant as she turned away for a moment. "I know I shouldn't feel this way, but it seems like it was my fault. I was away from home too often."

Hanson knew the feeling of guilt. "It was the opposite for me. I stayed at home too much."

He remembered his ex-wife's frustration, stuck at home weekend after weekend. She had taken to going out on her own, discovering a better life without him in it.

The plane banked a little to the east. Hanson looked over his shoulder. The pilot had his hands on the controls.

"She's programmed to make her way back home in the shortest route possible, but that takes us a little too close to Mount St. Helens. That's restricted airspace now," the pilot explained, looking back. "The only thing flying in there are helicopters picking up trespassers looking for Bigfoot. Can you believe it? Bigfoot!"

"No," they both answered.

"I've read your blog," she continued. "It's interesting and put together well. The cattle mutilation piece surprised me. I didn't realize it was so prevalent."

"I wrote that article a few years back. A few cows wound up dead over mysterious circumstances in one of Oregon's eastern counties. I had to explain that most cases are natural causes, and definitely not aliens."

"Were you always a skeptic?"

"I was the opposite. All the way up to a young adult, I read every book I could get my hands on when it came to the weird and unusual. The Bermuda Triangle, Loch Ness, Mothman. I ate that stuff up."

"Bigfoot?"

"That was my favorite. Bigfoot was popular in the seventies," Hanson explained. "The film footage was making the rounds. There were several movies. Even *The Six Million Dollar Man* fought Bigfoot. One of my favorite Saturday morning shows was *Bigfoot and Wildboy*."

"When did you stop believing in it?"

Hanson looked out his window. Mount St. Helens was nearby, to their west. There wasn't any snow on the mountain this time of year. The volcano was stark and grey except for the red in the cone.

"Bigfoot was the first casualty on my long road to skepticism. It started on May 19th, 1980," he answered.

She knew the date.

"The day after Mount St. Helens erupted?"

Hanson had a rueful look on his face.

"I was ten. I thought for sure the volcano would flush Bigfoot out," Hanson said.

"And it didn't," she filled in. She was also studying the mountain.

"I began to doubt. A few months later, I caught my classmate, Heidi Brookes, gleefully informing first-graders that there was no Tooth Fairy or Santa Claus. It brought the Bigfoot issue to a focus for me. Though I continued to believe in other nonsense, Bigfoot was over."

She refilled their glasses and held hers up. Hanson matched her.

"To Heidi Brookes then," she toasted. "For making you the skeptic you are today. I needed that a few days ago."

Glasses clinked.

Hanson glanced over his shoulder for one last look at Mount St. Helens. "So, you and your volcano squad are confident about your prediction?"

She grinned back at him. "We are. This is not without precedent. Twenty years ago we predicted the eruption of Popocatépetl, a volcano near Mexico City, to the day. As you can guess, the closer we get to the event the easier it is for us to narrow it down. I'll explain it in detail during my presentation."

They spent the rest of the trip making more small talk. Below them, the shadows deepened over the landscape.

Hanson felt and heard the landing gear deploy as they began their descent. The pilot had his hands on the yoke.

"She can land herself too," he said. "But, hey, I need to keep my skills sharp. Can't let *Skynet* do everything yet."

They came to a smooth landing and taxied to a rest near a half dozen Kesler corporate jets. The pilot opened the door for them.

The airfield was a private one that serviced the KET Observatory. Located nearby was the facility's expansive parking lot. Visitors parked their cars and took busses for the final ten miles to the tourist center.

Hanson looked around to orient himself. Mount Rainier rose to the west. South of them were low peaks known as the Berry Patch. Directly north was Mount Aix. The observatory rested on its northeast shoulder.

A runway tug was already maneuvering the Swift into a spot next to its siblings. The only structure nearby was a large hangar with a fuel truck parked next to it. Two guards stood at attention in front of the hanger's closed doors.

A blue SUV approached, its diesel engine rumbling. No busses for the party's rich and famous guests. The driver, a young woman wearing a white shirt and tie, stepped out.

"Doctor Bateman?" she asked, looking at a sheet of paper in her hand.

"Yes," Makani answered. "And this is my date, Steve Hanson."

Hanson liked the sound of that.

"Pleased to meet you," the woman said. She brought out two small pouches. They were black, and made of leather. They had two weird buttons at their openings. She held them out.

"I need you to surrender your phones and place them in here," she commanded.

Chapter 12

"I know it's just an antenna, but it's beautiful," Makani exclaimed.

Seated on the far side of the vehicle, Hanson leaned over for a look. The SUV was navigating a road cut into Mount Aix's steep east side. The area around them was stark and rocky, the trees small and scrub-like.

Though it wasn't quite sunset, the shadows were deep on this side of the mountain. The Galaxy Dish, the centerpiece for the observatory, was already lit up.

It was an enormous radio telescope, the dish three hundred feet in diameter. With its support truss, the whole structure stood four hundred and eighty feet tall.

The primary reflector, usually located in the center of the dish, was instead placed at the apex of the bowl, giving the array an asymmetrical look. Painted a stark white, and lit up the way it was, it appeared as a gleaming white jewel in a canyon of dark velvet.

"That thing can detect the energy of a snowflake hitting the ground a mile away," Hanson said. "And it's steerable; its operators can point it anywhere they want."

"Sounds like you know a lot about it. Did you do a little research before coming up here?"

"No, I learned all this a decade ago, when the thing was built. It was a huge story back then. One of the Microsoft founders, Paul Allen, had contributed millions to a Search for Extraterrestrial Intelligence program, the ATA project in California. It's a collection of smaller dishes configured to act as one big dish.

"Not to be outdone, Kesler started this project, but he copied something that already existed, the Green Banks Observatory in Virginia."

"I've heard of that. It's the location of the original NRQZ."

"The National Radio Quiet Zone," Hanson affirmed. He kept his eyes on the dish as he spoke. "That was the most difficult aspect of this project. Kesler wanted a NRQZ of his own. An area where he could regulate or ban transmitting devices to eliminate electromagnetic noise around his dish."

"What does it take to establish a quiet zone?"

"An act of Congress, the FCC, the Washington State Legislature, and a lot of money," Hanson answered. "Kesler succeeded, but at a square fifty miles on each side, this 'western' zone is roughly one-fourth the size of its cousin back east. Kesler's advantage is that this area is much more remote and underpopulated. The ravines are more profound, and the mountains that help block signals are taller."

"Is there cell phone service up here?"

"No, so phone calls and messaging won't work. But a phone's Wi-Fi feature, or Bluetooth, can still be a problem," Hanson answered.

"Hence, these," Makani said, holding up a pouch.

The pouches had a steel mesh lining to discourage someone from using a knife to cut them open. The mesh also acted as a Faraday Cage, which stopped any errant signals from escaping.

There were lockable magnetic tabs on top of the pouches, which could be undone with special keys. Hanson was familiar with the concept. Cosgroves used such keys for security tags placed on merchandise in its stores.

"So, besides phones, no digital cameras, microwaves, or garage door openers. This vehicle is diesel because even spark plugs are a problem," Hanson added. He nodded toward the SUV's front, where the driver was using a CB. "Though due to their low frequency usage, CB and ham radio equipment is okay."

"This is the last of them," the driver announced into her mike.

"Roger that," a male voice responded.

She turned around to them. "You're welcome to keep your phones close by, or you can check them in," she said.

They both handed over their phones, each receiving a numbered tag in return. The driver opened the door for them.

"Welcome to the KET Observatory," she announced.

They were in the parking lot for the visitor's facility. Besides being a research center, the KET was a popular tourist destination.

The visitor's building stretched north of them. Constructed of stone and concrete, it burrowed partway into the mountain. A half dozen phone booths stood at attention near the main doors. The front of the building curved and had huge windows that faced the dish itself. The radio telescope was a quarter mile away in a ravine two hundred feet lower in elevation. A large structure sheathed in aluminum siding, the research facility itself, rested below it.

A mile north were several dozen buildings where the staff for the entire facility lived. A small town that even had a post office, pub, and one-room school. The employees had named their village Aix.

Adjacent to the parking lot was a helicopter pad, most likely used in emergencies. It had a small hangar nearby.

Parked on the pad was a large semi-truck covered in a red shroud. The covering was enough so that Hanson couldn't even see the tires. Guards stood nearby, making sure no one approached. Journalists had speculated that a new business venture was to be revealed this evening.

"Impressive," Makani said, taking it all in.

"Kesler is known for having a flair for the dramatic," Hanson replied.

The parking lot was full of diesel SUVs and several large RVs for the caterers. Hanson and Makani weaved their way past them and made their way inside the main building.

"This is different," Hanson exclaimed.

Kesler's staff had changed up the tourist and information center. For normal business days the room was filled with kiosks selling coffee, books, Galaxy Dish statues, and souvenir shirts depicting a green, one-eyed alien holding a phone and asking '*Do you hear me now?*' They also sold disposable film cameras that one mailed in to develop. There were even interactive science stations scattered throughout the room.

For tonight though, these were all removed and stored away. The whole area now appeared as one grand ballroom. Small round tables covered with white linen now filled the area. Most of the lights were either dimmed or replaced with candles. And instead of piped in music over speakers, a string quartet played soothing music in a corner. There were about a hundred well-dressed guests mingling throughout the room. Servers circled them, offering drinks or hors d' oeuvres on silver platters.

"There's a lot of money in here," Makani said nervously. "Everyone looks like they stepped off the red carpet at the Oscars."

"The Pacific Northwest's elite," Hanson said. A server with champagne walked by, and Hanson snatched up two glasses and gave one to Makani. She downed it in one gulp.

She looked sheepish as she returned her glass to a nearby tray.

"I have to give a presentation to these people," she explained.

Hanson understood. Parties were not his thing, and he was feeling jittery also.

A man broke away from a group of people and approached them. Hanson knew who he was from news articles.

Wayne Kesler.

He was an inch or two taller than Hanson, six years younger, and his suit five thousand dollars more expensive. His hair was jet black and styled by professionals. He also sported a trimmed moustache, and his bowtie looked perfect.

"Doctor Bateman, thank you for coming," Kesler said, extending his hand.

She shook it. "Thank you, Mr. Kesler," she said, nodding toward Hanson. "This is my date, Steve Hanson."

Kesler's grip was firm. Hanson hoped his was the same. It was his first billionaire handshake.

"This is all quite impressive," Hanson said, opening with a well-rehearsed line.

"You like it? Good. Some of my guests feel that I am taking my quiet zone rules a bit too far with this Luddite display tonight," he replied, glancing at the candles.

"It's a nice change of pace," Makani said. "Nowadays, people look at their phones instead of interacting with each other."

"It is an interesting social experiment," Kesler acknowledged, smiling. "However, the lack of outside connection has some of my guests nervous about the upcoming eruption. I was hoping you could allay some of those fears?"

She produced a thumb drive from her clutch. "I have a small presentation on this. Is this safe to use?"

"Yes. Plugging something into a computer is no problem," Kesler answered as he motioned to someone nearby. A mountain of a man with a shaved head approached. Kesler's bodyguard. His dress shirt was bursting at the seams due to the bulletproof vest he was wearing.

"Give this to Rankin, have him queue it up on the overhead projector," Kesler instructed.

The bodyguard left.

"I'll make a short announcement," Kesler said, turning back to them. "Then I will introduce you. Your presentation will appear on that screen near the quartet."

He left. Makani cast her eyes about, searching for another glass of champagne.

"I'm so nervous," she said.

"I'm sure you'll knock it out of the ballpark."

"But these people, they're all so rich."

"Then look at me. I'll stand in the middle of the pack. Focus on me."

She seemed to relax at that thought. "I will," she said as she handed her small purse to Hanson.

The string quartet wound down. Kesler strode out in front of them.

"Distinguished guests, welcome to the KET Observatory," Kesler said, spreading his arms. He then gestured toward the room's windows. "Where humanity truly reaches for the stars, thanks to your contributions."

Outside, the massive radio telescope loomed in all its glory. Further east, over the Yakima Valley, a full moon was rising over the horizon.

Everyone applauded. Then a blonde woman dressed in an elegant white gown stepped forward.

"This is all nice, Wayne," she said, holding up her phone pouch. "But this is the longest I've been out of contact from my company in five years."

Everyone roared with laughter, most holding up their own pouches. The rich and powerful did not relinquish their lifelines to their businesses easily.

"Understandable, Madelyne," Kesler answered. "I'm sure most of us here are never out of touch with the outside world for any length of time. And now, those of us with assets in the Pacific Northwest have a new worry to consider, Mount St. Helens."

Everyone, including Hanson, turned and looked south to where, though out of sight, the volcano rested.

"Tonight, we don't have access to the USGS's app for keeping tabs on the volcano," Kesler said, holding up his own pouch. "So, to calm your worries for this evening, I have brought something even better. Let me introduce Doctor Makani Bateman of the United States Geological Survey."

Kesler held out his hand toward Makani. She walked toward him as everyone applauded. Hanson could see that all the men present were now admiring her as she moved across the room, while the women were giving him the 'who's this guy' stare.

Kesler moved away. Someone gave Makani a push-button device connected to a cord.

She looked up, locking on Hanson's eyes for a moment. He grinned back at her.

Behind her, the familiar photo sequence of the 1980 Mount St. Helens landslide and eruption sprang into view, and Makani addressed the crowd.

"Where were you when Mount St. Helens erupted?" she began.

Chapter 13

Hanson could tell she had done this sort of thing before, though most likely not so well dressed. Her confidence was back, and she had the crowd enthralled by her presentation. Behind her was a colorful diagram that illustrated volcanic eruptions of various magnitudes.

"We measure eruptions and what they project into the atmosphere with the Volcanic Explosivity Index," Makani explained. "Zero and one on the scale is gentle, eight is mega-colossal."

Behind her, computer animations of past volcanic eruptions were running.

"It's easier to appreciate this scale with examples," Makani continued. "Mount Pelee, in 1902, was a four. In 1883, Krakatoa, responsible for the loudest noise heard by mankind, was a six. Mount St. Helens, four decades ago, was a five. We expect Tuesday's eruption to be a three, which, though not catastrophic, is substantial. Let me show how we know that."

Video of volcano sensing equipment appeared on the screen.

Hanson glanced over at Kesler to see how he was taking the

presentation. It surprised him when he saw the billionaire talking to two Marines.

A man and a woman. Being a black-tie affair, both were in their dress blues and looked sharp, though out of place. Whatever they were discussing must have been important, for they had Kesler's attention.

Fisher had asked him to watch out for anything unusual. This fit the bill. Hanson kept his eye on them.

Up front, Makani was still talking. "Of course, instruments can't cover everything. Sometimes, we require a human touch."

The video changed to a montage of geologists in action. College students in t-shirts and shorts were guiding down equipment lowered by helicopter. An older couple was filming a pyroclastic cloud rolling down a mountainside.

The crowd gasped out loud at the next scene. It showed a geologist wearing a bulky, silver-colored heat proximity suit and air tank standing only a few feet from the edge of a roiling caldera of lava. Geysers of lava seemed to shoot over the figure's head, who looked vulnerable and insignificant against the display of Mother Nature's fury.

Hanson felt uneasy watching it, and he knew why. This particular video had sound, so a deep rumbling was coming over the speakers. Hanson amended what he had told the Garbers about earthquakes. Volcanoes also generated the 19Hz to 20Hz wavelength and caused feelings of foreboding. Coupled with the acute angle and long camera lens used to record the scene, it appeared that the silver figure was doomed.

Someone in the crowd voiced what everyone was feeling.

"My God, how long can anyone stand in that situation?" a man asked.

"I was only able to stay for thirty minutes before I had to retreat due to the heat," Makani answered.

There was a pause in the crowd.

"That's you?" another man asked.

"Yes," Makani answered, smiling. On her chest, the opal glittered, and now all the men in the room were viewing her with undisguised interest.

The video changed to the more familiar crater of Mount St. Helens. A drone was being used to view the lava dome. Glowing red cracks covered it.

These fissures also laced the floor of the crater, zig-zagging across the rocky terrain. Again, a silver-clad figure was present, this time bent near a piece of equipment.

"I was on the mountain a few days ago," Makani narrated for the crowd. "We had delivered what we call a 'spider,' a seismometer on tripod legs that can be rapidly deployed by helicopter. After Crater Glacier had melted and slid away we realized we could put equipment on the crater floor itself. But it didn't settle as we wanted. With magma near the surface, the temperature was uncomfortable, so they sent me in to fix it."

The drone pulled in closer. Hanson could see that the device had a bright yellow base with a bold identification number stenciled on it. Makani was working on the tripod base, twisting a knob to level it.

"But I'm not the star of this show tonight," she said. "Many of you are still wondering how it is we know when the volcano will erupt."

A still image of another geologist filled the screen. He was short, balding, and was wearing glasses. He was standing next to what Hanson recognized as a custom-made computer modem.

"This is Professor Donald Terrington, geologist and computer whiz. He's on loan to the CVO from the east coast, and he's the one that devised the computer program for predicting volcanic eruptions.

"But there's more to it than that. A few months ago, when Mount St. Helens was awakening, he traveled to Washington DC and sought aid from the President. He wanted access to the Stratton Institute supercomputer named Icarus, which already had simulation programs on it that modeled earthquakes.

"Remember, forty years ago, all we had was computers that still used floppy disks. Now we have a supercomputer that can perform twenty-five petaflops a second . . ."

She looked at the crowd. "Which I'm guessing is a lot."

Several computer company millionaires nodded their heads, as did Hanson.

"Icarus is our greatest asset. With it, Terrington has run thousands of complicated simulations, with the following scenario projected as the most likely."

The screen shifted to a cutaway view of the volcano displaying two primary magma chambers and the domes on the mountain.

The eruption simulation ran. First there was a decrease of magma near the top of the volcano, causing the floor of the crater to collapse, bringing the northern dome and southern dome with it. This changed the dynamics of pressure build-up within the volcano, and the southern half of the cone erupted, sending ash straight up. Soon after, what remained of the northern dome exploded, sending ash laterally outward.

"So that's why we are confident in our prediction, and we are all safe for tonight. Mount St. Helens will erupt four days from now. A category three event that will send a column of ash into the air and give . . ." she nodded towards the east, where the moon hung in the sky. "Eastern Washington a fair dusting."

An image of a young blond man appeared on the screen. His hair was longish, and he had a beard. He was sitting on a folding chair, writing on a paper tablet.

"I'll end on a somber note," Makani said, her voice softening a bit, her smile gone. "All this science comes with a price.

"There's a reason why the tourist attraction near Mount St. Helens is called the Johnston Observatory. This is David Johnston. He held a post six miles north of the volcano on May 18, 1980. He was aware of the danger, but felt human monitoring was necessary to keep the public safe. When the mountain exploded, his last message was 'Vancouver, Vancouver! This is it!'"

Makani paused a moment. The crowd was silent.

"This is it," she finished.

Another photo rotated into place. Kris Steinsson.

"Not all danger comes to geologists from Mother Nature. Our decisions, when it comes to safety, sometimes rub people the wrong way, with dire consequences. So when you look at our app, and you find yourself somewhere safe four days from now, remember that it came at a great cost."

The screen darkened.

Show over.

"So you don't think it was Bigfoot like everyone else seems to," a woman said. Everyone turned toward Makani, intent on her answer.

Makani looked at Hanson.

"I don't believe in Bigfoot."

Hanson felt a moment of panic as everyone present turned to look at him. Fortunately, Kesler saved the day by stepping forward.

"Thank you very much, doctor Bateman. We can all now be at ease for the rest of the evening, safe from both volcanoes and threatening cryptids," Kesler said.

He turned to face his guests. "Now, enjoy your refreshments. I will soon be making an announcement of my own," he finished.

The crowd shifted into mingling mode again, which Hanson hated. He started to make a beeline for Makani, only to notice the male Marine, a handsome Italian-looking guy, already talking to her.

Hanson squeezed the purse he was holding in annoyance. The guy was horning in on his date. He picked up his pace and continued toward them.

The female Marine intercepted him.

Chapter 14

First Lt. Kara Hamsfield forced herself to smile at Hanson. Making small talk at parties wasn't her idea of fun. She'd rather be up in the air, flying her jet.

But she and her partner had received a message a few days ago. Tonkov wanted intelligence on Bateman. The Russian general worried that the geologist could turn into a problem as Steinsson had. Due to her and Monetti's relationship with the billionaire, Kesler had listened to them and taken them up on their suggestion to invite Bateman to the party. And to find out what she knew, Monetti was doing what he did best—turning on the charm.

Though, now, with Hanson here as her date, the issue of Makani Bateman was moot in Kara's mind.

The geologist, along with Hanson, had to be eliminated.

But Monetti still had to make sure that Bateman hadn't compromised Terrington yet, so Kara now found herself in the position of distracting Hanson. For the tens of millions she and Monetti were about to receive, she could endure a few minutes of torture.

Strontium had a few photographs of Hanson from his daughter's Facebook page, so she was able to pick him out from the crowd. He was handsome, in a dull sort of way. He definitely didn't stand out amongst the rich and beautiful while wearing his off-the-rack tuxedo.

Hanson also looked confused with her standing in front of him. She hoped he was sharp enough to give her an opening.

He was now looking her over, noting her medals, rank, and wings. He stood a little straighter.

"Lieutenant," Hanson greeted her. There was respect in his voice.

Good. Once a Marine, always a Marine. She knew all about his past, but she couldn't let on.

"Oh, you've served," she said, making her smile larger. "I'm glad. I was beginning to feel like a fish out of water around here. I'm Kara Hamsfield. But please, call me Kara."

Hanson was nervously shifting Bateman's purse from hand to hand. He settled for holding it behind him.

"And you can call me Steve."

"When were you in the service?"

"Back in Desert Storm, oh, about three decades ago," he answered. He sounded a little surprised when he said it, as if he just did the math in his head and realized how much time had gone by. "I was part of the Marine forces there."

She knew this, as the Russians had gone digging. There was more to his story. Hanson had participated in the Battle of Kuwait International Airport and had received a Bronze Star. He had saved a group of Green Berets by using a steamroller he had found on the tarmac to take out an Iraqi tank.

But he was either modest or bashful, for he didn't elaborate.

"Where's your squadron located?" he asked.

"Yuma," she answered. "We were a Harrier group. We switched over to the F-35B Lightnings."

"I've heard of those. They're part of America's new fifth-generation jet fighters. The Lightnings, they're the ones that can hover and land vertically?"

"Oorah, Steve."

"How are they compared to the Harriers?"

"The Harriers were like riding a unicycle while juggling," she answered. "And could be scary at times. The Lightnings are a dream. They can even hover in place with no pilot adjustments."

Her distraction was working. Hanson appeared interested as she discussed fighter jets. But then his eyes flickered over her shoulder for a moment. Though that annoyed her, she kept her smile.

She was accustomed to men paying attention to her. Tall, blonde, blue eyes, and still slim at thirty-eight years of age, many had told her she was beautiful—even striking—in appearance.

But Hanson had eyes only for Bateman. Kara wasn't used to being second fiddle in any room. The volcano-exploring geologist was a tough act to follow.

She looked over her shoulder.

"That's Lt. Tony Monetti, my wingman," she said. "Doing what he does best, showing everyone that he's the real alpha wolf here."

Hanson stood there frowning. God, it was so easy to tell what the guy was thinking. He wore his heart on his sleeve.

"What do you do for a living?" she asked.

"IT support for our local supermarket chain, Cosgroves. You know, 'they come in droves, to Cosgroves!'" He sang the last part.

"That's fascinating," she said. She tried to sound interested, but couldn't quite pull it off.

"I write a blog also, I call it *The Unexplained, Explained*," he hastily added.

She improved her acting and leaned in a bit. "What's it about?"

"Exposing untruths of the weird, unusual, and paranormal. Though sometimes I dispel false notions about mundane things as well."

"I get weird, like this Bigfoot nonsense. But what would be mundane?"

"I have a good example right here," Hanson said. "This whole concept of alpha and beta behavior is baloney. It comes from a book called *The Wolf: The Ecology and Behavior of an Endangered Species,* written by David Meck back in 1968.

"Meck had referenced a German study of captive wolves. In zoos, the individual wolves seemed to struggle for dominance over each other. The study coined the term 'alpha wolf.'

"But later, scientists realized that life in captivity was different from living in the real world. Out here, there is no alpha and beta dynamic. Meck has been working these past decades on dispelling the myth, but it is too entrenched in popular culture."

Hanson nodded toward Monetti. "Your friend here is no alpha. He's just a jerk moving in on my date."

Kara had to stop herself from laughing out loud. Hearing this would amuse Monetti. This Hanson guy was a real nerd.

"How do you two know Kesler?" Hanson asked, changing the subject.

And now he imagined himself as one of the *Hardy Boys.* Tonkov suspected that there was a chance Hanson was continuing his aid to the FBI.

"He approached us a while back. We advise him on aviation matters, things like vertical lift," she answered. "As a matter of fact, we're going to help with his announcement later on in the evening."

"I'm looking forward to seeing that—"

She was getting tired of this conversation.

"And now I need to prepare," she said, moving away. "Take care, Steve. Maybe I will see you again."

That was not likely. Tonkov had been furious at the failed attempt on Hanson's life, thinking the skeptic as a threat to his grand scheme. But then the wily Russian had seen it as an opportunity. If done correctly, a second but successful attempt on Hanson's life would help promote the General's paranormal agenda to the American public. It would also keep the more pragmatic FBI focused on the protesters and away from the CVO, which was critical. The problem was how to lure Hanson into the trap.

But now the answer was obvious. There was already a plan in

play in which some random geologists would be attacked by Bigfoot tomorrow. All she had to do was make a call to Tonkov and have him arrange so that it was Bateman who showed up where Bigfoot was waiting. And Hanson, perceiving the potential danger, would be sure to follow. Threat or not, using Bateman was the best way to make this work and reinforce the protester connection. Kara wasn't remorseful. Hanson and Bateman were obstacles to her big payday.

She thought about how she started on this path. Years ago, she and Monetti had figured out that allegiance to a country wasn't a thing anymore. There wasn't a Russia, China, or America. There were only billionaires, oligarchs who ran the world.

She remembered frustration, and wanting to change the system, but it was way beyond her. She instead took to heart some advice her father had given years ago, and she and Monetti had gone searching for Russian contacts in the Dark Web.

There they found Tonkov. Or maybe he found them. At first, their treasonous acts were small, to prove their worth, such as low-grade cipher codes and troop movement secrets.

Tonkov was also after technology in the private sector. He steered them toward Kesler, and they ingratiated themselves as advisors to the billionaire. It thrilled him to have two Marine aviators helping.

Then came the announcement that the F-35Bs were arriving at Yuma. That caught Tonkov's interest. Now, with his two Marine spies, he had a bigger fish within his reach.

America's most advanced warplane.

The original plan was to defect while based overseas, making a quick run for Russian airspace with their stealth jets. They almost had a chance when F-35Bs were being shown off to Japan. Unfortunately, she and Monetti weren't part of that group, so they missed that window of opportunity.

Moscow was getting impatient, and Kara wondered if they would be able to pull it off at all.

Then the mountain stirred.

From what she understood, Tonkov was monitoring Mount St.

Helens for another project. Using what they knew of Kesler, Tonkov conceived a new plan for stealing the F-35Bs. It was an elaborate scheme, but it had a high chance of success and the added bonus of concealing their crime.

Pulling it off meant a considerable payout, forty million for her and Monetti to split.

She didn't feel guilty.

She didn't see it as treason but more as a business transaction. There weren't any nations any more, only a global network of the very rich watching each other's backs.

She started to make her way outside, where the phone booths waited. She moved through the crowd of millionaires, who were ignoring her.

Kara couldn't do anything to change their attitudes, so again she took comfort on her father's favorite motto.

If you can't beat 'em, join 'em.

Chapter 15

Hanson tried to mingle.

Makani was busy with admirers. Monetti was still talking to her, along with several millionaires.

He thought about butting in but realized it would be like competing with Maverick from *Top Gun* and Tony Stark and Bruce Wayne at the same time.

It was a party, so he tried to make small talk himself. The problem was, everyone else was already gathered in their social groups, comparing quarterly earnings or investing strategies.

Again, Hanson felt like he couldn't compete. He switched to his socially-anxious born party tricks instead.

He couldn't use his best one—there were no pets around. Hanson had spent many a party off in another room petting someone else's cat or dog.

He also couldn't pretend that he was busy texting someone on his phone.

So he went to the buffet table instead and loaded up, balancing his small plate on the purse he was still holding. Then he stood at the fringes of the various small groups, acting like he was listening but too busy eating to say anything. He nodded in agreement with whoever was talking as he stuffed his face.

But even that could work for only so long. Feeling drained by the endeavor, he soon found himself alone at the far end of the windows, nibbling on his last prawn.

"I've been looking for you."

Hanson looked to his side. Makani had broken free and was standing next to him.

"Just taking a breather," Hanson said, holding up his plate. He handed her purse back to her. "It's been a while since I attended a party."

"I know how you feel. All these millionaires are overwhelming."

"You did great on your presentation. They loved it."

"Thanks," she replied. "I'm glad that's behind me."

They both turned to study the nearby antenna shining in the dark.

"Has anyone detected an alien transmission?" she asked.

"Back in 1977, the Big Ear dish picked up a narrowband radio signal burst that lasted for seventy-two seconds. An astronomer, so impressed with the signal's output, circled the data on a paper hardcopy that displayed it and wrote the word 'Wow!' in the margin. It is now known as the 'Wow! Signal.' Though there have been theories to debunk it, it still stands as our best candidate for an alien signal."

"How do you know all this stuff?" she asked. With her heels on, Hanson realized she was standing eye to eye with him.

"Everyone has a superpower," he said, a hint of red rising to his face. "For everyone else here, it's making millions of dollars. Mine is repeating useless trivia."

"Trivia is my superpower also. Remember my volcano scale? The largest volcanic eruption in human history was Mount Tambora in Indonesia, back in 1815. Classified as a seven on the VEI scale, it sent so much ash into the atmosphere that it caused the 'year without a summer.' Crops failed, and horses died off. With the loss of everyone's primary source of transportation, the bicycle was invented."

Hanson put his plate down on a nearby table and took a step nearer to her. Her eyes were dark and were staring back into his with a playful intensity.

"The *New York Sun* published a series of articles about life on the Moon back in 1835," Hanson responded. "They said that a huge telescope with a seven-ton lens was powerful enough to see them. The *Sun* reported the existence of forests, pyramids, unicorns, biped beavers, and strange humanoids with bat wings. It was all a lie, but the masses couldn't get enough of it. The *Sun*, which was using innovative techniques such as a steam-powered printing press and newsboys on the streets to hawk their wares, experienced a sharp spike in sales. The viral story now known as the 'Great Moon Hoax' ushered in the era of mass media."

"Tambora had another effect on history," she countered. "It immediately caused an increase in rainstorms. Scholars note that bad weather was a big part of Napoleon's defeat in 1815. Because of a volcano, Napoleon met his Waterloo."

"I concede, you do have the gift for trivia," Hanson said, holding up his hands. "And more. Exploring the calderas of active volcanoes is impressive also. Weren't you scared?"

"It was frightening," she answered. "But I wasn't too worried. There's an old trope that when the angry volcano gods want a sacrifice, it's a virgin. I've given birth to twin sons, so I knew I was safe."

"I have a daughter, so I guess I'm safe too," Hanson said. "Well, I didn't give birth to her, but I am her father. I mean, I know I don't have proof, so I guess you're going to have to take my word for it that I'm not a virgin," he finished lamely.

She took a step closer, leaning in, her eyes looking back and forth between his eyes and mouth.

"I could take your word for it, or maybe we should—"

The ringing peal of a spoon tapping a crystal wine glass interrupted them.

Hanson and Makani, along with everyone else, turned to look at Kesler.

"Time for my announcement," Kesler said.

A server took the glass and spoon. From another angle, a different server approached with a tray that had a silver domed lid on it. A cord trailed behind it.

With an exaggerated flourish, the server raised the lid. The tray had an old-fashioned rotary phone on it, the handset resting on its side.

Kesler, who looked like he was enjoying himself, picked up the receiver and held it to his ear.

"Are we ready, Rankin?"

Everyone laughed as Kesler continued his old-fashioned phone call.

"Good. Call the crew at the dish. Tell them we will be generating radio signals for the next half hour."

He hung up the phone. The server replaced the lid and retreated.

"Now, everyone, if you would join me outside."

The crowd filed out the main exit into the crisp night air. Some of Kesler's crew were waiting at the door with faux fur stoles for the women to wrap around their shoulders.

Hanson looked up. Being in Mount Rainier's rain shadow, the sky was clear, and the stars brilliant. He could even pick out the Milky Way.

They gathered at the helicopter pad, where the shroud covered truck waited.

Kesler stood in front of it.

"I thought it would be appropriate to announce my next project here, near the Galaxy Dish," Kesler said, sweeping his arms to the distant radio telescope.

"You all have made my SETI project possible, so now I'm giving you a chance to join me on my next venture. I'm presenting it here so that what you witness is for your eyes only. There are no cameras at the KET Observatory. This show is for my most loyal investors."

A man in the crowd spoke up.

"My God, Wayne, are you getting into autonomous vehicle production?"

"Autonomous cars and trucks, Stuart?" the billionaire responded. "That's the stuff of yesterday. Kesler is the brand of the future."

He nodded, and the guards pulled the shroud away. Hanson's eyebrows shot up, and everyone around him gasped.

It wasn't a truck. It was a metal frame with the outlines of a semi to disguise what was inside.

The guards rolled the frame back, exposing a small white car. It had an unusual mass of equipment on top of it.

The equipment sprang into motion, unfolding as a butterfly spreading its wings. Hanson saw that they were a collection of propellers, nestled in frames and protective mesh, similar to a large drone.

The six propellers arrayed themselves around the top of the vehicle. They locked into place, and the vehicle's headlights snapped on.

Hanson looked on in awe. He had read about this, decades ago in science magazines. Magazines that had promised him that this day would come.

It was a flying car.

Chapter 16

It had a dragonfly hood ornament that glittered, jewel-like, in the light. LED lights blinked on the propeller housings. On the back was a Washington license plate.

"I call it the *Dragonfly*," Kesler announced as everyone gathered around it.

Without the propellers, it was about the size of a Smart Car, a two-seater with some luggage space in the back. With the props out, one had to stoop to get in.

"What can it do?" a woman asked from the crowd.

"It can fly at sixty miles an hour, with a range of seventy miles at the moment," Kesler announced. "That will change as battery technology improves."

"But telling you is boring," he added. "Let me show you instead."

He brought out a key fob and pressed a button. The *Dragonfly* chirped, and the door locks thumped.

"Lt. Monetti, if you please," Kesler said, holding up the key.

Monetti strutted forward, enjoying being on display. He stepped into the vehicle. Before he shut the door he turned toward Hanson with a smirk on his face and mouthed the word 'alpha.' Kara must have filled her partner in on their conversation. Hanson felt a wave of jealousy wash over himself and found himself disliking the Marine even more.

"I suggest we step back and give him room," Kesler advised.

Everyone did as he said.

Monetti started the car, letting it idle for a few moments. Hanson could see his mouth move as he issued verbal commands. The vehicle's rotors engaged. They sounded like a hive of angry hornets, and Hanson could feel the wash from a hundred feet away.

The *Dragonfly* sprang into the air and hovered nearby at fifty feet for a few moments. Then it took off and headed south. After a quarter of a mile it did a slow turn and came back, buzzing over the landing pad. Monetti banked it toward the telescope dish, reaching the structure in a few seconds. He circled it, appearing as a giant moth fluttering about a bright light. He then returned, and with a loud whine, settled the car back on the pad.

The props powered down. Everyone, except Hanson, clapped as Monetti stepped out and took a bow.

"The way of the future," Kesler said.

The woman named Madelyne stepped forward again.

"That's all well and good, Wayne, but not everybody is a military pilot. What good is a flying car if everyone has to learn to fly?"

Kesler's eyes were twinkling. "That's a good question. Let me answer with another demonstration."

He turned to Makani. "Doctor Bateman, may I request your help one more time?"

Again, all eyes were on them. Next to Hanson, Makani looked taken aback and uncertain.

"Me? I've never flown anything in my life."

"And that's the whole point. The *Dragonfly* is an AAV, or Autonomous Aerial Vehicle. It practically flies itself."

After taking a moment to hand Hanson her purse again, she traded places with Monetti, getting into the car as the Marine pilot stood next to Hanson. Hanson ignored him as he strained to hear the instruction Kesler was giving Makani.

"It has an automatic shifter for the ground, but engage this button instead to spool up the propellers and put it in flying mode. It follows voice commands, so state 'Dragonfly' and then tell it to rise to one hundred feet. From there, use your steering column for moving forward or backward. The pedals are like a car; you can increase speed, or even come to a hovering stop with the brakes. When you want to land, command the *Dragonfly* to touch down for you."

She still looked uncertain but nodded. Kesler stepped away. There was a hush in the crowd, and even Hanson felt unsure of what was happening.

The props spooled up again, but the car sat on the pad for a few moments.

"Looks like we may need another volunteer to fly that thing," Monetti said, low enough for only Hanson to hear.

"She'll figure it out," Hanson said, frowning at the tall Marine.

"Or maybe she just needs a real man to show her how to handle a stick," Monetti said, smirking. "Or at least someone who's primary function isn't to hold a woman's purse."

"Oh yeah?!" Hanson retorted, flustered and unable to come up with a snappy comeback. Fortunately, his feeble reply was drowned out as the *Dragonfly* rose and hovered.

Then it took off.

She flew it over the tourist facility and hovered there. Hanson guessed she was taking in the view. Then she came roaring back, overshooting the pad as she headed for the telescope. Like Monetti before, she orbited it, except she took a few extra spins, even dipping below the dish at one point. She then came back, hovering over where she took off. The dragonfly descended to a soft landing and came to a standstill. Makani opened the door.

"How was it?" Kesler asked as he offered her a hand.

"Shut up and take my money!" she yelled as she stood up.

The crowd once again roared with laughter.

"My God, Kesler. How's this possible?" someone shouted.

"It's like the driverless cars on the road today. The *Dragonfly* has a GPS and radar system processed by sophisticated software. That's why I warned my crew at the dish to ignore anything they detected for the next half hour. This car puts out a ton of signals. You can't wreck this thing. Even if it loses power, the propellers go into autorotation as the air passes by them, slowing its descent. It even has airbags on the outside to absorb any impact."

Everyone gathered around the car once more. Hanson practically threw Makani's purse into her hands as she came over to stand next to him.

"What was it like?"

"A thrill," she answered. "Kesler's right, it is easy. The dash is mostly one screen showing relevant information. With its onboard computer handling the details, flying it is simple."

Hanson looked at it again. God, he wanted to take it for a spin.

"When do you plan to announce this to the public at large?" someone called out.

"As I said, tonight is about you getting the first look, as my way of thanking you for your past support," Kesler answered. "Though there aren't any official photos or videos yet, I'm expecting your word of mouth to generate a buzz. Next year I'm going to capitalize on that buzz and announce the *Dragonfly* with a bang no one will forget."

"Musk put a Tesla into outer space, how are you going to top that?" Madelyne asked.

"I have a publicity stunt of my own," Kesler said, grinning. Hanson noticed him glance at the nearby hangar before turning around to the radio telescope. "Astronomers designed the KET to search for life in the cosmos. Come next June, there is an anniversary that will allow me to remind everyone that there is already proof of life from other worlds. And when I have everyone's attention, I will reveal the *Dragonfly*."

"And how are you going to remind everyone? What else do you have up your sleeve?" someone asked.

"You'll have to wait until next year," Kesler answered.

The landing pad was loud with chatter as everyone peppered the billionaire with questions. Hanson stole a look at Kara and Monetti.

They were both glancing over their shoulders at the nearby hangar. Hanson could guess why. Whatever Kesler was going to reveal next year was being stored here at the observatory.

And the two Marines were in on it.

Chapter 17

FBI Field Office, Portland, Sunday 10:06 A.M. PDT

"That's him," Hanson said.

The image of his attacker from two nights ago stared back at him. The artist had done a fantastic job of recreating the face from Hanson's description. He had expected to work with a tech that used a facial composite program but had found out that the FBI preferred the hand-drawn method instead.

"Good, print some hard copies for my team, I'm sending them back out to the Oregon Zoo," Fisher instructed the artist. "Then scan it for our facial recognition system. Also, send it out to Sheriff Hart and every other law enforcement agency in Oregon and Washington."

"Oregon Zoo?" Hanson asked as the artist left Fisher's office.

Fisher didn't answer. Hanson could tell that the FBI agent appreciated his help but was reluctant to share anything about the case.

So Hanson offered instead.

"It's the Bigfoot hairs from Steinsson's murder, isn't it?"

Now Fisher was glaring at him. It seemed to be his favorite

expression. But then the look softened, and he stood up and shut the door to his office.

"The hairs belonged to a primate," Fisher said, returning to his desk. "I sent some agents to the zoo yesterday. An employee saw someone suspicious around their composting area about a week ago. The incident stood out because the employee said it's not every day you catch someone digging around in the monkey shit. So now I'm sending your diagram out there."

"What primates does the zoo have?" Hanson asked. Images of chest-thumping gorillas flashed through his mind.

"Some Colobus, chimps, a De Brazza's monkey, and even an orangutan," Fisher replied, looking at a sheet of paper on his desk.

"Do you think your labs will make a match?"

"I'm hoping so," Fisher answered. "If it turns out that way I'm reporting it to the news. That would help bring this Bigfoot crap to an end."

Hanson doubted that. In the face of proof, people with opposing views usually elected to disbelieve the evidence, thinking it was all conspiracies and lies.

"What about the gun? And my attacker's truck?" Hanson asked, changing tack. He had handed over the pistol, sealed up in a sandwich bag, to Fisher in the parking lot when he had arrived at the FBI building.

"We're still going over the pistol," Fisher answered, "I do know that it is a Taurus Model 85. It holds five .38 Special rounds and sports a two-inch barrel and a shrouded hammer."

Hanson remembered how fast the intruder had whipped out the gun and had seemed willing to use it.

"The truck was stolen. Oregon State Police recovered it in the parking lot of Oxbow Park," Fisher continued. "We're still going over it. What my techs can tell me is that from the truck's cab they picked up on the same smell you mentioned, a 'garage' like odor."

"Like the service bays of an oil changing business," Hanson reaffirmed. "Could this guy be some sort of mechanic?"

"Or he was under the hood of the truck when he stole it," Fisher said. "Describe last night to me."

Hanson's first thoughts were of Makani, and of how beautiful she looked throughout the evening. They had taken their plane back home shortly after Kesler's flying car reveal. That trip was pleasant also, most of it discussing family, or her work, since her job was much more interesting.

Unfortunately, a colleague was waiting with a running car when they landed at Pearson. She was breathless with excitement. Something had happened to equipment on the mountain, and Makani's boss was quickly putting together assignments with his laptop at his home. Makani was needed at the CVO as soon as possible.

"Volcanoes can be so demanding," she said, standing in front of him.

"I have the same problem," he said. "Registers break down all the time at Cosgroves."

She smiled at that and stepped closer, her eyes still at a perfect height, pupils wide in the dim light.

"I hope we can do this again," he added.

"I'll call you when I get a break," she replied.

Even an introvert like him could pick up on her cues. He leaned in, kissing her, their mouths also at the same level.

Her lips moved against his, giving him the subtlest of suggestion that she wanted more. He held her close in his arms, his hands on her bare back, feeling the smoothness of her skin—

"Hanson!"

He snapped back to Fisher's office, blinking.

"What happened at the KET?" Fisher prodded.

"Kesler's coming out with a flying car," Hanson said, shifting in his chair.

"I know that. One of the guests gave an interview here in town on one of the morning news shows," Fisher said.

"He's planning something big for next year. And it involves a couple of Marines. They're both F-35B Lightning pilots, based out of

Yuma. One is named Kara Hamsfield. The other is a guy named Tony Monetti. Both lieutenants."

"What's their relationship with Kesler?" Fisher asked, writing at his desk.

"I don't think they're giving away military secrets," Hanson answered. "But Kesler's *Dragonfly* moves like a helicopter. So does the F-35B. They must be giving him advice."

Fisher frowned, tapping his pen on his pad of paper.

"You like Kesler for this, don't you?" Hanson asked.

"I'm not excluding him," Fisher answered. "Your 'someone's upset because they have something to lose in the eruption' theory is a good one, and businesses on Highway 12, including the KET, will soon be closed down for a few days. And almost everyone on his guest list is affected one way or the other by the volcano. They all bear watching."

"So now what are you going to do?"

"The usual. Gather more evidence," Fisher answered, standing up. "I appreciate your help, Hanson, I really do. And I hope you realize that me sharing all this is not normal."

Hanson stood up also, his heart rate increasing as the FBI agent fixed him with a stare.

"But someone is interested in you and Doctor Bateman, and that makes you a part of this investigation," Fisher added. "And only by working together will we get to the bottom of it. So don't hesitate to call me if you think of anything else."

Authority figure. Anxiety. Hanson's heart was pounding in his chest again.

"I can do that," Hanson answered.

An agent arrived and escorted Hanson through the building and to the front door. Heat blasted Hanson as he stepped outside. The forecast for the area projected low nineties for the afternoon.

Hanson made his way to his van, giving voice commands.

"Computer, unlock doors, and engine start."

The van started up.

"Engage air conditioner."

Hanson waited in his vehicle as it cooled down, wishing that the van could fly. That would be something.

His phone vibrated and chimed in his pocket.

Makani.

"How's the volcano?" he asked, turning towards Mount St. Helens to the north.

"The mountain's fine," she answered. "And is behaving as predicted."

"How are you doing?"

"That's why I'm calling you," she said. "Protesters have messed with some of the seismometers we have around the mountain and they need repair. The rest could use recalibrating, so they are sending a bunch of us out to do it. Like Steinsson did a few days ago, out in the forest."

Though she didn't say it, he could tell she was worried, and Hanson understood what she was implying in her last sentence from the sound of her voice.

Out in the forest.

Bigfoot country.

Chapter 18

Mount St. Helens' Eastern Shoulder, 5:45 P.M. PDT

"I think we're getting close," Hanson said.

"Good. This next seismometer station is our last one. When we are done with it, we get to turn back home," Makani responded, grunting as the pickup truck she was driving lurched over a pothole on the dusty road.

Hanson looked out his window as the trees passed by. The logging road they were on was deep in the Gifford Pinchot National Forest, approximately twenty miles southeast of Mount St. Helens.

"What do you see?" she asked.

"Not Bigfoot," Hanson answered.

"You sound almost disappointed."

"It's something I used to do as a kid when my mother and I travelled to Portland from Astoria," Hanson answered, turning towards her. "I would stare into the trees, hoping to catch Bigfoot unawares. One glimpse was all I wanted."

"And Mount St. Helens erupting killed the dream for you," she said. "How did other people rationalize the lack of any Bigfoot sightings that day?"

"Back in the seventies, some Bigfoot enthusiasts thought Bigfoot was an alien, and he bugged out on flying saucers before the eruption," Hanson said, grinning. "But the more common thought is that Bigfoots did perish on the mountain. There's a conspiracy story on the web that black helicopters were seen hauling away the charred remains of large creatures."

"And people believed this?" she said incredulously.

Hanson thought about his ten-year-old self, clinging to those ideas for several months.

"Yeah," he answered, bracing himself as they bounced out of another pothole.

After Makani's phone call, Hanson had used the Glenn Jackson Bridge to drive to her building, which was just across the Columbia River from the FBI field office. He was going to try to talk her out of it.

Reaching her wasn't easy. A small group of protesters had been keeping vigil at the CVO for the past week, and getting past them was nerve-wracking. People gave him dirty stares and waved signs as Vancouver Police escorted him through their line. Makani had cleared him to be let in. Hanson took better looks at their signs as he inched by.

End The Tyranny

We Are Not Prisoners

President's Puppets

Once past that, Hanson had found a crowd of volcanologists standing in the back parking lot. Makani's bosses had mustered most of the CVO crew for the project, and they were taking precautions.

The geologists were going out in seven pairs to repair and fine-tune equipment dotting the mountain. Some of the geologists were locals, and were experienced hunters in their free time. They had brought their own hunting rifles, so some of the small groups had their own protection. Hanson felt reassured by that. Even if one took the possibility of violent protesters posing as Bigfoot out of the equation the area still had a population of black bear and cougar. It was a reasonable precaution.

But Hanson's alarm returned as he watched someone hand Makani's partner a bolt action 30.06. At some points the geologist had the rifle pointed at several people as he turned with the weapon in hand. Hanson guessed it was the guy's first time handling firearms.

Hanson volunteered to go with Makani instead. Makani's boss, the CVO's Scientist in Charge, Doctor Owen Livken, had balked at the idea for insurance and legal reasons. But Makani, and the Professor Terrington guy, who Hanson had recognized from Makani's video, argued for and secured Hanson's inclusion. Makani's original partner joined a small group that had the heaviest workload of the day. Hanson, thankful for Terrington's help, signed some waivers and also exchanged numbers with Livken. The geologist wanted to be able to contact him.

Each team was either going to repair a piece of broken equipment or service three intact ones. Cell coverage was spotty at best in the deep woods, so each truck had a radio. To boost the radios' effectiveness, a CVO helicopter would be circling the volcano. Any truck in sight of the chopper would gain better range and reception. In addition, a contracted helicopter would be ferrying one of Sheriff Hart's deputies. The sheriff wasn't keen on the idea of armed confrontations. If any protesters tried to block their way, the repair crews were to back off and call in the deputy.

The departure of seven CVO trucks took the protesters by surprise. They quickly recovered, and Hanson was dismayed as he watched several of them make calls on their cell phones. His anxiety faded when he spotted the helicopters in the air as he and Makani left Vancouver. The helicopters would also be in contact with deputies on the ground, who were clearing the way by chasing out trespassers. The eyes in the sky ignored the CVO trucks since they had distinctive markings on top of their cabs.

So far, their afternoon had been uneventful. Makani was on tune-up duty and she had already serviced two stations. Between the maintenance stops, she drove while Hanson acted as navigator. When needed, he would hop out of the truck to open Forest Service gates with a master key they possessed. The only other rig they passed on the road was a deputy driving the other direction. Helicopters had passed several times over their heads.

Hanson put down the GPS unit he was holding.

"Park here," he said.

She pulled over into a small clearing. Hanson hopped out and surveyed their surroundings.

The dark-sided volcano was about twenty miles northwest of them. Mount Adams, with a bit of snow still on it, was twenty miles northeast.

It had been hot all afternoon. For this last job, with the sun lower, it was starting to cool off. Hanson looked up into the sky. It was still a bright blue, and he saw two helicopters floating nearby.

"Aloha, Vancouver, we're parked near our third station," Makani said into her radio.

"Two hours until check-in then," a male voice responded. "Good luck, Makani."

Makani shouldered a pack with her tools. "It's about a half-hour walk in, one hour to work on the equipment, then a half-hour walk back."

"Uuf da," Hanson sighed, shouldering his own pack with hiking supplies. "We better get going. The sun will be close to setting when we get back to the truck."

"But it's still up now, so hold still a moment," she said, approaching him with a tube of suntan lotion in hand. She rubbed it on his skin. Hanson waited quietly, enjoying the feel of her hand gliding along his arm. She lifted the left sleeve of his t-shirt a bit to put some on his shoulder. It exposed a tattoo of an eagle driving a steam roller. On the steam rollers side were the letters USMC.

"What's this?" she asked.

"I got that after the war—long story," Hanson answered.

She worked the right arm, finding the tattoo of the d20 die on that shoulder.

"And this?"

"That's a natural twenty on gaming dice," Hanson grinned. "Twenty always succeeds. If anyone touches it, whatever I do next with that arm will always succeed. It's my good luck charm."

She shook her head. "Skeptic, but still superstitious."

"Some things are hard to let go of," Hanson confessed.

She put the last bit over his face, leaning in for a quick kiss when she finished. He savored that also.

"Not my idea of a second date," she said ruefully.

They were hot, sweaty, and dusty from their afternoon hiking.

"I know a nice place for cold beers if they let you go this evening," Hanson said.

"I'm looking forward to that. Let's finish this," she said.

She took up the GPS device, Hanson, the rifle. He was familiar with the weapon; he had inherited one from his father when he had passed away in the mid-seventies. Hanson had used it when elk hunting with his uncle during his teens.

The rifle was single bolt action. Back at the CVO, ammunition had been parsed out. Hanson had a dozen cartridges. He slid one into the rifle and split the rest in his front pockets. He hoped no protesters found them. Things could go south real quick if that happened.

They started out. Though there wasn't much of a path, there were markers on the trees, reflective disks with yellow ribbons fluttering below them.

He and Makani also stood out. They were wearing jeans with bright yellow t-shirts the USGS had provided them. Makani had her hair in a ponytail and was also wearing a blue cap with 'USGS' in white letters across the front.

They plunged into the woods that surrounded them. Again

Hanson peered between the trees, only this time with a rifle in his hands.

"Hypothetically, if you saw Bigfoot, would you shoot it?" Makani asked.

"If there was such a creature, no," Hanson answered. "And even if I was so inclined, I would still hesitate. They passed a law here in Skamania County. Killing one carries a one year in jail penalty."

She raised her eyebrows. "You're kidding."

He grinned back at her. "No. In this area, Bigfoot is officially a protected species."

They climbed down a steep embankment. At the bottom, they turned south. After fifty yards they came upon a small log cabin with an outhouse nearby. The slope, which they had been keeping to their right, was higher and steeper here. It loomed over the structure.

"Is this for the Forest Service?" Makani asked.

"I'm guessing it's for campers," Hanson said. "Some trails reach out this far from the Mount Adams recreational area to our east."

They marched southwards. After a quarter of a mile, Makani found what they were looking for.

It was a rugged, brown-colored plastic casing about five feet high. Its angled top faced south and had solar panels mounted on it. An antenna rose two more feet on its west side.

Makani had explained beforehand that it was a seismic and deformation station. It transmitted data in real-time and was part of the Pacific Northwest Seismic Network. The upcoming eruption was a rare opportunity, and geologists had focused a record amount of equipment toward the volcano. Livken wanted everything in top-notch condition for the next few days.

Makani had a key for the case and she opened it up and went to work. Though Hanson wanted to watch, he turned away instead, his eyes on the forest.

She made small talk while she worked.

"How are the cats during all this?"

"This was an unexpected trip, so I called in Tolmany to feed them," Hanson answered.

"How's he doing?"

"He's fine," Hanson answered. He didn't tell her that Tolmany had informed all their gaming buddies that Hanson had been out on a date. Hanson's texting app had been active all morning as his friends discussed Hanson's social drought coming to a three-year end. The upcoming volcano eruption was also brought up, and parallels were being made.

It was cooler out, and the sun was much lower when she finished. They buttoned up the unit and made their way back to the cabin, pausing to use the old fashioned outhouse.

"I guess that's one thing off my bucket list," she said in disgust as she exited it.

They climbed the hill and followed the markers back. Makani, who was out in front, stopped at the forest's edge when they made the road.

"Steve," she gasped.

Something had damaged the truck by smashing in the windows and headlights. One door hung askew, and the flattened tires sagged to their rims. Large human-like footprints circled the vehicle.

Makani took a step forward, but Hanson put a hand on her shoulder and pulled her back into the trees.

"Don't go out there," he whispered, looking all around him.

"But we need to get to the radio."

"It's most likely destroyed also," he said. "Don't go out into the open, they might be watching."

"Who?"

In answer, a strange hooting reached their ears. An eerie whistle followed it.

"What the hell?" she whispered. Now her eyes were wide.

"How long until Vancouver considers us overdue?" Hanson asked.

"We made good time on this last station, so check-in time is twenty minutes from now," she answered, looking into the woods all around her. "If the chopper is on the other side of the mountain with the other repair crews, it could be another thirty to forty minutes before it checks in on us."

"But the deputy's helicopter has been making regular rounds all day," she added. "It should be swinging by real quick."

They both looked up. The only thing in the air was a circling hawk.

Makani's thinking was hoping for the best. Glancing back at the wrecked truck, Hanson realized they needed to prepare for the worst.

"Our phones aren't getting any signals out here, so we need to hold out for that hour," Hanson said grimly. "Come on; let's go back to the cabin."

"Shouldn't we wait here, near the truck?"

"We're too exposed." More hooting sounded off, this time closer. "Remember, this can't be Bigfoot. It's men, and they most likely have guns. We need some cover."

It was getting dark, but Hanson refrained from breaking out their lantern. For a few moments he contemplated firing a shot into the air, as there was a small chance a random deputy was within hearing range. He held off on that and instead led them away from the truck.

In the distance he could hear tree branches rustling and twigs snapping.

The whistling and hooting increased. At one point, Hanson thought he saw a large shadow flit from tree to tree. Again, he refrained from firing his rifle.

He stopped often to listen. Makani would keep close whenever he did this. She was trembling.

Hanson could understand. Even though he knew the history and all the lies of Bigfoot, it was easy to imagine the creature out there.

They made the embankment. Here, they were out in the open, so Hanson led them both in a rapid zig-zagging dash to the bottom. The cabin was less than fifty yards away. The foliage was sparse, but

Hanson used whatever cover he could find. As they moved, the background noises increased in intensity.

They made the outhouse. Hanson took a moment to judge the distance to the cabin.

"Above us," Makani moaned.

Hanson followed her gaze.

The hill above the cabin loomed. It was to the west, so the few trees that lined the ridge line were in silhouette with the setting sun behind them.

As were the three giant hairy figures that were standing up there, watching them.

Chapter 19

For the third time, Hanson considered lifting up his rifle and snapping off a shot. For the third time, he held off.

"Makani, bring out your phone. Take a photo with the flash enabled," Hanson commanded as he kept his rifle pointed at the ground.

He heard her reach for her phone in her pocket. Above them, the three hulking forms watched. After a moment, a bright flash went off behind Hanson, along with a synthesized sound effect of a camera shutter.

The Bigfoots retreated from the ridge line.

"Let's get inside," Hanson said, making for the door.

The door had a single cylinder dead-bolt installed. It was unlocked, and they both pushed in. The interior was dark. Hanson pulled out a small LED lantern from his pack and switched it on.

The cabin was one room. A fireplace was in the corner to their right. A kitchen countertop stretched out from it. It had a stainless steel basin inset, but no faucet. Cupboards lined the bottom of the counter.

The wall across from them had a shuttered window with a two-by-four barring it. Below that were a rough table and two chairs. A broom leaned nearby against the wall.

The last wall to their left had two beds end to end. Together, they stretched the entire width of the cabin. Thin mattresses were on both.

Hanson placed the lantern on the fireplace's mantle and stood guard at the door.

"Makani, break out the glow sticks," he said, peeking outside.

She pulled four out of the backpack, bending and shaking them to life.

"Steve, why didn't you shoot at them when you had the chance?" she asked as she handed them to him.

"I think it would have changed the rules of engagement," Hanson answered as he jammed one of the light sticks into the eave above the door, making a crude porch light.

"What do you mean?"

"They're going through a lot of trouble to promote their Bigfoot narrative. It's important to them. They had plenty of chances to shoot us out there, but they didn't."

"So they're trying to scare us," she said, her face relaxing with relief.

Hanson was hanging two more light sticks on nails above the window. He turned toward her.

"No, Makani, they will try to kill us. But they're going to make a big show of it, whistling and hollering while they pound on the door. They're hoping that we're recording everything on our phones. That's why I asked you to make it clear that we were. They'll keep up their act as long as they think we have our cameras on. Then, at the last moment, they will switch to their guns."

Her eyes were wide again. "But won't that show that they are human?"

"They'll take our phones and edit out the last few moments. When the authorities get here and go over this place, all they will find is a wrecked cabin, our blood for DNA matching, and a whole hell of a lot of large footprints. They will assume the bullet holes in the cabin walls came from me. Our phones will be amongst the debris, and on them will be recordings of our last terrifying moments. Found footage, like *The Blair Witch Project*. We'll be famous."

"So if you use your rifle—"

"Then they switch to plan B that much sooner and simply use their guns. There was a chance I could have attracted the attention of a deputy if I had fired a shot into the air by the truck. But if I had, we would have died under a hail of bullets. When they bust out their guns, we won't have a chance. We have to hold that moment off and go along with their charade for . . ." Hanson glanced at his watch. "Thirty-five more minutes."

From outside they could hear hooting with some growling thrown in.

"Maybe less," Makani said hopefully. "That helicopter with the deputy is still making the rounds."

Hanson paused as he was locking the door but didn't answer.

"You don't think help is coming, do you?" she asked.

"I don't," Hanson answered. "Doing all of this is a huge risk for these guys. They must have a contingency plan for keeping the helicopters off their backs."

Makani stopped in the middle of the room, despair on her face. Hanson stood in front of her and put his hands on her shoulders.

"It's going to be okay. Put everything we have on that mantle, including your phone. Set it up to record, so that we have something to show Fisher the next time we see him."

"You think we're going to make it?" she asked.

"We have a big advantage," Hanson replied as he scooted one of the beds toward the door. "I've read their script."

Makani dug into the backpacks, setting up water bottles and health bars. There was even a flare gun with two flares.

As she was loading it, Hanson moved the second bed. As they

were earlier against the wall, Hanson laid them out end to end in the middle of the room against the door, bracing it.

It was getting noisier outside and they could hear stomping sounds. Their attackers were trying to leave as many footprints as they could.

Hanson grabbed the broom, snapping it off at the bristles. He brought out his Leatherman multitool and selected the knife blade. He whittled down the broken end.

"What are you doing?" Makani asked.

"Making a spear," Hanson said. "I took javelin in track and field. Back in the day, I could sling one of these babies a couple of hundred feet."

"All I took was the triple jump in high school," Makani confessed. "No one else did it, so I thought I could excel in it."

Hanson gave her a small smile. "Well, I can't think of any real-world applications for the triple jump," he said, holding out his knife. "So take this and keep it handy."

She took up the knife. Outside, things quieted down for a moment.

Then something crashed into the side of the cabin with a resounding boom. A log shifted a few inches from the force of the impact.

Makani, who was standing nearby, yelped in fear and jumped away from the wall. Hanson snatched up his spear and faced the door.

Like Ape Canyon a century before, the assault had begun.

Chapter 20

Outside, the Bigfoots roared in anger.

Crashing noises came from the roof. Heavy objects were impacting it.

"They must have someone up on the hill; he's throwing rocks down on us," Hanson said, looking up.

"Will it hold?" Makani yelled over the din.

"I don't know," Hanson replied, his voice raised also.

Dust was filtering down on them from the rafters. Hanson had to rub the irritation out of his eyes.

Another blow struck the side of the building, but the log siding held. The cabin was sturdy. At least they had that going for them.

After a few minutes, the rain of stones stopped. The howling and grunting continued.

"I think the hilltop guy is coming down to help out," Hanson said to Makani's questioning look.

"What do you think is next—" she began.

The sound of glass breaking made them turn away from the door and look at the window behind them. The shutter covering the window heaved, and the two-by-four cracked.

"Stay by the corner," Hanson commanded. He flattened himself against the wall next to her, a few feet from the window.

There was another blow against the shutter, and it burst open. Hanson saw the end of a two-foot diameter log extend into the room and then draw back. Their attackers were using a ram.

"My God, did you see that?" Makani gasped.

Hanson nodded. For a brief second, a few feet back from the window, he had glimpsed a simian face in the darkness.

"They're fully costumed for our camera," Hanson muttered. "Turn off the lantern."

The cabin plunged into near darkness, the only illumination being the two light sticks over the window and the one on the mantle.

Hanson tossed the mantle stick outside. It landed twenty feet away in the dirt.

He took a quick look, wary of anyone waiting with a gun. Outside, two shambling forms dropped a ten-foot-long log and ran into the darkness.

"Caught two of them," Hanson told Makani with some satisfaction. Without their ram, Hanson was hoping that would stop their attacks on the cabin for a few minutes.

Outside, the howling continued.

"I heard this pattern a few minutes ago," Makani said. "They must have some sort of recording of monkeys on a loop."

"Must be on one of their phones," Hanson whispered back. "It's connected to a blue-tooth speaker."

That gave him an idea. But before he could act on it, something crashed into the door.

Hanson faced toward it, crouching, so no one outside had an easy shot. Makani pressed herself against the wall near the window.

Again, there was a crash against the door.

"It sounds like someone's trying to kick it down," Makani said.

A long, hairy arm snaked from the window and grabbed her.

"Steve!" she screamed.

Hanson turned toward her, shifting his spear for a quick jab.

A softball-sized stone sailed through the window, glancing off of Hanson's left arm. Its jagged edges tore a deep gash into his bicep. Hanson stumbled back with a grunt of pain.

The Bigfoot arm dragged Makani toward the window.

"Back off!" she yelled, plunging her knife into the arm holding her.

Window Bigfoot gave a muffled yell and snatched back its arm, its scream of pain sounding much different from the recording blaring outside.

Standing back up, Hanson caught a look at the second one. It was winding up for another pitch.

He heaved his spear at it.

The spear shot out the window and connected with its target, piercing the creature's right leg. Hanson shook his head and corrected himself. Man's right leg. He was surprised at how easy it was to think of their attackers as real Bigfoots.

The speared figure howled in anguish and retreated into the shadows.

Again something heaved against the door. Hanson took up the rifle.

"We hurt them," Makani said.

"But not enough," Hanson replied, grimacing in pain. Blood was running down his left bicep.

"Steve, your arm."

"I know, one of them tagged me."

"Watch the window, let me work on it."

She took up the first aid kit and water bottle. They huddled on the fireplace's low hearth as she washed away the blood. She then placed a thick wad of gauze on that, securing it with several of the larger bandages.

He took out his phone and turned it on. He handed it to her.

"How much time?"

"Fifteen, maybe ten minutes," she answered.

"Go to my phone's settings. Try to pair with that speaker out there."

While she did that, Hanson took an oblique look out the window. The battering ram was gone. They had used the past few moments to secure it.

Next to them, the door boomed as something crashed into it. The top half shifted, but the bottom half, braced by the beds, didn't budge.

"I have it," Makani said, holding up the phone.

The door heaved again. A crack was forming at its midpoint. The top half was going to break off before the bottom yielded.

"Rest my phone next to yours for now," Hanson yelled. "Grab the flare gun and shoot it out the window."

Makani snatched the flare gun off the mantle and spun around, bringing it up to level with the window ten feet away.

She fired.

The flare shot out the window, lighting up the cabin's interior as a camera's flash. Hanson and Makani closed their eyes to save their night vision.

Outside, the flare crashed into an isolated stand of trees fifty feet away, sputtering and sizzling against the trunk of a Douglas Fir.

Then it exploded.

Flames began spreading.

The ram crashed against the door again. Hanson guessed it could take two more blows, and then it would crack open.

Setting the stage for their attackers to catch them in a crossfire.

Game over.

"Load the next flare, and give me your hat," Hanson yelled.

Makani pulled her hat off and handed it to him. She then turned her attention to the flare gun.

Hanson wanted a flare shot up into the air, but leaning out the window would expose her to the enemy.

"Shoot the flare up the chimney," Hanson commanded.

She got on her back and scooched into the fireplace. She held the pistol up with both hands upward.

"It's clear," she yelled.

She turned her head to the side and closed her eyes. Light blazed from the fireplace as she fired.

The door boomed.

Hanson tossed the hat at the window, giving it a slight spin. It landed on the sill.

Someone on the outside shot it off. The hat fluttered back into the cabin.

Hanson shifted to the window, his rifle up. He could tell Makani's chimney shot was successful. The second flare was casting shifting shadows as it climbed into the sky. That, and the nearby growing fire and rising moon, lit up the outside to almost twilight conditions. He spotted a shaggy figure holding an automatic pistol in its right hand.

Hanson snapped off a shot, the rifle roaring in the tight confines of the cabin.

Bigfoot was already ducking, and Hanson's bullet gouged into a tree behind it.

"Holy shit," Bigfoot screamed as he ran into the woods behind him. It looked like it was wearing snowshoes as it lurched away.

"Makani, grab my phone, join me over here," Hanson said as he hopped over the beds and went to the cabin's far corner. He overturned the table to make a small barrier.

Makani kneeled next to him as he was reloading.

"Crank the volume, start a song from my playlist," Hanson yelled as the top of the door exploded inward.

Hanson fired a round into the door frame. Again, the rifle's report was deafening. Their attackers returned fire, pouring bullets through the door and into the kitchen wall.

Outside, the sound of howling monkeys stopped. The voice of Rick Astley singing 'Never Going to Give You Up' filled the area.

"Rick Astley is the first artist on your playlist?" Makani asked.

"Do you keep it there so that you can Rickroll people whenever you want?"

The truth was that he enjoyed the song, and listened to it every day. But she looked incredulous.

"Yeah, of course," Hanson answered.

He shot a bullet into the window sill, hoping to make his message clear to those outside. Stick your head in here and you'll lose it.

Outside, things were getting brighter, and Hanson and Makani could smell the fire.

The gunfire from outside stopped. For a few moments, the only sound was Rick Astley's voice, but that also ended when someone switched the speaker off. In the sudden quiet, Hanson could hear the clomping of large feet as the costumed men retreated.

"Stay here," Hanson said.

He moved one of the beds away and opened the door.

The battering ram was on the ground nearby. Large footprints trailed away from it.

Hanson peered around the corner.

He spotted the shaggy backsides of the trio as they plunged into the woods, heading east. Hanson guessed they had their vehicle parked in one of the Mount Adams' campsites.

The fire caught his attention. It was growing. Fortunately, it was in a small group of trees surrounded by a scree of rocks from the nearby hillside. With luck it would burn itself out without spreading.

Makani joined him outside. She had the recording cell phone in her hand, scanning the area.

"Looks like they're gone," she said.

Hanson was about to reply, but a strange buzzing sound from above made him pause. They both looked up.

A large disk was hovering several hundred yards up in the sky. A ring of thrusters on its underside glowed red and the outer rim strobed blue. At its center was a circle of intense white light. It was pointed at Hanson, and for a moment he was fearful that it was some sort of tractor beam emitter. Not wanting to be drawn up toward the light, he dodged a few feet to the side.

He needn't have bothered. With a loud whine the saucer darted away, disappearing beyond the treetops to the north.

"What the hell?!" Makani shouted, her camera held over her head.

Hanson didn't answer. He stood there, his mouth agape, dumb-founded.

He couldn't believe what he just saw with his own eyes, but there it was.

A flying saucer.

Part Two

PANIC

Chapter 21

Portland, Sunday, 9:35 p.m. PDT

F isher adjusted his pillow so that his head was at a more comfortable angle as he read the next file off of his tablet.

He felt guilty at that. Usually, he tried to keep his home life separated from work. His wife, Jessica, a lawyer with a downtown firm, did the same. They wanted to focus on each other while away from work.

But this case was proving different.

It was the pressure from Washington. His SAC was in daily contact with the Director himself, who, in turn, was updating the White House. After the hurricane, President Sandra Hayes wanted to improve her administration's record on dealing with natural disasters. She didn't want the murder of a prominent Icelandic national clouding that in any way.

So Fisher was going through the case late at night in bed, his last bastion from work.

His wife murmured sleepily as he shifted around in bed.

"Almost done?"

"Only a few more files, honey. Go back to sleep," Fisher answered.

She rolled back over. Fisher opened up the ballistic report and read that again.

They had caught a significant break. The gun traced back to Columbus, Ohio, where it had been used in a murder. Someone had shot a drug dealer named Stan Humphry two years ago. Three bullets to the chest, one of which tore through Humphry's pulmonary artery.

A junkie named Adam Ruck was the chief suspect, but the murder weapon was never found. Fisher studied Ruck's mug-shot. A bald, wild-eyed man in his twenties with several Swastikas tattooed on his face stared back.

The photo helped Fisher guess what had happened. The smart move for Ruck would have been to drop the gun off a bridge over the Scioto River. But someone desperate enough to kill a drug dealer was most likely also low on cash, so he sold the gun instead.

Now it was here, in Portland.

Fisher wanted to talk to Ruck, but Humphry's associates had killed him in a drive-by shooting.

So he turned to his files of geologists at the CVO offices in Vancouver and looked up the home bases of visiting specialists, as Steinsson had been.

There was a strong international presence, with Italy, Japan, Ecuador, and Indonesia represented. As for domestic visitors, a few were from Alaska. But there was no one from the Midwest, where the gun had come from.

There weren't any volcanoes in Ohio.

Fisher sent the ballistics report to Sheriff Hart, hoping he would have some success cross-referencing that information with his interviews.

Next, he turned to the sketch they had from Hanson's description of his attacker.

They had some luck there also. Agents Stillwell and Catling had passed the image of the unknown subject at the zoo. Employees there had recognized him as a guy spotted near the compost and waste removal area.

That confirmed a connection between Steinsson's murder and Hanson's break-in. Whoever this person was, it was clear that he felt that Hanson was a threat worth eliminating.

He felt a pang of guilt over that. He had brought Hanson into the case.

Fisher left-clicked the next icon. He had downloaded the sketch into ViCAP, the FBI's directory for violent criminals. Impaling a man to a tree fit Fisher's idea of a violent crime.

He scanned the file's summary. There were no matches. For a moment Fisher wasn't sure what he was expecting. A mug-shot of Bigfoot standing next to hash marks on the wall that measured him at eight feet and two inches in height?

Fisher moved on. He had also submitted the sketch with the National Crime Information Center, a criminal database that law enforcement agencies across America contributed to and referenced.

Again, nothing. Hanson's attacker was a ghost.

As was the shadowy group astroturfing the protesters. Their manifestos were easy to find on the web. But whoever was behind them remained hidden. National news outlets were speculating big business, and social media was a battle ground as counter protesters blamed the anti-closure group of putting money before people's lives.

Fisher sighed as he closed the file and prepared to drudge through photographs of CVO protesters when the messenger app on his phone pinged.

It was Hanson's number. Earlier in the day, Hanson had let him know that he was accompanying Makani into the forest for volcano fieldwork.

Fisher guessed that Hanson wanted some alone time with the Hawaiian geologist. He was worried at first but had felt reassured when he reviewed all the precautions Sheriff Hart was taking.

Hanson's message was alarming.

We were attacked. Both of us are okay. Forest fire is out. You need to see this.

Fisher swore out loud, and his wife stirred next to him. There was a video file included with Hanson's message. Fisher started it.

Makani and Hanson were in a darkened cabin. There was howling and hooting outside.

Then something powerful and substantial threw itself against a wall with a loud booming sound. Makani screamed, and things were hard to follow from that point on.

Next to him, Jessica was awake. She had rolled over and put her head on his shoulder so that she could watch.

"Dan, what is this?"

"Trouble," Fisher answered, alarmed at what he was seeing.

In the video, a window burst open. Jessica gasped out loud.

"Did you see that?" she asked.

Fisher nodded his head.

They both caught a glimpse of an ape-like face peering into the cabin.

More chaos followed. Music filled the Fisher's bedroom.

"Is that Rick Astley?" Jessica asked.

"I think so," Fisher answered.

The song seemed to work, for it quieted down after that. Hanson crept out the door, rifle in hand. Makani, and the camera, followed. Relief washed over Fisher. Hanson and Makani had weathered the assault.

A strange buzzing filled the audio, and the camera pointed up.

A glowing flying saucer could be seen withdrawing into the distance.

Makani was yelling, and the camera's view swung down, the screen freezing on a motion-blurry image of Hanson's wide-eyed, confused face.

"Did I just see what I think I saw?" Jessica asked next to him, sitting up.

"You did," Fisher answered. The covers flew as he stood up from bed. As he replaced them he put his hand on his wife's knee. "Tell no one," he added.

She nodded her head.

One more text message from Hanson filled his phone's screen.

We need to talk.

Chapter 22

St. Petersburg, Monday 7:45 p.m. Moscow Standard Time

"Are there any updates with Bigfoot reportings?" Tonkov asked as he stepped into Gontarev's office.

"No, sir, the media is shifting to UAPs now," Gontarev answered.

The GRU General tilted his head quizzically at Gontarev and frowned.

"I mean UFOs, General," Gontarev explained. "The American government is trying to change 'unidentified flying objects' to 'unidentified aerial phenomena' when reporting encounters."

Tonkov snorted. "Of course. The term 'UFO' carries the implication of aliens these days. The US military has always tried to distance itself from the concept of other world visitors coming to our planet. I remember back in the 1950s when everyone was calling unknown objects in the sky 'flying saucers'. The men behind Project Bluebook came up with 'unidentified flying objects' as a more encompassing expression."

For Gontarev, the 1950s was ancient history. It was easy to forget how old Tonkov was.

"Their morning news shows led with the volcano," Gontarev continued. He punched up the recordings he had made from the network broadcasting a few hours earlier, putting them up on the six large screens on his wall. They all started out with a screenshot of the USGS app.

The digit '1,' red against a black backdrop, dominated the screens. One day left. The volcano was to erupt sometime Tuesday.

Computer graphics of the eruption appeared on the screen. When that played out the studios switched to the weather.

Wind direction was important. Where was the ash going? At the moment, every network's weatherperson was the most valuable employee in the room. The projections had a high chance of afternoon lightning storms for late Monday afternoon on the mountain. Tuesday's forecast was clear skies with winds aloft blowing eastward.

Gontarev fast-forwarded through his recordings. "All the networks then rehashed the Steinsson murder, reporting no headway in the investigation. But talking about Steinsson allowed them to segue to this . . ."

Now all the screens showed dark, grainy video of a flying saucer moving across the night sky. It lasted only a few seconds before the craft disappeared over the horizon.

"This came from the previous evening from one of the major networks. A cameraman of theirs saw the saucer and recorded it. Even though the video is brief and low quality because of darkness and distance, there's a lot of excitement on the web because the footage comes from an 'official' source, and not amateur photography," Gontarev said.

"Any announcements from airports or the military?" Tonkov asked.

"Journalists interviewed both. They reported that there was nothing on their radars."

"Good. She told me she was going to avoid radar by keeping to canyons and ravines and flying near tree level," Tonkov revealed.

Gontarev wondered who 'she' was. "So, this is our doing?"

"As I have said, I have many assets in play in the Pacific Northwest," Tonkov said. "What is the web saying about the UFO?"

Images filled the screens, amateur illustrations of Bigfoot catching rides on open-topped flying saucers with the likes of E.T., Baby Yoda, and a green-skinned man with antennae coming out of the back of his head. Another meme had Bigfoot beaming out with Spock at his side.

"Don't know who the antenna guy is," Gontarev admitted.

"It's Ray Walston from *My Favorite Martian*," Tonkov volunteered. "From before you were born."

"Anyway, UFOs are starting to bubble up to the top of American consciousness," Gontarev said.

"That's something, at least. We need the Americans to be in the right frame of mind for tomorrow. How are your people doing?"

Gontarev thought about his answer. The work was exhausting his trolls. They all had been stuck in the building for the last forty-eight hours, fanning the internet fires raging between numerous American factions. The trolls were expected to do this for two more days. Cots were set up in the basement, and food was being ordered in.

But Tonkov was present for the duration also, and no one was complaining as long as he was present.

"Everyone is doing fine," Gontarev lied.

"And how about Hanson's website?"

"Under control, General," Gontarev answered. "I have a group countering his posts through legitimate accounts."

That was another lie. To make sure *The Unexplained, Explained* was properly squashed, Gontarev was allotting more bots than he should. Normally he would be more careful, but Tonkov wanted results, and Gontarev didn't want to explain any failures to the old general.

"Good. Now, do we have anything on Hanson?"

"What we know came through Terrington," Gontarev replied, calling up a series of texts on the upper right screen. "He overheard Batemen requesting her building's break room for a meeting with the FBI and Hanson."

Tonkov looked thoughtful at that. "She and Hanson are going to discuss what happened to them overnight."

Despite his fear of overstepping, months of cloak and dagger were catching up with Gontarev.

"What did happen last night, General?"

"We failed. We wanted a scenario like what happened to Steinsson, but once again, Hanson has tempered that narrative. We don't have any recordings of Bigfoot in action, so we have to settle for a few brief videos of UFOs and those internet cartoons you showed me."

"Will it be enough?"

"It will have to be, though Hanson and Bateman are still a problem. Because of them, our groundwork for this project is much more fragile than I would like." Tonkov answered. "With the volcano erupting tomorrow, I'm guessing that Doctor Bateman will be out of our reach. Contact Terrington. Tell him to find out Hanson's future movements. I need Foster to take one more attempt at him before tomorrow. We need the FBI to think the protesters are now focused on Hanson, and how he will harm their anti-shutdown cause."

Tonkov was being a bit more forthcoming. Gontarev decided to risk one more question.

"And what exactly happens tomorrow?"

Tonkov fixed him with a stare, and for a moment, Gontarev's heart dropped down to his stomach as he feared that he overstepped his bounds. But then the smallest of smiles crossed the old man's face.

"History repeats itself."

Chapter 23

CVO building, Vancouver, Monday, 11:40 a.m. PDT

"After the Bigfoots left, the flying saucer showed up and headed northwest," Makani told Fisher, thinking it was the craziest thing she had ever said in her life.

Crazy or not, it had been amazing to see. Crappy video from documentaries was one thing. Witnessing an UFO with one's own eyes was another. She had been struck by the wonder of it.

As had Hanson. She had expected him to explain it away, to rationalize it. But he had grabbed her hand and dragged her to the other side of the cabin, hoping for another glimpse. It was gone, but that didn't stop Hanson's excited chatter. Makani realized that, for a few moments, she wasn't listening to the skeptical man she knew but the boy he had been—someone who had believed in everything beyond the ordinary.

But then the CVO helicopter showed up, looking much as an UFO itself as it approached with its spotlight on. Hanson had calmed down as he watched it arrive. When he turned back to her she could see that his wonderment was gone. He had been quiet for most of the flight back home.

That was last night. This morning she and Hanson were with Fisher in the CVO's breakroom. The welcome smell of coffee filled the area from the brewing machine on a nearby counter. The remains of a fellow employee's birthday cake rested there also, and a small clutch of Mylar balloons floated in a corner, adding color to the room. A muted television mounted on the wall was running a commercial promising updates on the volcano in the next few minutes.

Makani stretched a bit, trying to relieve her aching back. After reporting what had happened to Livken, Makani had spent a few hours going over the data from the equipment she serviced. Then she had slept on an uncomfortable cot in a back room.

She woke up when Fisher had called. The FBI agent wanted to discuss the previous day's events. Since she had a busy day ahead of her, he and Hanson met at her work. Both men had arrived in Fisher's SUV, and Fisher had carefully driven through the protester's gauntlet while Hanson kept out of sight behind the backseat's tinted windows. Adding to the confusion around the CVO was the arrival of the network news crews. Television journalists were gathering nearby in the building's conference room for a noon briefing.

"How many other people saw the saucer?" Hanson asked.

"At least a dozen," Fisher answered. "Three of them recorded it." He had his tablet out with a small keyboard attached. "And that's not all that happened last night."

He turned the screen toward her and Hanson. Fisher's tablet was running a video that had been posted online. A drone had recorded an image of a corn field from above. A large circle of knocked-over corn stalks, along with smaller circles radiating out from it, could be seen.

"A crop circle? Where was this filmed at?" Hanson asked.

"A few miles west of Pendleton, Oregon, near an overpass for

Interstate 84," Fisher answered. "A trucker discovered it this morning."

Makani studied the circle, which was being explored by the drone from different angles.

"I've seen that M. Night Shyamalan movie. People think they're left behind by aliens, a code for others of their kind to read from the air," she said.

Hanson snorted. "It's not aliens," he said. "All it takes is a board to flatten the corn stalks and some rope to keep the circle round. Two guys in England made several hundred of these back in the 1980s as a hoax. It's been in our collective consciousness since."

"Why do it now?" Makani asked.

"It helps reinforce the UFO sighting last night," Hanson answered. Makani could tell his skepticism was back in full force. "Whoever is behind all this had a busy evening."

Makani turned to Fisher. "How are you going to handle these events?"

"With a 'no comment,'" Fisher answered, turning the screen back to him. "And we are going to try to keep the attack on you two under wraps for now also. If anyone were to hear of another Bigfoot assault, even with us explaining it was men in costumes, more people would flock to the mountain. At this point in time, that would prove disastrous." Fisher looked at her. "What does everyone in this building know?"

"I told my boss what had happened," Makani answered.

"The pilot that picked us up saw the mess we left at the cabin," Hanson added. "But we felt the same as you do, so we put the 'angry local residents' spin on our story, and told him that three men showed up, firing guns into the air to scare us. We retreated to the cabin, using the flares to signal for help."

"And, of course, our pilot talked, so that's the gossip that's going around the office," Makani said.

"Where's your Outreach Coordinator right now?" Fisher asked.

"Shirley Wright is only a few feet down the hall, waiting for her turn at the podium during the news briefing."

"I'm going to give her a quick message," Fisher said, standing up. "After the Steinsson murder, I instructed the staff here to not share anything related to the case with the public. I need to make sure she doesn't put out an official statement of your recent attack."

As Fisher left the room, Makani watched Hanson get up to refill his coffee. He was wearing a plain, dark green shirt this morning, and his left arm had a large bandage on it. While she worked last night, he had taken off to have it stitched up. He had then gone home to take care of his cats and arrange some time off from his work.

She found herself staring at Hanson longer than intended. She remembered the feel of his bicep under her oiled hand yesterday, and she had looked forward to sharing those promised cold beers with him last night. And maybe a bed instead of the uncomfortable, lonely cot she had to settle for.

Hanson caught her watching him. He held up the pot of coffee.

"Need a refill?" he asked.

"No, I'm good," she said, glancing away.

While Hanson seemed oblivious to what was going through her mind, Fisher wasn't. The FBI agent had returned, and his eyes were roving back and forth between Hanson and her.

Fortunately, he ignored the situation with a question. "Who knew where you two were going yesterday?"

"Everyone," Makani answered. "Our assignments were even posted on our bulletin board."

"Who made those assignments?" Fisher asked.

"Dr. Livken. The tune-ups had been scheduled for a week now. But when the protesters damaged some of the equipment last night he had to make some adjustments so as to send specialists to repair the damaged equipment. He shuffled our missions last night by using his laptop at his home."

Fisher's brow furrowed in thought for a few moments.

"You think someone hacked his laptop?" Hanson asked.

"That's my guess," Fisher answered. He tilted his head northward, where the protesters were gathered outside. "The anti-closure movement is getting their marching orders from someone online. An organization sophisticated enough that even we at the FBI can't figure out who they are. Fortunately, our cyber unit has determined that the firewalls here at the CVO haven't been penetrated, so no one can mess with the prediction algorithm. But Dr. Livken's router at his home is another story. It's possible that while he was distracted with his equipment crisis, someone outside his house logged onto his computer and switched Makani to the cabin's location."

"They killed Steinsson. Does someone want me dead also?" Makani asked, a chill running down her spine.

"As a volcanologist representing the closure of Mount St. Helens, yes," Fisher answered. "But I also think that Hanson is the main target."

"Me?" Hanson exclaimed.

"Yes," Fisher answered, shifting a bit in his seat and looking away for a moment. "Steve, I'm sorry. I didn't realize when I brought you into this I would be putting you in jeopardy."

"No need to apologize, Agent Fisher," Hanson said, grinning. "Even knowing the danger, I'd pay money to be in on this if I wasn't already here."

Fisher's posture relaxed a little and relief washed over his face. Makani could tell the FBI agent had been stressed out with concern for their well-being.

"Do you have any theories on why all this is happening?" Makani asked.

"I do," Fisher answered. "A lot of people don't believe the volcano is going to erupt anytime soon, and they don't like being kept off their property or losing money with their businesses. These interests want things back to normal, and everyone here at the CVO is an obstacle to that."

"So they killed Kris," Makani said.

"And they made a statement doing so," Fisher continued. "Bigfoot is now an icon of freedom for them."

"And I'm a threat to that," Hanson guessed.

"Yes," Fisher answered. "I've interviewed Nesbitt. He admitted that he discussed his night at the murder scene with his friends online. Though I don't think Nesbitt's a part of this, someone in his Mount St. Helens circle decided that Hanson needed to be taken care of."

"But they didn't want to tarnish their cause, so the first attempt was made to look like a burglary gone bad," Hanson filled in.

"Finding Hanson at his home sounds easy enough," Makani said. "But how did they catch him on the mountain?"

"With you. I think the cabin scenario was something planned a while back. The Bigfoots were to ambush random geologists near the cabin, hoping that it would be recorded on phones. To make sure the victims had no help, fires were lit on the west side of the volcano, a distraction to bring all of the helicopters that direction when the attack happened. Killing or scaring anyone at the cabin would have worked out for the attackers. But then Hanson came along, and now they wanted him. The Bigfoot skeptic killed by Bigfoot fighting for the local people's rights would cement the protester's cause."

"So anyone at that party the other night would have seen us together and thought there was a chance Steve would accompany me to the cabin," Makani said.

"Yes," Fisher replied.

"I was at the KET because of an out-of-the-blue invitation from Kesler. Is he part of this?" Makani asked.

"Could be," Fisher answered. "Or, like Nesbitt, he has a bad apple in his circle of friends. Anyway, the UFO you and Hanson saw last night makes him someone worth looking into."

"Batman," Hanson interjected.

"I don't follow," Makani said.

"There's a wry observation amongst comic book fans that though

Batman is flying around in multi-million dollar jets, no one in Gotham suspects their resident billionaire, Bruce Wayne," Hanson answered.

"Hanson told me about the flying car. The KET is less than fifty miles from where you were," Fisher said. "It's not inconceivable that Kesler is capable of making a saucer-shaped flying aircraft."

"But why would he have one of those?" Makani asked. "A flying saucer makes no sense."

"Kesler told us the reason," Hanson answered. "He has a splashy publicity event scheduled at the same time as an alien-related anniversary next year. He must be shooting for June 24th, the date of the Kenneth Arnold incident. His publicity campaign will most likely end two weeks later, on July 8th, when the Roswell press release came out."

"I'm familiar with Roswell," Makani said. "But who's Kenneth Arnold?"

"He's the man who started the modern era of UFOs nearly seventy-five years ago," Hanson answered. "And it all happened right here in our own back-yard."

Chapter 24

I *t began near Mount Rainier.*

Kenneth Arnold was a salesman for an airport fire suppression company out of Boise. His region was the Pacific Northwest, which he covered with his own private plane.

Arnold was flying from Chehalis to Yakima on the afternoon of June 24th, 1947. The sky was blue, and the air crystal clear, perfect conditions for visibility. Arnold decided to take a detour by Mount Rainier to help search for a wrecked military plane. A substantial reward of five thousand dollars was being offered for its discovery.

Instead, Arnold found something else.

He noticed bright glimmers of light from something near the mountain, like the reflection of the sun off of large mirrors.

The flashes were coming off a series of flying objects twenty-five miles away. There were nine of them lined up in a straight formation. They had a chrome-like finish, which reflected sunlight as they wobbled in their flight.

Arnold studied them. Eight of the aircrafts were formed like a partial disk with an angled-off backside like the heel of a boot. The second to last was crescent moon-shaped with the barest hint of a tail. All objects were incredibly thin, almost disappearing from view when observed edge on.

Their flying, though straight, was erratic. The airships seemed to 'skip as a saucer on water' and lurch about like the tail of a kite.

They moved away from Mount Rainier and headed for Mount Adams. Arnold timed them. It took them a little over a minute and a half to cover the fifty miles. He considered that and made a conservative estimate that they were flying at 1,200 miles per hour. This was at the time when the military had yet to break the sound barrier.

He lost sight of them as they passed beyond Mount Adams. He continued on to Yakima in central Washington, where he shared his story with airport employees.

The next day he flew to his next stop; the town of Pendleton, located in northeast Oregon. He at first made a trip to the local FBI office to report what he had seen, but the agent was out. So he went to the local newspaper, the East Oregonian, and talked to a reporter there. It was almost noon, and deadlines needed to be met. The reporter wrote a quick blurb, a few paragraphs long, which described Arnold's encounter with nine saucer-like aircraft. The story ran on the bottom of page one. The reporter also put it out on the national wire service, where other newspapers picked it up.

And history was made.

"Now wait a minute," Fisher said. He was looking at the screen of his pad. It had the black and white image of a man holding a painting of a UFO, a flying crescent with a dark spot for a cockpit. "I have Kenneth Arnold here with an artist's rendition of his UFO. Where did 'nine saucer-like objects' come from?"

"The reporter misunderstood him. He had taken Arnold's description of their movement for their shape," Hanson answered. "Other newspapers soon described them as 'flying saucers,' coining the term we use today."

"So when we use the words flying saucer—" Makani began.

"It's a mistake," Hanson finished. He held up his hand and made the pincer gesture. "We were this close to calling them 'alien boomerangs.' People seeing flying saucers worldwide is the power of suggestion at work."

"They must have treated him as a crackpot back then," Fisher said, scrolling through the website he was looking at.

"It was the opposite. People treated Arnold's sighting with seriousness. He was a respected businessman with thousands of hours of flight experience and considered a reliable witness. Journalists conducted many follow-up interviews with him."

"That's different from today," Makani said. "Networks occasionally report UFO sightings, but it's usually done tongue-in-cheek, like when those kids staged a gathering at Area 51."

"The shift to downplay sightings wouldn't occur until the following July, but for a few weeks after Arnold's sighting, the public treated UFO sightings as real occurrences."

"You said UFOs. Plural," Fisher noted.

"Arnold's encounter caused an increase in UFO sightings," Hanson said. He gestured to Fisher for his tablet. The FBI agent slid it toward him. Hanson called up his blog and pulled up his UFO article.

He tagged one of the illustrations embedded in it. A simple bar graph appeared, showing UFO sightings over a two week period. Its shape was like a tall, thin skyscraper.

"This is a graph of the 'UFO Wave of 1947.' In the mid-sixties, there was a study done on newspaper reports of flying saucers right after Arnold's sighting."

Fisher's eyebrows arched up. "It starts from less than five sightings per day in mid-June to over 150 sightings a day in early July."

"Reporting flying saucers at face value had the effect that we all here can guess. It caused a panic. Remember, it was only two years after the war, and the dropping of two atomic bombs. It was the dawn of the nuclear age, and the Cold War was starting. And now everyone was seeing flying saucers all across the United States, flying with impunity."

"People must have been terrified," Makani said.

"They were. Arnold once told the story of a preacher informing him the end was near, and he was preparing for Armageddon."

"But isn't this like the Bigfoot story you told us? After the 1967 film, there was an increase in Bigfoot sightings in the seventies," Makani noted.

"Yes. Only this time it's weirder because people were seeing something based on a misunderstanding, flying saucers."

"So fear was gripping the nation," Fisher observed. He pointed at the graph. "But what happened later in July? The graph falls off just as fast as it rose. By mid-month, the UFO reporting is back down to under five per day."

Hanson was back at the coffee, pouring himself another cup. Nearby, the cake looked good, sweet vanilla frosting over chocolate. He took a moment to cut off a piece and put it on a paper plate.

"Roswell," Hanson answered, turning back toward them.

He could see the confused looks on their faces. He didn't blame them. He knew his answer was counterintuitive.

"Roswell?" Makani responded. "Now that one I know. That's when the US military captured a flying saucer."

Fisher was nodding his head in agreement.

Hanson wasn't surprised by that either. Decades of rumor had ingrained the myth deep into the American psyche. Hanson put down his cake and coffee and moved to the cluster of balloons in the corner.

"Roswell wasn't an alien spaceship," he began, taking one of them by its dangling ribbon and pulling it down to him at chest level.

"It was a balloon."

Chapter 25

"What do you know of Roswell?" Hanson continued, letting the balloon go. It rose back up to the ceiling.

"During the night of a freakishly powerful lightning storm, a spaceship crash-landed in a farmer's field near Roswell, New Mexico," Makani answered.

"There was a military base in town, leftover from World War II. The farmer told them what had happened the next day. They all went out to the crash site," Fisher added. "Debris littered the field. Metal chunks that were lightweight but could withstand tremendous force, or struts with alien hieroglyphics printed on them."

Makani jumped back in. "They even found alien pilots. They took everything back to the base and announced it to the world. But then men in black suits showed up and changed the story. The next day there was a press conference. Military personnel posed by scraps of foil and rubber and told everyone it was a downed weather balloon. The cover-up began."

"Where did you guys hear all this stuff?" Hanson asked.

"Same as Bigfoot," Makani answered. "From television documentaries about the paranormal."

"I first saw it on an episode of *Unsolved Mysteries*," Fisher confessed. "Robert Stack was the host of that show."

"I remember, I saw that episode also," Hanson said. "But let me explain what truly happened."

The Roswell press release occurred on July 8th. This means by your stories, the crash happened on July 7th.

That wasn't the case. William Brazel, a farm hand who worked a patch of land outside of Roswell, discovered a pile of debris near his home on June 14th. He gathered some of it together into boxes and stored it in a shed.

Fisher interrupted. "The farmer sat on the wreckage of a UFO for three weeks?"

"Yes. He didn't feel what he had found was important at the time. It was just a mess of rubber, tin foil, tape and sticks," Hanson answered, sitting back at the table with his cake in front of him.

But later that month, stories of flying saucer sightings across America reached Brazel in his out of the way homestead, and he began to wonder what exactly had crash-landed onto his field. On July 6th he took his boxes of debris and drove into town to show the sheriff at the Roswell county courthouse. At the same time a local radio journalist, as part of his daily routine, called the sheriff for regional news updates. The sheriff handed the phone to Brazel, and Brazel told the reporter what he had seen and had in his possession. The reporter advised Brazel to call the 509th. Brazel did so, and he was put in contact with intelligence officer Major Jesse Marcel.

"What was the 509th?" Makani asked, eyeballing Hanson's cake. He slid his piece over to her and stood up to get himself another slice.

"They were the airmen that dropped the two atomic bombs. The military based them in Roswell after the war, where for the next several years they were our only atomic bomber squadron."

"That sounds like an elite group," Makani said.

"They were. Roswell was a bustling military community, with its base being one of the most important in the States, and used to operating under a blanket of secrecy."

As I said, the UFO hysteria was starting to hit its fever pitch, and now intelligence officer Marcel had a farmer on the phone with an unusual story. Marcel drove to the sheriff's office to look for himself. What he found was wreckage with strange markings on them, hieroglyphics that no one could decipher.

Marcel, and the 509th, were interested in what they were seeing. For the rest of that day, and the next, military personnel made several trips to the debris field, and more material was gathered. An investigation was started.

This activity brought the 509th under a unique form of pressure. It was now July 7th, and newspapers across the nation were running banner headlines of flying saucers being sighted over America. And since Brazel had talked to the sheriff and a member of the press, rumor of the wreckage was making its way around Roswell, heightening the flying saucer scare at the local level. In a small town where everyone knew each other, residents were demanding answers from their military neighbors.

Colonel William H. Blanchard, the commander of Roswell Army Air Field, was aware of this. He also felt that the military had lost control of the narrative. Orders were put out to find and bring in Brazel. Military police located the farmer while he was giving an interview to the radio journalist he had first met. Brazel, and his recorded interview, were brought to the base.

But even with Brazel under control, the rumors would still persist. Blanchard wanted to put a different spin on things, one that showed that the military was still in control of America's security. So he called up the base's public information officer and dictated, considering how you view it, the most important statement of the millennia.

The United States Army had a flying disc in their possession, a bonafide extraterrestrial spaceship.

"You're right," Fisher said. "I've never thought about it that way. If the report is true, it's the story of our lifetime, of the entire history of humanity."

"What happened after that announcement?" Makani asked.

"The shit hit the fan," Hanson answered, pointing to the bar graph. "As you can see, the flying saucer reporting peaks on July 7th, the day the debris was being collected and brought back to base. The press release came out on July 8th, which also has a high number of sightings. There looked to be no end in sight for flying saucer sightings."

But then the military top brass stepped in, for they knew something that the officers of the 509th were unaware of.

Roswell had the wreckage of a top-secret program on their hands.

Project Mogul.

The Cold War was starting, and our government wondered about the Soviet Union's nuclear program. We wanted to know how far along they were, and when they would detonate their first atomic bomb.

But this was the time before satellites or spy planes like the U-2 or SR-71 Blackbird. We had no eyes to confirm the advent of Soviet nuclear testing.

But we had ears.

Scientists had figured out that high in the troposphere is a layer of air in which sound propagates much further, an 'acoustic duct' for low frequency pressure waves. The faint echoes of a Soviet nuclear test could reach halfway around the world if we placed microphones at the right altitude.

Weather balloons were the obvious answer, but the sound layer was narrow, and the equipment had to maintain a precise altitude for extended lengths of time.

Scientists devised a more complicated arrangement. They suspended microphones under a train of twenty-four weather balloons. Air pressure sensing devices would release ballast to maintain a constant altitude. They added radar reflectors, box-like contraptions of foil and sticks that were taped together. This allowed the launch crew to track the balloon train, which stretched for several hundred meters.

"That whole thing must have been huge," Fisher said.

"It was, and now it's easy to see why the wreckage in Brazel's field was so vast," Hanson said. "Also, remember those hieroglyphics? The crew that put together the radar kites had limited resources. Some of the tape they used came from a toy store, which had a fanciful flower-like decoration on them, almost emoji-like."

Usually the Mogul squad recovered the equipment when it came down. But on June 4th, out of Alamogordo Army Air Field, Flight No. 4 was launched. It went off course in a storm, and its last known position was seventeen miles from Brazel's ranch.

"America's intelligence agencies must have found themselves in a tight spot," Fisher observed.

"A tight and dangerous spot," Hanson clarified. "Mogul was a top-secret project. And now it was being displayed by the gang at Roswell for the world to see. Something had to be done to throw the Soviets off the scent and calm down the UFO hysteria gripping the nation."

So the government created a cover-up.

A simple one by using a white lie. A half-truth. The military arranged a photo-op and displayed the wreckage and called it a downed weather balloon. They also took the stance that all the sightings for the past two weeks were also misunderstandings. It was the start of a campaign to discredit UFO sightings. It was all everyone's overwrought imaginations. The campaign worked, and interest dropped off. UFO sightings flat-lined.

And history forgot Roswell, the incident being dismissed as an example of military miscommunication.

Makani was looking over Hanson's website. It showed a black and white picture of a military officer holding up a swatch of tinfoil.

"So how did it become the conspiracy juggernaut it is today?" she asked.

"As I said, no one remembered Roswell. I'm old enough to recall a time when it wasn't a thing," Hanson answered. "But Blanchard's press release and the military's quick turnaround caught some people's eyes in the seventies. A few of them called up Major Marcel and re-interviewed him. The interviews focused on things like the sheer amount of wreckage and the hieroglyphics. UFO researchers published books, some rather loose with the facts. Someone started the rumor of the military hiding alien bodies. The concept caught on, for the conspiracy theorists were right about one thing. There was a government cover-up, but it would take fifteen more years for the government to declassify Project Mogul. So the myth of Roswell took hold, and despite what we currently know, it stays with us to this day."

"So why did a flying saucer and a crop circle show up last night?" Fisher asked. "I think we have a handle on the reasons for Bigfoot, but UFOs don't fit."

"As I told Makani, there are theories about a relationship between Bigfoot and flying saucers," Hanson answered as he leaned back in his chair. "So the UFO reinforces the Bigfoot sightings. It could be that my website counteracts that. But I don't see how that would be much help. The number of people who believe in this crap is overwhelming. My website is being spammed into oblivion by nutcases."

Fisher perked up as he typed out Hanson's revelation on his tablet's keyboard. "Is that normal?"

"No. But then again, this is the first murder case involving Bigfoot."

"What about Kesler?" Makani asked.

"He's not returning my calls, but I'm working on getting a warrant to search his complex," Fisher answered. "He's a billionaire, so you can imagine what his lawyers are like. Fortunately, I have the President of the United States behind me on this. She's scheduled to give a presidential address during the eruption tomorrow, and she wants results on this case. My paperwork is being expedited at the highest levels."

Hanson couldn't keep his disdain for Monetti out of his voice. "What about those two Marine pilots?"

"They're back in Yuma as of this morning," Fisher answered. "Their records are clean. I'm not sure if they have any part in this, apart from giving Kesler technical advice."

Hanson scowled as he ate his last bite of cake. He had been looking forward to seeing Monetti busted for something. Over the past few days, Hanson had had several long stints of daydreaming up imaginary arguments with the sneering Marine. In each one, he made Monetti look like an idiot in front of an appreciative Makani.

"What do you need us to do now?" Makani asked. Her talking snapped Hanson out of his reverie.

"I've been in contact with Sheriff Hart," Fisher answered. "He's taking a team to the cabin before it gets covered in ash tomorrow. He's requesting Hanson to join him and help out."

"Me?" Hanson asked, alarmed.

"They want to find all the bullets, and hear from a witness where each one came from," Fisher answered. "You also need to tell him what really happened. I'm arranging for our helicopter to take you out there later this afternoon."

Hanson leaned back in his chair and groaned. "God, I haven't ridden this many helicopters since Desert Storm." He then turned around and gave Makani a questioning look.

She got the hint. "You're safe. At this point, we're narrowing down our prediction to the hour. We have a little over a day before the eruption."

She turned to the television on the wall. The news was on, and the lead was the press conference occurring a few rooms over. Hanson recognized the Terrington guy. An animated cross-section of Mount St. Helens was on display behind him. It was being fast forwarded through the volcano's next twenty-four hours.

"Good," Hanson said. "I don't want to be anywhere near when that volcano blows."

"What about me?" Makani asked Fisher.

"Stay here for safety," Fisher said. "I have agents doing more interviews and making sure the computer systems remain untouched from hackers. They will be keeping an eye on you also. Check in with my people often."

The thought that someone was out there seeking harm didn't sit well with her. "I hope you find out who's behind this," she said.

Fisher leaned back in his chair. "So do I," he answered. The FBI agent then held up his arms as if he was trying to encompass everyone outside the building to the north.

"But right now, it could be anybody," he finished.

Chapter 26

"Any more questions?" Terrington asked.

A brunette stood up. Terrington recognized her as Jennifer Steel, a national news correspondent from New York. She was the most attractive reporter in the room, and also the most sensational.

"Have you heard anything on the Bigfoot murder? Or the UFO that was seen last night?"

The other reporters looked shocked that she had asked such silly questions but also thankful that she did. All eyes turned back to him.

A drop of sweat trickled down Terrington's back. The question was innocent, but his guilt and the live television cameras pointed his way made him imagine that somehow she knew Steinsson's death was his fault.

He couldn't let on his distress. Not when he was so close to the end.

"That's for the FBI to say," Terrington answered her, not missing a beat. "Obviously, the volcano is commanding all my attention now."

Shirley Wright, the CVO's Outreach Coordinator, was edging closer to the podium. Terrington switched places with her and shuffled to the side of the room. He made his way along the perimeter to the door in the back, hearing one last question as he left the room.

"Will the forecasted lightning storms be a problem for your equipment this afternoon . . . ?"

Terrington sighed in relief and loosened his tie as he made his way toward his office.

He spotted Makani leaving the break room. She was wearing a blue shirt with stylized sea turtles printed on it. Accompanying her was the head FBI agent and that Hanson guy. They were all deep in conversation.

Most likely talking about last night's attack, which he had helped set up by changing Makani's assignment on Livken's computer. The plot had failed, though, for which he was glad. He couldn't stand the thought of Makani, or any more of his other colleagues, getting hurt.

He felt guilty for all the trouble he was causing, but his back was against the wall.

It had all started several years ago. A man had approached him in a supermarket parking lot, with a manila envelope in hand. Inside the envelope were printouts of all the child pornography websites he had perused over the previous year.

He thought he was being careful by using VPNs and the Dark Web to mask his movements from the authorities. Instead he had attracted the attention of Russia's most elite hacking unit, Strontium.

They offered him a choice. Utter ruin and humiliation, or riches and all that he desired. All he had to do was their bidding when they needed him.

He chose the latter.

He was already modeling volcanoes on university supercomputers, so he had guessed that sometime in the future the Russians would want access to one.

But when Tonkov had called him up two months ago and told him about Project Front Door, Terrington had been surprised as to the why.

Terrington passed through the building's main area. Volcanologists from around the globe crowded the room as they prepared for the event of the decade. He walked by them and approached a steel cabinet that was bolted to the wall.

The cabinet door had a complex locking mechanism on it, one that required both a retinal scan and a code to open.

And he was the only person in the building that the retinal scan was configured for.

He leaned in, his right eye watering a bit as he stared into the light. He then punched in his fourteen-character code into the keypad. The sound of several large pins sliding into the unlocked position let him know he was successful. He pulled the heavy door open.

Inside was the object that was the center of his upcoming betrayal.

The Stratton modem.

It was an unassuming thing, no larger than a shoebox. It had a few blinking lights up front and fiber optic wires sprouting out of the back. It allowed the CVO servers to connect directly to the Icarus supercomputer at the Stratton Institute. Petabytes of computing power to guess what Mother Nature was up to next.

All of that was straightforward enough. But there was a potential problem with the arrangement. A matter of national security. A few astute reporters had even asked him about it.

Terrington remembered reassuring them with a lie.

A lie reinforced by the President herself a few months ago.

And the only person here at the CVO privy to that secret was him.

The Russians had coached Terrington in his application for the Icarus connection, though it appeared to everyone that it was his idea. A simple and logical request to ensure the safety of citizens in the Pacific Northwest.

The Russians knew American intelligence agencies would vet him, so they backstopped his internet history. They also instructed him to abandon his dark web habits and instead switch to the more common use of 'incognito' mode while on the internet. So now, when the FBI, CIA, or whoever did this sort of thing looked into his internet history to see if anyone could compromise him in any way, they would discover an ordinary guy doing volcano research, purchasing bowling shoes online, and having a preference for tall women on porn sites.

To satisfy his true appetites, though, the Russians provided him with his viewing preferences on thumb drives. Terabytes of video given to him risk-free.

Terrington found himself warming up to the arrangement.

"Professor Terrington, may I have a moment of your time?"

Terrington snapped to attention. One of the FBI agents had approached him. Terrington remembered him from earlier in the week.

"Yes, Agent Stillwell, how can I help you?"

The tall agent looked down at him. For a moment, Terrington imagined him being the one going through his internet history while having a good laugh at his fictitious kink for tall women.

"We're doing another round of interviews," Agent Stillwell answered. "I know you're busy. Can I schedule you for two o'clock?"

The modem was nearby, its fans purring. For Terrington it seemed like they were getting louder, as in Edgar Allan Poe's *The Telltale Heart*. In that story, the murderer was being interviewed by constables. The victim's heart, hidden under the floorboards nearby, was still beating, reaching a crescendo that the killer thought impossible to miss.

It was the same here. Steinsson was dead, and the modem was roaring, its lights blazing. This FBI agent must suspect something. Terrington opened his mouth to blurt out his confession.

"Or four o'clock if you want," Stillwell added.

The roaring disappeared. Stillwell was unaware. Everyone nearby was going about their business.

"Four o'clock would be great for me," Terrington answered, his own heart beating hard.

Terrington walked away from him as a female FBI agent approached. He overheard them talking as he quietly shut the cabinet door.

"I have six interviews lined up, how many do you have?" she asked Stillwell.

"Five. Is Fisher doing any today?"

"I'm not sure. All I know is that he is arranging a flight for Hanson back to the cabin this afternoon . . ."

Their conversation faded as they walked away. Terrington walked into a short hallway and entered his office. He sat down at his desk to collect his wits.

Steinsson's death was his fault. The Icelander had begun to guess that there was more to the Stratton connection than met the eye. Terrington knew that if the White House suspected that someone was looking into it, no matter how innocently, the President would pull the plug.

Terrington couldn't let that happen. Moscow would ruin him if he lost the Stratton connection. He had made a phone call to Tonkov. A man named Foster called him back later that day. Terrington told him of Steinsson's movements. The Russian agent informed him that he would take care of it. He had laughed when he added that it would be 'a two birds with one stone' sort of thing.

Terrington took out his phone. The Russians had supplied it to him. It looked like a normal cell, but it was two phones in one case. The first was legitimate and registered under his name. He surfed the web and paid his bills on it. The second had components to encrypt calls and wasn't traceable to him. He entered his code to unlock the hidden half. He had been instructed to phone in if he learned anything about Hanson's movements.

Again, he felt guilty. Again he justified it by telling himself that his own future was on the line. He focused on the rewards promised him. Ten million dollars deposited in an offshore account. A new identity, and transportation to an Asian country known for its looser sex trafficking laws. A place where desperate parents brought their children to the city for a price. A price that he would be able to comfortably afford for the rest of his life.

He calmed down with that thought and made the call.

Chapter 27

Fisher met up with his two FBI agents in the CVO's parking lot for some privacy. It was already hot outside, so they sought out some shade. North of them gathering clouds obscured Mount St. Helens.

"Do you have your interviews lined up?" he asked them.

Catling, a woman with her blonde hair up, spoke first. "I have most of them. With this volcano going off tomorrow, it wasn't easy."

"Understandable," Fisher said. "A lot of pressure is on these volcanologists right now. But we can't let that stop us."

Fisher turned to Stillwell.

"There are some other things I need help with. Contact our cyber department," Fisher said. "Hanson mentioned that his website is being overwhelmed by commentary. I want to know by whom. Maybe our mysterious astroturfers made a mistake when they went after him."

"What's on your plate?" Stillwell asked.

Fisher held up his pad. "Going over all these files coming in and making my own report to the director himself." Fisher looked north again at the brooding mountain on the horizon. "And arrange for our helicopter to ferry Hanson to last night's crime scene."

Stillwell gave a grunt. "I don't envy that. With that storm brewing, it looks like it's going to be dicey up there."

Fisher studied the building clouds. It looked like they were over the cabin's location. For a moment he felt like calling the trip off, but he thought of his upcoming call with the director. Everyone was under a lot of pressure to solve this case.

As he followed Stillwell and Catling into the air-conditioned offices of the CVO, he took a moment to message the pilot of the FBI's helicopter to arrange the flight.

* * *

Portland International Airport, 12:32 p.m. PDT

"Terrington says that the FBI is flying Hanson back out to the cabin," Foster reported as he put away his phone.

Cooper limped over to him. "What are we going to do about that?" the other Russian agent growled.

Foster knew the source of Cooper's anger. Hanson had wounded him with a makeshift spear that had penetrated deep into Cooper's leg. They had field dressed it the best they could on their hasty retreat last night, but it still caused Cooper a lot of pain.

"And no more costumes," Cooper added, "It's too goddamn hot."

Both men were baking in the early afternoon sun. They were standing on a huge concrete pad on the airport's southern edge. The area had been repurposed for the half-dozen helicopter companies present to help during the crisis.

There was no real shelter out here, only parked helicopters and fuel trucks. A line of portable bathrooms rested on the pad's eastern edge. A nearby hangar to the south was on loan for everyone, but it contained another company's helicopter that required repairs.

"I agree. It's time for a more direct approach," Foster said.

He, too, was fed up with the theatrics. He knew it was essential to the mission, but it made carrying out their duties damn near impossible. He remembered following Hanson and Bateman last night while sweltering in his costume, all the while wondering if Hanson, a former Marine, was going to start taking pot-shots at them with his hunting rifle.

In the end, they had herded the two into the cabin, but Hanson had mounted a defense that they couldn't break through. And now all they had was Cooper's wounded leg and Smith's slashed arm to show for it, and he couldn't get that catchy song out of his head.

Shooting Hanson right from the beginning would have been so much easier.

Foster nodded to his side. "We'll sabotage their helicopter this time."

He was looking at the FBI's parked Bell 407 helicopter. It was on the opposite side of the pad, near the portable bathrooms. Three other helicopters separated them. Though there was some activity in the area, the FBI's section was quiet at the moment.

"Any security nearby?" Cooper asked.

"No. They all left when the last of the 142nd flew out earlier this morning," Foster answered.

The 142nd was part of Oregon's Air National Guard. They patrolled the Pacific Northwest's Coastline twenty-four hours a day, protecting that part of the border from any threat. To do that, they stationed nearly two dozen F-15 Eagles at the Portland Airport.

Until today.

For the past few weeks, the weather report had predicted an eighty-five percent chance of winds aloft pushing the ash cloud east.

That left a fifteen percent chance that the ash could go elsewhere.

And with over a billion dollars' worth of jets parked nearby, those odds were too high for the United States military. The 142nd base was being temporarily moved to California to keep those assets safe. Once the dust settled they would come back home.

It was what Moscow had been hoping for. Project Rod wasn't

going to work with twenty high-performance jets parked a few minutes away from Mount St. Helens.

That left the Oregon National Guard's airfield a ghost town. Several rows of open-sided sheds and smallish hangars stood empty only a couple of hundred feet away.

Foster stared at the blue and white helicopter sitting all alone.

"I'm going to plant one of our charges on it," Foster said.

"We need to be within a hundred yards to set one of those off," Cooper pointed out.

"We'll follow them in our own helicopter. When the time is right, we'll trigger it."

Next to them was their company's aircraft, an eight-seater that was slightly larger than the Bell 407. The white-colored helicopter had the image of a Northern Cardinal painted on its side.

They had put their helicopter to good use last night, as the Skamania County Sheriff had contracted them to fly their deputy around the mountain. That allowed one of their pilots, Williams, to control what the local authorities were seeing, and spend a little extra time hovering over the small brush fires that another Russian agent was setting off on the west side of the mountain.

Cardinal Air had a crew of six. As the helicopter's company's chief mechanic, Foster was servicing the helicopter today. The other two mechanics, Grey and Johnson, had already departed in two modified tractor-trailers. They were driving east, out of state, where they were to prepare for their next task. Back up pilots Williams and Smith were resting back in their hotel room.

Foster moved over to Cardinal Air's small service truck and removed several large toolboxes from a compartment. The compartment had a false bottom which concealed a locked case. Inside that were his spare revolver, ammunition, and a trio of explosives. These were small portions of C-4 attached to a detonator and battery; the whole arrangement was the size of a cigarette pack. They were each paired with a radio switch. Their original use was for blowing up the helicopter if their cover was blown, giving them time to escape during the confusion.

Foster took one. He also selected a screwdriver and electrical tape from a toolbox. He then grabbed a roll of toilet paper from the cab and made his way east.

Cardinal Air and the other helicopter outfits had been here for several weeks, and everyone knew that the portable toilets were notorious for running out of toilet paper. Each outfit had their own supply. Foster returned waves to a few smirking helicopter pilots who noticed him making a trip to the bathroom with a bit of the roll trailing behind him.

Satisfied that his ruse had worked, Foster turned away from the latrines when he reached the far side of the FBI's helicopter. A quick look showed him that no one else was making a similar run. Foster grabbed a nearby stepladder and placed it under the tail boom. He climbed up to within reach of an access plate and removed that with his screwdriver.

He used the electrical tape to secure the bomb inside and replaced the cover panel. With his roll still in hand, he returned to his side of the helicopter area.

"No one looked your way the whole time," Cooper told him. "Though you're most likely on several cameras."

"That shouldn't be a problem," Foster said. "With that storm, everyone will initially think it was an accident. When they finally look at the tapes, we'll be long gone."

Chapter 28

Mount St. Helen's airspace, 3:32 p.m. PDT

"Have you ever seen this many helicopters in the air before?" Hanson asked Spiros.

It was his attempt at small talk. Hanson was back in the FBI's helicopter, only this time he was alone with the pilot. It was the same young man that had flown him to the mountain earlier. Fisher had used his badge to expedite getting through security and had then driven to an area where a half dozen helicopters rested. After dropping him off, Fisher headed back for the nearby FBI office.

That left him alone with a near stranger. At least this time Hanson caught the pilot's name. They were both sitting in the front seats. Hanson could have made the entire trip in silence, but he figured he should say something.

"No," Spiros answered. "I'm guessing most of them are news helicopters. I bet they're frustrated by this storm, though."

Hanson looked ahead. Though the sky was clear above the Vancouver/Portland metro area, clouds shrouded Mount St. Helens.

Massive cumulonimbus formations that were spreading into anvil shaped heads as they reached the upper atmosphere.

The bad weather stretched from the volcano to nearby Mount Adams. Hanson could see similar clouds around Mount Rainier and behind him on Mount Hood. All the peaks had storms forming on them in the hot summer afternoon.

The towering clouds were brilliantly white. And they were blocking the view of the volcano.

"It's supposed to clear up tomorrow," Hanson said.

"Good. I've seen my share of storms. I'm looking forward to witnessing a true volcanic eruption."

Hanson noticed something unusual. "Those other pilots are pointing their choppers at us."

"That's because they know this is a FBI helicopter," Spiros answered. "They're guessing that we are either searching for Bigfoot or looking for UFOs. We'll be on the news tonight."

Hanson wondered how powerful the cameras were on the nearby helicopters. He leaned back, trying to hide his face behind a wall panel.

"I wouldn't mind seeing a UFO," Spiros continued. "Imagine, a volcano and a flying saucer in the same week!"

"You're in the right place," Hanson said. "Washington is the number one state for UFO sightings."

"Why here?

"Scientists reason that it has to do with upper atmosphere mirages caused by tall mountain peaks," Hanson answered, sweeping his hand at the Cascade Range in front of them. "Such as these volcanoes."

"Agent Fisher told me that you're some sort of skeptic," Spiros said. "What do you think about all this Bigfoot business?"

"That's easy. It's all some sort of hoax."

"You're sure?"

"I saw three of them last night. They shot at me with semi-automatic pistols," Hanson answered. "Bigfoot is known for a lot of things. Packing heat isn't one of them."

"So it's men in disguise, like a *Scooby Doo* episode. Where does one get a Bigfoot outfit?"

"The hunt for the costume of the Patterson film, and who made it and who wore it, is a story in and of itself," Hanson said. "These days, it's easier. Anyone could order something up online."

"We can look into that. Bigfoot costumes can't be that common. It would be easy for the FBI to trace."

"I told Fisher that," Hanson said. "I pointed him toward some cosplayer costume suppliers also. There's a chance that our hoaxers are using Chewbacca costumes instead, and they swapped out Chewie's face with gorilla masks."

"Cosplayers?" Spiros snorted. "You mean those nerds that hang out at conventions pretending to be superheroes?"

Hanson didn't answer. He had been to a con a few years ago, dressed up as Luke Skywalker. The older, bearded version from the sequels.

Spiros didn't notice the sudden silence. He had shifted his attention to his flying.

They were west of Mount St. Helens. From what Hanson could tell, the storm was most furious in a southern area between Mount St. Helens and Mount Adams. It looked like Spiros was going to hook around north of the volcano, passing over Spirit Lake while heading east. Then he would turn south toward the cabin, where Sheriff Hart was waiting.

They left the news helicopters behind as they plunged into the dark clouds.

"Hold on, this is going to be a little bumpy," Spiro warned.

* * *

"Don't lose them," Foster urged.

He and Cooper were a half-mile behind the FBI's tactical helicopter, blending in with the journalists. When their target disappeared into the clouds, they moved forward.

"Storm looks troublesome," Foster added.

Cooper threw some switches on his panel. "This is nothing. You should try flying in a blizzard in Siberia."

Foster felt reassured with that. Both of them were Spetsnaz, and Cooper was also a trained military pilot. There wasn't much that could deter him.

"At least it will give us some cover," Foster said.

Cooper didn't answer. He was busy talking to the tower at PDX, explaining to them that he was flying north to search for trespassers near the Johnston Observatory. It was a good lie. Foster could see a few helicopters northwest of them doing the very same thing.

Then they plunged into the clouds. Heavy rain pelted the helicopter. A blinding streak of lightning arced in front of them, followed by a shuddering roar of thunder.

* * *

Hanson grabbed his hand rests, his knuckles white.

"That was close," he said into his headset.

A bolt of lightning had gone off behind the helicopter. Judging by how fast the thunder had reached them, it had happened close by.

Spiros didn't immediately answer him. Both of them had headsets on, allowing them to communicate over the roar of the helicopter's rotors. But the pilot was also tied into the airport tower back in Portland. He was listening in on something for a moment. He then turned toward Hanson.

"Sorry, I'm not ignoring you. Someone else is flying in here with us," Spiros answered. "That's good news; it means they think as I do. This is the safest passage through the storm. The real mess is southeast of us."

* * *

The rain was coming down in sheets. Cooper had his wipers going at full speed. And though it was still mid-afternoon, it was as dark as twilight around them.

Foster brought out the bomb's trigger mechanism and flipped the safety cap off of it.

"Bring us in closer."

* * *

Now it was Spiros was making small talk. Hanson realized he was doing it to distract him. He welcomed it.

"So Bigfoot lore all began around here with Ape Canyon?" Spiros said, pointing at the general area ahead of them.

"Yeah, nearly a hundred years ago," Hanson answered. He had a death grip on a strap near his shoulder. The helicopter was bucking in the wind and rain.

"Is this the first time the FBI has investigated Bigfoot?"

"No. Back in 1976, a group of hunters thought they spotted Bigfoot in Tillamook County. They tracked it, but all they came up with was some hairs. They sent it to the FBI to be analyzed."

"What'd they find?"

"Forty years later the FBI revealed it was deer hair."

"Forty years?" Spiros laughed. "That's the FBI for you. Let's hope they're faster this—"

Hanson heard something explode behind him. Lightning strike?

The helicopter lurched and started violently spinning.

Centrifugal force threw Hanson to his right, his face pressing against the glass as the chopper whirled out of control.

They were in a brief area of clearing. Hanson spotted a nearby helicopter, white, with a splotch of red.

Then it was gone, replaced by rain and grey.

"I've lost the tail rotor," Spiros yelled.

* * *

Foster watched the stricken helicopter turn away from them, spinning like a top. It disappeared into the clouds.

"How long will it take NTSB to figure out there was a bomb involved?" Cooper asked, swinging their helicopter away.

"I don't think that's going to be an issue," Foster said, a smile on his face. Luck, for once, was with them.

Foster's last look at the FBI helicopter was of it falling to the south.

Into the volcano's crater.

Chapter 29

Another flash of lightning dazzled Hanson's vision. The crash of thunder that immediately followed sounded like an explosion.

The helicopter was still spinning. Hanson had to push himself off from the side to resume a normal sitting position.

Visibility was crap. If lightning wasn't flashing, the view was a wall of grey. Hanson had no idea where they were, or how close the ground was.

Spiros was screaming into his microphone, fighting with the controls.

"Mayday! Mayday! Tail rotor gone! Can anyone read me?"

Hanson watched as Spiros flipped a couple of switches, shutting down the engine.

The helicopter stopped its frantic spinning.

Turning off the power removed the torque the main rotor was producing. It was only a small improvement, though. They were still caught in the storm. The wind was tossing around the helicopter like a leaf in a hurricane.

Hanson could also feel them dropping at a much faster rate.

Again, lightning flashed around them.

"One at a time!" Spiros yelled.

Though Hanson was hearing only one side of Spiros's conversation, he could guess what was happening. The helicopter pilots were all chiming in.

"I don't know where I am," Spiros shouted. "I've cut power and am now in autorotation. I repeat, I don't know where . . ."

Below them a red glow replaced the grey.

"Chopper's in the crater!" Spiros shouted. "Mayday! Chopper's in the crater."

Hanson grabbed his armrests. The glow was more defined now. He could pick out the fissures that crisscrossed the lava domes and the bottom of the crater. It looked like they were going to land close to one of them.

Hanson found himself thinking of a prayer. The short one that everybody used when they found themselves in immediate danger for their lives.

Please—

Then his world was one of bone-jarring pain and ear-deafening noise.

* * *

Makani loaded the last of the groceries into the back of the van.

It was her turn to get food supplies for the CVO. Dozens of geologists spent most of their day at the office. Their little kitchen required constant replenishing.

She looked at her watch. The lines at Cosgroves had been huge as locals made a run on stores and gas stations to prepare for tomorrow. It also didn't help that all the metro area's hotels were booked. People from all across the nation had flocked to the region to witness the eruption. At least past lessons had been learned and the local supermarkets weren't running out of toilet paper.

She turned to scan the parking lot as she returned her cart.

During the entire trip she had made sure no one followed her. She had also changed up the store that the geologists used and had instead gone to a Cosgroves on the city's northern edge.

She started up the van. Excited chatter from the radio immediately filled the cab.

"—chopper is in the crater!" Mark Buchanan said.

Buchanan was one of the USGS helicopter pilots. Makani turned up the volume on the radio.

"Tell the other pilots not to go in there!" Livken responded. "They might land in a fissure, or get dashed against the crater wall in this weather!"

Makani didn't hear Buchanan answer. He must have switched back to the channel the helicopters were sharing.

She grabbed her mike. "Owen, what happened?"

"Makani? It's the FBI's helicopter. It had some sort of mechanical problem. It went down in the crater itself."

Steve!

"Has anyone heard from it?" Makani asked, fear creating a lump in her throat.

"Not for a while. But before it went down, the pilot radioed that he was attempting a landing."

Makani felt some relief wash over her.

There's a chance.

"Owen, order Mark to come to pick me up," she said, looking behind her. "I'm in the supply van. My protective heat suit and a couple of spares are still in the back."

"Makani, I can't let anyone up there. Buchanan says the storm is making it impossible to navigate the crater. Visibility is almost nonexistent, and the winds are worse against the crater walls. Chances are you'll smash into the cliffs."

"He just has to get me close," Makani responded. "He can drop me off on the north side, where the crater wall was blasted away in the 1980 eruption. I'll hike the rest of the way in."

"Makani, the rock slides. You won't see them coming—"

"Owen, I'm the only one who can do it. I was in the crater a few days ago. I can find that downed helicopter with my eyes closed."

Buchanan must have finished talking with the other pilots, for he was back on their channel.

"Sounds like a plan. Where are you, Makani?" Buchanan said.

"Owen?" Makani prompted.

Her boss still sounded reluctant, but he acquiesced.

"Do it."

Makani had a map up on her phone. "Hockinson School is a few miles north of me; can you pick me up on their football field?"

"I'll meet you there," Buchanan replied.

* * *

Water on his face woke him up.

Hanson groggily looked around him. Rain was blowing in from a broken window to his right.

Though it was still mid-afternoon, it was dark outside due to the thick clouds. Visibility was around fifty feet due to the storm's raging downpour. Lightning flashed every ten to twenty seconds and Hanson could detect the iron like tang of ozone in the air. He also smelled helicopter fuel. There was a leak somewhere.

He looked left. The mist glowed red in that direction. A flash of lightning gave more detail. A fissure was about seventy feet away.

The helicopter rested at a twenty degree tilt to the left, causing Spiros to lean out of his seat. Only the pilot's seat belt kept him from tumbling out.

Hanson undid his own belt as he remembered the crash. It had been loud and violent. The strain from the impact must have caused him to black out for a few moments.

But at least their landing had been survivable. At the last moment, they had entered an updraft from the heat rising from the fissures. It had slowed their descent right before impact.

But they had landed on their left side, and Spiros had taken the brunt of it. Hanson moved over to him.

The pilot had a cut on his head, and blood matted his hair. Hanson removed Spiros's headset and lifted up each eyelid. He found the pupils unequally dilated.

Concussion? If it was, it was a bad one. Spiros was showing no signs of waking back up. Hanson crawled toward the back to where the first aid kit was. He groaned a bit as pain flashed across his chest from when he had strained against his seat belt during the crash.

Ignoring the pain, he made his way back with the kit. It contained smelling salts, and he tried those first.

Spiros didn't flinch.

Hanson turned to the wound, washing the worst of it away with a bottle of water. He then dressed it up the best he could by wrapping a bandage around the pilot's head.

He coughed. The reek of the smelling salts still filled the helicopter's cabin. As that dissipated, the odor of sulfur replaced it.

He glanced at the fissure.

Was the lava closer?

Hanson knew that poisonous gas was an issue with volcanoes. At the moment, the storm was a mixed blessing. It made visibility lousy, but the swirling wind was scouring out the sulfuric gas that was issuing out of the ground near him. And the heavy rain was keeping the temperature down. It felt like a sauna here in the crater, but at least it wasn't the unbearable griddle top it could have been.

Again, the sky lit up.

Something loomed out of the haze in front of the helicopter, about a hundred feet away. Hanson recognized it was one of the USGS's spiders.

It was similar to the one in Makani's video, a cluster of seismic equipment supported above the volcano's floor by a tripod. It was bright yellow and had the number '581' stenciled on it.

He turned back to the fissure.

The lava was definitely closer. The crack it issued out of was a bit above them. He was next to one of the volcano's domes.

The flow was a bright five-foot-wide ribbon that moved like cold molasses as it wound through the rocks. Hanson estimated twenty minutes before it would reach them.

They would have to leave the shelter of the helicopter. Hanson thought of the nearby spider. Could a rescue team find them through that?

He grabbed up the pilot's headset and put it on. Though Spiros had cut power to the engine, the radio still had battery power. Hanson could hear a cacophony of voices as nearby pilots tried to reach out to him.

He almost responded, but paused to think about it. This was no accident. Something had exploded behind him in the tail section.

He recalled spotting a nearby helicopter as they went down. Did it have something to do with his current predicament? If it did, he didn't want to advertise to them that he was still alive.

During yesterday's road rip Makani had pointed out the radio channel that the USGS used. Hanson dialed it up on the panel in front of him.

"Anyone out there?"

For a few moments, nothing. Then a familiar, welcome voice.

"Steve! Thank God," Makani answered.

Hanson was surprised to hear her.

"Makani? Where are you?"

"I'm in a USGS helicopter about ten minutes south of the mountain. We're coming to get you."

Hanson looked out the window. The rain was coming down harder, and the wind was rocking the helicopter. The spider wasn't even visible at the moment.

"It's a bit rough down here," Hanson said.

"Do you have any idea where you are?"

"I think so. I'm about a hundred feet away from one of your spiders, number 581."

"I know that one. I was there last week. You're near the base of the south rim and the cryptodome forming there. We have a makeshift landing area to the north. I'm going to hike toward you with air and a spare heat suit for you. Is the pilot okay? Do I need a suit for him also?"

"The crash knocked him out," Hanson answered. "I'm going to have to carry him."

"A suit for him may be out of the question, then. I'll think of something else. Stay where you are, but keep your eyes open for rock fall. I'll be there as soon as I can. Stay in radio contact with my pilot."

Hanson looked to his side. The lava was five feet closer. Despite the sheeting rain, he could feel the heat.

"Negative. We're abandoning the helicopter and radio and moving to the spider."

"Why?"

"Lava," Hanson yelled, ripping off his headset.

* * *

"Steve! Can you read me?" Makani repeated.

There was no answer.

Livken responded instead.

"Are you sure you can make it, Makani? Station 581 is a little under a half-mile from the landing site," her boss said.

"I've done it before," she answered. She didn't mention she would be carrying a spare suit and air tank with her this time around.

"Makani, remember the volcano computer model. You don't have much time. I would feel better if you had someone with you to speed things along."

"I have an idea about that," Makani said. "Mark can't leave the helicopter on the mountain. He says the winds could topple it over. Can you head up here in our other chopper? That way, you can assist us on the way back. I'll leave the third suit at the landing site for you."

"That sounds good. Parker is lifting off right now from the airport. I'll have him pick me up in our parking lot."

"I'll be looking for you on the mountain then," she said.

She took off the headset and moved to the back of the helicopter. She had placed three duffel bags back there.

She opened one of them up. It had her silver bunker suit, a custom job designed for her small frame.

She put it on as Buchanan entered the storm. High winds rocked the helicopter, and she fell down while adjusting her pants' suspenders.

"It's a mess out there, Makani," Buchanan yelled. "Are you sure you don't want to wait for Livken to walk in there with you?"

"Every second counts," Makani yelled back. He still had his headset on; she didn't. "Terrington predicted the crater bed would collapse this afternoon. According to his timeline, it's going to be close even if we don't wait for Livken."

She pulled on her jacket and secured it. She then turned to her Self Contained Breathing Apparatus. It was a mask and tank similar to what firefighters used to breath in smoke-filled buildings. She buckled into it, slid the face piece on, and attached the regulator. She took a moment to check her airflow. On the volcano, carbon dioxide was the silent killer, while sulfur dioxide was the painful one, searing the lungs as the gas converted to sulfuric acid inside one's body.

The helicopter had a backup SCBA in it also. It was for the pilots as they waited on the ground in dangerous situations. It had a smaller air bottle. She took it and placed it in the empty duffel her suit had been in.

She also placed a fire-resistant blanket in the same bag. Designed to shelter fire jumpers if caught in a forest fire, the blanket was compact while folded up, and lightweight. It would offer the pilot some protection while they carried him out. She used some bungee cords to secure the two bags she would be carrying together.

The sky flashed a brilliant white, and the chopper shuddered as thunder crashed around them. Buchanan checked a GPS unit in front of him and angled left.

Blinking lights, arranged in four points like the corners of a square, were strobing below them. The USGS's makeshift landing area on the mountain. The pilot settled the helicopter within them.

Even on the ground, Buchanan was fighting the weather. The helicopter shook in the whipping winds.

"Make your way back here. We'll be waiting!" he shouted.

Makani pulled her head shield on and locked it into place with hook and loop fasteners. She gave him a thumbs-up sign.

She slid the door open. The wind almost knocked her over. She threw the duffels out on the ground. She then took a walking cane from the very back of the helicopter and jumped out herself.

The helicopter rose away. Makani half expected the wind to abate as it did, but the gale still tore into her when the aircraft disappeared into the clouds.

She hooked the strap of a duffel bag to one of the flashing beacons and shouldered the other one and the extra gear. She grunted under the weight.

Makani turned to the south. For a moment, fear froze her in place. Complex algorithms from a distant supercomputer had predicted that the crater floor would collapse at any moment. Entering Mount St. Helens now meant a high probability that she would die under crushing rock, or by falling into the magma below.

She put the thought out of her mind. Steve was in there. Gripping her walking stick, Makani took her first steps into the crater, using the red glow in front of her as a guide.

* * *

"She's going after Hanson," Cooper said.

He and Foster had been eavesdropping. Ever since their attack on

Steinsson the Russians had been monitoring the USGS's channel. What they heard now dismayed them.

"We can't let that happen," Foster said, rage building inside of him. *What did it take to kill this guy?* "Can you take me down to that same spot?"

They had watched where the USGS helicopter had landed. Cooper had been careful, using the cloud cover and keeping to the other helicopter's backside to keep their presence cloaked.

"You want to go into the volcano?" Cooper said in disbelief.

"I'd rather face the volcano than Tonkov," Foster said. "They left a spare suit down there. I'll put it on and surprise them halfway."

Cooper moved in for a landing, the storm masking their approach. Foster looked around the cabin for something he could use as a weapon. Since he had thought he wouldn't need it, he had left his pistol in his truck.

He found the pole they had used on Steinsson earlier in the week. It was a long, sharpened stake about five feet long.

He held it up and slapped Cooper on the leg. The pilot at first scowled and groaned in pain, but his face lit up when he saw the weapon's pointed end.

"An eye for an eye, comrade," Foster said, grinning. "He skewered you. Now we'll skewer him."

"What about Bateman?"

"She won't be a problem," Foster said, a hard glint in his eyes. "Just get me down there."

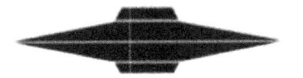

Chapter 30

With a groan, Hanson laid the pilot's limp form at the base of the spider. Metal stakes anchored the apparatus to the ground. It provided some relief from the wind if one stood on the leeward side.

Hanson huddled over Spiros, doing his best to keep the pilot protected from the elements. They were up in mountain elevations, and the rain was cold.

Hanson had been prepared for that. Expecting rain at the cabin, he had brought a heavy raincoat with him. To protect Spiros from the elements, he had put it on the pilot before they left the helicopter.

But it was the ground that was their best ally against exposure. It was warm, and steam rose up off of it as the rain pelted the hot rocks. Temperature-wise, Hanson realized he was in some sort of sweet zone.

He looked at the device near him. Was it some sort of seismometer? He grabbed one of the legs and shook it.

"I'm here," he yelled.

In answer a boulder the size of a basketball appeared out of the mist, bouncing off the ground and streaking by his head. Hanson ducked as it hurtled by.

He stood back up and looked south. He could barely detect the crater wall looming above him.

While on their repair run yesterday, Makani had explained that the greatest danger she had faced inside the volcano was falling rocks from the crater's steep sides. The USGS had deployed drones to be her spotters when she had entered the area earlier in the week.

Hanson had no such help. He would have to be more alert, and keep his head up.

Nearby, he heard a hissing sound. He looked toward the downed helicopter.

The lava had reached it. Smoke was billowing from the cabin.

Hanson dove on the ground, covering the pilot's body with his own.

The helicopter exploded, the fireball briefly illuminating the area. One of the rotors spun toward Hanson, passing a few feet above him and shearing off the spider's antenna.

Shaking, Hanson looked up. The seismometer was cut in half. Nearby, the fire from the helicopter raged.

"Jesus Christ," muttered Hanson, thankful to still be alive. At least it couldn't get any worse.

Then the ground shook.

Makani kept to a southwesterly direction.

Fissures laced the area she was approaching. These crevices were hundreds of feet deep and thick, viscous dacite lava flowed at the bottom of some of them. Poisonous gasses rose from the cracks, deadly if one didn't have a mask on.

Her colleagues called this area the Cracks of Doom, after the volcano in the *Lord of the Rings* trilogy. The last time she had traversed them, they had asked her if she had spotted Gollum, or any hobbits.

At least the ground was reasonably clear. A few months ago, before the mountain stirred, the crater's floor was covered with a young glacier and rocky debris from landslides. Even without volcanic activity, exploring Mount St. Helens' crater with unstable ice under one's feet was one of the most dangerous hikes in the world, if not impossible.

But the rising heat had changed that. The horse shoe shaped Crater Glacier had begun rapidly melting when the mountain reawakened. And when the southern bulge had risen from the ground, the glacier had broken in half like a turkey wishbone on Thanksgiving.

Riding the layer of melt water under them, the two glacier halves had swept down the sides of the older, central dome before coming to a rest on the mountain's lower northern slope.

Besides being a major geological event in and of itself and causing a dangerous flood on the Toutle River, the glacier's exodus had scoured out the crater floor. And any water that had remained had rapidly evaporated, or flowed into the one of the newly appearing fissures. The end result was a crater surface that was easier for Makani to navigate.

She approached the first fissure. It radiated out from the old central dome, almost reaching the crater's west side, leaving only a ten-foot-wide ledge that one could use to get around it.

Her ears straining, she studied the cliff above her. Nothing seemed to be falling her way. She quickly navigated the narrow, thirty-foot-long path.

Though the danger was real, she felt at home here. Since that day, when she was six years old, she had spent her childhood visiting the Kilauea Volcano National Park whenever she could. In college, she focused on becoming a geologist, specializing in volcanology.

Volcanoes fascinated her. Was it their power? Or did it make her feel closer to Pele, the Goddess of fire and volcanoes? Her father had raised her Christian, but her mother, native to Hawaii, had also introduced the Goddess to her. Growing up, Makani had found herself in the confusing situation of worshipping both, depending on the circumstances.

To her southeast something exploded and a fireball rose into the sky. It appeared to be several hundred yards away.

Steve's helicotper.

Beneath her, the ground shook as an earthquake rocked the crater. She kept on her feet with the help of her walking stick. Lightning struck the lava dome nearby, and boulders bounced by. As the thunder rolled over her, she uttered a quick prayer.

To Pele.

* * *

Foster struggled to put the gear on. As a Spetsnaz soldier, he had experience with radiation containment suits, but it had been a while. His time in America had made him soft and out of practice.

He had the pants and shirt in place, both layered with an aluminized coating. He then donned the SCBA, making sure his regulator was secure. He pulled on the silver helmet.

Because of the rain, the damn thing was steaming up. Foster wiped at the large, square window that let him see out. With that and the storm, he could barely see ten feet in front of him.

To his south was an explosion. It had to be the other helicopter. Then the ground shook from an earthquake, and he fell to the ground.

It lasted several seconds. With a curse, Foster picked himself up, second-guessing his decision.

He stuck to it. At least here, he had a small chance. Facing Tonkov after failure was inviting sure death.

Using the sharpened pole as a walking stick, he strode into the crater.

* * *

Hanson kept his breathing shallow.

Despite the wind, he could still detect whiffs of sulfur. The gas was venting from the same crevice as the nearby lava flow. He wondered if it was at dangerous levels.

The fire around the helicopter was dying down. And the lava, now on level ground, wasn't seeping his way.

The storm still raged, though. A brilliant flash lit the area, and Hanson once again glanced north.

Where was Makani?

* * *

Makani came up on the second fissure and followed it east.

It was really two fissures. One stretched from the crater's west wall for several hundred feet.

Another fissure reached out from the lava dome to meet it but came up short from intersecting the first by about twenty feet.

This left a bridge-like path between them. Makani took a moment to study it.

Despite all the earthquakes the mountain had suffered since she had last been here, it still looked solid.

As thunder and lightning crashed around her, she hustled over it. She knew the heat was strongest here, and Hanson and the pilot would need protection to cross it. When she made the other side, she turned right to get around the third and final crevasse.

* * *

Foster found himself blocked by the first fissure.

He looked into the glowing abyss. Lava pooled a hundred feet below. Even with his suit, he could feel the heat emanating from it.

To his left the fissure stretched upward, onto the volcano's older central dome, which was riddled with even more smaller fissures.

He reasoned that the fissure in front of him terminated somewhere short of the crater's west wall to his right. Cursing at his bad luck and loss of time, he turned and began hiking that direction.

* * *

Another earthquake rocked Hanson. He wondered how powerful the now-broken seismometer would have measured it. Again, boulders bounced by him. He wondered if he should move back a bit.

The rain was letting up for a moment, and he detected movement to his north.

A figure clad in a bulky silver-colored suit was moving through the hellish landscape toward him, a large bag over its shoulder. It looked like some sort of alien astronaut with its large, square face-plate. It covered the remaining one hundred feet in a lurching manner. When the figure reached Hanson, it knelt next to him and removed its bulky helmet.

Makani.

"What's a nice girl like you doing in a place like this?" Hanson asked with relief in his voice.

* * *

Hanson looked pretty roughed up. He was also soaked to the bone. The pilot lay still on the ground, his face ashen.

"Are you hurt?" she asked.

"I'm fine," Hanson answered. "The pilot took the brunt of it. He might have a concussion. We're going to have to carry him out."

"I'll get an air mask and this blanket on him," Makani said, rolling the duffel in Hanson's direction. "Put these pants on first."

As Hanson worked with the suspenders, she tightened the face mask on Spiros and checked his air. Though the air was breathable here, the noxious fumes in the crevasse area were too much, even with the wind. The heat at the bridge would be overwhelming also. Even with the heat blanket wrapped around the pilot, Hanson would have to cross it in shifts, once with her silver helm on the pilot, then again to return the helm to her for her passage.

"Jacket next," she ordered.

When Hanson finished that she helped him with the SCBA. She attached the regulator. They then both worked on the pilot, wrapping the bungee cords around his body to hold the blanket she had cocooned around him.

The ground shook beneath them for a few seconds. She kept an eye out for falling debris.

"Is this normal?" Hanson shouted through his mask.

She shook her head. "Not at this frequency. Remember my presentation?"

Hanson shook his head and smiled ruefully at her from behind his protective cover. "I was distracted by your dress."

He looked so embarrassed at admitting that. She wanted to kiss him then and there, but the masks were in the way.

"Well, since I'm now in this shapeless suit, I'll explain it to you again. The pressure beneath us is about to give way, and the crater's floor will collapse."

Hanson looked alarmed. "Has this happened before?"

"It happened in Kilauea in 2018," she answered. "When the caldera collapsed back then, it sent the lava flowing to an alternative vent, where it caused millions of dollars in damage to homes and property. Here it will result in tomorrow's eruption."

"So this area—"

"—is going to sink down a few hundred feet," Makani said.

"And us with it," Hanson said, standing up.

They both got their hoods on. As Hanson had instructed, she had kept one of the pilot's arms free of the foil blanket. Hanson now grabbed it and pulled him up to a sitting position. Hanson then carefully bent the unconscious man's legs at the knees. By bracing the pilot's feet with his own foot, Hanson hauled him up into a fireman's carry.

Hanson grunted in pain when he did so.

"You're hurt," Makani said with concern in her voice.

"Don't worry," Hanson said, his voice muffled behind the two layers of protection. "If Sam Gamgee can do it, then so can I."

It took her a moment to realize he was making a *Lord of the Rings* reference. The pilot's body was across Hanson's shoulders. The legs draped to his left. She helped by placing herself at Hanson's side and taking on their weight on her shoulders. She held the spare air bottle in front of her, and Hanson took up the walking stick. Like some sort of ungainly example of the three-legged race, they moved away from the spider.

And toward the Cracks of Doom.

Chapter 31

Hanson could only bear the pilot's weight for a few minutes at a time. The combined weight of the suits and air tanks were too much. He was also in pain. He must have bruised his ribs in the crash, and the stitches on his left arm had broken apart. The gash from yesterday's fight throbbed.

As in a nightmare, each step was an effort. Visibility was crap also.

He was wondering how soon till they should take their next pause when the volcano decided for them. An earthquake knocked them all to the ground.

"Break time," Hanson groaned.

"Don't have to tell me twice," Makani said.

They had rounded the corner of the first crevasse, and the ledge was behind them.

Again the ground shook, and lightning flashed.

They both made ready to stand back up, using each other for support. The foreheads of their suits touched as they leaned into each other.

"So, you do this for a living?" Hanson said. He could barely see her face through the four layers of protective gear between them.

"Just another day at the office," she answered.

"And I thought Black Friday at Cosgroves was bad."

They stood back up and shouldered Spiros. Hanson knew that carrying the wounded pilot with his head hanging down wasn't good for his concussion, but he had no choice. Getting him off the mountain was the first priority.

His burden secure, he took his next step.

* * *

Makani did her best to help Hanson. She could tell he was at the end of his rope as he stumbled every other step.

They were walking along the edge of the central fissure. The bridge was only a hundred feet away. Makani looked across the crevasse to their north, wondering where Livken was.

In answer, a figure clad in silver stepped into the garish red light coming out of the crevasse. Hope soared within her. That disappeared when the figure waved at them.

"Is that help?" Hanson asked.

"Steve, Owen is known for giving a goofy salute when greeting someone in one of these suits. I don't know who that is."

With a grunt, Hanson laid Spiros on the ground. He turned to face her. She could see a grim look on his face.

"It's one of them. He's here to finish the job," Hanson said. "Stay with the pilot."

"What are you going to do?"

"That bridge is a choke point. I have to get there before he does."

Clutching the walking stick in his hand, Hanson turned from her and lumbered for the bridge.

* * *

Foster spotted them on the other side.

They were carrying the pilot out. He watched the smaller one, who he guessed was Bateman, look his way.

He gave a friendly wave. Surprise was his best weapon now. He planned to strike first when they were close together.

But they put the pilot down, and Hanson began running.

Foster looked to his left. A small bit of rock spanned the crevasse.

His ruse was over before it began, and Hanson was trying to make the bridge before he did.

Foster broke into a run.

* * *

Hanson got there first.

The land bridge arched up ahead of him. His breath coming to him in ragged gulps, he used the walking stick and moved up the slight incline.

His opponent was waiting for him at the bottom of the other side. He had a long, staff-like pole in his right hand. And even though the heat suit covered all of him, Hanson could tell who it was from his stance.

The man who had invaded his home.

Blondie slowly started making his way up the slope towards him.

Though it was not as long as his opponents, Hanson brandished his walking stick as a weapon.

"It's over, asshole," Hanson shouted. "I have the high ground!"

Blondie responded by sweeping his staff at Hanson's legs. Hanson yelped in pain as the wooden pole whipped against his shin, knocking him to the ground on his back.

His air tank jarred into him. Hanson floundered like a turtle balanced on its shell.

The other man adjusted his grip, leaning in for a spearing thrust at Hanson's chest.

Hanson parried it to his right, and the pointed end of Blondie's weapon jammed into the ground a few inches from Hanson's head.

Hanson kicked out with his right leg. The heat suit made the move almost impossible, though, and he barely connected on the other man's right thigh.

With a grunt, Blondie stumbled a bit back down his slope. Hanson used his walking stick and pulled himself back up.

Blondie crashed into him, knocking him back down, this time close to the bridge's west side edge. Hanson was only a few feet from the precipice. He could feel the heat from the lava below.

His arms feeling like lead, he tried to use his walking stick to ward off the blows raining on him.

* * *

Foster kept on swinging his staff at Hanson.

He could tell that the American's strength was all but gone. All he could do was to keep his own staff up in a feeble resistance.

He knocked Hanson's weapon out of his hands. It fell into the abyss, incinerating halfway down. Foster aimed for Hanson's head next. His goal now was to beat him unconscious and roll his body into the fissure.

Something slammed into his back, driving the air tank painfully into his spine. Foster gasped out loud and dropped his staff as he turned to face what had hit him.

It was Bateman.

* * *

Makani couldn't stand by as Hanson dueled with his silver-clad opponent on the bridge. Even though the fumes rising from the fissure shrouded them, she could tell Hanson was getting the worst of it.

As lightning flashed around her, she dashed forward.

Whoever this guy was, he had his back to her as she ran up the slope. Unlike the men fighting before her, her heat suit was tailored for her. It allowed her to maintain a sprint-like pace as she crashed into the man raining blows on Hanson.

He yelled in pain and stumbled forward, dropping his staff.

Then he spun toward her.

She could see his face, a feral mask of rage.

He lurched toward her. She aimed a kick for his crotch and connected.

His baggy heat pants acted like armor, absorbing most of the blow. With a grunt he moved forward and grabbed her on both sides of her body, right below her armpits.

He lifted her slightly and kept walking. She felt herself losing ground as her scrambling feet couldn't get any traction under her.

He was carrying her to the east side of the bridge. She could feel the heat building at her back.

She tried pounding on his chest, but he was so much bigger and stronger than her.

She could see his face. It had a wicked smile.

"Live by the sword, die by the sword," the man shouted through his mask.

They were almost at the edge.

She reached up and twisted his outer hood to the side, hearing the hook and loop fasteners tear free as she did so.

Blinded, he let go of her and raised his hands to readjust the outer layer of his head protection.

Makani leaped forward and snaked her hand under the man's face shield, finding the hose and regulator connected to his breathing apparatus mask.

She pulled the regulator free.

* * *

Foster felt a tug at his face mask.

The smell of a thousand matches being lit filled his nose. Something in him warned him not to breathe, but he was already panting from his exertions. He gulped in the hot, poisonous air.

Pain seared his lungs, and suddenly it felt like they weren't working. Every gasp only seemed to make it worse. He needed air.

Ignoring Bateman, he fumbled with his regulator.

* * *

Hanson tried to stand back up but almost blacked out from doing so.

He didn't have any strength left. He looked to his side, spotting Makani nearby. She had ripped away Blondie's air hose.

Blondie looked to be in distress, but Hanson knew he still could be a threat, so he did the only thing he was capable of at the moment.

He began crawling towards them.

* * *

Their attacker was stumbling back, but he still remained standing.

He would be incapacitated in a few minutes, but in that time, he could still kill both of them.

In the background, Makani saw Hanson stumble back down. Then he shuffled forward on all fours, placing himself behind the other man.

Makani guessed what he was doing. She charged forward.

* * *

His regulator reconnected, Foster took a few deep breaths. The air from his tank helped, but he was still in pain.

Bateman would pay for that.

He finished twisting his outer hood into place.

The geologist was rushing him.

He braced himself, and her impact barely forced him back a step.

The back of his leg met unexpected resistance.

Hanson was behind him. Foster tried to recover, but the weight of the air tank threw him off. He flipped over Hanson into empty air.

He had been too close to the edge. His flailing hands reached out, finding the ledge. He grabbed at it and hung on for dear life.

He was a few feet down from the bridge's west edge. He could feel the heat through the suit's protective material.

His feet took the worst of it. The heat rising from the lava below him seared into them.

Foster screamed in agony.

Above him, Hanson's helmeted head peeked over the edge. He was on his stomach, and his hand stretched out toward Foster.

"Hold on," shouted Hanson.

Hope sprang in Foster. Maybe he'd survive this yet. He extended his right hand to Hanson.

Hanson batted it aside and reached further. He snatched the outer cover from Foster's head.

"I need this," Hanson said.

Waves of intense heat burned away Foster's hair. His air mask melted around his face. He screamed again and lost his grip on the ledge and plummeted into the crevice.

As flames consumed him on the way down, the last thing he saw was Hanson's face in the red glare from the lava below, and the final sound he heard was Hanson's mocking voice, shouting out one last word.

Precioussssss.

Chapter 32

Makani dragged Hanson back from the edge. He remained on the ground for a few moments, panting from the heat.

"I have a helmet for the pilot," Hanson said, holding up the hood.

"That's good, this bridge is the hottest point on our path," Makani said, holding out her hand.

She helped him up, steadying him as he swayed a bit. Hanson also picked up the staff that their assailant had brought and used it as a walking staff. They made their way back to Spiros.

"Who was that?" Makani asked. She couldn't get the man's face, or his dying shriek, out of her mind.

"It was the same guy that attacked me in my house," Hanson answered. "And I suspect he participated in all the Bigfoot encounters this past week."

They reached Spiros. He was still wrapped up like a mummy on the ground.

The rain continued to pour down. She made Hanson rest on the ground and cool off in the downpour. She took off one of her gloves and felt for a pulse on the pilot.

It was weak and thready, but he was still alive. As Hanson recovered his strength, she worked the extra hood over Spiros's head and shoulders.

The ground shook again for a longer period of time.

"Let's go," Hanson said.

* * *

The rain was lessening up as they crossed the bridge. Visibility improved, and it brightened as sunlight began to penetrate the clouds. That surprised Hanson. He had forgotten that it was only late afternoon.

Each step was still a struggle, though. Hanson found himself with his head down, focusing on putting one foot in front of the other. He didn't know how much longer he could keep this up.

"There's Owen!" Makani yelled next to him.

Hanson wearily looked up. The tall form of Makani's boss was on the other side of the last crevice, giving a jaunty salute. He wasn't wearing a heat suit, but he had on SCBA gear. He was as close to the final ledge as the temperature allowed.

Hanson stumbled.

Makani prodded him on. "We're close to the finish line, soldier! Don't quit on me now."

The pep talk worked. Hanson surged forward with Spiros on his back.

They cleared the final ledge. Livken rushed over and helped ease the pilot to the ground.

Hanson dropped the staff and ripped off his outer cover from his head. The heat was tolerable here. He also peeled off his air mask. For the first time since he crash-landed, he had a clear view of the crater.

The cloud ceiling was now a few hundred feet above the volcano's floor. The upper edges of the crater walls were still shrouded, but the domes could be seen. They looked like islands in a sea of steam.

Makani had her gear off also. He felt her hand on his face as she leaned over him.

"Take it easy, Steve. Owen is calling the helicopter to us."

Hanson could hear it approach. "Makani, what you do next is very important," he said.

"What is it?"

He gave her his instructions. Makani's look of understanding was the last thing he saw before he passed out.

* * *

The helicopter landed nearby. Makani could see that the chopper's external camera was focused on the center of the crater. The pilot was recording as he flew. She and Livken stripped the heavy breathing gear and jacket off of Hanson. His eyes fluttered open as they did so.

The wash from the rotors slung the light rain into Makani's face. It felt like she was back in the storm. She and Livken stood up a delirious Hanson. They supported him to the helicopter and shoved him through the rear right side door. He passed out again on the helicopter's floor.

The ground rocked underneath them. This quake was the strongest yet, and the two geologists struggled to remain upright.

"Guys, you're going to want to see this," Parker yelled.

Makani moved to the other side of the helicopter and gasped.

The crater's floor was sinking. It was slow and deliberate, but the lava domes were definitely lowering into the mist.

Next to her, the pilot raised the helicopter a foot off the ground and hovered there.

"Move it!" he yelled.

Livken was staring at phenomena like it was the most beautiful thing he ever saw. She slapped him on the side of the head and they both moved to pick up Spiros.

They carried him around the front of the helicopter, passing in front of the camera. The blast from the rotors was more intense as Parker hovered over the shaking ground.

Makani looked over her shoulder. The domes were almost gone, as was the crater floor. The newly created void raced toward them with a loud roar.

Livken leaped in first, so that he could bodily drag Spiros in with him.

"No time!" Parker shouted.

She felt the ground giving beneath her. She jumped up on the strut and held on to the side of the open doorway.

At first she thought she was rising but soon realized that that was an illusion. Parker was holding the helicopter steady as the ground fell away from her.

Livken pulled her in. She shut the door behind her.

"We made it," she shouted with relief.

"And I have it on tape," Parker whooped as he increased power and rose from the crater. He kept the helicopter out of the clouds as he filmed the spectacle below them.

Livken fumbled his way to the right forward seat. Makani turned to the two stricken men, trying to make them comfortable on the helicopter's floor.

Livken had his headset on and was talking on the radio, announcing on the USGS channel their success.

"Vancouver, we were successful. We're flying straight to the hospital now."

She knew what the next logical question from Vancouver was, so she moved forward and put a hand on Livken's shoulder. He pulled the left side of his headset away from his ear. As per Hanson's instructions, she told him what to say next.

Livken looked confused, but he did as she said.

"Call ahead to the hospital and tell them to prepare for only one head trauma case," Livken said. He turned to her to make sure he got the next part right. "The pilot was the only person we retrieved from the FBI helicopter."

In the back, Makani nodded her head.

Chapter 33

Emmanuel Hospital, Portland, 11:13 p.m. PDT

"Is there any word on Spiros's condition?" Fisher asked.

Vinsant shook her head. "They're still operating on him," she answered.

Sabrina Vinsant was the Assistant Special Agent in Charge at the Portland Office. When word that Spiros was being brought in to Emmanuel, the Special Agent in Charge, Lewis Jacobs, sent her and Fisher to debrief Hanson and overlook the hospital's security.

"How's he holding up?" she added.

Fisher looked toward the waiting area outside the hospital's operating rooms. Hanson was sitting alone on a couch, his gaze shifting back and forth from the operating room's door to the television mounted on the wall.

Fisher and Vinsant were standing in the back. A tall redhead nearing sixty years of age, her bearing commanded respect.

"Physically, he's fine," Fisher answered. "He had passed out from heat exhaustion on the helicopter. But he recovered enough to walk in on his own once they landed here. He blames himself for Spiros, though."

"That's on us," Vinsant said, scowling. "We should have anticipated they were still gunning for Hanson and watched our own backs closer."

Anger was on Fisher's face also. Whoever attacked the FBI had made a huge mistake.

"What do we know about the other helicopter?" Fisher asked.

"We quickly narrowed it down to two companies here for the emergency effort," she answered, pulling up images of helicopters on her phone. "The red 'smudge' that Hanson said he saw was either the mascot from Cardinal Air or the large, red ampersand from Lewis & Sons." She looked back at Fisher. "Guess which state where the cardinal is a state bird."

"Ohio," Fisher answered.

"Where the gun from Hanson's home invasion came from," Vinsant said. "Their headquarters is in Columbus."

"We need agents in there."

"Jacobs is already working on that."

"What about our end?"

"We're searching the area where they parked their helicopter. That, and their service truck, are gone. We have agents checking in at every domestic and military radar station in Washington and Oregon. Whoever their pilot is, he's good. They tracked him for a while but lost him somewhere in the Yakima Valley. With half that area emptied out, they could be anywhere."

"Descriptions of their crew?"

"The other helicopter ground crews interacted with them, so our artist is working with that. Our best description is coming from one of Hart's deputies. Cardinal Air was the contracted chopper that was flying him around yesterday."

"Shit," Fisher said. Whoever these guys were, they were bold. "What are we telling the press?"

"Hanson set that up for us. To the world at large we're reporting it as a mechanical failure and Makani Bateman of the USGS rescued the only person onboard, our unconscious pilot."

"Hanson had made a call over the USGS radio channel. Everyone at the CVO must be wondering about him."

"They did for a while, but I had agents Stillwell and Catling inform them that Hanson perished in the crash, and that we wish to keep that quiet until next of kin can be reached."

"So whoever is behind this will think that Hanson is dead, and was unable to provide a description of their helicopter," Fisher observed.

"If these bastards at Cardinal Air think that we don't suspect them, then maybe we'll be on top of them before they realize we're pursuing that angle." She started walking off. "I'm going to do one last check on the men we have posted around the hospital. You good here?"

"I'll keep an eye on him," Fisher said, glancing toward the couch.

* * *

"Comfortable?" Fisher asked as he sat down.

Hanson looked down at the hospital scrubs he was wearing. He had asked for something to change into once they landed. His rain soaked shirt and pants were in a plastic bag next to him.

"I feel like I'm wearing pajamas out in public," Hanson admitted, his face red.

"Have they said anything about Spiros?" Fisher asked.

"Only that they would know more in another half hour," Hanson answered.

The news on the television shifted back to the afternoon's events. Hanson raised the volume a bit.

On the screen was the video from the USGS helicopter as it approached for a landing in the crater. The camera's lens kept focused on the lava domes, which soon began sinking.

"Good God," Fisher said next to him.

Makani and Livken were shouting off-camera. Hanson guessed it was while they were struggling with moving him. Then they appeared in front of the camera carrying Spiros. There was more yelling, and the collapsing crater could be seen closing on them as the helicopter rose away from the destruction.

The face of national news correspondent Jennifer Steel filled the screen.

That was the scene this afternoon from the USGS helicopter that flew in to mount a rescue effort for the pilot of a downed FBI helicopter in Mount St. Helens' crater. As predicted, the crater floor collapsed, but that didn't stop volcanologist Makani Bateman from entering the area and rescuing the helicopter pilot.

The background video changed. Hanson recognized the scene as the one Makani had used in her presentation, where she was standing on the edge of the lava lake of the Marum Volcano in the Vanuatu Island region.

Doctor Bateman is no stranger to the perils of volcano exploration. With her experience, she saved the pilot, and the presence of the USGS also gave us astonishing footage of today's events, which everyone had at first thought we would miss due to the storm.

The crash is being attributed to mechanical failure. As to why the FBI's helicopter was there in the first place, we only have a 'no comment'. But speculation is growing across the nation. Were they investigating the recent sighting of a flying saucer? Already sightings of UFOs are growing around the United States. Is this all some sort of cover-up? More after this.

The news broke to commercial.

"How'd you keep off camera?" Fisher asked.

"Makani and her boss must have done some editing at the USGS office before they released the tape," Hanson said, relief in his voice. He didn't want to be on television.

"Good," Fisher said. "Whoever's targeting you thinks you're dead."

"It might give us some breathing room," Hanson said. The image of Blondie's face withering in the heat filled his mind. "Any word on the guy who attacked Makani and me?"

"They're part of a helicopter outfit from Ohio," Fisher answered. "We're checking on it now."

"What's up next for you?"

"My warrant for searching those hangars at Kesler's Galaxy Dish site should come through tomorrow. Do you want to come?"

Hanson's eyebrows shot up.

Fisher gestured around them. "Normally, I'd schedule someone to watch you until this is all over, but we're coming up short-handed. We have people guarding this hospital, the CVO, and investigating every radar site in the Northwest. I'd feel better if I knew where you were."

"Count me in."

"Good," Fisher said. He pointed at the television, which was running a story on tomorrow's pending eruption. "How's Makani doing?"

"I talked to her a while ago," Hanson answered. "I guess that since she was a first-hand witness to the caldera's collapse, they want to record her account as fast as possible at the CVO."

Fisher stood up, looking at his watch. "Understandable. Tomorrow is a big day for all of us." He turned toward Hanson. "Will you be okay here while I check on Spiros?"

Hanson held up his phone. "I'm good. I have a phone call to make anyway."

Hanson hit a quick dial number on his cell as Fisher walked away. Despite the late hour, she answered on the first ring.

"Is everything all right?" his mother asked.

Chapter 34

"I'm fine, Mom," Hanson answered. "I hope I didn't wake you."

"We're watching the news," his mother answered. "The volcano's collapse is something else."

In the background a young and excited voice piped up. "Is that Dad?"

"I'll put Elanor on first," his mother said.

His daughter's rapid-fire questions came over the phone. "Dad! When are you coming over?"

"Soon, sweetheart. Work at Cosgroves is hectic right now with all these people here to watch the volcano."

He felt guilty about not being over there. After his divorce, he spent every other weekend and school breaks with his seventeen-year-old daughter. These past few weeks, she had been staying at her grandmother's place in Astoria. Hanson was supposed to swing up there last weekend.

At least she was safer there. Hanson wondered how long it was going to take to resolve this case, though. He couldn't keep her there forever.

She didn't seem to mind his absence. She was describing a budding summer romance with a local boy.

"Oh, my phone's ringing, it's him," she said. "Hope to see you soon, Dad!"

"Me too, sweetheart. Don't hang up! Put your grandmother back on."

Again, the phone shuffled hands.

"Is he a good kid?" Hanson asked.

"He is," his mother answered. "Your daughter is an excellent judge of character. Where are you at right now?"

Hanson paused. He could never lie to his mother. "I'm at the hospital, waiting for someone to get out of surgery."

"Steve, I'm sorry. Is it someone I know?"

"It's the pilot you're watching on television. I was there also."

She didn't miss a beat. "It's this Bigfoot and UFO business, isn't it? You're caught up in the middle of it."

Lyca Hanson had raised him on her own since he was in first grade when his father passed away from cancer. A tall, strong woman of Scandinavian descent, she knew her son.

"I'm advising the FBI," Hanson said. "I was on that helicopter."

"Were you hurt?"

"No. But the pilot has a bad concussion. I don't know if he's going to make it."

"Then I'll say a prayer for him."

Again, Hanson hesitated.

"It wouldn't hurt if you said a prayer also," she said quietly.

Hanson knew his faith was a point of concern with her. She had raised him Lutheran. He remembered going to church, Sunday school, Confirmation, the whole bit. Belief was easy back then.

Then he started his road to skepticism. As the Loch Ness Monster and pyramid-building ancient aliens fell by the wayside, he also began to look at the events described in the Bible. Worldwide flooding? Water to wine? He had his doubts about it all.

His mother worried about him.

"I will. I promise," he said.

He and his mother spent a few more moments arranging for Elanor to stay for a while longer in Astoria.

"Steve, take care," his mother finished.

"Love you too, Mom, I'll call soon," Hanson said.

Hanson stood up. He had made a promise to his mother. He went looking for the chapel.

* * *

He found it on the building's ground floor; it was a small room off to the side of a large hallway. Still feeling dehydrated, he took a moment to get a bottle of water from a vending machine before entering. Inside were several rows of pews, and a backlit cross on the front wall.

The chapel had a handful of people in it. Hanson sat a few rows back from the front.

It was his sweet spot, where one could blend in and escape notice. He hated the first row, where all other eyes focused on the back of his head. It also ran the risk of being singled out for questions by the speaker.

The very back was no good, either. Lecturers would always proclaim that they can't talk that loud, and would everyone please move closer. What followed was an embarrassing game of musical chairs when selecting another seat.

Hanson looked up at the cross in front of him. What to say? Did it matter? He thought about earlier, when the helicopter was plummeting through the clouds and the brief moment when his thoughts on the issue were clearer.

Please.

Someone sat down next to him. It annoyed Hanson for a second that somebody was sitting close to him, but that emotion softened when he realized that his comfort zone invader also had a small dog.

It was a Maltese, a tiny white dog smaller than his cats. It had on a red vest with white medical crosses printed on it. The dog was looking up at him with dark eyes, and it put a paw up on Hanson's leg.

The dog's companion, sitting on its right side, spoke up.

"I hope you don't mind. She's trained to do that. She can sense a person's distress."

The speaker was an old woman, her frame shrunken with age. Hanson guessed she was in her mid-eighties. Deep wrinkles crisscrossed her tan face, and her long white hair was in a braid. She had on a red shirt, and like the Maltese, a red vest with a white cross emblazoned on it.

Hanson was already petting the dog. It had a calming effect.

"What's her name?"

"Mitzi," the old woman answered.

It was like his cats back home. Hanson felt better around the dog.

"She's part of the hospital's animal-assisted therapy program," she explained. "I take her into rooms for people looking for comfort." She nodded to the cross. "Are you here for a loved one?"

Hanson looked to the cross also, feeling bad about his answer.

"I barely know the guy," he admitted.

"And yet, here you are."

"It's my fault," Hanson said, getting to the heart of his guilt. "People are being hurt because of me."

"People? As in someone else is involved?"

"There's this geologist," Hanson replied, his confession now gushing out. It was easy to talk to this woman and her dog. "I've put her in danger twice now."

The woman nodded her head. "Doctor Bateman," she said.

"You know her?" Hanson asked, surprised. The dog put a paw on his hand so that he would resume petting it.

"I'm aware of her," the woman answered. "She's been all over the news. She seems quite exciting."

"There's more to it. Makani . . . Doctor Bateman . . . knew that the volcano was going to collapse, but she went in there anyway to save me."

"She must care for you very much."

At a loss for words, Hanson didn't reply.

"And I can see you care for her. Maybe someday you can return the favor."

He hadn't thought of that. Hanson grinned at her. "Are you this good with all your patients?"

She smiled back, an expression that added more wrinkles to her face. "The dog carries most of the load."

She had a small dish out for Mitzi, but she was busy looking for something in her bag to fill it with. Hanson held up his water bottle.

"Is she thirsty?"

The woman's eyes lit up in appreciation as Hanson poured out some water. The dog lapped it up.

"Thank you," she said. "Do you know which room your friend will be in?"

"Not yet. But if it helps, his name is Spiros. I guess you can look him up that way."

She was standing up and making ready to leave. "I will. Tomorrow morning."

Hanson's phone vibrated. He dug it out of his pocket and looked at it. It was a text from Fisher.

Spiros pulled through. Moving him to his room now.

Hanson typed out a response.

Thank God.

He looked up at the cross, his thumb hovering over the screen. Did he believe that?

He pressed send.

He turned to the old woman to tell her the good news, but she was already gone. Hanson realized he didn't know her name.

He messaged Makani to give her an update. She responded a few moments later.

I'm glad to hear that. Busy at work again, spending another night here.

She immediately followed up with another message.

Thinking of you.

She had hiked into an unstable volcano for him and also saved his life from an assassin's killing stroke. The old woman was right. They did care about each other, and tonight should have been theirs to share. Unfortunately, urgent responsibilities kept them apart. Quick messages to each other didn't feel near enough, but it was all they had at the moment. He sent his reply.

Same.

Hanson spent a few moments looking at that, feeling the single word's weight, knowing she would also. Then he glanced at the clock on his phone. Again, he was having another late evening. It was almost midnight.

He switched to the USGS app. Front and center on its home page was the digit '1' in a large, red font.

It changed to '0'.

Part Three

HYSTERIA

Chapter 35

St. Petersburg, Tuesday 6:55 p.m. Moscow Standard Time

"Are all these UFO sightings our doing?" Gontarev asked as he read the information on his computer screen.

Graphs and charts displayed trending keywords and subjects on the web's social media sites. There was a noticeable spike in flying saucer commentary.

"No. American citizens are reporting these on their own," Tonkov said behind him. "Already, a mild panic is setting in."

Tonkov looked up at the monitors on the wall. Most were tuned into American network news channels, and they all showed the same thing; steam rising from Mount St. Helens in the distance. Yesterday's rain had settled the dust in the region, and the mountain could be seen crystal clear against a blue sky.

The USGS app was on one of the left screens. It was now displaying hours. It was 9 a.m. in the United States' Pacific Northwest region; the volcano was set to erupt sometime close to noon.

Tonkov was thankful for that. Everything that was happening

now was from under his direction, but he had no control over Mother Nature. With or without the eruption, this plan was moving forward. Mount St. Helens made it much more manageable.

"And now it's time to fan the flames," Tonkov added.

Gontarev sent out the command to his squad. Outside the office, one hundred Russian trollers went to work.

Tonkov knew their script. They were to first find and bury any opinions contrary to their own with bots, programs designed to run automated tasks. In this case to spam any sites like Hanson's *The Unexplained, Explained* so much that they crashed under the increasing traffic.

Then the trolls were to add their own accounts of witnessing UFOs, backing it up with links to websites that detailed the original Mount Rainier UFO sighting, the Roswell cover-up, and a news article in which a former US senator tied to the recently revealed Ariel Unidentified Phenomenon Task Force claimed that America was in possession of alien hardware.

Bots, and American personal computers slaved to them, would augment the troll's postings from hundreds to millions.

"Anything else you need, General?"

"Put up a map of the United States."

A satellite image came up. Gontarev already had several pins marked on it.

His agents were in place. Grey was waiting in Eastern Washington, while Johnson was somewhere northeast of Billings, Montana.

Cooper, Williams, and Smith were hiding out with the helicopter on an abandoned farmstead outside of Goldendale, Washington.

Tonkov scowled. Foster should have been there also, but Cooper reported that he didn't make it out of the crater.

On the wall, the newsfeeds were showing yesterday's video of the crater's collapse. There was no way Foster could have survived that. At least Hanson perished there also.

But the pilot had survived. That was why he had Cooper abandon their station at the airport. Tonkov didn't know the pilot's condition. He might have been aware of the Russian helicopter nearby, and reported it to his superiors.

He glanced over southern Nevada on the map. Hamsfield and Monetti were in position at Nellis Airforce Base, and the President of the United States was set to give an address in a few hours.

Years of planning, coming to fruition.

Success today was critical. The Su-57, Russia's addition to the world of fifth-generation fighters, was floundering. Their largest collaborator on the project, India, had recently pulled out of the joint effort out of dismay toward the Su-57's performance. His cash-strapped country desperately needed those sales to finance its own military programs. Without outside money, there was a chance the Su-57 program would never get off the ground.

Acquiring two F-35s would fix that. He had contacts with several cash-rich countries that were eager to pay billions for the American technology. Billions more would be saved on research and development as they reverse-engineered the jet's advanced systems. Russia's stealth program would be back on track with a stealthy supersonic jet of their own; an aircraft that could take off and land on almost any battlefield.

And with both Russia and other governments that were opposed to America in possession of this technology, the balance of world power would shift in their favor.

All in one afternoon.

But F-35s weren't the only prize he had his sights on. Tonkov pulled out his phone and made a call.

"Siberia here."

Tonkov snorted at that. These kids were so full of themselves.

"Chernov, contact Terrington. It's time."

"Understood."

Tonkov put away his phone. In front of him, Gontarev was excited.

"Results are already coming in, General. Mount St. Helens, Bigfoot, and UFOs particularly, are trending."

"Good, it was what we were hoping for," Tonkov said. "The heist of the century begins now."

Chapter 36

Portland, Tuesday, 9:10 a.m. PDT

"And Bingo is her name-o!"

Hanson finished dishing up the can of cat food, splitting it between Sebastian and Bingo. The cats showed their appreciation by ignoring him as they ate.

Hanson shouted over to his phone on the counter.

"Remember, feed them around six!"

Tolmany's voice came over the speaker. "Got it. Anything else?"

"Change the litter box?" Hanson asked hopefully.

"Only if you promise me you'll ask Makani out for a date," his friend responded.

Hanson picked up the phone and switched it off the speaker. "Dude, volcano."

"I know, but after yesterday, she's all over the news. Everyone wants to interview her. She's a genuine celebrity now. Steve, don't let this one get away."

"I promise, after she deals with the volcano's eruption, I'll ask her out."

"That's not the only eruption she—"

"Just watch the cats," Hanson cut in. "I'm going north on another advisory mission for the FBI. I have no idea what traffic on I-5 is going to be like."

"Is this about the UFO? What do you think everyone saw? A helicopter?"

Hanson thought about his own experience. "I don't know. That's why we're going to talk to the man behind the search for alien intelligence himself."

"Drive safe. Talk to you tomorrow."

Hanson said his goodbyes to the cats and headed out to his van. It was going to be another hot day, so he was wearing a plain dark grey t-shirt with his jeans.

"Computer, open back hatch," he commanded.

The van's rear door swung upward. Hanson loaded a small cooler packed with bottled water and sandwiches. He wasn't kidding when he told Robert today's trip worried him. The KET Observatory was several hours away by road, and an exploding volcano was in the middle of that. He had no idea how long this trip would take.

Then he took his Glock 17 and holster that he had retrieved from his gun safe and placed that under the driver's seat.

He was going on a simple trip to question Kesler, but after all that had happened the past few days, Hanson wasn't taking any chances. He also laid two loaded magazines next to the automatic pistol.

Traffic was light, and the trip to the FBI field office went quick. It was if Portland was holding its breath. People were at home glued to their televisions or already had strategic hilltops staked out.

He was on time and Fisher met him out front as he pulled up. Fisher had a briefcase with him, and his phone was to his ear. He hung up when he got in.

"How are you doing?" Fisher asked as Hanson pulled onto the road.

"Fully recovered," Hanson said. "Plenty of fluids like the doctor ordered. The only thing that aches is my arm. How's Spiros?"

"He's still in an induced coma, but the swelling is down," Fisher answered. "Have you heard from Makani?"

"She called this morning," Hanson said, glancing to his right. They were crossing the Glenn Jackson Bridge, so the CVO was just a few miles away. "They're in full swing over there. Though I'm surprised the news hasn't done a full-on interview with her."

"That's our doing. We told the networks that she's a witness for our investigation into the crash, and she's hands-off. Dr. Livken is also doing his best to keep her out of sight in the building."

"What about the protesters?"

"They're not there today. I think no one wants to look stupid on camera when the volcano goes off today."

"Good, as long as she's safe."

Fisher gave him a sidelong look. "You two have been spending a lot of time together since this all started."

"Well, yeah," Hanson said. He wasn't sure how to respond to that.

"She asked you out the first time. You should ask her out."

"I'm going to," Hanson said, his voice raised a little. "I'm not completely helpless around women. I've been busy with Bigfoot and UFOs chasing me."

Fisher raised his hands up. "Hey, I believe you. I didn't know it's a touchy subject." The FBI agent looked around him. "So, a van."

"The doors open on voice command," Hanson revealed.

"Is your daughter part of a soccer team?"

Hanson looked over at him, debating whether to tell Fisher the truth.

"I bought it because its shape reminds me of the *Galileo 7*, the shuttlecraft from the original *Star Trek* series."

Fisher stared at him in disbelief. "My God, I knew it. You're such a nerd. No wonder you haven't asked her out yet."

"We'll get there."

"She's crazy for you, you know."

"I said we'll get there. These things take time," Hanson said. Now he wanted to change the subject. "Why were you interested in my van anyway?"

"It's a three-hour trip, and I was hoping you had also had a sports car," Fisher said. "I'll make a call and let the State Police know that we're on the Interstate. You don't have to drive five miles per hour under the posted limit."

"You're telling me to speed?" Hanson said, his eyebrows raised.

"Yes. Maybe we can make this a two and half hour trip."

"I'll do it if you give the order."

"What?"

"You know what to say," Hanson said, grinning.

Fisher turned to look forward, sighing as he did so.

"Make it so," Fisher commanded.

Hanson pressed down on the gas pedal.

Chapter 37

CVO Building, Vancouver, 11:05 a.m. PDT

"How much time now?" Livken asked.

"Somewhere between one or two hours," Terrington answered. "I'm using the data from yesterday's event to augment my prediction."

"Too bad we lost all that equipment."

Terrington agreed. The volcano had swallowed several hundred thousand dollars' worth of survey devices.

"But it wasn't in vain," Terrington said, pointing to his monitor. "I was able to take all the incoming information and route it to Icarus in real-time. It processed the collapse as it was happening. With that as a reference, we can use the data coming in from our equipment at the base of the mountain to fine-tune today's prediction."

"Remarkable, Terrington," Livken said, straightening up and patting him on the shoulder. "It was our lucky day when you arrived a few months ago. You're going to receive the Vetlesen Prize for this."

The Vetlesen was the highest honor awarded to scientists like them. It was the Nobel Prize of geology. Terrington had been looking forward to winning it and making a name for himself.

But now that wasn't going to happen, and history was going to remember him for something else.

Treason.

As Livken left his office, Terrington took two thumb drives from his pocket.

The first was a complicated affair, having an alphanumeric keypad built into it and some LED indicators. It was his own, and he had a ten-digit security code already programmed into it.

The second flash drive was unremarkable in appearance, but he knew it held a 'zero-hour' Russian hacking program—something so advanced that no one had ever even seen such a thing in action, and as of yet had no defense against it.

One of Strontium's more infamous hackers, Siberia, had designed the program. Tonkov's agents had delivered it to Terrington a few weeks ago, showing up at his house in the middle of the night.

He stepped out into the main room.

It was a madhouse. Geologists packed the CVO. Some of them were newly arrived this morning to help out. Everyone was either at their stations or gathered around in small groups, catching up with each other.

A sizeable crowd was circled around Makani as she described her adventures from yesterday.

Again, Terrington was glad she was unharmed. Steinsson's death was all on him. He couldn't stand the idea of anyone else he knew getting hurt because of his actions.

He skirted around her group and approached the cabinet that housed the modem. As he opened it, Agent Stillwell walked up.

Besides the geologists, several FBI agents were present, squeezing out interviews with the newcomers. Though with the absence of the protesters the agents were more relaxed today.

"Professor, may I ask you something?" Stillwell asked.

"How can I help you, Agent?"

"Are you sure when the volcano is going to erupt in a few hours? I want to time my break so that I can be outside when it happens."

Terrington smiled. The FBI still didn't suspect him. He was coming to realize that the best way to conceal his actions was to hide in plain sight. With the agent standing nearby, he plugged his thumb drive and the Russian hacking program into several USB ports on the modem.

"I'm sure, Agent Stillwell," Terrington said, patting the modem. "Icarus is giving me all the power I need to calculate today's outcome."

Which was the lie that had caused Steinsson's murder.

The modem wasn't just connected to Icarus, the world's ninth most powerful computer.

It was also connected to Icarus's big brother, Apex.

Apex was the number two ranked supercomputer in the world, with a 135 petaflop processing speed. It shared the same Stratton campus as Icarus and could be tied into the smaller computer if need be.

Normally, Apex was air-gapped, or cut off from the outside world, due to the importance and sensitive nature of its primary function. Tonkov wanted the data located on Apex, and he had instructed his puppet Terrington on how to go about securing it.

President Hayes had fumbled early in her term by not responding fast enough to a devastating hurricane in Florida. That, and the idea of closing off the Mount St. Helens area, so close to the specter of COVID, had dropped her approval ratings to dangerous levels. It also didn't help her cause that Tonkov was using Russian trolls to fan the flames of American discontent with her.

Tonkov had extensive psychological profiles on Hayes, and he coached Terrington on how to approach the President and secure an audience. Tonkov also instructed him on how to convince the President that Terrington required the computing power of Apex to pull off his prediction miracle.

It worked. Hayes was hoping to convince the American public that she cared about safety. But she also wanted a solid date of when things would return back to normal. And, as Tonkov had guessed, she was willing to take a significant security risk in doing so.

The authorities put Terrington through normal background checks, though the usual step of interviewing his coworkers was skipped. The government didn't want anyone at the CVO having a hint that there was more to the Stratton connection. The government gave him clearance and access to Apex. The air gap was quietly withdrawn, and Terrington was provided the Stratton modem. The device had the ability to encrypt the CVO's communications with Stratton over an unsecured network using a socket shell protocol. Without it, no one on the outside could penetrate Stratton's NSA-grade firewalls.

As he and the FBI agent made small talk, Siberia's program went to work.

This was the perfect time for it, as the USGS was sending tremendous amounts of data at the moment. The Russian program tagged along, part of the sheer volume of information.

Not that it mattered at this point. At the primary gateway, there were no protections to overcome. Hacking was more than an exotic code overcoming existing defensive programming. There was a human element, individuals tricked into giving up passcodes, or compromised into opening those pathways.

Terrington fell into the latter. He had been given the key, and he left the front door wide open for the Russians.

Once inside, accessing what the Russians wanted was still a problem. Terrington had plenty of computer memory allocated to him for his volcano algorithms, but the data Tonkov craved had been partitioned off and protected by internal firewalls, and still out of reach.

Siberia was prepared for that.

The Russian hacker had earlier in the year pulled off the amazing feat of breaking into nearly a dozen European supercomputers.

At the same time.

His on the ground spies had secured credentials to bypass barriers and log in. Once inside, Siberia launched codes that changed the elite system of computers into run-of-the-mill, but powerful, cryptocurrency mining farms.

Or least on the face of it. That was a diversion. The truth was the attack was a dry run for today. Siberia used his time inside studying the internal workings of Western supercomputers. From what he learned, he devised his zero day hack.

It went to work within Apex's cores and storage drives, ferreting out the information Tonkov was looking for. After thirty seconds, it sent off what it had found, and terabytes of data flowed through Stratton's outgoing connection.

And into Terrington's flash drives.

LED lights blinked on both of them. Terrington pulled them out and held them up to the FBI agent.

"Like I said Agent Stillwell, two hours," Terrington said.

"Thanks, Professor," the agent said, grinning. "I don't want to miss it."

Stillwell walked away. Terrington remained by the modem for a moment.

Though everyone else at the CVO accepted what he did at face value, Steinsson had a stronger computer background and had pressed him on details about his dealings with Stratton. He suspected there was more than Terrington was letting on. He also had figured out that Terrington's contact with the Utah computer center was a man named Phil Jacobs. Steinsson was planning on making a phone call.

His questioning would have been innocent, but it might have been enough to spook the US government and sever the connection to Apex. Terrington couldn't let that happen, and he had contacted Tonkov to update him and await instructions.

Instead, the Russians killed Steinsson that very afternoon.

Terrington went back to his office, the guilt washing over him in waves. He took the Russian flash drive and placed it on the ground.

He then stomped on it a few times, grinding it into bits. He kicked the debris under his desk.

He took his cell and accessed the hidden, secondary phone and texted a message.

Coming out.

He looked up at the shelf behind his desk. It had a framed photograph of the CVO crew from a month back. Steinsson, being taller, was standing behind him.

For a moment, he imagined the Vetlesen Prize, a large, bronze medallion, framed and placed on a spot next to the photograph.

Then he stepped out of his office. Everyone was gathered around the main screen, once again watching the crater collapsing.

Unnoticed by them, Terrington exited through the back door and left his life behind.

Chapter 38

A few minutes earlier...

"I better get back to work," Makani announced.

Her coworkers gave her small waves and smiles. Others clapped her on the back and told her they were glad she was okay.

Makani appreciated the sentiment, but she was finding it all overwhelming. Seeking escape, she made her way toward a back hallway and ducked into an empty office.

Steinsson's.

She was surprised to find herself here. For the past few days, yellow police tape had blocked the door. Fisher's FBI crew must have taken it down earlier in the day.

She turned on the light and reminisced about the last time she had visited the room.

It was the morning of the day of his death. Steinsson was sitting down in his chair with his laptop open before him, and they had talked about family and the demands of the job. They also compared their small volcanic islands, hers of fire, and his of ice. He joked that

Kilauea had too many vowels. As she left his office, she retorted that Eyjafjallajokull had too many consonants, and was unpronounceable.

Fifteen minutes later, he left for the mountain, never to return. She had been one of the last people here to talk to him, and when he didn't check back in, she had gone out and discovered his body.

It had seemed so wrong to see someone that had been so full of life mere hours earlier appear so empty in death.

She sat down in his chair. The laptop was gone, taken by the FBI. Other desktop items remained—a pen and pencil holder, stapler, a cube of sticky notes, and a framed photo of his family. He and his wife were standing in a rift with their two teenage children. Makani recalled Steinsson telling her it was Thingvellir National Park, where the American and Eurasian tectonic plates met in Iceland.

Steinsson also had a bulletin board sandwiched between his desktop and shelves mounted on the wall. It was covered with notes, calendars, and maps.

It was also subtly different from the last time she was here.

A sticky note was in the upper right corner. It was square in shape and colored purple. Written on it with felt pen ink were two words.

Call Phil.

During their interviews the FBI had asked her if she had known anyone named Phil. She hadn't. She thought little of it, though, since they had asked her a thousand other things that afternoon.

Looking at the bulletin board, she could now see the source for many of their questions. The names of geologists from all around the world peppered it. The FBI was following up on everyone that Steinsson had had contact with.

It hadn't bothered her that she didn't know who this Phil was, for she had no context. But now she knew something that no one else was aware of.

Writing this note was one of the last things Steinsson had done.

She studied the sticky note cube. It had hundreds of different colored sheets that formed thick layers on its sides. It wasn't a perfect cube anymore due to usage, and the top color of the moment was yellow.

When she was in his office earlier, the top color had been purple, and only one sheet remained. That had bothered her. Purple notes were the worst; one could barely see the writing on their dark surface. She had wanted to reach across Steinsson at his desk and rip it off and throw it away.

She hadn't, and now, there it was, one of his last actions. A reminder to himself for when he returned from Mount St. Helens.

Call Phil.

Was it important? Was this Phil worth killing for? Or was he someone who watched Steinsson's dog back in Iceland or dry cleaned his clothes here in Portland?

She knew everyone else on this board. The volcanologists were a tight-knit group, and she was acquainted with everyone they dealt with.

She heard an exit door open. Glancing out of the office, she caught sight of Terrington's back as he went outside.

Terrington.

The CVO's computer genius wasn't based in the Pacific Northwest. He was from the east coast, and thus a long way from Hawaii. She didn't talk to him that often, and her chief impression of him was that he was always on his phone, talking to his contacts at the Stratton Institute.

What he did with computers was way over everyone's head. They let him deal with it, and they were all happy to live with the results.

She realized she had no idea who he talked to when he called Stratton.

No one did.

She impulsively leaped out of the chair and followed him outside. It was already warm, and she was glad she was wearing shorts and a dark blue t-shirt with 'Hawaii Volcanoes National Park' circling an image of Kilauea itself printed on it.

She couldn't see Terrington at first so she stepped further out into the lot until she located him. His car was parked on the far side of a small white delivery van. He was pulling a small suitcase from the trunk of his car.

She decided to be direct as she approached him from behind.

"Donald, who's Phil?" she asked.

His face gave her all the answers. He may have been ready when the FBI questioned him, but he wasn't prepared for her. Guilt covered his face as his eyes widened, and his jaw dropped.

"Who's Phil, Donald?" she repeated.

"Makani—" he began.

She didn't let him finish. "Why did Kris have to die?"

A hand clamped down on her left shoulder, and she felt the barrel of a gun press against her back.

"Because he asked the wrong questions, Doctor Bateman," a voice hissed behind her.

* * *

It took them twenty minutes to reach Pearson Field. The gunman, a tall, muscular guy with dirty blond hair and a full beard, gave Terrington directions the whole way there. Makani guessed that he was to be the original driver, but he was now busy pointing an automatic pistol with a suppressor attached at her. From the conversations she was overhearing, it was also clear her kidnapper was a Russian agent, and Terrington was providing something that he wanted. That filled her mind with questions but she refrained from asking them. The Russian was wearing a heavy bandage around his arm for the stab wound she had given him back at the cabin, and he didn't look like the forgiving type.

Terrington drove the van out to a circular patch of asphalt, where a helicopter was landing. The chopper was white with a decal advertising a company name in blue letters: *Vertical Lift Enterprises*.

They all got out of the van, her captor pushing her ahead of him with the gun at her back. Terrington followed.

She looked around for help. There was some activity on the airfield, but Terrington had parked the van so that it would block witnesses in the flight center. And the noise from the helicopter warming up would drown out the suppressed gun.

They herded her into the back of the helicopter. Two men were already sitting in the front. The pilot, a clean-cut man that was shorter than the gunman but just as muscular, looked her over.

"What's she doing here?"

"She followed Terrington out. She knows," the gunman said.

"Shoot her now," the man in the other forward seat said. "We'll drop her body out on the way to the observatory."

Fear gripped Makani as the gunman raised his weapon a bit higher.

"Don't let him do it, Cooper!" Terrington screamed. He was in one of the very back seats, and he was holding up a thumb drive, his thumb hovering over a small button.

Cooper turned out to be the pilot. Makani watched his hand drift toward his own gun.

"What's that?" Cooper growled, his eyes on Terrington's hand.

"My own drive with the data your boss wants," Terrington said, sweat beading on his forehead. "I was running it parallel with Tonkov's. That one is in a million little pieces. Mine's encrypted, and only I know the code. I can also destroy what's on it with the press of one button. It will fry the chip inside."

Cooper's eyes narrowed. "Smart. You covered your ass."

"You bet I did. Only when I was away safe from you and my money was in the bank would I text the code to Tonkov. It's my insurance. But now, it's for both of us," he said, looking at Makani.

Cooper turned to the gunman.

"Put it down, Smith."

Makani realized she had been holding her breath. She let it out with a sigh as the gun lowered.

The helicopter rose from the pad. Terrington and the Russian she now knew as Smith took a moment to put on headsets. She didn't have one, so she could barely follow their conversation over the noise of the rotor.

"Okay, Terrington, what do we do with her? I can't have her in the way at the KET," Cooper said.

"There's a place where we can lock her away for a few hours, it's on the way there."

"Where?"

Makani's heart went cold when she heard Terrington's answer.

"The Johnston Ridge Observatory."

Ten minutes later they passed through a phalanx of news helicopters hovering south of Mount St. Helens. There was a no-fly zone for them over the volcano itself and to the north of it. Portland air control didn't want the ash plume between them and anyone nonessential in the air. Only search and rescue helicopters were allowed close to the mountain, and they would soon be pulled back also.

Makani could see several such craft from where she was sitting, flying over the lower slopes. Back at the office, the television news crews reported that authorities were still rounding up Bigfoot rescuers from the forests around the volcano.

"The FBI must have alerted everyone to look out for this helicopter," Terrington asked from the back. "Aren't you worried you'll be caught out here?"

"We prepared for this contingency," Cooper answered. "Thanks to Strontium, *Vertical Lift Enterprises* was slotted to fly in from Seattle today. We even changed our transponder. With everything happening today, we'll blend in."

They passed west of the crater. It was almost unrecognizable since the crater floor was now a steaming depression. But the lava domes could still be seen, and they looked even more massive than from the previous day.

Cooper turned to look at her.

"What happened to Foster down there?"

She looked straight back at him.

"He got a preview of what hell was going to be like."

He glared back at her and then turned around.

"At least he took Hanson with him."

Makani hung her head and didn't respond. She didn't want them to guess that Steve was still alive.

Cooper approached the Johnston Ridge Observatory. Makani could hear him explaining to air traffic control that he was investigating a report of trespassers at the tourist center.

They landed on a paved pathway west of the edifice. The Russians in the front seats stayed with the helicopter as the man named Smith shoved her toward the building. Terrington, still clutching the flash drive, followed.

"You're right, this will do," Smith said.

The building was an imposing structure built into the hillside. A concrete bunker, designed to survive a day like today.

It had massive windows facing the volcano. These were all covered with bolted down plywood, as were the air intake vents. With the building sealed tight, the hope was that the center would remain intact during the nearby eruption and be recoverable in the future.

Terrington, keeping a wary eye on the other man, brought out a set of keys. As part of upper management at the CVO, he had a few master keys for places the USGS needed to access.

He unlocked the padlock that held a chain securing a side door. He then unlocked the heavy door itself and opened it. With all the center's windows boarded up, it was dark inside.

"Get in, Makani," he ordered. The guilt on his face was stronger now.

"Donald, please, don't do this," she pleaded.

"Makani, I'm trying to save your life," Terrington answered. "No one else has to die. The north eruption is a few hours away. We'll send someone to pick you up once we've made our escape." Terrington looked at Smith, who gave a curt nod, his face showing no emotion.

With the gun pointed at her, she had no choice. She took a few short steps into what looked like a utility hallway and turned around.

"You better, Donald."

"I will, I promise," he said, shutting the door and leaving her alone in the darkness.

Chapter 39

Highway 12, Washington, 11:45 a.m.

Fisher looked up from his tablet. "You can slow down for this part."

"You don't have to tell me twice," Hanson agreed, easing up on the gas.

They had left the town of Packwood twenty minutes ago and were now climbing the steep grade of the White Pass area. The highway here cut into the side of a steep canyon carved out by the Clear Fork Cowlitz River. At some points of the road, the shoulder was only a few yards wide and dropped hundreds of feet into the torrent below.

But though the drive was white knuckle inducing at this point, it was still a picturesque trip. The trees were still tall and thick here and numerous lakes dotted the scene. Hanson could even see Mount Rainier in his rearview mirror.

He focused on the road, though.

"Anything in those files you received?" Hanson asked, taking a drink from a bottle of water.

Packwood was on the southwestern edge of the National Radio Quiet Zone. Its enterprising citizens had signs posted throughout the town.

Last chance to make a phone call.

Fisher had asked Hanson to pull over while he downloaded last-minute files from his FBI bosses and coworkers. Hanson parked the *Galileo 7* at a closed gas station that had two Bigfoot statues in front of it, one carved of wood and the other covered in fur. Due to the recent news, the wooden one had a sign hanging off of it.

I'm innocent.

Hanson had busted out his cooler with sandwiches and water, and the two men ate in the van. After the progress bars made it to the one hundred percent mark, they had set off again.

"Something you'll find disappointing," Fisher answered, reading off his screen. "Your Marines are now at Nellis Air Force Base for some Red Flag exercises for a few weeks. I don't see how they fit into the picture."

Hanson shook his head. Finding Monetti guilty of something would have made his day.

Fisher picked up on Hanson's discouragement, for he continued. "But the 'Bigfoot' hairs are from chimps."

"No surprise there, we thought as much," Hanson said, perking up. "What about the costumes?"

"Your advice paid off. USPS delivered three Wookie costumes to a Post Office box in Columbus, Ohio."

"Columbus? You mentioned earlier that Cardinal Air was from there."

"Yes. And it's also where the gun used in your home invasion came from."

Hanson raised his eyebrows. That was news to him.

"Something else of note was shipped directly to their hangar," Fisher added. "They received several dozen weather balloons, radar reflectors, and helium canisters."

"All of that brings Project Mogul to mind," Hanson said.

"Yes, but for what purpose?"

"I have no idea," Hanson answered.

Fisher held up his tablet. "Does this man look familiar to you?"

On the screen was a blown-up image of an Ohio driver's license photograph. A recognizable face stared back at Hanson.

Blondie.

"It's the guy who attacked me at my house, and in the volcano," Hanson said.

"His name was Trent Foster. He was a helicopter mechanic employed at Cardinal Air."

"That explains the 'garage' like odor I got off of him. Does anything else stand out?"

"No," Fisher answered. "He was born and raised in the Midwest. A model citizen, he doesn't even have any parking tickets."

"But you do not like what you're seeing."

"The other employees at Cardinal Air are the same. But get a load of their names. David Cooper, Mason Grey, Jim Johnson, Ken Williams, and Stanley Smith."

Hanson snorted. "Sounds like someone didn't have much of an imagination when handing out identities."

"You're right. This entire helicopter company is populated by men with generic, but false, identities. They're some sort of airborne mercenaries with made-up backgrounds, designed to fly under the radar."

Fisher paused a moment.

"No pun intended," he finished.

"Good one, though," Hanson said, grinning. "Any ideas on the identity of the shadow organization that hired them?"

"Still nothing. Whoever they are, they're good. They're bouncing off server farms across the globe. We can't pin them down."

Fisher returned to his reading. Hanson focused on driving, thinking the FBI agent was going to be intent on that for the rest of the trip. That lasted for only thirty seconds.

"Holy shit," Fisher muttered.

"What?"

"Your website is down because of a Denial of Service attack out of Russia."

Hanson almost swerved off the road at that. Fisher grabbed his armrest as a precipice loomed to his right.

"Sorry," Hanson apologized as he corrected. "A DoS attack? Are you sure?"

"I've had our cyber department studying your website for a while now. It's sophisticated, so they're still not sure where exactly it's coming from, but it carries a Russian signature."

Hanson thought back to earlier in the morning. He had checked on his *The Unexplained, Explained* blog. He couldn't access it because the server it was on had crashed. Hanson had thought it was because it had finally become popular.

"What does that mean?" Hanson asked.

Fisher was quiet for a while, staring thoughtfully out the front window.

"We've been looking at this thing all wrong," Fisher finally said. "Whoever's behind the protesters is powerful, and we've been thinking it's business interests. But what if it's the Russians? They have the know-how. With preparation, they could cover their tracks as they goad the protesters on. But, unfortunately for them, you showed up. A wild card with his own website. They had to react to you, and they made a mistake doing so. This may be our biggest break in this case."

"Are you sure?" Hanson asked. "Seems like a stretch to me."

Not if you add Cardinal Air into the picture," Fisher said. "Their false identities now make more sense. They're some sort of Russian sleeper cell."

"So you think the guy from the volcano—"

"Was a Russian agent."

Hanson grunted his agreement. The man had fought like he had combat training.

"But that means that Russian agents are dressing up as Bigfoot. Why?"

"I don't know," Fisher answered, looking at his cell. It had no bars. At the moment, they were cut off from the outside world. "We need a phone. I personally ordered the cyber department to look at your website. You and I are the only ones putting this together!"

"The KET has land-lines," Hanson said, increasing his speed. "We'll make some calls from there."

* * *

CVO building

"Where's Doctor Bateman?" Agent Stillwell asked Livken. He had spent the last hour going over a report on his phone that described the FBI's search results in Columbus, Ohio. It had the driver's license photographs of the employees that worked at a helicopter company over there. Still angry about Spiros being in the hospital, he had burned their faces into his memory.

But now he realized he hadn't seen Bateman for a while. He had found Livken in the building's control room, a small office that controlled the monitor's in the main bullpen.

"I don't know," Livken answered. He had a worried look on his face. "I also can't find Terrington, he's gone too."

"*Shit,*" thought Stillwell. He saw Catling across the room. He waved her over, hoping that nothing else would occur before he could contain this thing.

In the bullpen, dozens of voices yelled out.

"It's happening!"

On the room's main screens, Mount St. Helens erupted.

Chapter 40

Mount St. Helens, 12:11 p.m.

The southern dome gave way.

The pressure below it couldn't be contained anymore. In 1980, it was the northern landslide, the greatest ever observed by humanity, that set off that eruption. The sudden removal of the weight of millions of tons of rock allowed the pressure building under the mountain to burst free, like a cork popping off a bottle of champagne when the wire basket was removed.

Today, there was no landslide. Instead, it was the rapid increase of pressure from the crater collapsing that induced the eruption. It was as if someone had shaken the champagne bottle and both cork and cage burst off.

The ash column clawed its way up into the sky from a vent covering the southern third of the crater. As a category five on the Volcanic Explosivity Index, the ash column from the 1980 eruption had risen to a height of fifteen miles. As a category three eruption, today it would only reach somewhere around seven miles to ten miles.

The crater walls directed the ash, and none of it spilled down the mountain's southern slopes at the moment. On the open north face, the ash flowed out of the north gap, seeping down into the canyon west of Spirit Lake.

* * *

New York City, the studio of World News This Evening

"You're on," the studio director said.

Doug Morgan looked up to the camera with a smile. Nearing sixty years of age but still possessing a thick shock of white hair, he exuded paternal authority.

"Good afternoon, everyone. World News This Evening is breaking early today due to the eruption of Mount St. Helens. We are also scheduled to cut to the White House for President Hayes' Oval Office address. But for now, let's switch to Portland, Oregon, where national news correspondent Jennifer Steel is standing by."

The studio director signaled to Morgan, and he relaxed. He turned to a nearby monitor to watch Steel's broadcast.

Her location was a hilltop. Behind her, ash rose from the volcano.

Thank you, Doug. I'm standing here at the top of a Portland landmark known as Rocky Butte. It commands a view of the surrounding area.

As predicted by the United States Geological Survey, Mount St. Helens has erupted. Behind me, the ash plume is rising into the atmosphere. The weather forecast has the plume drifting into the eastern half of the state of Washington.

And while the eruption is exciting to witness, people will remember this day as a triumph of science. Mount St. Helens erupted within a half hour of predictions. The geologists involved must be very excited at this very moment . . .

* * *

CVO building

"Have you seen Doctor Bateman?" Stillwell asked, his voice raised in near-panic.

Catling shook her head.

It was pandemonium in the CVO at the moment. Geologists were shouting and rushing back and forth in the building.

Livken wasn't much help at the moment, either. He had way too many things on his mind.

Stillwell leaned in closer to Catling.

"Take over the security cameras," he said, pointing to a small office down the hall. "I saw Bateman and Terrington a little while ago. Go back an hour and see where they went."

Agent Catling sped off, and Stillwell turned to the main room, spotting another FBI agent.

"Burns, you're with me."

He and Burns burst out into the back parking lot on the building's south side. There was an enclosure for USGS vehicles nearby so he sent Burns over there. He swung over to the parking lot on the east side.

It gave him a view north. As he had desired earlier, he could see the rising ash column.

Stillwell ignored it and turned to his phone. It had been too loud in the CVO, but outside it was peaceful. He looked up and then dialed Doctor Bateman's phone number.

No answer. He almost put the phone away in frustration, but the faint sound of another phone ringing reached his ears.

He searched for it, tracking the sound to some bushes at the lot's edge.

Underneath the foliage was a phone. Stillwell picked it up, recognizing the incoming phone number on its display.

It was his.

* * *

Johnston Ridge

Holding up her small penlight attached to her key ring, Makani put her hand against the wall. It was vibrating.

Mount St. Helens was erupting.

Though she couldn't see it, she could feel it. The ground was shaking, and a faint rumble filtered through the thick walls.

It was dark inside the building, power having been shut off several days ago. The boarded-up windows didn't let in any light. Fortunately, the LED flashlight didn't consume battery power at a fast rate. She had illumination for several hours.

She had checked all the building's exits. They didn't budge. Johnston Ridge's staff had chained and padlocked them shut.

She was sealed in.

She explored the main lobby. Many of the building's exhibits still remained, being too large to move. A tree blasted by the 1980 eruption stood prominent. A large, octagon-shaped table with a huge relief map of Mount St. Helens and the surrounding area was still there also. It had buttons on the side where a tourist could turn on small lights that highlighted areas of interest on the map.

She pressed a button. The map remained dark.

A nearby kiosk had a seismometer built into it. It was supposed to register vibrations when a child jumped on the floor mat in front of it. With the current eruption, the needle should have been fluctuating like crazy at the moment.

But without electricity, the needle remained still.

She turned to the souvenir shop. The shelves were bare. Electronic equipment, like the till, credit card machine, and phone, were also gone.

She had peeked into the restrooms earlier. The water was shut down, but some still remained in the toilets. She wondered how thirsty she would have to be to turn to them.

She wasn't there yet.

Back out in the central area, she moved over to some equipment that looked out of place.

It was a USGS camera unit, video gear inside rugged plastic housings to protect them from the elements.

The housing was roughly three feet by three feet and six feet tall. On its front face was a Plexiglas window for the camera to look out of.

Solar panels covered the sloped roof, placed there to recharge the batteries stored at the base. An antenna, designed to communicate with a satellite above, stuck out a further yard above the whole thing.

It was the reason upper level managers like Terrington possessed a key to this place. The observatory was under the care of the US Forest Service. But the USGS had struck a deal with them to store their expensive camera equipment in the building when not in use. The USGS was afraid that looters would truck them away if left out for weeks at a time.

Two such units were outside at the moment, placed on the observation deck to the east and the amphitheater to the west ten days ago. Both spots were on the lip of a cliff face across from the mountain. She had a key to the east one still in her pocket. She had used it a week ago when she had transmitted an educational video live to schools across the nation. The camera units also had a screen, microphone, and speakers so that she had been able to take student questions.

Though she didn't have a key for this one, its front panel door was already open, and ajar. If it had power, she could call for help.

Inside, she knelt down and found the power switch, only to discover the reason why it was stored in the building.

USGS techs had stripped it down. Even the batteries were missing.

Frustrated, she stood back up. The walls still rumbled around her.

She was in no danger at the moment. The ash plume was rising skyward.

But soon, the northern dome would erupt. That would send a blast of hot ash her way, covering Johnston Ridge in a thick layer.

The building would protect her, but not for long. Covered in a blanket of superheated ash, the ambient temperature of the building would rise. And though she wouldn't be smothered as most people who died in volcanic eruptions, the building would turn into an oven, slowly roasting her alive.

She imagined people finding her weeks later, a mummified corpse hugging a toilet in desperation.

Not how she wanted to be remembered.

Terrington may have had good intentions, but she didn't like the look on the other man's face. If she wanted rescue, she would have to find it on her own, or this place would be her tomb.

Chapter 41

KET Observatory private airfield

For a few minutes before they landed, Terrington had a view of Mount St. Helens erupting in the distance. He felt a small measure of pride as he looked at his watch. He had been only fifteen minutes off, the scientific achievement of the decade.

The pride evaporated when they landed and made ready to exit the helicopter. His accomplishments this day would soon be overshadowed by his traitorous acts. He wondered if the name Terrington would be uttered in the same breath as Benedict Arnold.

Terrington looked around the small airfield. They were near a hangar with several fuel trucks and SUVs parked nearby. A Kesler brand corporate jet was there also, parked on the far side of the building. The Russians looked concerned at that, and Terrington overheard them discussing how it came to be here, since all flights in the Pacific Northwest were grounded. Cooper blamed it on capitalistic billionaires doing whatever they wanted. With that mystery solved they turned their attention to the small side door of the hangar.

It was locked and made of reinforced steel. Cooper took something the size of a pack of cigarettes and stuck it near the knob. The four of them moved around the corner, Cooper bringing up the rear since he was limping. When they got far enough away, Cooper pressed a button on another small device. An explosion went off on the door. When they returned to it, they found the door hanging ajar.

Smith went inside while he, Williams, and Cooper waited on the tarmac. Terrington envied Smith, despite the heightened elevation of the place; it was hot out here in the sun. A mirage appearing as a sheet of water shimmered at the far end of the runway.

The main hangar doors rose up, and Terrington gaped at what he saw.

It looked like a spaceship from an old *Flash Gordon* movie. It was a smallish flying wing, all silver, like an Airstream camper trailer, and it had a dark-tinted, oval-shaped cockpit window.

"What is that thing?" Terrington asked.

Even the three Russian soldiers were taken aback a bit.

"It's a functional prop for one of Kesler's upcoming commercials. He calls it the *Alpha-47*, because it's the UFO that started it all, and '47 is the year that it happened," Cooper answered, running his hand over the skin of the craft. He looked over at Smith. "You sure you can fly it?"

"Yes," Smith answered. "From what our defecting Marines report, this plane has a cockpit like that Kesler Sparrow parked over there. I have over three hundred hours of experience with Sparrows."

Smith moved over to the fuselage and ran his hand over it also. "Though, from what I understand, that doesn't matter. Even a sixteen-year-old kid whose only experience is flying X-Wings in *Star Wars Battlefront* games could operate this plane."

Williams wheeled over a step ladder, and Smith climbed it and made his way across the top of the strange aircraft. A small keypad was near the cockpit hatch. Whatever the code was, Smith seemed to know it, for the hatch sprang open, hinged at the back.

The flying wing powered up with a low whine. Cooper pushed

Terrington ahead of him, and the three men stood to the side as the jet taxied from the hangar. Out in the open, the sun's dazzling reflection shone in Terrington's eyes. He was hard-pressed to find a spot where the sun didn't reflect from the plane's mirrored surface.

The jet began moving down the runway, heading south, so Terrington could also see the ash plume of Mount St. Helens behind it as it took to the air. It banked west and headed for Mount Rainier.

"Why that direction?" Terrington asked.

"History," Cooper answered.

Still mystified, Terrington was going to ask a follow-up question but stopped when Cooper and Williams both pulled out automatic pistols. Terrington held up the flash drive, his thumb once again near the abort button.

They were just checking the ammunition in their gun's magazines.

"Relax Professor, before we reached this cell phone dead zone, I texted Tonkov," Williams said, returning his weapon to a clip-on holster at his back. "He's instructed us to make sure that you and the data remain safe. He said it would ruin his reputation in the espionage world if we killed you."

Terrington wasn't convinced. "Then why the guns?"

Cooper nodded toward the Sparrow. "This jet means that Kesler is here for some reason, so his armed bodyguard is also nearby."

"Why does that concern us?"

"If Kesler finds out that his UFO is up in the air, he may call out and tell people its true nature. We can't have that happen. My job is to knock out the phone lines and the short wave radio antenna at the observatory. That way we can isolate this whole area."

Cooper stepped back into the hangar and plucked a set of keys from a hook mounted on the back wall. He stepped back out and waved them over to one of the waiting SUVs.

It was blasting hot inside, and Cooper ran the air conditioner.

"No one's going to get hurt, right?" Terrington asked.

The Spetsnaz agents gave him hard looks.

"That depends on them," Williams said.

* * *

Once he reached a point south of Mount Rainier, Smith banked the aircraft around and pointed its nose at Mount Adams to the southeast.

The view was amazing. Arrayed in front of him were the snow-capped volcanic peaks of the cascades, and the plume of St. Helens was already three miles in height. He realized this was one of those moments that one would remember for the rest of one's life.

He programmed his course onto a map displayed in one of the two main screens in the cabin. His flight path was to take him over the Yakima Valley, all the way to a town named Connell in Eastern Washington.

With his course laid in, he sat back and looked at his watch, wondering where the Marines were at this moment.

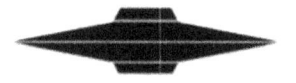

Chapter 42

Nellis Air Force Base, Las Vegas, Nevada

"Come on people, we're on the clock, let's show them what we can do," Kara said into her mike.

Next to her, in his own F-35B Lightning, Monetti barked like a dog on his radio. "Just make sure you guys finish me up before her," he yelled out to his crew.

Kara shook her head. No matter what the situation, Monetti had to be the first and best at everything. Such persistence had earned him the call sign 'Alpha Wolf.' He had it emblazoned on the side of his jet, near the cockpit. Kara had told him that the theory his nickname was based on was all bullshit, according to Hanson. Monetti was still pissed about that.

Kara decided to lead her crew with a carrot instead of a stick. "And remember, the sooner we get this done, the sooner we all get to go inside and watch the volcano on television."

She and Monetti were in the middle of a hot load exercise on the tarmac. As guests at Nellis Air Force Base, they were demonstrating to other visiting brass what the Marines were capable of.

It was all part of the current Red Flag exercise. A half dozen times a year, military pilots from all around the United States and a few select foreign nations came here to hone their combat skills. Their foes were the Red Team, Nellis's elite squad of F-15 and F-18 pilots. Kara and Monetti were part of the Blue Team.

"And make sure my heaters are in place," Monetti yelled.

Kara watched his crew double their efforts as they lifted heat-seeking Sidewinder missiles into his weapon bays. As part of a hot load demonstration, the engines of the F-35Bs were still on, giving off a loud whine as they idled. Keeping the jets running while rearming and refueling saved on the wear and tear of coming to a complete stop and follow up restart. It also produced a faster turn-around time.

Her crew continued on with a professional manner, knowing that everyone was watching. As the military's newest and most advanced asset, the F-35Bs were the stars of the event, and she and Monetti had worked hard to manipulate their commanding officers to make them the marquee players of today's demonstrations.

For the dogfights, Nellis outfitted visiting jets with equipment that simulated weapons fire and hits to a computer. Kara had put forth a suggestion that since she and Monetti were late to the event, and still equipped with standard weapons, they would be perfect candidates to demonstrate the Marine's abilities to pull off a hot load.

The brass bought it, and now she found herself here with an audience as her crew topped off her fuel and installed air to air missiles into her own weapon bays.

Her crew was also double-checking her gun pod. Due to size and space restrictions from the F-35B's vertical lift components, the jet didn't have room for a built-in cannon. Military engineers had designed an external pod. It hung from the bottom of the plane, a 25mm gun that held 220 rounds. The gun pod was a recent addition, and everyone watching was eager to see it in action. Tracer rounds were being used today to highlight its abilities.

The crew was wrapping things up and was signaling her off. With a mocking wave to her scowling wingman, she moved away first.

Once in place at the end of the runway, she opened the fairing right behind her cockpit, exposing her vertical lift fan. Spectators always liked this part. The vertical lift drastically shortened her takeoff length. After a short few hundred feet of hurtling down the runway, she took off.

Monetti was right behind her. They made a few passes for the audience below and then climbed to several thousand feet.

"Two angels," Monetti said over his radio, using pilot slang for their current altitude.

She looked to her side, not seeing him. He was flying in her blind spot.

She fixed that.

One other component that made the fifth-generation fighter aircraft unique was that it didn't have a Heads Up Display, where vital information was projected on a transparent screen near the canopy for easy viewing.

The F-35s had a HMDS, or Helmet-Mounted Display System. It showed off tactical information more readily and even allowed the pilot to switch to infrared mode without the burden of attaching other equipment.

But that wasn't the helmet's best feature. Kara toggled the DAS, or Distributed Aperture System.

The cockpit disappeared from her sight. Her helmet display was now tied into sensors and cameras located throughout the jet, seamlessly blended together by the onboard computer. From her point of view, it was as if the plane had turned invisible.

She looked back to her right. Though her wing should have been in the way, she could see Monetti behind her. She looked through the floor of the jet. Nellis's location was near the northern boundary of Las Vegas. She could pick out the black pyramid of the Luxor Hotel below her.

She still remembered her excitement the first time she had experienced the helmet. She had exited the plane, gushing on the tarmac on how she felt like Wonder Woman flying her invisible plane.

Everyone had laughed at her excitement, and the name had stuck. They had stenciled *Wonder Woman* below her canopy.

She toggled the DAS off and pulled a satellite phone from her pocket, texting the top number programmed into it.

Monetti acknowledged their illicit communication by sending a smiley face emoticon back at her, along with the emoji of a bag full of money.

She smiled and put down the phone. A part of her was going to miss all this, but twenty million was twenty million. She was looking forward to retiring at the tropical paradise of her choosing.

She and Monetti made a long, leisurely turn north toward the gunnery range. They wanted to be as far along in this direction as possible when the text came in from Tonkov.

Ordering them to begin their defection.

Chapter 43

Highway 12, Washington

"You can barely see it," Fisher said.

Hanson checked his rearview mirror. Highway 12 was closed to nonlocal traffic, so they had the area to themselves. He pulled off to the side, hugging the guard rail that prevented vehicles from plunging two hundred feet off the road.

Hanson stepped out and took a look. The ash column, fifty miles away, was rising over a nearby ridge.

"Son of a bitch, they did it," Hanson said, looking at his watch.

"To within a half hour," Fisher noted. "I wonder if they'll get this good with predicting earthquakes."

"Someday," Hanson replied. "It's amazing what that Terrington guy pulled off. He was on a *National Geographic* special last week. I've taken my share of computer science courses, but what he did was way over my head."

Hanson got back in his van and set off again. They still needed to get the word out about their theory about Russian involvement.

Fisher was intent on his tablet, opening more files.

"Now what is it?" Hanson asked.

"What you said about Terrington has me thinking, so I'm looking into my agent's interviews and background checks into CVO employees," Fisher answered, his eyes scanning his screen. Hanson could tell he was reading at an incredibly fast rate. "Someone local got into Dr. Livken's computer—"

"And you think it was Terrington, the computer expert that's the hero of the day?" Hanson interjected.

"He would be the perfect inside man . . ." Fisher muttered as he read. After a few moments he straightened up, a frown on his face.

"Dammit. Terrington's squeaky clean."

"But that's good, right?"

"It's how I know that worries me," Fisher replied, holding up the tablet. "My people didn't do the background check. A comprehensive background check, done by another agency in Washington, DC, was handed over to us. Not only is Terrington clean, he also has a high security clearance issued by the White House."

"Do you know why?"

"I don't," Fisher continued. "All I do know is that the background check was done by the Department of Energy seven weeks ago."

Hanson did some mental math. That, along with the introduction of Russian spies into the equation, made him feel cold as dread washed over him.

"I think I know what this is all about," Hanson said. "On that documentary they mentioned that Terrington had traveled to Washington DC to ask the President herself for help around that time."

"With what?"

"He wanted her to expedite his request to hook up with the Icarus supercomputer."

"How is that a problem?" asked Fisher.

"Terrington has been telling everyone that the CVO is running its simulations over the Stratton Institute's supercomputer named Icarus, the ninth most powerful computer at the moment.

"But Stratton also houses the world's second most powerful

computer, Apex. In the past, scientists used computers like Apex to work on the world's more difficult questions, like how to predict the weather or decode the human genome.

"Lately, though, the priority has changed. Governments are using supercomputers for the military's most pressing issue: how to deal with our aging nuclear stockpile."

"How can they help?"

"The same way Terrington came up with his Mount St. Helens prediction: by running simulations. Our nuclear weapons are over fifty years old, as are the ICBM's they're sitting on top of. Everyone is wondering how well they will perform, or even work."

"And we've signed treaties. No one can set these things off in controlled tests anymore," Fisher responded.

"So we blow nukes in cyberspace instead and measure the results. I read about it when Apex came online. You wouldn't believe the complex—"

"Hanson, if this threat seems so obvious, why did it take a computer geek like yourself so long to figure this out?"

"Because it should be a non-issue. Apex is air-gapped, cut off from the outside world."

"So dealing with Stratton doesn't set off any alarm bells."

"Exactly. But now you're telling me that one of the agencies watching over the nuclear stockpile, the Department of Energy, gave Terrington a once-over. That changes everything. It has to be because he was to be granted access to Apex, though I don't know how he convinced the President."

"I can guess at that. Before steam began rising from Mount St. Helens' crater, President Hayes was taking a beating in the polls from her handling of Florida, and COVID."

Fisher glanced out his window toward the ash column.

"Then the mountain stirred," he continued. "And Hayes, along with Washington's governor, had to set up the 'Red Zone' and keep locals out for an undetermined amount of time. Spurred on by astroturfing by the Russians, the President was once again faced with outcries of basic human rights being trampled by the government."

"And along comes Terrington, throwing her a political lifeline," Hanson said, following Fisher's line of thought. "If she agrees to give him access to the world's second most powerful computer, he can hand her a prediction of when the volcano will erupt. She can now promise a date when everyone can go home."

"President Hayes used her Executive Privilege. She quietly gave Terrington access to Apex and swore him and the crew at Stratton to tell no one," Fisher added. "She must have figured that secrecy was her best defense against foreign hackers. If no one knew that Apex was connected to the outside world, they wouldn't even think to try to access it."

"Unfortunately for the President, Terrington himself must be compromised."

"Steinsson also had a computer background. He might have guessed about the Apex connection. They killed him to keep Terrington's secret, and keep the protester pressure on the President. Steve, how detailed and important do you think this nuclear information is?"

"Vital. To put it into perspective, older computers working the same nuclear simulations have been replaced by Apex. Engineers have since decommissioned them and taken them apart. Rather than taking the risk of foreign agents sifting the garbage created and even gleaning a fraction of information, our government had all the debris ground to dust."

Fisher grabbed his armrest. "Floor it, Hanson. We need to warn people. We can't let the Russians steal our nuclear secrets."

Hanson complied, tires screeching as his van took the road's curves. His mind raced as he rehashed everything that had happened in the past week. Monetti's sneering face cycled through his train of thought, and once again, Hanson found himself wondering how the two Marine pilots fit into everything. Though Fisher didn't think they were part of it, Hanson still felt that they were overlooking something about them. As he dwelled on that, the road straightened out in front of him, giving him a clear view of the sky. The answer he was looking for hit him like a flash.

Literally. Something flashed in the sky above him.

Hanson stomped on the brakes, and the van came to a screeching halt to the side of the highway, blue smoke rising behind it. Fisher's tablet almost went flying as he lurched forward in his seat.

"What the hell?" Fisher yelled.

Hanson didn't answer. He was looking upward through the front windshield.

A boomerang shaped aircraft was flying low above them. The sun reflected off of its silvered surface as it banked toward the east and receded in the distance.

It was the UFO that had started it all, flying the same route, nearly seventy-five years later.

Fisher was also looking up, his mouth open in confusion. Hanson turned toward him, certainty painted across his face.

"That's not the only thing the Russians are stealing today," Hanson announced.

Chapter 44

Central Washington

S mith left the forested mountains of the Cascades and entered the semi-desert landscape of the Yakima Valley. Thirty miles ahead, he could see more green, though. Farmland, irrigated by the Yakima River.

He steered for the populated oasis, flying only a few hundred feet above the ground. Tonkov wanted as many witnesses possible for this stage of the mission.

According to GPS, he was over the towns of Toppenish and Zillah. Crowds of people were below him. They were already standing outside, looking west at the ash cloud that was approaching.

They were all waving at him in excitement and pointing cameras his way. He was an added bonus to an already momentous day.

He didn't waggle his wings. He didn't want anyone to think that there was a human pilot inside.

Interstate 82 stretched out in front of him, surrounded by irrigated fields and small towns. He followed its southeast direction.

St. Petersburg

"Reports are coming in now, General," Gontarev said.

He put up a twitter post, labeled *#AreYouSeeingThis?* The tweet was a video of Mount St. Helens' ash column from seventy miles away.

Then a silver airship glided over and the camera followed it. In the background, people were screaming 'Oh my God, oh my God.'

"It looks like the real thing," Tonkov commented.

"There's more, General. Similar postings are occurring on other media sites. Megathreads on UFOs are popping up. I expect UFOs to leapfrog over Mount St. Helens in popularity in a few minutes."

"Excellent. Send out information on how to effectively report UFOs to civilian airport towers and military bases. Reinforce that with your bots, and your army of zombie computers in the states. I need it to spread like wildfire. Continue to promote the airship's historical origins, and keep playing the *War of the Worlds* videos and those clips of Americans storming their shopping marts for toilet paper."

Gontarev issued the commands to his trolls. He also told them to make sure they had the right keywords in their searches to look for any dissenters on social media. He didn't want anyone derailing the story they were trying to weave.

* * *

Seattle, Washington

Kevin Patel finished up his tweet and sent it out.

#ItIsNotaUFO

I work for Kesler Aviation. What you are seeing is a prototype we are unveiling next year. It is human in origin.

266

Patel hoped he wouldn't get fired for this. As a Kesler employee in research and development, he had signed strict confidentiality agreements with heavy financial punishments. It was why he, and others tied to the project, hadn't said or posted anything about the UFO seen in Washington a few nights ago.

But now things were different. People were panicking online because someone was taking the *Alpha-47* out for an unauthorized joyride.

The web was exploding with misinformation from frightened people. He couldn't let that happen. He sent out similar posts on his other social media sites, hoping that others who were in the know were doing the same.

Certification for Kesler's projects, both the promotional aircrafts and the flying car, was a complicated and time consuming procedure. And besides the Federal Aviation Administration, the *Dragonfly* also had to pass muster with the National Highway Traffic Safety Administration. Though Kesler's flying car project was secretive, hundreds of people were aware of what he was doing. With their help, he should be able to squash this UFO rumor online.

He cycled back through his accounts. He was surprised to see that he had hundreds of comments but no likes. He read through the first post, his confusion rising as he did so.

Typical. I'd expect nothing less from a Holocaust Denier.

I bet you think the earth is flat.

Another entry had GIFs of young people running across a desert landscape, their arms stretched out behind them. Patel recognized the meme. The runners were people protesting the government hiding aliens at Area 51. The arms behind their backs emulated a cartoon running style in which the sprinters could outrun bullets.

The GIFs had a header.

You can't silence us.

The rest of the comments were similar, and they were growing. Patel wondered why they thought he was a Holocaust Denier. He didn't believe that, and he certainly had never posted such a lie.

He posted his own comments, trying to refute the fabrications against him, hoping to convince others of the truth. Instead, he was overwhelmed by an avalanche of lies and personal attacks.

He switched back to his other sites. The same thing was happening. Feeling helpless, he sagged down onto his couch as the negative commentary piled up.

* * *

Nellis Air Force Base

A text came over Kara's phone.

Now.

It was from Tonkov. It meant that the *A-47* was halfway over Washington.

She and Monetti were lining up for their first run on some old shipping containers stacked up in the Nevada desert. She took a moment to call the tower.

"We're kind of out of touch with the news up here. What's happening with the volcano?"

The tower was quick to respond. She could detect excitement in the man's voice.

"Mount St. Helens went off right on schedule, Lieutenant, but that's not half of it. A genuine UFO, um, I mean a UAP, was filmed flying over the state of Washington."

"A spaceship?" Monetti yelled, trying to sound surprised. Kara thought he was shitty at it.

"Do you know what our response is?"

"That's just it. They moved all the planes from Lewis-McChord and Fairchild. Portland's National Guard F-15s are down in southern California. Even commercial flights are being directed elsewhere. It's all empty airspace over there."

"We can be there in under an hour, tower. Request permission to—"

"Fly up there for some close encounters of the kick-ass kind," Monetti finished.

The radio went quiet, and Kara held her breath. This was it.

A half minute passed before she had her response.

"Affirmative. I took it upstairs. We need a presence up there."

"Let's go show these aliens what we can do," Monetti said for the tower's benefit, turning north and climbing. Once they reached cruising altitude, they both set off sonic booms as they broke the sound barrier.

* * *

Central Washington

Smith figured he had hundreds of cameras on him at the moment.

He was over the confluence of the Columbia, Snake, and Yakima Rivers. The cities of Richland, Kennewick, and Pasco hugged the banks of the three rivers.

The *A-47* had the same engines as Kesler's newest corporate jet. He was taking it easy with it, cruising at a comfortable three hundred miles per hour.

That meant that he had spent around forty minutes in Washington airspace. At this point, military jets or even curious civilian helicopters or single-engine planes, should have risen up to intercept him.

But there was none around.

The warplanes of Joint Base Lewis-McChord in Seattle and Fairchild AFB in Spokane had been shifted east. Both weren't much of a factor anyway since McChord was an airlift wing populated with massive C-17 Globemaster IIIs. Fairchild stationed equally large planes tasked with refueling, KC-135 Stratotankers.

Portland's F-15s were an issue, though. Had they been still stationed there, they would have been scrambled and on his tail in minutes. Fortunately, the military had moved them to Southern California for a few weeks.

Still, at least two were currently cruising up and down the west coast. If ordered, they had a chance of reaching him.

Tonkov had a plan for that. A Borie class submarine was lurking two hundred fifty miles off the coast of Northern California. When Cooper's helicopter had entered the KET Observatory's airspace the old general had routed a message that the stealthy submarine had been waiting for. Its crew released a few weather balloons with large radar reflectors attached. Once the balloons reached a high altitude they were destroyed with explosives. The hope was that it would be enough to draw the F-15s away to investigate.

Smith turned away from populated areas and flew above what looked like dryland wheat country. He kept the Snake River to his right and in view as he took the *A-47* even lower, skimming the fields like a crop duster.

He made a quick U-turn and approached the small town of Connell from the east, still keeping to the wheat fields. One mile east of the small town was an airfield with a short landing strip.

It was going to be tight. Smith slowed the plane as much as the onboard computer allowed and landed the fake UFO. He taxied back to the small hangar, turning the aircraft into it, pushing toward the rear of the building.

Johnson was waiting for him with a ladder, and Smith scrambled off the plane. Both men stepped outside. It was even hotter here than back at the KET airfield.

"Anyone see me?" Smith asked.

Johnson, a burly man with short, curly red hair, shook his head.

"All the media sites have been guessing that the airship was going to pass west of here," Johnson said. "They're all looking the wrong way."

There was a semi-truck with a large, canvassed topped trailer idling nearby. Both men boarded it, with Johnson driving. He kept to little-used dirt roads that followed the edges of fields as he drove east.

"Was the crop circle difficult to pull off?" Smith asked.

"Yeah, the corn stalks were a pain in the ass," Johnson answered. He gestured to the rolling hills of wheat surrounding them. "This would had been much easier. With the corn I had to put all my weight on the plank and jump on it a few times to keep the stalks down."

"Well, it worked. I heard someone is already making a documentary on it."

Johnson snorted. "Americans! I guess I'm a famous artist now."

After fifteen minutes of driving, Johnson pulled to the shoulder. No one was in sight.

Smith helped Johnson with removing the canvas covering, absent-mindedly humming the catchy song Hanson had played during last night's attack.

"Stop that," Johnson growled. "Or I'll never get it out of my head."

With the cover gone, nine giant weather balloons bobbed up, coming to a stop a few feet above the trailer walls.

They were all secured by a framework of pipes at the base of the trailer. With a grunt, Johnson pulled a lever.

As had happened out at sea, balloons rose to the sky. Beneath each one hung a large radar reflector, foil-covered plastic with as many exposed surfaces as possible.

Johnson texted a quick message to someone, then both men watched the balloons rise into the sky for a few moments. Johnson pulled out his phone and dialed a number. When he saw that he had a connection, he pressed a button.

All nine balloons and reflectors exploded from the C-4 charges also attached to them. Smith watched with satisfaction as the debris rained down on a field nearby.

"That should keep the F-15s off our back," Smith said.

"As long as Grey is on time," Johnson responded, checking his watch.

* * *

Central Montana, five hundred forty miles away

Mason Grey looked up from the timer on his phone. He had started it a few minutes ago when Johnson had texted him that he had released his array of balloons.

Grey checked the rigging on the back of his semi. It was the same set-up that his Spetsnaz colleagues had used in Connell. Nine weather balloons with reflectors and explosives attached to them, all still held in place by the rigging at the base of the trailer.

He and Johnson had taken off in the two balloon laden tractor-trailers last night. They had headed east, pausing only long enough to make the crop circle. Then they pushed on to motels near their designated target areas. His spot was a dirt road twenty-five miles east of Billings.

He was excited that Projects Front Door and Rod were almost done. He was looking forward to dropping his American alias, Mason, and once again using his real name, Dimitri.

He checked his timer. The release time was coming up. When the count reached nine minutes, or five hundred forty seconds after the first balloon launch, he pulled the lever that released his.

They rose into the sky. A few minutes later, as his comrades had done in Connell, he blew them up.

He jumped into the cab of this truck and headed west.

Chapter 45

Johnston Ridge Observatory

"I'm sorry about this, Smokey," Makani said as she ripped the shovel out of the bear's paws.

Like the other sizable exhibits in the tourist center, employees had left the large, wooden statue of Smokey the Bear behind during the exodus from Johnston Ridge. The figure itself wasn't useful to her, but the shovel he was holding was.

Smokey had a tight grip on it, though. His hand broke apart as she wrenched the shovel free. A wooden squirrel had been resting on the bear's arm. It fell to the ground.

She picked the squirrel up and put i back in Smokey's hand. Even a statue shouldn't be alone in this oppressive dark.

Her small flashlight was still working, but it only cast its illumination in a ten-foot radius. She had it clipped to her necklace, next to her fire opal. Occasionally it would flip behind the gem and cast a multifaceted yellow light on the walls.

She took up the shovel and walked toward one of the many sets of windows that stretched from floor to ceiling. She swung her newly-won tool and smashed one of the lower panes.

Though built like a World War II bunker, half of the place was still windows. It should have been easy to break out of here.

But thick plywood panels were fastened over them for protection. She spent a few moments kicking at the impenetrable barrier.

It didn't budge.

She used the shovel's metal edge and gouged at it. After a few minutes, she gave up, her arms numb. It would take all afternoon to break through.

The ground shook below her.

She didn't have all afternoon.

She left Smokey to the shadows and made her way back to other exhibits.

Out of the dark, a man's face appeared.

It was a mannequin, part of an open diorama set up of three men hard at work repairing the damage caused by the 1980 eruption. Two of them were on the ground, clearing toppled timber with a chainsaw. The third was about ten feet about her, standing on the shattered remains of a bridge. He was setting up a block and tackle to move the debris away.

All three were wearing rugged clothes, suspenders, tool belts, and hardhats. The two on the ground even had filtered face masks. They all reminded Makani of the titular character from her twin's favorite cartoon growing up, *Bob the Builder*.

The first time she had come across the trio, it had startled her. After she recovered, she took stock of what they had to offer and had come up with a plan.

It was a dangerous, complicated one, though. That's why she had made the futile attempt of busting through the windows.

That hadn't worked, so now she was back to Plan A.

She took the suspenders off of one of the mannequins. His pants fell down.

"Sorry, I'm not that kind of girl," she muttered.

She put the suspenders on and cinched them up.

At her feet was a second shovel, a prop for the two lumberjacks. She picked it up and sheathed it against her back with the suspenders.

The handle flopped around against her lower spine. She secured it with the other guy's suspenders wrapped around her abdomen.

That done, she picked up Smokey's shovel and clambered up the 'wreckage' depicted in the exhibit. It was designed to look like broken-up concrete supports that had toppled over.

She joined the third man up there. He was holding both ends of a rope that looped into a pulley about ten feet away.

She worked the line free from his hands and pulled it through the pulley. She now had two shovels and twenty feet of rope.

She took a moment to reorient herself. The ceiling here in the main hall came to a vaulted peak of around twenty-five feet. A complicated array of rafters held up the roof. These were fifteen feet off the ground and set ten feet apart. Standing up here in the exhibit, one of them was now a few inches from her head.

Since the nearby mannequin was in the way, she shoved him off of his perch. He crashed into the ground below her.

"Sorry, Bob."

She tied one end of the rope at the base of the blade of Smokey's shovel. She then laid it on top of the beam near her head.

She jumped up, hoisting herself up to her armpits. She held that pose for a moment as she worked up the strength to swing her legs up to the side. After a minute of grunting and straining, she found herself on top of the beam also.

She lay there, panting for breath. She was too old for this crap.

She inched toward the side, where the beams came together in a joist. Once there, she took a moment to shine her light down the hall.

Two joists away, the grill of a large vent cover was set in the wall.

While Terrington was herding her into the building, she had noted that while the window coverings were large and massive, the external air-intake vents had thinner plywood sheets over them, and they looked more manageable to remove.

If she could get to them. The interior vents were almost twenty feet off the ground. She had considered looping her rope around the joist and climbing up the wall to this one, but she doubted she had the upper body strength to pull that off.

The set-piece below had been much simpler to scale. She was now even with the vent, though still twenty feet away. She took up the shovel like a harpoon and aimed for the next rafter over.

She threw.

It came up short and fell out of sight to the dark below. Makani hauled it back up, remembering what Hanson had said back at the cabin that, unlike her triple-jumping, his javelin throwing had real-world applications.

She held the shovel above her shoulder, and with a deep breath, threw again.

It sailed over the nearby beam.

She pulled it back. Like a weighted grapple, it jammed up into the joist's corner and held.

She stood up and looped the other end of the rope around her arm. She didn't want it dragging behind her, its friction slowing her down.

Her plan was to swing, pendulum-like, to the far beam. It was all math and physics now. Her mass times gravity, allowing her matching amplitudes on her swing. Discounting negligible friction from air and the pivot point, she should be able to reach the far rafter.

On a schoolroom blackboard, it all seemed straight forward. Here, where her little light, now half-buried in the folds of her shirt, feebly pierced the darkness, the concept seemed dubious.

She steadied herself. Ahead of her, the vent was lost in inky blackness, as was the ground below.

She entertained the notion of waiting for help. Again, she talked herself out of it. Mount St. Helens was due to send ash blasting her way in little under an hour.

Saying a prayer to Pele, she stepped off into the void.

She was falling, and she sensed the ground rushing up at her. She held on for dear life as she began her arc upward.

A beam appeared out of the darkness. Makani stretched her legs for it and hooked it at the knees.

For a moment she hung there precariously, stretched between the rope and beam. With an effort, she reached for the beam with one hand and pulled herself onto it.

As before, she lay there, recovering from her efforts. Then she inched over to the wall, where the vent cover was.

Using her second shovel, she pried it open. Her light showed that the air duct inside was large enough to accommodate her.

Shovel in hand, she crawled in.

Chapter 46

KET Observatory

Hanson rammed the gate.

A large cross guard had been resting across the entrance to the science and tourist complex. An electronic sign announced the site as closed due to Mount St. Helens.

Hanson reached forward and patted the dashboard in front of him.

"Sorry, baby."

Fisher, who was looking over his shoulder at the wreckage behind them, turned back to Hanson.

"Why do you think the Russians are also going for the F-35Bs?"

"That mock UFO can't be for Terrington. He must already have what he wants. But speaking of Russians and seeing a UFO makes me think of something that happened decades ago. In 1952, there was a second major UFO scare. People saw mysterious lights and objects over Washington DC, and everyone went nuts. In the aftermath, the CIA concluded that there were no UFOs; it was all caused by the weather. But they identified another serious problem from the event."

"It was the panic itself that worried the CIA," Fisher guessed.

"It caused confusion and hampered the military's ability to determine what was real and what was the imagination of a credulous American public. The CIA postulated that the Soviet Union could take advantage of such situations, and thus it was a matter of national security. Our government felt that there was a need to educate everyone on UFOs, to take away the mystique. The plan was to do this through Hollywood with movies."

"Have you seen any of these movies?"

Hanson gave him a sidelong glance. "There's a rumor that *Close Encounters of the Third Kind* was designed to make aliens, and UFOs, appear less threatening."

"It seems like that didn't work," Fisher said, shaking his head. "Belief in weird crap seems stronger than ever these days. We've been seeing it in real time with all the Bigfoot reporting."

"I think Bigfoot was to soften us up mentally and get us all in the right frame of mind. Now everyone is more open to accepting UFO sightings, and the Russians are taking advantage of that. You said they're spamming my blog. Most likely they're attacking similar websites," Hanson explained. "That means they're coordinating all of this on the internet. Seventy years ago, all we had were newspapers and radio stations. Now we're saturated with dozens of media platforms. Fear is going to spread like wildfire."

"I can see the nation running out of toilet paper, like the COVID scare, but how does that get the Russians a couple of fifth-generation jets?"

"By forcing our military to chase ghosts, and giving the Russians an opening."

"I don't know. It all sounds pretty thin to me."

They crested a hill. It brought the area's small airfield, and Kesler's corporate jet, into view. Hanson slowed down and pointed at something beyond the small plane.

"Recognize that?" Hanson asked.

"It's the Cardinal Air helicopter," Fisher answered, calling up a file on his tablet. An image of the same model resting on the tarmac appeared. "They changed the decal, but it's the same craft."

"And the hangar is empty," Hanson replied. "That's where the UFO we saw was kept. That means it has a Russian pilot."

"There are also a couple of fuel trucks down there," Hanson continued. "The Russians must have something up north, a freighter maybe, anchored somewhere off of Canada's west coast, where the F-35Bs can vertically land. We're at about at the halfway point between Nellis Air Force Base and the Gulf of Alaska, and those two Marine pilots are familiar with this area. This is the perfect place for them to refuel, right in the middle of a no-fly zone due to the volcano, and a dead signal zone so that some random witness can't call someone and say that he saw an F-35 fly over."

"Okay, the Russians being here adds weight to your theory. But I'm still not buying that a couple of Marine defectors can simply fly a couple of jets out of here. What's their plan for when the military notices that they aren't checking in and sending everything they have after them?"

Hanson was increasing his speed as he drove the van toward the visitor center still ten miles away.

"You almost guessed it. The military will send everything they have. But they're going to send it to the wrong place."

NORAD and USNORTHCOM Headquarters, Peterson AFB, Colorado Springs

General Nolan Mitchell and Admiral Vincent Yardley didn't like what they were hearing.

"Reports of UFOs are coming in from all over the lower forty-eight states," Lt. Easton reported as he looked up from his monitor.

"People are swamping military bases with phone calls across the country, worried that something is attacking us."

"Then why are we not seeing anything on the main screen?" Mitchell asked.

"Maybe we don't have the technology to track them," Yardley answered.

Around the two officers stretched the integrated control center of NORAD and NORTHCOM. It was a large, wood-paneled room filled with officers sitting at desks with multiple computer monitors and large screens mounted on the wall.

Though impressive, it didn't measure up to Hollywood's vision. In movies and TV, the North American Aerospace Defense Command's control center was always depicted as a cavernous room with shadowy corners due to poor lighting. Scaffolding supported monitors the size of movie screens.

That wasn't the case. The room was more like a bank's lobby in scope, with sports bar-size mounted monitors.

Its location was another thing most people had wrong. Though NORAD had been initially based deep in the granite of Cheyenne Mountain, its expanding role had forced it to outgrow the Cold War bunker. After 9/11, people had realized that threats could originate from inside the states. President Bush had created USNORTHCOM, a command that was tasked to watch over the entire North American continent.

Created as separate entities, NORAD and NORTHCOM were all but fused together and were thus commanded by Mitchell, a four-star general, and his Canadian counterpart, Admiral Vincent Yardley.

But though he and Yardley performed their duties here at Peterson, Cheyenne Mountain hadn't outlived its usefulness. The bunker still served as the alternate headquarters should the need arise. Its two blast doors, each three feet thick and weighing over twenty tons, could still be closed in case of a significant threat. The last time they had done so was during the confusion of 9/11.

Both men were looking at a screen showing North American airspace. It displayed aircraft without a registered flight plan.

As it should be, it was all but void of activity.

Yardley, a tall man who was in his mid-sixties but still looked youngish, continued his analysis.

"Or they don't exist."

"I agree with your second assessment," Mitchell concurred.

"But General, these reports, there's so many," Easton said. "How can you be so sure?"

Mitchell had put Easton, and several other officers of his age group, on an unusual assignment a few hours earlier. Though against policy, Easton and the others had their media accounts called up on their computers.

Due to a morning briefing with the UAP Task Force, Mitchell was aware of the swelling tide of UFO sightings, and he wanted to keep a close eye on the situation. The younger officers had been keeping abreast of flying saucer reports across the US.

"This has happened before, Lieutenant," Mitchell answered. "Back in 1952, there was a rash of UFO sightings over Washington DC. The 'strange lights' seen over the Capitol were also detected on radar. It created quite a scare."

Yardley continued the historical lecture. "Subsequent investigations showed that the radar blips were caused by pockets of air trapped in temperature inversions. The reported 'sightings' of UFOs were the result of mass hysteria."

"Though the UFOs weren't real, a detailed analysis by the CIA of the event came to a chilling conclusion. Americans are gullible, and since visual observation and reporting, by pilots and citizens alike, is part of our air warning system, it's possible for our enemies to overwhelm us with false information while the real attack comes from elsewhere," Mitchell finished.

"You think someone is behind this?" Easton asked.

"I do. And the scale suggests a player on the national level."

"Are they also behind that?" Easton asked, pointing at one of the large screens on the wall.

It was tuned to a news station. On it, a wedge-shaped silver UFO was gliding across a blue sky.

At first, Mitchell had discounted it as a coordinated release of prank videos posted on social media sites. But several of the helicopters filming the eruption of Mount St. Helens had caught it on their cameras also. From their locations south of the ash plume, it was a tiny, silver speck moving to the right of Mount St. Helens.

The lieutenant was right. Hearsay on the internet was one thing; this was another. It was real. He had no idea what to make of it.

For a few moments, it had shown up on the unregistered aircraft screen, but they had lost it over Yakima. A pulsing dot of its last ping on the radar remained on the monitor.

"I don't know," he answered. "We need eyes on it before we can even begin guessing."

He looked at another screen, which was also a source of his frustration.

It showed all the registered flights they were tracking across North America. Icon of jets all but covered the map as civilian aircraft made their flights.

Except for the Pacific Northwest. Due to Mount St. Helens, there was a noticeable absence of air traffic over Washington, Oregon, and Idaho. A gaping hole devoid of aircraft, and their pilots, who could have called in visual confirmations.

Another screen showed military activity. It displayed the icons of two Marine jets that were hurtling across the Oregon/Nevada border. F-35B Lightnings, the military's most advanced weapon. Fortunately, they had been in the air and armed for a Red Flag exercise.

That would give them eyes they needed in Central Washington. Looking at the same map, he could see that two F-15's from the 142nd were about two hundred miles west of Brookings, Oregon. Something had popped up on the radar out there an hour ago and they had vectored that direction to check it out. He almost gave the order to recall them and have them join the F-35Bs when Yardley interrupted him.

"What the hell is that?"

The Canadian was looking back at the unregistered flight screen.

Nine blips appeared over Eastern Washington.

"Enlarge," Mitchell ordered.

Someone zoomed in on the area in question. Mitchell could see that it was near Spokane, Washington.

"Fairchild's radar just picked it up," Easton reported.

As quickly as they had appeared, the nine blips vanished.

"Can we get anything in the air from Fairchild?" Yardley asked.

"No," Mitchell answered, rubbing a hand over his cropped gray hair. "Geologists forecasted Spokane to receive a quarter-inch of that ash. If that stuff gets into jet engines, it fuses into glass in the heat. We couldn't risk leaving the Stratotankers, or any support craft, there."

The two men spent a few moments discussing the merits of sending something down from Canada when Easton interrupted them.

"There it is again."

This time the nine blips were near Billings, Montana. They were in the same configuration. Like the first sighting, they disappeared.

"That's not air pockets—" Yardley began.

"How fast?" Mitchell interrupted.

"If they're the same objects, a mile per second," Easton replied, intent on his screen.

Everyone in the room was familiar with that rate of speed.

Mach Five.

When he had asked for Intel on the unusual craft spotted in Washington, someone had pointed out an article circulating on the web of a man named Kenneth Arnold, who had witnessed a crescent-shaped aircraft flying at impossible speeds. Was he supposed to believe that alien spaceships were flying over Montana?

He didn't. He had a more earthly threat in mind, the real danger that these UFO reports were supposed to mask.

"They could be hypersonic missiles," Mitchell said.

"Impossible," Yardley said. "Not even the Russians have that range."

"That we know of. Their Zircon hypersonic missile is reputed to approach Mach 10, but it needs to fly through the upper atmosphere to do so. Their Kalibr missile flies low and subsonic, and it has the range we're seeing here. Maybe these radar hits are of some sort of stealth hybrid of the two, launched from a Yasen class submarine off the West Coast and carrying nuclear warheads. They timed it to take advantage of us clearing out of the western airspace. We got lucky and spotted them a couple of times."

"My God, Mitchell, why?"

"We're not here to guess why . . . wait a minute, pull the map back out."

Once again, the screen showed the entire North American continent. It still displayed the point where the UFO was first seen. The locations of the mass radar signatures were also shown.

What Mitchell had guessed at was now apparent to everyone else. The three locations, like the three stars that depicted the Belt of Orion in the night sky, formed a straight line.

"Extrapolate that," Mitchell ordered.

A red line connected the points. It continued on through the United States. Whoever was drawing it stopped near the east coast.

Over Washington DC.

"How much time?" roared Mitchell.

"From when the radar signature disappeared and current speed, twenty-five and a half minutes," someone else in the room shouted back.

"How about our location?"

"Less than five minutes."

There was the chance that some of them had peeled off and were heading their way. For a brief moment, Mitchell thought about the CIA report he and Yardley were just discussing.

The CIA had come to a sobering conclusion about nationwide UFO panics. In the heat of the moment, how could the US military determine which threats were imagined, and which were real?

General Mitchell faced that now. With ICBMs, reaction time used to be in tens of minutes. In this age of hypersonic missiles, he had only seconds.

And he didn't know if it was real or not.

Any other person would have hesitated in a situation like this. Mitchell was a four-star general. There was a reason he was put here to do this job.

"Someone secure me a line to the White House," Mitchell shouted. He turned to Yardley. "Admiral, contact Cheyenne Mountain. Order them to close the doors!"

Chapter 47

KET Observatory

"Don't pull all the way down into the parking lot, Hanson," Fisher instructed. "I don't want anyone seeing us from inside the tourist center."

Hanson pulled off to the side of the driveway, about fifty feet south of the concrete building where Kesler had held his gala event a few evenings ago.

"That's the *Dragonfly*," Hanson said excitedly, pointing at the white car parked on the pad in front of the nearby hangar. Its propellers were in the open position. He had spent the first hour of their road trip explaining to Fisher the merits of flying cars.

Hanson gazed around the rest of the lot. A large, blue diesel SUV was parked in front of the center's main doors. A quarter-mile away, to the east, the four hundred foot tall Galaxy Dish dominated the skyline. Another SUV, along with a golf cart, rested in front of the observatory's command center.

"Those SUVs are part of the airfield fleet," Fisher said. "Kesler's group used one. The other must belong to the Russians."

"Kesler's here because of you, but do you think he helped the Russians get that flying wing in the air?" Hanson asked.

"I don't know, but we should assume he did."

"What next?"

"We make a phone call," Fisher said, pointing at the pay phones lined up outside the main doors.

They both got out. Before Hanson closed his door, he reached under his seat and pulled out his gun and spare ammunition.

"Don't be mad," Hanson said, noticing Fisher's stare.

"Hanson, look," Fisher said, his expression softening. "I came up here to simply serve a search warrant and look for evidence of Kesler's mock UFOs. I didn't even bother bringing a satellite phone. I wasn't expecting armed Russian spies. I can't ask you to do this—"

"Agent Fisher, that kid is in the hospital because of me," Hanson interrupted. "I'm not standing on the sidelines now. And we both know how much is at stake."

Fisher still looked conflicted, but thankful that he had some backup. "Good. Cover me while I contact my boss."

They made their way across the shimmering hot parking lot to the phones. Fisher stepped into the first one while Hanson kept watch.

"Been a while since I've used one of these," Fisher said, picking up the handset and putting it to his ear. He held it there for a moment, then reached up and toggled the hook switch on the phone's cradle a few times.

"Dammit."

"What?"

"The phone's dead," Fisher said, slamming the handset back into the cradle. "We're two decades into the twenty-first century, and we can't make a call because the phone lines are out."

"They must have a communications nest nearby," Hanson said. "Let's check the back."

The building was the size of a large grocery store. Hanson and

Fisher turned away from the east-facing windows and made their way down a service driveway on the building's south side.

The outer wall here had no windows, but several emergency exits. Fisher tried a door. It was locked.

They rounded the corner to the building's backside, where they found a loading dock and back door. Both couldn't be opened from the outside.

On the small lot in the back, several large dumpsters were set side by side. The mast of a radio antenna rose up behind them.

They cautiously made their way around the dumpster, their pistols up.

Twenty feet away was a small fenced-in enclosure with a gate. The fence surrounded an antenna, television satellite dish, and several medium-sized utility boxes.

A diesel golf cart was nearby. A man was also there, kneeling at one of the boxes, his back to them.

Hanson hung back, keeping an eye on the building as Fisher approached the man.

"This is the FBI, hands where I can see them," Fisher commanded.

The kneeling man raised his hands and slowly stood up.

"Please, don't shoot, I work here," the man said in a quavering voice.

"Turn around," Fisher ordered.

He did, and Hanson saw that he was an older man, somewhere in his upper sixties. He kept his white hair long, and he was wearing a long-sleeved green shirt with a blue patch that had the white image of the radio telescope stitched into it. He was also wearing a green hat with the same logo.

He didn't resemble anyone from Fisher's photographs of Cardinal Air employees. After Fisher patted him down, both men lowered their guns. Hanson still kept a lookout behind them.

"What's your name?" Fisher asked.

"Logan," the old man answered, his hands dropping a bit as he relaxed.

"What are you doing here?"

"Those men cut the lines to everything; I was trying to see if I can fix them."

Hanson took a quick look. A cable from the satellite dish had been cut. The boxes for the short wave antenna and landlines were in the worst shape. Someone had smashed the delicate connections housed inside of them.

"Tell me what the situation is," Fisher said.

"Most everyone has a few days off due to the volcano," Logan said, glancing at the ash plume to the south. "I was here securing everything when Mr. Kesler arrived. He looked angry, and I overheard him complaining about being here, but he wanted to be present because someone was arriving with a warrant to search the entire property."

"That would be me," Fisher said.

"Makes sense," Logan said, looking over the FBI agent's suit and tie. "Though at first, I thought it was the other guys that showed up after Mr. Kesler."

Fisher held up his phone.

"You can't use that," Logan said out of habit.

Fisher shook his head at that as he scrolled through some photographs. The groundskeeper pointed out Terrington and two Russians.

"Did they see you?"

"I was keeping out of sight. I thought they were you. Mr. Kesler didn't want me saying the wrong thing to you guys," Logan said, looking guilty at revealing that.

Hanson butted in. "What did they do?"

"They came to our communications array first," Logan answered, scowling. "Phone lines are down. We have several ham radio operators in Aix, but we had connected them all into this main antenna here. As you can see, we're cut off. When they finished here, they split up. Your geologist guy and one other just went into the tourist facility. The third guy drove down the hill to the dish complex itself."

Fear set in the pit of Hanson's stomach. He had seen first-hand what these men were capable of.

"Agent Fisher, they might be trying to eliminate any witnesses to what they're doing around here."

"Or they're trying to cut off all communication," Fisher argued. He looked back at Logan. "What is the protocol when you lose radio and phone lines?"

"There are two satellite phones. One is here in the tourist center. The other is down below with the dish."

Fisher gave Hanson a 'told you so' look.

"We can't take that risk," Hanson said. "We can't let anyone else get hurt."

"What do you propose to do about it?" Fisher asked.

Hanson turned to the groundskeeper.

"Agent Fisher is going to need the keys to your cart," Hanson said.

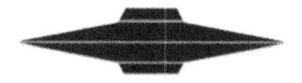

Chapter 48

Gainesville, Virginia

"Could you turn up the volume on the TV?" Amy asked from the kitchen.

Ted Wright set down his phone and took up the remote. Soon the voice of anchorman Doug Morgan filled the living room.

"*—As of yet, no one has stepped forward claiming to know the origin of the UFO seen over Washington—*"

"That's because it's aliens," Adam, his fifteen-year-old son, said as he came down the staircase. Polly, the family's Boston terrier, followed him since he always snuck her food.

"We don't know that," Ted said. "And look at those two air intakes. It looks like it has normal jet engines."

"Maybe it's a stunt." Amy offered. Ted could hear some worry in his wife's voice.

He was also concerned. The web was rife with reports of UFOs seen from all around the country. Brad Hogan next door claimed that he saw three unusual lights in yesterday's night sky.

Was something going on that the government wasn't sharing?

Their twelve-year-old daughter walked in with her phone.

"Dad, have you seen the *War of the Worlds* movie?" she asked.

"Which one?"

She appeared confused. "The old one, with Tom Cruise."

He frowned at that. He was thinking about the 1953 version with its manta ray shaped ships.

"Yes. Why?"

"It's all over the internet," she answered, her fingers flying on the screen as she looked for the next thing the web had to offer.

Ted's concern grew. Alien invasion was trending online. He took up his phone, which was still logged into a social site. A meme had bubbled to the top of the front page, a captioned image of two large-eyed grey aliens instructing the population to make a run on toilet paper since they appreciated clean asses for their exploratory probing.

Jennifer Steel was on the television now. She was still at her Rocky Butte location, and she was shading her eyes as she looked up.

"For the past few minutes, we have been receiving tweets from Oregonians south of us. Two jets are coming this way. And . . . wait a moment, here they are . . ."

The camera moved off of her and pointed to the Portland skyline. Two military jets soared above the city. The camera tracked them as they continued north toward the ash plume rising from Mount St. Helens.

"My producer has informed me that they are F-35s, fifth-generation aircraft that only recently came into service."

Steel turned toward the camera.

"The government has yet to acknowledge the existence of the UFO. What we do know is this. The military has sent two of its most advanced warplanes to check it out."

Doug Morgan reappeared on the screen.

"Thank you, Jennifer. We are now preparing to join President Hayes for her address from the Oval Office."

Amy sat down on the couch with him.

"Maybe Hayes will talk about the UFO also," she said.

"Why is she doing it from the Oval Office?" Adam asked.

"They do it there for the more serious stuff, like natural disasters," Ted answered. "She's trying to make up for that hurricane thing."

The screen showed the presidential seal for a few moments. Then it changed to the scene of President Hayes sitting at her desk in the Oval Office. The late afternoon sun was casting long shadows on the lawn behind her.

As it had been during her campaign, her brunette hair was cut short. She was wearing gold wire-rim glasses. Her jacket was dark, and the collared shirt cream colored. Two buttons were undone at the top of the shirt. Ted wondered how much thought went into how she buttoned her blouse. He felt guilty about that. His young daughter continually admonished him for wondering about her clothes. No one worried about buttons with male presidents.

My fellow Americans, thank you for joining me. Today, at this moment, we are witnessing a spectacle of Mother Nature that we haven't seen for four decades—"

"She's just talking about the volcano," Adam complained.

"It's what this speech is for. Give her a few minutes," his mother said.

President Hayes did focus on Mount St. Helens. She announced that she was declaring the state of Washington a disaster area and that FEMA would be there to help. She called on everyone to think of how they could help their fellow Americans in the Pacific Northwest.

President Hayes' eyes flicked down to her desk.

Ted guessed that her speech, which was on the teleprompter, had come to its end. She was now reading off of a piece of paper on her desk.

"And now I have something to add. A little while ago an Unidentified Flying Object was videotaped flying near the volcano. And as you all know, the rumor of UFOs have been rampant on the web these past few days.

I am here now, as your president, to tell all of you not to worry. My advisors tell me that sightings of UFOs are from our imaginations and that we will soon have identification on the craft flying over Washington.

So please, don't pan—"

Chaos erupted in the Oval Office. A crowd of Secret Service personnel swarmed Hayes, shouting as they did so.

"Get Paladin out of here now!"

"Call ahead to Air Force One! We need Paladin in the air in twenty minutes!"

They dragged the president off camera. Only the desk, and the chair behind it, remained on the screen. The last thing the audience heard from the president was her shouting in the distance.

"Where's my family?!"

The broadcast cut to an alarmed-appearing Doug Morgan, then to commercial. Since it was the news, the advertisement was for arthritis.

The Wrights sat there, shocked.

"What just happened?" Amy asked, fear in her voice.

Trish held up her phone. "Now everyone is talking about *Independence Day*. Did you ever see that movie, Dad?"

Outside, Ted could hear the sound of the Hogan's garage door opening. He went to the window. The Hogan's SUV was speeding away down the street.

Ted looked east. As the crow flies, the White House was only thirty-five miles away.

He grabbed his keys. "Everyone, into the van. Adam, grab the dog."

Amy was already dragging Trish to the door that led to the garage. Adam ran by, Polly in his arms.

"Where are we going, Dad?"

Ted Wright vocalized what most likely was going through everyone's mind in the DC metro area.

"Anywhere but here."

Chapter 49

KET Observatory

Hanson moved into the gift shop area and hid behind a display case. Rows of green, one-eyed plushy aliens stared back at him.

The visitor center was back to normal. Racks of souvenir t-shirts and hats stood where cocktail tables had been several nights ago. Interactive kiosks showing the wonders of space rested where the string quartet had played.

He had already passed through the café and its kitchen. No one was present.

His heart racing, he cautiously approached the entrance to a back hallway. It was labeled 'Employees Only.' His gun held out in front of him, Hanson entered it.

Doors to utility rooms lined the hall. Partway down, a hallway jutted off to his left to an emergency exit door. A small nook was on the left also, designed for temporary storage. A couch with a small tear in the cushion rested there.

A bit further and on the right, a door stood open. Voices were coming from inside.

Hanson peeked in.

It was an employee break room. The walls were yellow, and the lights fluorescent. A half dozen tables with chairs filled the area. The far side had a countertop and sink. A refrigerator anchored one end of it. Monitors hung on the wall. One was for cable television, but its screen was blue since the Russians had cut the line to the satellite dish. A smaller monitor displayed the main room of the tourist center.

Kesler and his entourage were present. The billionaire had the handset of a wall-mounted phone to his ear. A man wearing an expensive suit was standing next to him, checking the wire running out of the phone. The pilot was there also, but she must have been hungry, for she was off by herself, pulling a boxed frozen dinner out of the freezer and reading the back of it.

Hanson was relieved to see that they were safe. But since he was unsure on how Kesler fit in all this, he strode into the room with his Glock held up.

"Mr. Kesler—" Hanson began.

A gun pressed into the right side of his head.

"Hand over your weapon, slowly," a voice growled next to him.

Fisher drove the diesel-powered cart down the slope, approaching the building serving the Galaxy Dish. He had one hand on the wheel and the other gripping his Glock 19, which he held low but at the ready.

Hanson had volunteered him for the science building in case the Russian inside was monitoring his approach. If worse came to worse and the Russian popped out of the front door, Fisher was the better shot in a long range gun battle.

Fisher parked the cart. He could see no movement at the doors, so he risked a glance upwards.

The massive structure of the radio telescope loomed above him. Girders and trusses supported the three hundred-foot diameter dish. More trusses stretched toward the sky at the top of the bowl. This extension held the feed horn at its apex, the telescope's focal point being off-center so that it wouldn't interfere with incoming radio waves. The whole thing was painted a stark white.

Though awed, Fisher looked away from it. A man with a gun was somewhere nearby.

Fisher entered the aluminum-clad building through a glass-fronted door. Up close he could see that the glass had some sort of coating. A label affixed to the window's corner touted it as a material designed for electromagnetic shielding. A larger label on the door instructed visitors to close it behind them.

Inside was a small air-conditioned lobby that had a desk. Like the door, the windows to the outside had a shielding layer on them, and the frames were trimmed in metal. No one else was in the room. Fisher guessed that on ordinary days a guard sat here, making sure no tourists snuck into areas where actual work was being done.

A heavy metal door was behind the desk. The guard room also acted like some sort of radio signal airlock. The doors were not to be opened at the same time.

Fisher cautiously went through and shut the door. The hall behind it was empty. Posted signs reminded employees to always keep the door shut. Fisher realized it wasn't to keep signals out but to keep transmissions from high tech equipment in.

Office doors with large windows lined the hall, and Fisher could see that they were empty.

A bit further down, a door on the right had a curtain instead of a door. Fisher peeked in. It was the building's break room.

He moved on and the hallway turned right. An open doorway was set in the left wall twenty feet away. He looked in.

The ceiling was higher in here. A dozen desks, each one laden with several large monitors, occupied the bulk of the floor. Behind them, on the far wall, a door opened out into another hallway.

To his left he detected more exotic equipment resting on a far counter. The wall above the work area had several large screens. Printers with large rolls of paper recorded the radio telescope's readings.

An astronomer in a lab coat was studying the paper strips. She was a petite woman with long black hair pulled back in a ponytail. So as not to alarm her, Fisher held his Glock behind his back as he entered the room. She saw him and pointed toward the door behind her.

"Your friend is in the back," she said.

It took Fisher a moment to process what she said. The Russian must have used the pretense that he was part of Kesler's group, and now this woman thought he was also.

Fisher held his badge with his left hand. "I'm with the FBI. I need you to get out of here—"

Before he could finish, a tall, lean man with black hair combed to the side walked in from the back hall with a smile on his face. That disappeared when he saw Fisher's held up badge.

He dove toward the nearest desk, pulling an automatic pistol from behind him. He fired off a few shots as he hit the floor.

"Get down," Fisher yelled at the astronomer. Shouting in fear, she ducked under a table.

Fisher fired off three quick shots at the Russian as he too sought cover behind a desk. His bullets plowed into the backs of monitors, shattering them.

Fisher recognized the other man and even had a name for him from his Cardinal Air files; Ken Williams.

The Russian agent fired more shots, and bullets flew over Fisher's head. Williams was trying to keep him pinned down.

On his hands and knees, Fisher noticed that the desks all had eight-inch legs. This led to a large gap between the bulk of the office furniture and the floor.

Crap.

Fisher flopped down and stretched out entirely on the floor on his side. Through the forest of desk and chair legs and cable pylons, he could see Williams was doing the same.

Then the real shootout began as the two men opened fire on each other, both squeezing off shots as fast as they could, sending their bullets skimming inches off the floor toward their targets.

Bullets ricocheted off the furniture legs, and sparks flew as they hit electrical pylons. Finding an unblocked path between the two of them was nearly impossible.

Fisher ran out of bullets. It was quiet on the other side also. As he switched out magazines on the ground, he risked a look through the haze of gun-smoke.

He could see William's face through a gap, slack in death. A bullet hole gaped on his forehead. One of Fisher's shots had made it through.

Fisher could also see that his survival had been a near thing. A bullet was buried in the backside of a desk leg inches from his chest. As he stood back up, the support gave way, and the desk leaned over, spilling its monitors to the floor.

The astronomer was standing back up also. She appeared shocked at what was going on around her.

"What's happening?" she gasped.

Fisher kept it simple. "He was trying to steal something from Kesler." He went to the body, moving the man's gun, a Heckler & Koch VP9, to the side, and began searching the Russian's pockets. "Is there anyone else here?"

"Only myself. Almost everyone has the day off. A few technicians maintaining the dish are working also, but they're at Aix on their lunch break," she answered shakily. "I drew the short straw, so I'm stuck here keeping an eye on the dish until everyone returns." She approached Fisher. "Is that man dead?"

"Yes. I think he was here for the same thing I am. Is there a satellite phone nearby?"

She looked at the back door. "He was in the main office looking for it. He might have it on him."

Fisher continued searching the body. The satellite phone wasn't there, and Fisher guessed it was most likely destroyed. He found Williams's cell phone. Fisher powered it up, hoping to find some information on what was going on around here.

"You can't use that around here," she scolded. "Unless it's important, like a matter of national security or something."

Images of Russians making off with the bulk of American nuclear secrets flashed through Fisher's mind.

"It's a matter of national security," he deadpanned.

Chapter 50

Cooper slammed the satellite phone against the side of the desk. It broke apart into several pieces.

"Couldn't we use that?" Terrington asked.

"Someone might track it," Cooper said. "And we can't let anyone else here use it. Destroying it is the best option." He dropped the pieces into the security office's trash can.

He and Terrington had lost some time avoiding Kesler and his crew. The billionaire wasn't supposed to be here today, and Tonkov had in the past stressed that no harm was to come to him. An alive and well Kesler would help convince the authorities that he had something to do with what happened today, and they would focus their investigation on him.

Fortunately, it was a large building with many halls and corners, and they had made it to this back room undetected. All that remained was to sneak back to their vehicle.

"The FBI agent is here," Terrington said.

The geologist was at the security monitors. Cooper joined him. One of the cameras showed a man wearing a suit and tie making his way to the radio telescope in a golf cart.

"Are you sure?" Cooper asked.

"It's Agent Fisher, he's interviewed me several times," Terrington said.

This Agent Fisher was heading right for Williams. Cooper regretted smashing the phone, as it would have been useful at the moment. He needed to get down there and back Williams up.

Other activity on the monitors caught his eye. Kesler's crew was in the employee break room.

Along with Hanson.

Cooper swore under his breath. Hanson was supposed to be dead.

He took one last look at the screen, memorizing where everyone was standing. It looked like Kesler's bodyguard had the only gun in the room, and it was pointed at Hanson, whose arms were up in the air.

Cooper pulled out his own semi-automatic pistol and set off limping down the corridor.

"Wait a minute, you said you weren't going to hurt anyone," Terrington said, shuffling after him.

"That was before I knew Hanson was alive," Cooper snarled, rubbing his wounded leg.

* * *

His arms held up in the air, Hanson watched with frustration as Kesler's mountain-sized bodyguard put his Glock into the lower-right pocket of his suit's jacket. He kept his own gun pointed at Hanson.

"What the hell is going on here?" Kesler asked, his voice raised.

"It's over, Kesler, we know you're working with the Russians," Hanson shot back.

"What are you talking about?" Kesler said. Recognition crossed his face. "Wait a minute. You're Doctor Bateman's date from the other night."

"I'm here with the FBI now."

"FBI? What are you, exactly?"

Hanson hesitated. That was a hard question to answer at the moment. He fired back with a question of his own.

"Never mind that. I'm here because of your UFOs."

Hanson could see from the expression on Kesler's face that he had struck a nerve. "I can explain," the billionaire said. "Someone who is helping with my flying car program took one of my aircraft for one last spin before she returned to duty. No one was supposed to see her."

Hanson could guess who 'her' was. It was Kara in the air that night. But that wasn't the airship that concerned him at the moment.

"Why is your flying wing UFO in the air right now?"

"What are you talking about?"

The man at Kesler's side leaned in. "Mr. Kesler, remember, you don't have to reveal anything about your advertising campaign until we have proof of their warrant."

Kesler waved his lawyer off.

"You saw the *Alpha-47*?" Kesler asked.

Hanson was beginning to get the idea that Kesler was unaware of his role in all this.

"I saw it right before I got here. It was heading for the Yakima Valley," Hanson said. He lowered his hands, though the bodyguard still kept his gun on him. "Kesler, what exactly are the Marines doing for you?"

"They helped out with the *Dragonfly*, and gave some advice on my other projects."

"Is that the only reason you approached them?"

"They approached me. They told me they were UFO fans. They were eager to help."

Now it was clear he had been wrong about the billionaire.

"Kesler, they were using you."

"What? Why?"

"They're working with the Russians."

"What Russians?"

In answer, a Russian limped into the room.

Hanson recognized him as a pilot named Cooper from Fisher's photo line-up. From the way he was limping, Hanson guessed he was also the fake Bigfoot he had skewered with his spear. Cooper looked pissed. And he had a gun.

Without any preamble, Cooper began shooting.

Everyone yelled in fear and scrambled as the first bullets exploded out of the weapon. Kesler dove to the floor. The lawyer went left, the pilot right.

Hanson ducked behind the bodyguard.

He guessed the Russian was a soldier like Foster and was no fool. His first course of action was to take out anyone holding a gun.

Bullets slammed into the bodyguard's chest as Cooper shot him center mass.

But due to his bulletproof vest, the bodyguard remained standing, though he staggered back. He swung his gun around.

Cooper's next shot tore into his target's right arm. The bodyguard's hand whipped back, his weapon flying behind him.

Cooper kept shooting. Hanson heard the pilot scream in pain behind him.

A bullet hit the bodyguard in the leg and he began toppling back onto Hanson. Cooper paused a moment, waiting for Hanson's cover to fall away.

Desperate, Hanson jammed his hand into the bodyguard's pocket, his fingers finding and wrapping around the grip of his Glock.

He returned fire with the gun still in the pocket, wildly pumping out bullets as the bodyguard's weight pushed him back. Both of them wound up on the floor.

Cooper dove back through the door as bullets tore into the wall around him. Hanson drew his gun forth and took better aim, snapping off shots behind the Russian's retreating form.

The door to the hall closed. For a brief moment, Hanson caught a glimpse of Terrington pushing it shut.

Hanson kept his Glock pointed at the door.

"Who's hurt?" he yelled.

"Judy's hit," Kesler said. Hanson to see Kesler bent over his wounded pilot, a worried look on his face.

"It's bad," Kesler said.

Hanson moved over to them. The pilot had passed out and was bleeding from her abdomen. He couldn't tell if the bullet had hit any vital organs.

"Jesse's also been shot," the lawyer said.

The bodyguard's vest had spared him the worst of it, but he had taken bullets in his arm and leg. The big man was sprawled on the ground, reaching over with his left arm to assess his own wounds.

"Who was that guy? Why was he shooting at us?" Kesler yelled. Hanson felt everyone focus on him.

Keeping half an eye on the door, Hanson turned back to Kesler.

"Your Marines are defecting with their jets, Kesler," Hanson answered. "And there's several Russian spies here helping them. I think your mock UFO is in the air to draw our military away from this location."

Now everyone stared at him as if he was crazy.

"Look, I know it's a lot to take in, so let's just focus on our immediate concerns," Hanson instructed. "Mr. Kesler, keep pressure on her wound. Is there a doctor nearby?"

Kesler pressed his handkerchief on the bullet hole. "There's a clinic in the employee's village, a doctor is over there. But we can't reach her. The phone lines are down for some reason."

"Is there a satellite phone option?"

"Yes. It's in the back security room."

Hanson glanced at the room's back corner. "Where does that door go?"

"To a utility hallway that leads to the building's rear exit."

"I left a groundskeeper back there; he's hiding behind the dumpsters. Send your lawyer to the door to open it and let him in to help find the satellite phone, if it is still in one piece."

Kesler nodded to his lawyer, who got up and left the room.

Hanson stood up and went to the bodyguard. The big man waved him off.

"Get me my gun," he growled.

Hanson found the weapon, a Beretta M9, under a table and handed it to him. Hanson also took a moment to reload his Glock.

With the bodyguard able to back him up from the floor, Hanson cautiously tried to push the room's front door open. It didn't budge. He guessed that Cooper and Terrington had braced it with the broken-down couch out in the hall.

Hanson checked the monitor that showed the gift center. He could see Cooper and Terrington exiting the main doors. The closed circuit camera also captured part of the outside lot. Cooper ignored the *Dragonfly* and went for the SUV. It must have been locked, for, after a few moments, he left it, and he and Terrington set off on foot toward the dish.

"Dammit," said Hanson.

"What's wrong?" Kesler said.

"The gunman is heading for the dish. Fisher's down there. They might get the jump on him." Hanson walked over to the wall-mounted phone and picked it up. No dial tone. He looked at his own cell. No bars.

"Nothing works," Kesler said. He was still on the ground, keeping his blood-soaked handkerchief on the pilot's wound.

"I need to warn Fisher," Hanson said desperately. His eyes fell on a small box on the counter. It was the TV dinner the pilot had taken out of the freezer. "Wait a minute!" he shouted, hope back in his voice as he grabbed it up.

"What is it?" Kesler asked.

"Salisbury steak and mashed potatoes," Hanson answered.

"How does that help us?"

"The 'Wow! Signal' isn't the only famous transmission that astronomers have detected . . ." Hanson began.

Chapter 51

Air Force One

FBI Director Palmer Knox fumbled with his Ethernet cable. The large table in the 747's conference room had numerous ports to plug into. He wasn't sure which one was his, or if it mattered.

The last half-hour had been a whirlwind of fear and confusion. With reports of UFOs increasing across the United States, he was already in the White House to attend a briefing with the president after her address.

As a result, he had been swept up in the scramble to get the President out of Washington. She and her family had been shoved into 'The Beast,' the heavily armored limousine used to move the President on the ground. He, along with a few other high ranking officials, rode with the Secret Service in their SUVs.

What came next was a mad dash across town to Andrews Joint Base, where Air Force One was being warmed up. The impromptu motorcade was smaller than usual but more nimble. Washington DC police also helped, blocking side traffic so that their path was clear. Knox had gasped aloud when, on several occurrences, Secret Service vehicles had swerved out of the motorcade and crashed into cars that had wandered out into their way. It reminded him of NFL linemen protecting their quarterback.

Air Force One was waiting for them on the tarmac. Secret Service rushed everyone up the steps to the airliner, and it began moving even before staff shut the door.

Then they were climbing in a steep emergency ascent as the pilot pushed the engines and brought the 747 to an altitude of 45,000 feet. They were high above a layer of clouds. Knox had no idea which part of the US they were over at the moment.

President Hayes walked into the room. She had been in the presidential suite, making sure her husband and son were safe.

"What do we know?" she asked, standing at the table.

There were only a few other people in the conference room. Fortunately, they were the right ones.

Hayes' Chief of Staff, Elaina Prichard, was busy setting up a laptop for the President. The Secretary of Defense, General Douglas Thorpe, was sitting close by. Next to him, in uniform, the Chairman of the Joint Chief of Staffs, General Martin Lampard, was setting up a station for himself. Like Knox, they had been nearby to attend the same meeting after the President's televised address.

Against the wall, a Navy officer quietly sat in a side chair. She had an briefcase handcuffed to her. Knox knew she was the aide-de-camp assigned to guard the Football, the small case that held the United States' nuclear launch codes and targets should the president deem a nuclear strike necessary. She lightly held it in her lap.

"The Vice President has made it to the Presidential Emergency Operations Center below the White House," Thorpe said. "Senate and House leaders have made it to their bunkers also, as have your Cabinet members. We're setting up links now."

Lessons had been learned after 9/11. Many officials in high positions had ignored protocol and not fled to bunkers. Communication had been a mess also. Intel had been hard to come by in the hours after the attack on New York.

Today it was different. Air Force One had secure connections to military satellites. They were able to communicate in real-time to anyone they wanted and tap into any news channel.

"Mitchell made it to Cheyenne Mountain. Yardley transferred NORAD and NORTHCOM command there once he arrived," Lampard added.

"Peterson Airforce Base?" the President asked.

"Still there, Madam President," Thorpe answered. He looked at his computer screen. "As is Washington, DC."

Relief washed over the President's face. She glanced over at the large monitor mounted on the wall. It displayed the unregistered flights radar screen from Cheyenne Mountain.

The two patterns of nine blips, along with the extrapolated line, were still on it.

"So we're past General Mitchell's forecasted missile strikes."

"But not out of danger," Lampard said. "These hypersonic cruise missiles can change course. There's a chance they are circling out there, positioning themselves so they hit everything at the same moment."

"Wouldn't anyone notice them?" she asked.

"That's the problem. People are noticing something. Calls are coming in from people claiming to see UFOs, or UAPs, or whatever the hell we're calling them now. We don't know if they are mistakenly seeing cruise missiles instead."

"Recommendations?"

"Madam President, being the chance this is some sort of nuclear first strike, we should put everything on Defcon 2," Lampard advised. "We need our bombers loaded and in the air, and have everything else ready for that matter. We need as many military pilots' eyes over the eastern seaboard as we can get."

"What about the west coast?"

"Mitchell already ordered the 142nd to send all their F-15s over the Pacific Ocean. They're looking for signs of any Russian subs capable of launching missiles. Two F-35Bs are above Mount St. Helens right now, where that UFO was first seen."

President Hayes shook her head. "The volcano. Strange how it's the least of my worries right now." She looked at Knox. "You have an investigation going on there. What do you know?"

Knox cleared his throat. "Madam President, there's a good chance that the Washington UFO we're seeing on the web belongs to Wayne Kesler."

"The billionaire?"

"Yes. My agent and the man advising him think that Kesler owns several prototype aircraft that are to be used in an advertising promotion. An attention-grabbing stunt, like Elon Musk sending his Tesla into outer space. Their guess is that Kesler designed the aircraft to look like past UFOs."

"Who's this advisor?"

"His name's Steve Hanson; he's some sort of paranormal debunker," Knox said, looking at his notes on his computer.

"Can this Hanson and your agent confirm this theory?"

"I don't know. My Special Agent in Charge in Portland has been trying to reach them all afternoon. For some reason, they've been out of touch."

"I hope he succeeds in contacting them, Knox," the President said grimly. "Because, without answers, my only choice is to bring the entire United States to Defcon 2 for the first time in its history."

Behind the President, Knox could see the young woman guarding the nuclear codes clutch the Football closer to her.

Chapter 52

Mount St. Helens

"Tell those helicopters to back off," Kara ordered the tower as she banked her F-35B around the column of ash rising from the volcano. She orbited it to the south side, giving her a view of Portland. Monetti kept on her tail.

She watched with satisfaction as the news choppers dropped further south. She and Monetti had been riding herd for the past few minutes, driving the overzealous newscasters back. They didn't want any witnesses on the north side of the mountain when they made their break into Canada.

It also let them show off for the cameras. Tonkov had advised them that their presence would add validation to the UFO reports across the country. Their being here made the government response to the UFO hysteria 'official.'

She engaged the DAS and took in the view. The ash column was now seven miles high and spreading out like an anvil head in the upper atmosphere. The ash was also drifting east because of prevailing winds.

"How much more time?" Monetti asked on the satellite phone.

"Soon," she replied. "Tonkov just texted me. The Russians should be in position to refuel us in a few minutes." As she swung around the column, she looked north. At this altitude, she could see a small white dot fifty miles from her. The Galaxy Dish. She would use that as a guide when she and Monetti made their way in that direction.

She looked down through her feet. The Johnston Ridge Observatory was directly below. She wondered how it was going to weather the eruption.

* * *

Johnston Ridge

Ten thousand feet below the jet, Makani was wondering the same thing. She was on her back, kicking the grill that covered the vent on the outside of the building.

She had lost some time navigating the fans in the air passages. She was too large to crawl between the blades. She had to use the shovel to bend an edge back and squeeze through the gap, getting rid of the suspenders she was wearing as she did so.

The plywood she was working on was screwed on tight, but at least it wasn't as thick as the plywood on the windows. It must have been a leftover piece of scrap, attached as an afterthought. She could feel it giving away. With renewed determination, she started kicking harder.

* * *

St. Petersburg

"Air Force One is in the air," Gontarev said. He had one of his screens tuned to an American news channel. On it, anchorman Doug

Morgan looked worried as the President's jet took off in a video playing behind him.

"As I thought it would," Tonkov said.

"What happens next?" Gontarev asked.

"With the threat presented to her, Hayes will most likely order her forces to Defcon 3, maybe even Defcon 2. Russia, of course, will notice their change of defensive stance. Our President, acting concerned, will call their President through the direct line, asking her what is going on."

"Won't they blame us?"

"They will, but they won't have anything to back their claims. When the dust settles, all they will have is some phantom contacts on their radar, the false reports of UFOs from a hysterical population, and a billionaire thought to be part of a publicity stunt gone wrong."

"What of the F-35Bs?"

"It will appear that the volcanic ash claimed them. If they ever do figure out what happened, it will be far too late."

Gontarev looked to the screen again. It showed wrecked cars at intersections as panicking Americans tried to flee their capital.

"How did you come up with this plan?"

"It was the CIA who thought it up. There was a scare in 1952. People thought aliens were attacking Washington DC. A panel was convened. Their government determined that people panicking in the face of a 'perceived' threat could mask a 'real' attack. The intelligence branches of the United States were afraid that we Russians would someday take advantage of this."

"You'd think their government would be ready for us."

"I'm sure they were," Tonkov replied. "But the general population isn't. Their memory is short, and they've forgotten their past scares with UFOs. And, as I've observed, Americans are mentally conditioned to the acceptance of the incredible. They believe that men never walked on the moon, or that alien corpses are stored in government facilities. They doubt their doctors and turn away from vaccines. They think the worst of their neighbors if their political or religious views are not the same."

The rioting on the monitor was growing.

"They will always fall for our lies," Tonkov continued. "And today that will bring us their deepest nuclear secrets and two of their most advanced warplanes."

A car exploded onscreen.

"And there's no one to stop us."

Chapter 53

KET Observatory

Fisher walked back into the main room. After determining that the Russian phone he had was locked and useless, he had gone down the hall to the break area to retrieve the curtain hanging in the doorway. He wanted something to cover the Russian's dead body.

He studied the woman standing near him as he shrouded Williams. She looked to be recovering from her initial shock. Her named tag identified her as Professor Debbie Oaks.

"Professor Oaks, I'm sorry about what happened here," Fisher said. "But I need to go back to the tourist center. Are you going to be okay?"

Oaks looked at the body. "Is anyone going to take care of that?"

"As soon as possible," Fisher said. "I'll make sure no more of them—" he glanced at the dead Russian, "—comes in here to bother you."

He made his way to the doorway, but a sound made him pause.

One of the many devices that translated signals from the telescope to hard copy suddenly became more active. The needles were recording pulses of energy from somewhere. Fisher didn't know what transmissions the piece of equipment was detecting, but he recognized the cadence of the signal.

Dot-dot-dot, dash-dash-dash, dot-dot-dot.

SOS.

Oaks noticed it too. She was walking over to one of the printers.

"This is morse code," she said, puzzlement in her voice. The needles were still scratching on the paper.

"SOS is all I know, Professor. Can you read it?" Fisher asked.

"Of course, signals are my specialty," she said. She looked at the strip. "The next word is 'gun.'"

Fisher drew his own Glock forth. "How's this being broadcast?"

"The wavelength is 2.45 gigahertz."

Fisher looked blank.

"Someone's running a microwave oven."

That made sense.

"Hanson," Fisher said.

"Who?"

"Someone I know. This is something that he would do. What does the rest say?"

"Coming your way."

Gun coming your way. Hanson was trying to warn him.

"Professor, stay here and secure the door behind me. More of these men are coming."

She followed him to the door. Fisher heard her engage the lock when she shut it behind him.

He moved down the hall to the 'air lock' door and carefully opened it. The small guard room was empty. Fisher looked out the front window.

Terrington and a limping Russian he recognized as Cooper were approaching the building, keeping to the side of the road. They were almost out of view. Fisher realized that if Hanson hadn't warned him, the Russian would have surprised him. They were still a hundred feet away, and Cooper had a gun in his hand.

Fisher had the advantage of cover from the building. He pushed the door open with his own weapon held up.

"Drop the gun, Cooper!"

The Russian brought up his weapon and fired as he limped along. Terrington yelped and dashed off the road.

Fisher ducked down. Cooper was moving way faster than he had anticipated, and was shooting his pistol as if it was second nature to him. Bullets gouged the wooden door frame near his face.

Fisher knew the Russian's attack was designed to make him flinch and keep him off balance for a few moments. He disregarded the flying splinters and took a half-second to make sure his aim was true before he returned fire. The Russian spun around as a bullet caught him in the chest, and he cried out in agony as he fell to the ground.

Terrington kept on running. He disappeared around the side of the building.

Fisher left the doorway and advanced on Cooper's prone body. He kicked the Russian's semi-automatic gun away and felt for a pulse.

The man was dead. Fisher picked up Cooper's pistol, a SIG P226, and put it in his suit jacket's pocket. He took off in pursuit of Terrington, cursing the hot weather.

The geologist was nowhere in sight. Fisher continued to the back of the building.

It was empty there also. The base of the radio telescope was fifty feet away to his left.

The whole thing rested on a circle of tracks that allowed it to rotate on its azimuth. The base of the frame was positioned so that the elevator to the telescope's elevation drive level was behind the control building.

The elevator began rising.

Again Fisher swore out loud. Terrington was going to try to make his escape by losing himself in the structure itself.

Fisher sprinted to the radio telescope's base.

* * *

Hanson closed the outer cover to the microwave oven.

He had guessed that the breakroom had a microwave oven from the presence of the frozen meal. It was in a special cupboard with a fine steel mesh insulating it, a custom built Faraday Cage to catch any rogue radiation that leaked out as the appliance was running.

He had set the timer for five minutes and then let it run. By quickly opening and closing the outer door, he was able to control the frequency of escaping microwave emissions.

He hoped Fisher got the message.

"How'd you know to do that?" Kesler asked from the floor. He was still tending to the pilot. Her face was ashen. She needed a doctor, and soon. Hanson rushed over with a towel from the kitchen counter. He knelt down and handed it to the billionaire, who used it to replace his blood-soaked handkerchief.

"Like I said, there's another strange but true story dealing with radio telescopes," Hanson explained. "The Parkes Radio Telescope in Australia was picking up unusual signals on a regular basis. Lore had it that the astronomers thought they had alien transmissions on their hands.

"The truth is less sensational. They always knew the signal was local, but they didn't know exactly from where. After some equipment upgrades and experimenting, they found their culprit. It was their breakroom microwave."

Kesler snorted. "And the morse code?"

Hanson shrugged. "I was a boy scout."

The lawyer came in with Logan, who had pieces of a satellite phone in his hand.

"They destroyed the phone, but the back is clear," the lawyer said.

"Thanks, Luis," Kesler said. He turned to Hanson. "What next?"

Hanson took up his Glock. "Follow me. We'll circle to the front and get your SUV. We'll pull around back and use it to get these two to the medical center."

Luis and Logan took over caring for the pilot and bodyguard. Hanson and Kesler made their way out the door and down the side of the building. The SUV chirped as Kesler used a fob to unlock it.

Hanson took a moment to look at the *Dragonfly* parked next to it.

"Why did you have this out here?"

"I was hoping it would be enough to satisfy your FBI agent's curiosity, and he wouldn't look further into what else I was storing here," Kesler admitted, looking toward the closed door of the nearby hangar.

"And what exactly are you storing here?" Hanson asked as he slid into the SUV's passenger seat.

Kesler started up the vehicle. "I have an aircraft shaped like a flying saucer behind us," he answered. "It has sixteen propellers to keep its lightweight aluminum frame aloft, like a large drone. And even though it has two jet engines to give it some zip, it's still as easy to operate as a car. I call it the *Roswell*. You've seen the *Alpha-47*."

"Why here?"

"I flew them out here at night a half a year ago. With no cameras functioning in this area, I figured they would be more secure until I revealed them. After my ad campaign, I plan to display the *Roswell* right here where the *Dragonfly* is sitting. The *A-47* would be kept at the airfield."

"That would be a draw," Hanson agreed.

"There's another reason I have them here," Kesler added. "We're in the area where Kenneth Arnold saw his UFOs." The billionaire looked up and to the south. "If we were present that day seven decades ago, we could see them from where we're sitting. Nine bright airships, skipping across the blue sky. Can you imagine that?"

Hanson could.

"So keeping these ships here, and near the Galaxy Dish, just feels . . . right," Kesler finished, turning to look at the radio telescope. He put the rig in drive and started forward. He had only moved a few feet before he slammed on the brakes.

"What's going on over there?" he exclaimed. Hanson followed his gaze.

In the distance, Terrington was moving along a catwalk immediately below the dish. He was having a difficult time of it since the catwalk was tilted. Sixty feet behind him, a second man was beginning the ascent.

Fisher.

"That catwalk's designed only to be used when the dish is in a flattened out resting position." Kesler said, concerned. "It's now at a thirty-degree angle. They'll both get themselves killed."

Hanson glanced at the *Dragonfly* parked nearby.

"Mr. Kesler, I'm going to ask you a huge favor . . ."

Chapter 54

The catwalk to the next elevator was at a steep angle, so Fisher had to use the rails to pull himself forward.

Ahead of him, Terrington was already riding a second elevator up to the dish's feeder arm. Fisher noted that it stopped at the catwalk at the top of the bowl for a few moments and then continued its way to the very top, where the signal receiving unit was located.

He made the elevator and called it back to him. He risked a glance down. He guessed he was a dizzying two hundred and fifty feet up.

The elevator reached him. Inside, an alarm bell was ringing, protesting the use of the elevator at the structure's current angle.

Fisher ignored it and pushed the button for the dish level. The elevator's tilt caused him to press against a wall.

The door opened. Fisher was on another catwalk that ran along the top of the dish, terminating at the bowl's apex.

No one was nearby. He looked up. The framework of the feeder arm that supported the receiving room rose two hundred feet above him.

The elevator had gone all the way up. Was Terrington up there?

Or was he still on this level, hoping to make a dash for the ground once Fisher committed to searching the top?

Fisher stepped out onto the catwalk. The dish's tilt seemed more acute up here. He clutched at the rails and made his way across.

A noise made him turn his head. In the distance, Kesler's flying car, the *Dragonfly*, was rising from the ground. It pivoted in the air and started coming his way.

It had to be Hanson. He wouldn't shut up about the thing on the drive up.

Fisher made the apex of the dish. The catwalk had a few steps down to the dish itself, whose white bowl stretched out three hundred feet to its far rim. The control building was below and off to the side.

Directly below him was Terrington.

The geologist had undone a safety chain and lowered himself a bit off the catwalk. He was hanging onto the edge of the dish. Fisher guessed Terrington was hoping to be out of his field of view when he glanced down the catwalk from the elevator.

The man looked terrified. He had overcommitted to his plan, and he was losing his grip.

Fisher put away his gun away and held out his hand for Terrington.

"Can you reach me?" Fisher yelled.

The geologist stretched for it but lost his grip with his other hand. With a yelp of fear, he slid away, barely managing to grab the chain at the last moment.

"Help me!" he cried out.

Terrington was now three feet from the edge. Fisher leaned over, grabbing ahold of the chain halfway down and reached out for him.

"Take my hand!" Fisher commanded.

The geologist grabbed it. Grunting, Fisher, who was almost upside down, began hauling him up. Cooper's gun, which he had tucked away in his suit's pocket, fell out and clattered down the slope. Fisher watched it gain speed and launch away into space at the bottom.

Then the chain gave way, and he and Terrington followed it.

* * *

Professor Oaks turned down the volume of the various alarms going off in the control room.

Judging by the amount, someone had taken off in the *Dragonfly*. Electronically, that aircraft was the noisiest thing in the area. It was overwhelming the bulk of her sensors.

How can this day get any worse?

With most of the alarms turned down, she heard an unfamiliar beeping. It drew her to the station where they kept tabs on the physical structure of the antenna.

Someone had been using the elevators while the dish was at a thirty-degree angle.

That was dangerous. There were cameras on the dish, so she looked at the monitors.

The FBI agent and another man were at the apex, hanging on for dear life.

With a cry of disbelief, she leaned over a keyboard, engaging the motors that ran the elevation gear. She had to reduce the dish's angle.

It began moving.

On the screen, the men broke free and began sliding down the face of the dish. The telescope continued to lower its pitch. She wondered if she had reacted in time.

* * *

Hanson pushed down on the pedal and forward on the yoke. The flying car leaped forward for the radio telescope.

Kesler was right the other evening. The car was easy to operate.

Video game easy. Hanson had it figured out in seconds. It also helped that he had flown this thing before, thousands of times.

In his dreams.

He still remembered reading about them in the seventies. Back when tech magazines predicted a flying car in every garage.

The future is here.

He banked toward the dish, hoping to help Fisher by locating where Terrington was going.

Instead, he saw the two of them at the top of the dish, dangling over the edge.

Tapping his right shoulder for luck, Hanson angled the wheel on the steering column downward.

The *Dragonfly* went into a dive. Warning bells went off, and a soft voice from the car spoke up.

"Exceeding safety parameters."

Hanson felt the car's onboard computer fighting him. The steering wheel was moving on its own, bringing him out of the dive. Ahead of him, he saw Fisher and Terrington begin their slide down the dish.

"*Dragonfly*, disengage safeties," Hanson yelled, pressing the gas pedal down.

* * *

Fisher turned over on his back.

He and Terrington were hurtling down the face of the dish. Due to the sun, the aluminum panels that covered the thing were scorching hot. He couldn't use his hands to slow him down.

He bent his knees so that the soles of his shoes met the dish's surface, but it wasn't enough. He was still gaining speed.

He felt a vibration below him. The dish itself was moving, trying to lessen the steepness of the angle they were sliding down.

He and Terrington passed the halfway point. The dish was still moving, and the bottom lip was now rising up, becoming more like a ramp.

It slowed them down, but it wasn't enough. He and Terrington flew off the short incline and became airborne, the geologist shrieking the whole way.

The *Dragonfly* appeared above them, pulling up into a hover. Air blasted Fisher as the downdraft from its six rotors drove him and Terrington back, and they tumbled down to the dish, now sliding a short way in the opposite direction before coming to a rest.

The dish was now almost flattened out, bowl-like. Fisher shakily stood up from the hot surface as the flying car landed near him.

Hanson, with the biggest grin Fisher had ever seen, opened the door.

"Need a lift?" Hanson asked.

Chapter 55

Hanson eased the *Dragonfly* onto the pad.

"Good to be on the solid ground again," Fisher sighed, pushing Terrington out in front of him. The geologist was in handcuffs. Fisher had searched him and found a flash drive with a security lock. Terrington had told Fisher he wasn't saying anything until he had a lawyer.

It had been a tight fit with all three of them, and the small flying car had strained with the weight, but Hanson managed to get them back to the tourist center.

The SUV was gone, but Kesler was waiting for them at the door. Everybody piled inside, into the cool interior of the facility.

"How is everyone?" Fisher asked.

"Luis is transporting my pilot and bodyguard to the clinic down below," Kesler answered. "I don't know if Judy is going to make it." The billionaire looked distressed that one of his employees had been grievously hurt.

Fisher saved any questions he had for Kesler. On the way over, Hanson had told him that the billionaire had been clueless about what was going on.

"When the SUV comes back, you can go and check up on her," Fisher told him. Kesler appeared relieved at that.

"We should make a few calls. Does anything work around here?" Hanson asked.

Logan walked in from a back hallway and answered. "Communication is still down, but I have satellite TV connected," the old man said. "Give me a moment with this television so we can see what's up with the volcano."

Nearby, Terrington perked up.

Logan turned the television on, but it still had a blue screen. He spent some time running his fingers up and down the side of it.

"Use the remote, it's faster," Hanson said.

"We don't use them around here," Logan said. "You younger generations don't remember a time when there were no remotes. When I was a kid, we had to stand up and turn on the television."

The old man found the button he was looking for and began flipping through channels.

"Now, everything is wireless and fits in the palm of your hand," Logan continued, shaking his head. "Always connected. Look at you. You're acting like if you're out of touch for an hour, it's the end of the world."

A news channel came up. It showed an aerial scene of Washington DC. Smoke was rising from a half dozen locations.

A scroll was running along the bottom.

Thousands flee the capital as citizens panic, wondering if an alien, or foreign, attack is imminent . . .

There was a small box inset on the right side of the screen.

Coming up next:

Will the volcano erupt again?

Are there aliens amongst us?

How Air Force One keeps the President safe.

What is Defcon 2?

Logan stood back from the television, stunned.

"Fucking A!" he exclaimed.

"It's worse than we thought," Hanson said, gaping at the screen.

Fisher turned toward Kesler. "I have to call DC and tell them what's really happening out there. Where's the closest cell tower?"

"Turn left at Highway 12. There is a directional cell tower thirty miles down the road. But it only works if you get on the east side of it," Kesler answered.

"Dammit, and your driveway into here is a bit over ten miles. It'll take us a half hour to get there."

"Not as the crow flies," Hanson said. "I have a plan. I'll fly you over on the *Dragonfly*. It will save us some time."

"I'm good with that," Kesler said.

Hanson was already moving for the door. On the television, the next news story cycled up. The screen now showed Mount St. Helens.

Terrington spoke up with worry in his voice. "Agent Fisher, I need to tell you about Doctor Bateman."

Next to Fisher, Hanson stopped and turned around.

"She followed me out when I left with the Russians—"

Hanson ran back and grabbed ahold of Terrington by the lapels of his shirt and pulled him up so that the geologist was balanced on his toes.

"What did you do, Terrington?" he yelled.

The geologist was shaking. "I saved her," he whimpered. "They were going to kill her, but I convinced them to lock her away somewhere secure."

Hanson looked like he was going to tear the geologist apart. Fisher put a restraining hand on his shoulder.

"Where, Terrington?" Fisher asked.

The geologist turned toward the television. "We locked her in the Johnston Ridge Observatory. After we escaped from here we were going to send someone for her. I left a key right outside the west utility door."

Everyone was looking at the screen now. Two F-35Bs could be

seen circling the ash column like a pair of sharks. The scroll on the bottom displayed a warning.

Volcano is due to erupt a second time at any moment . . . .

Next to Fisher, Hanson dropped the geologist, who fell to the ground with a grunt. He turned to the FBI agent, a desperate look on his face.

"New plan," Hanson announced.

Chapter 56

Johnston Ridge

Makani lowered herself to the ground, free of the building. In her line of sight was the outside amphitheater. On it rested a USGS camera unit.

Not the one she wanted. She moved around the corner of the building, stopping in her tracks as she did so.

Mount St. Helens was only six miles away, and the eruption was playing out in front of her. Ash rose from the crater, stretching seven miles above her head. Lightning bolts danced across the face of the column.

The sound was overwhelming. It was a distant, crackling roar that not only assaulted her ears but seemed to pass through her body.

Several miles up, the ash was flowing away, forming a curtain that drifted eastward. Gravity was pulling it down also, and it was already covering the floor of the Yakima Valley. Near the mountain itself, the ash cloud had yet to reach the ground, so a gap remained. She could see blue sky on the other side.

To her north, the ash flowed down into the canyon below. Unlike 1980, which produced the destructive flash of pyroclastic clouds and flooding lahars, the ash here only dusted the ground below, though its heat killed the flora and fauna that had returned from the last eruption.

Shaking her head from the mountain's spell, she turned away. The northern dome was still a threat. She sprinted toward the camera unit placed on the observation deck two hundred feet to her east.

* * *

Highway 12

Fisher skimmed the treetops. The cell tower he wanted was ten miles south, then thirty miles east by road.

He was taking the hypotenuse, flying over the scrub tree terrain.

Hanson was right; the *Dragonfly* was a kick to fly. Something like this would be cool when commuting to work. Or chasing down fleeing criminals.

Ahead, he could see the mast of the cell tower. He circled to the far side of it.

"*Dragonfly*, hover here," he commanded.

The onboard computer took over, and the car held its position fifty feet away from the cell tower, and one hundred feet off the ground.

He was consuming a lot of energy doing so. He knew that when he finished, he was going to have to return to the observatory the old fashioned way by landing the thing on Highway 12 and driving back.

He took out his phone. For the first time in several hours, he had bars. He quick dialed his boss.

"I've been trying to reach you all afternoon!" Special Agent in Charge Jacobs yelled when he answered.

"I've been stuck in the Radio Quiet Zone," Fisher explained. "Sir, we need to reach the President. I have vital information—"

"Knox is on Air Force One with her, I'm going to connect you to his phone now," Jacobs interrupted.

A few moments passed. Fisher watched the indicator for the *Dragonfly's* battery level tick from twelve percent to eleven percent.

"Knox here."

"Sir. It's Agent Fisher. I have news for the—"

"One moment agent, I'm going to tie you into the conference room's comm system," Knox said. Fisher heard some shuffling in the background. "You're on speaker. And Agent, you're talking to the President of the United States."

Fisher sat up a little straighter.

"Can you hear me?" he asked.

"We can hear you, Agent Fisher," President Hayes answered. "We're hoping you have some answers for us."

"Madam President, I do. There's no attack, and there are no aliens. The whole thing is a Russian hoax."

"How do you know this?"

"I've talked to Wayne Kesler. The UFO is his, a prop for an upcoming commercial. He was storing it here because he also planned to display it near his KET observatory after his publicity campaign. The man flying it now is a Russian sleeper agent out of Ohio. I've already had to kill two other Russian agents trying to stop me."

A man's voice came over Fisher's phone. "Agent, this is General Lampard of the Joint Chiefs. We detected several unexplained radar signatures east of you earlier this afternoon."

Fisher thought about it for a moment. "Sir, in our investigations, we discovered the Russians invested in weather balloons and radar reflectors. Your radar was picking up on those."

Hayes was back on. "To what end, Agent Fisher?"

"Madam President, the Russians are doing something the CIA predicted seventy years ago. They're using mass hysteria to force our military to do what they want. I'm guessing the bulk of our forces are over the eastern seaboard, looking for threats to Washington DC."

"You're correct there," Lampard said.

"That, along with the volcano, leaves the Pacific Northwest wide open. There are only two F-35Bs here at the moment. From what I know, it's my feeling that the Marine pilots are defecting, and delivering the F-35s to Russia."

On the phone, he could hear Lampard swearing in the background.

"You're sure, Agent?" the President asked.

"It's only a guess, Madam President. We'll only know for sure when their transponders switch off in the next few minutes. All I'm suggesting is that you guys should send a few more jets our way just in case."

"I'll have the entire 142nd there in twenty minutes," Lampard yelled.

The President's calm voice took over again. "Is there anything else, Agent Fisher?"

"Yes. There's a third aircraft in the air near the volcano. It's a friendly. Please instruct our pilots not to shoot it down."

"Understood, Agent. What does this aircraft look like?"

"I'll describe it to you, you can't miss it . . ." Fisher began.

Chapter 57

Johnston Ridge

M akani bent over the door to the camera's housing and unlocked it. Inside, she could see everything had power.

There was a keypad with this unit, designed so that it could call the CVO and establish a link.

She reached for it but stopped for a moment. She was trembling, and her hand was shaking too much.

She looked over her shoulder at the rising ash column. She had been close to other volcanoes, like Kilauea, but this was different. The noise coming from Mount St. Helens was shaking her to her core. She'd never felt so small.

Taking a deep breath, she turned back and keyed in the quick code. #1. On the speaker, she could hear the other end begin ringing.

"Pick up, pick up . . ." she pleaded.

* * *

CVO Building

It was chaos around Shirley Wright as geologists scrambled amongst their stations, making sure they didn't lose one bit of data during the eruption. The whole day had been an enormous success so far, except for the mysterious disappearances of Makani and Terrington.

Through the window of her office, she could see Livken working on that issue, talking to an FBI agent.

She turned back to her monitors. One screen was split into twenty smaller screens that displayed views of all the cameras they had pointed at the volcano. By tapping them, she could select which image went to the primary monitor in the control room. At the moment, she had the west camera at Johnston Ridge up and running. It had the best angle on the northern dome, which was due to go at any time. She wondered if the other perspective was worthwhile. She looked at the thumbnail for camera east.

There was movement on it. Someone was there, waving at the camera.

Makani!

She reached for her desk phone. It had six lights on the bottom for the lines dedicated to it. All were flashing, including the little-used one on the right. She punched it and picked up the handset.

"Makani!"

"Shirley! Thank God," Makani answered back.

"Makani, how—"

"It was Terrington. He killed Kris, and he betrayed us all. Shirley, can you get a helicopter to me?"

"Parker's in the air on the south side. I can get him there in twenty minutes," Shirley said. She selected Makani's camera for her screen only and expanded it to full size. She also put the phone on speaker.

Nearby, Livken was now on his cell. He had Parker's phone number on his quick dial. She frantically waved him over.

* * *

Mount St. Helens

Kara read the text on her satellite phone.

Now.

She called Monetti.

"Time to go, Alpha Wolf."

"Roger."

They both took their F-35Bs close to the ash cloud on the north side. Kara looked above her. The plume was spreading in the upper atmosphere. In the future, when the military began its investigation, she and Tony's initial movements would be hidden from satellite cameras. No one would be sure what had happened at this moment.

"Mayday, mayday!" Kara yelled into the microphone in her helmet. "Engine is blowing out!"

"Losing power!" Monetti yelled into his radio. "Mayday! Ash in the engine. Mayday!"

Both cut off their radios and turned off their transponders. Their stealth jets were all but invisible to the world.

They turned north. Ahead, she could see the white dot of the Galaxy Dish. She lined up her F-35B with it.

After refueling, they would continue on to the Gulf of Alaska, where a Russian freighter waited.

On paper, the plan to fly out undetected seemed flawed. Though invisible to radar and flying through unpopulated areas, chances were good that someone the ground would witness their flight and report it to the authorities.

Tonkov had assured them it wouldn't be an issue. At the moment, reports of UFOs and the planes chasing them were overwhelming the government. Phone calls about two jets heading north would be lost in the chaff.

Kara felt reassured, and she was counting her money already.

An alarm from the DAS was pinging. The sensors ringing her jet were detecting something. She engaged the cameras tied to her helmet, and the cockpit disappeared. She took a look around.

Movement caught her eye. The computer already had it singled out. Something was flying below her, heading toward Mount St. Helens. It was flying low, keeping to the canyons. She was surprised when she recognized it.

What's that doing here?

* * *

CVO

"Owen, get in here!" Shirley yelled.

Livken heard her and hustled her way, his cell still up to his ear. Whoever he was talking to on the phone, it seemed important to him.

But so was this. She needed Parker over there, now.

In the main room, alarms went off. The crowd in there whooped and hollered. Someone yelled, "It's happening!"

Looking out her window, she could see the main screen, and her heart sank.

The north dome was erupting.

* * *

Johnston Ridge

Makani heard Shirley moan in despair over the speaker.

Knowing what it meant, she turned around.

The anticipated eruption was happening. An ash plume, several shades darker than the column rising above, was now heading toward her and expanding rapidly.

She spent a moment observing the spectacle. Then she turned to the camera.

"It's happening, Vancouver," she said, looking straight into the lens. "The north face has given away."

Shirley's grief-stricken voice came through the speaker.

"Makani—"

"Shirley, I need you to do me a favor. Record my last words," Makani said. Her voice was even, the fear gone.

"Yes . . . it's ready."

Makani knelt down, taking a breath to compose herself. Memories of her sons filled her mind.

"Kai, Makaio, I'm hoping this message reaches you soon in your time of grief. I want you to know that I've always loved you and that I will always keep on loving you. Please realize that I died doing a job that has brought me much happiness and satisfaction, and that the knowledge gathered this day will help save the lives of thousands in the future."

Makani looked over her shoulder. A wall of ash filled half of her view now.

"My only regret is that I didn't live long enough to see you both grow up into the men you are destined to be. And now all I can ask is that sometime in the future when you stand near the slopes of Kilauea with your families, and the red fountains of lava stretch for the night sky . . ."

She paused for a moment, trying to get the last words out.

"Think of me."

Below her, the ground shook. Her hand stretched to the keypad.

"Shirley, please cut the recording to this camera. I don't want anyone to see what happens next."

On the speaker, Shirley was crying. "Of course, Makani."

Makani's finger rested on the off button for the microphone. Shirley didn't need to hear her cries of pain and terror.

Livken's voice came through, he was excited, shouting.

"Makani! My God, Hanson was right. He told me you were there. Don't hang up!"

"Hanson?" she exclaimed, puzzled.

"He's on my phone, I'll put him on speaker," Livken added.

Hanson's voice came next. It sounded distant.

"Makani? Where exactly are you?"

Since he was on speaker talking to another line on speaker, his voice echoed.

"The east observation deck. Oh, Steve, I'm sorry, the mountain is erupting—"

"I know, I see it. I'm coming to get you, I'm almost there."

She looked up. Behind the camera to her north was the parking lot and road leading up to the observatory. Her despair deepened. If Hanson was driving toward her, there was no escape for him either.

She stood up and looked south. The ash cloud was a wall now, and it filled her entire vision.

They were both doomed, but they wouldn't be alone. She wanted to be near him.

"Do you need me to run for the road?" she asked. It would give them a few seconds.

"No! Stay there . . ." Hanson began.

The wall was closing in, a roiling mass that reached for her.

In front of it, something rose from the canyon and hung above the cliff face and observation platform.

A flying saucer.

It was large, at least forty feet in diameter. It was lit up like a Christmas tree.

Hanson was in its domed topped cockpit, and she could hear his voice coming out of the speaker behind her.

"I'm not using roads," he finished.

Chapter 58

"You're going to have to jump," Hanson commanded.

The flying saucer was level with a fence that kept tourists from falling off the observation deck, but still a hundred feet away. Hanson was coming in fast, and he kept the front end of the saucer down as he approached.

As she did back in high school, she took a brief moment to assess the distance to her mark.

Then she was off.

She raced for the fence thirty feet away. When she got close, she planted her right leg and hopped for it.

She kept her right leg extended and landed on the wooden railing, her left leg up out of habit. She used her forward momentum to step off of the fence with a strong push.

Hanson was still fifteen feet away from the edge at this point. As she hung in the open air, she was briefly cognizant of the two hundred foot drop below.

Then she touched down on the saucer itself with her left foot. It was fifteen feet from the saucer's outer edge to the domed cockpit.

Hanson had it open, and he was stretching his hand out for her. Behind him, the entire world was ash.

She jumped with her left foot and sailed into the rear of the cockpit, a confusing tumble of arms and legs as she rolled around in the back.

Hop. Step. Jump.

"Real-world application!" she yelled.

"Touché," Hanson responded. "Computer, close hatch, and full power to main thrusters!"

The saucer surged ahead, and the wind in Makani's face went away as the Plexiglas dome closed around them with a pneumatic sigh. She pulled herself forward into the copilot's seat.

The cockpit reminded her of the *Dragonfly*, only more. It had three screens instead of one, and it looked like the yoke had more controls.

Hanson was focused on the landscape ahead as he skimmed the ground. One of the screens had the view from a ventral camera. They were passing over the parking lots. Another screen showed what was behind them, and she could see why Hanson wasn't climbing for altitude.

The ash was almost on them. Bits of gravel rattled against the fuselage as the backside of the saucer was partially engulfed. Hanson didn't dare lose speed by climbing.

"Come on, baby," Hanson said through gritted teeth.

Makani reached over and rubbed Hanson's shoulder for luck. They needed all they could get now. He noticed it and gave her a quick grin.

The rattling became louder. Then, inch by inch, they pulled out of it. Hanson pointed the nose of the aircraft up and gained some elevation.

She looked to the rear viewing screen. Johnston Ridge was gone.

Shirley's and Owen's voices were coming over a speaker, crying out her name. She noticed Hanson's phone on a clip.

"Vancouver, I have her. She's okay," Hanson said, leaning toward his phone. "We'll get back to you. All's well that ends well," he finished, looking at her as he hung up the phone.

She stretched over and hugged him.

"How?" she asked, gesturing around them.

"It's the same craft we saw the other night. Kesler calls it the *Roswell*. Fisher and I caught Terrington at the KET site. He told us about you. I convinced Kesler to let me borrow it to go get you. Thank God you were already outside."

They were at a thousand feet, and Hanson eased off on the throttle. Below them, ash swept over the landscape.

"Computer, hover mode," Hanson commanded.

The saucer held its position.

Safe from the volcano, Makani took a moment to study the saucer. Its skin was dark in color, and it had a large tailfin behind the cockpit. On each side of the fin were jet engines, the same that Kesler used on his corporate jets. They provided horizontal thrust.

Built into the saucer were sixteen propellers that gave the craft its vertical lift. Their intakes topside were protected by metal grills, and lit up by red LED lights that lended to the saucer's alien appearance.

An acrylic dome covered the cockpit. It gave the ship a *Jetsons* vibe.

"How does it handle?"

"Like a dream," Hanson answered. "It's a glorified drone, but with a sophisticated computer to cover all the details that come with flight. All I have to do is control the stick. It used to respond to the command word 'Roswell,' but I changed that to 'computer.'"

"Like *Star Trek*," she observed.

"Easier for me to remember," Hanson admitted with a grin.

"You have Terrington. Do you and Fisher have any idea what this is all about?" she asked.

Hanson looked up and nodded ahead of him. She followed his gaze.

High above her, she could see two delta-shaped military jets make a long sweeping turn and point their noses toward the saucer.

"Them," Hanson answered.

Chapter 59

K ara enhanced her helmet display to binocular view, not believing her eyes.

It was the *Roswell,* as she had glimpsed earlier. She was familiar with the hobby airship, as she had given Kesler advice during its construction. She had even taken it out for a spin the other day under the pretense of giving it a test drive before she returned to base. What Kara truly had wanted was a view of the Russians as they attacked the cabin, and to let witnesses record the saucer and seed the hysteria to follow a few days later.

"Why is the *Roswell* here?" Monetti asked on the phone.

"I don't know. I flew it a few days ago, so I know the frequency it uses. I'm switching to that now."

She spoke into her comms. "Cooper, is that you?"

It was quiet for a moment; then she heard a familiar voice.

"Cooper's dead, Lieutenant. *Earth vs. the Flying Saucers* is over," Hanson answered.

Kara couldn't believe it. "Hanson? They told me you were dead."

"Reports of my death are . . . well, you know the rest," Hanson responded. "Kara, listen carefully. The US military knows about you, and everything in the air right now is heading your way. You need to surrender."

Monetti's voice exploded on the comms. "You gotta be kidding me!" he yelled.

"Is that Monetti?" Hanson asked.

Kara heard Makani's voice in the background. "He told me everyone calls him Alpha Wolf."

"Alpha Wolf?" Hanson said, sounding amused. "You know that's not a thing, right? Maybe he should change it to Alpha Chump, the guy who believes everything he hears."

On the radio, Monetti yelled something unintelligible.

Kara spoke over him. "Hanson, we can't turn ourselves over. The military can't take any chances that we will slip away, or fire off a first shot. They are going to shoot us down as soon as they make contact. Even if we land and give ourselves up, the penalty for treason is death."

Hanson was quiet on his end. He most likely realized the same thing.

"But before we go, at least we will have the pleasure of seeing you die first," she said.

Next to her, Monetti howled into his mike as his jet surged forward.

* * *

"Here he comes," Makani said. "What are they flying?"

"F-35Bs," Hanson answered grimly. "The most advanced weapon on the planet."

He spun the *Roswell* around and put it in a steep dive toward the billowing blanket of ash below them.

"What are you doing?" Makani yelled as the air began to whine around them.

"Evening the odds," Hanson answered. Alarms in the cockpit were sounding off. He ignored them. "If we're to survive this, I need to bring this ship as close to the volcano's event horizon as I possibly can."

"What's the event horizon?"

"The point of no return," Hanson answered. "Fasten your seatbelt!"

Again, ash filled their entire view. Hanson skimmed above the top of it and continued toward the crater itself.

She hoped he knew what he was doing.

* * *

Monetti switched to DAS and focused on the saucer in front of him. Hanson was hugging the layer of ash below them, and he had also turned off the saucer's flashing lights. Was he trying to blend in?

It didn't matter. His F-35B was currently equipped with Aim-9 Sidewinders, air to air missiles that homed in on enemy aircraft's heat signatures. The display on his helmet visor already showed weapons lock.

The missile wasn't hanging off a hard point on his wing. It was kept in a weapons bay in his jet's fuselage to help maintain his stealth profile.

The bay door opened, and the Sidewinder rolled out. Its rocket engine ignited, and it streaked forward.

"Fox two," Monetti shouted gleefully. "Eat that, you beta-cuck!"

* * *

"He's fired something at us," Makani yelled.

"It's a heat seeking-missile," Hanson said, concentrating on his flying. The vertical column of ash was fast approaching. "It's locking onto our engine."

"Can we avoid it?"

"That depends, Doctor, on hot that ash is!"

Hanson knew the weapon. After meeting Kara the other night, he had looked up F-35Bs online out of curiosity, going through *Wikipedia* articles and *YouTube* videos on their capabilities and armament.

The Sidewinder had forward scanning infrared scopes that could discriminate against background signals as it homed in on its target's heat plume.

But Hanson was betting nobody had taken a volcano into consideration when they designed the thing.

He banked the *Roswell* hard left. The ship protested the move as its propellers strained to follow the instructions he and the airship's onboard computers were giving it.

The missile rocketed past them by a few feet, unable to track the saucer's heat signature.

For its sensors, this close to the volcanic ash, the entire horizon was a heat signature.

It plowed into the ash column, exploding as it did so.

"You missed, Alpha Chump," Hanson goaded.

"Then let's make this up close and personal," Monetti's voice roared over the ship's speaker.

Hanson looked at his rear scope. The F-35B was closing, slipping in behind him.

Hanson kept close to the column, heading east along the volcano's crater.

This near to the edge, he noticed it was more than ash. Huge, house-sized boulders were being flung into the air. They reached their apogee at several hundred yards above the volcano, hung there a bit, and then fell back to the earth. Hanson adjusted his altitude to match where the debris field of slow moving boulders was forming.

"What are you doing?" Makani asked, her eyes wide.

"Don't worry. Back in the day, this used to be my best game," Hanson answered.

He flew the *Roswell* into the debris, dodging boulders as he did so. He kept half an eye on the ventral camera and jinked left as smaller and faster rocks went hurtling past. For another, he had to lower his profile to the ground by tilting the airship seventy degrees. Next to him Makani yelped in fear at each near miss.

"Is he still behind us?" Hanson asked.

She turned. "Yes!"

"Computer, launch flares!" Hanson commanded.

* * *

Monetti accelerated toward Hanson. He didn't want to lose him in this mess.

Hanson was flying through a stream of boulders hanging in the sky, slowing down a bit as he navigated them.

Monetti took it as a challenge from Hanson.

Come in here if you dare.

He closed the gap and pressed the trigger.

The gun pod mounted below the F-35B sprayed a hail of 25mm shells at fifty-five rounds per second. Having only 220 bullets on board, he kept it a short burst.

He was dead on target, but a boulder passed between him and Hanson and blocked his shot, fracturing apart as his bullets tore into it.

Monetti swore as he dodged another boulder. The invisible cockpit gave him an advantage; he could see the rocks approaching from below.

Ahead of him, three bright points of lights launched from the *Roswell*.

A weapon? To Monetti, they looked like photon torpedoes from a *Star Trek* episode. It took him half a second to process what he was seeing, and determine that they were harmless flares.

But that half a second of distraction was enough. As Monetti glanced back down, he could see the instrument of his death racing up to meet him. He cried out in rage as a boulder slammed into the bottom of his jet and his F-35B exploded.

* * *

"Unbelievable!" Makani shouted. She was looking over her shoulder at the remains of the jet that had been behind them a moment before.

"I know," Hanson answered excitedly. "Usually, I'm rooting against the saucer!"

Shaking her head, Makani was about to respond but Kara screaming over the radio interrupted her.

"You'll pay for that, Hanson!"

The second F-35B dove toward them

"I hope you have a few more tricks up your sleeve," Makani said, looking over her shoulder again.

"I do, but you're not going to like it," Hanson replied. He kept the *Roswell* pointed east.

They came alongside the gap in the ash curtain stretching toward Central Washington. Gravity was causing it to collapse, and it looked like it would continue to exist for only a few more minutes.

He steered into it. The 'wormhole' through the ash was about a mile long, and only a few hundred yards across. With the sun blotted out, the world darkened around them.

"Steve!" Makani yelled out in fear.

He sensed it too. This close to Mount St. Helens, he could both hear and feel the volcano's roar. It seemed to pass through him. He felt the same as he had back at the Garbers, and again goosebumps rose on his arms. The mountain was generating infrasound, causing unreasoning terror.

"Don't worry, she'd have to be crazy to follow us in here," Hanson told her.

He steered the *Roswell* through the vortex. Above and around them ash swirled. Below, on the volcano's south slope, a pyroclastic cloud flowed downward.

"Look out for those rocks!" Makani warned. She was looking to the side.

Hanson looked over also, ready to dodge, but he saw nothing. She must have imagined it in her excitement.

Hanson began relaxing as they neared the other end of the ash tunnel. They were going to make it.

"She's behind us," Makani said.

Hanson checked the monitor. Kara's jet was racing toward them. She would reach the far end at almost the same time.

"Time for Plan B," Hanson announced.

They exited the wormhole's far side, and warm sunlight and blue sky greeted them. Hanson could see the Columbia River and the metro area. News helicopters were distant specks.

He banked left. That was for show for the pilot behind him. Out of Kara's view for a moment, he dropped down and swung back right. He held the *Roswell* there, hoping that when Kara shot out of the vortex, she would miss him and continue on east.

The F-35B came screaming out, keeping its bottom to Hanson as it turned away.

"What now?" Makani said.

"Now we pass through one more time," Hanson answered. "When the wormhole collapses behind us, we'll have a curtain of ash between us and her."

Hanson entered the vortex again, leaving the warm sun behind. Inside, the tunnel was already smaller, giving the illusion that the far end was further away. He pushed the yoke forward.

"Steve!" Makani yelled.

The F-35B drifted into the ash cavern with them. It was only a few hundred feet away.

It didn't shoot past their position. Kara was transitioning into hover mode. Several panels were open on the jet's topside, exposing the intakes for vertical thrusters, and the rear exhaust nozzle was now pointed downward.

Kara's mocking voice came over the radio. "Sorry, Hanson, but this jet has no blind spots."

Hanson jinked right as the gun slung under the F-35B's belly roared as it spat a burst of bullets. They were tracers, and Hanson could see them slide along the *Roswell's* fuselage.

Both airships danced with each other, Hanson doing his best to keep out of Kara's sights while she tried to track him. She fired off another burst, and bullets screamed past the saucer's cockpit dome.

"Computer, route power to vertical thrusters," Hanson yelled.

Hanson knew he had several advantages. The *Roswell's* multiple fans and light airframe gave him more maneuverability.

And Kara was limited in the number of rounds she had. And with her gun's high fire rate she only had two shots left.

Hanson tried to move around to her backside, minimizing his profile to her as he did so.

She followed him, firing off a burst. Some of the bullets tore into the *Roswell's* left side, taking out a propeller. The saucer began to feel sluggish in Hanson's hands, and smoke trailed from it.

"You're like a forty-foot bullseye, Hanson," Kara shouted.

"Look out for the rocks!" Makani warned again.

Makani yelling wasn't helping. Hanson was going to tell her to quiet down, but then he finally picked up on what she was seeing. The volcano's infrasound was messing with their eyes. He, too, was seeing the grey blobs at the edge of his vision. He remembered how Calderone had terrified the Garbers with his ghost stories.

The power of suggestion.

Hanson dropped below Kara, hoping that he would have to time to pull off what he was thinking. It was getting tighter in the wormhole, and darker. And the opening to the outside world was closing.

"Call them out to me, Makani. Between the two of us, we should be able to dodge them!"

* * *

Hanson slipped below her. With her helmet, Kara was able to follow him as once again he tried to get around her.

She held back on her last shot and let him dance. She was

stalling. Soon the volcano would have them both. If he tried to make a run for it, she would shoot him in the back.

Through her radio, she could hear the geologist yelling in terror.

"Hanson, boulders to your right! More below you!"

Kara looked around her. Flying debris had brought Monetti down. Was the same thing happening here?

It was. Car sized rocks were raining out of the ash, and Kara jinked right as one crossed her vision and almost hit her.

Now the boulders were all around her. With a cry of fear, she pulled up on her stick and rolled left and up. The rock she dodged went whizzing by.

Sighing with relief, she brought her yoke back before she got too close to the ceiling of ash above her.

She kept drifting the wrong way.

Hanson was still below her, the saucer visible under her cockpit. He had the *Roswell* pressed under one of her wings, adding to her momentum toward the ash. The *Roswell's* cockpit must had been right next to one of her DAS cameras, for she could see Hanson's face clearly. He had the grim expression of someone who knew exactly what he was doing.

"Computer, more power," Hanson shouted over the radio.

She tried to compensate, but with Hanson pushing, she couldn't stop her drift. The swirling ash caught her tail fin.

Then, in an instant, it pulled her in. Everything that she could see with her helmet went dark. She became disoriented as her jet spun around.

The engine shut down as the ash overwhelmed the intakes. Her canopy collapsed from the pressure, and she screamed as the searing ash filled her lungs.

* * *

The F-35B disappeared from their view, and Hanson eased back from the edge.

"Now, to get out of here."

"Oh, no," Makani moaned.

He saw the reason for her despair. A hundred yards away, the wormhole closed, and darkness engulfed them.

They were too late.

On the rear camera monitor there was a small, bright circle.

The proverbial light at the end of the tunnel.

Hanson spun the saucer one hundred eighty degrees.

"Hang on," he yelled as he pushed the yoke forward.

One mile away, the far end was still open. The *Roswell* raced for it.

"Computer, max power to forward thrusters," Hanson commanded.

The airship leaped forward. Around them, the wormhole was collapsing. The swirling walls were now only a hundred feet apart from each other.

Makani was leaning into him again, rubbing his right shoulder. They needed all the luck in the world right now.

"Come on, come on, come on!" Hanson yelled.

Gravelly bits of the ash was raining on the fuselage. The *Roswell* was shaking, and for a moment, everything was grey.

Then they shot out of the ash curtain's north side. Both Hanson and Makani shouted in relief as the saucer gained altitude.

Hanson took them several miles away. They were down one prop, but the *Roswell* seemed to be holding up. He ordered the ship into hover mode. Nearby, Mount St. Helens continued erupting. Lightning bolts lanced up and down the massive ash column. Awed, Hanson took in the view, remembering his helicopter trip a week ago. This wasn't something that one saw every day.

Next to him, he heard the sound of a seatbelt releasing. Then, warm lips on his.

The spectacle of the century was playing out before him. He turned from it and focused on her. His arms wrapped around Makani, her hair tickling his forearms, and he held her close as he returned her kiss.

After a long moment, they separated.

"Thanks for the lift," she murmured.

"Now see, you get it," Hanson said, gesturing at the flying ship. "I had to explain it earlier to Fisher—"

A half dozen F-15s roaring by interrupted him. They swung back and circled the flying saucer. Hanson could see one of the pilots tapping his helmet near his ear.

"Computer, scan radio channels, strongest signal," Hanson commanded.

Soon, a voice reached them.

"—can you hear me?"

"We hear you, Eagle," Hanson answered.

"We're looking for two F-35s," the Eagle pilot announced.

"The volcano has them, it's just us," Hanson answered.

The pilot didn't immediately respond. Hanson could see him, and the others, study the flying saucer as they took turns making passes.

"Understood. The President wants us to make sure you make it home safe. She wants to talk to you when she can."

Hanson looked over at Makani with a grin. She rolled her eyes. She knew what was coming.

"Then take us to your leader. We come in peace," Hanson responded.

Chapter 60

Portland, Wednesday, 3:10 p.m. PDT

"You look good on TV," Hanson said.

"Thanks," Fisher answered. He was petting Bingo at the cat tower in the corner of Hanson's living room. He and Hanson, along with Makani, were watching the FBI's earlier press conference held outside their field office.

"Though I still feel you two should get some sort of recognition," Fisher added.

"I'm good with how things stand," Makani said. She was scratching Sebastian's forehead, who was lounging on the couch's backrest. "I have more exposure than I want with the pilot rescue a few days back. I don't need any more attention. Fortunately, the deal Steve swung with the President keeps me out of some of the limelight."

"The President told me over the phone that she owed me a big favor, and asked me what I wanted," Hanson explained further, shrugging his shoulders. "I asked her to leave us out of it."

"And I'm grateful," Makani said. She was wearing her khaki

shorts again and the blue t-shirt with Mount St. Helens on it. At the moment, the message printed below seemed more poignant.

Where Were You When Mount St. Helens Erupted?

"But still, it can't be easy to hide your involvement," Fisher said.

"Not really," Hanson answered. "Except for Russian spies, no one else was at the cabin when they attacked as Bigfoots, and I'm off-camera during the crater rescue. Cameras were also kept on the wrong side of the ash column yesterday. As far as anyone knows, I'm just a guy who couldn't keep his skeptical blog up and running during this crisis."

On the television screen, Fisher was standing behind SAC Jacobs, who was talking to the press.

"Also, the Apex computer connection was already a matter of national security, and the President swore us, and everyone involved, to secrecy," Hanson added. "Even Livken and Wright, the only two at the CVO who knows what happened, can't talk about it. That helps set up the FBI's cover story. Who came up with that?"

"Director Knox," Fisher answered. "From the public's point of view, the FBI cracked the case of the Russians trying to steal our F-35Bs. The 142nd was called in at the nick of time and downed them at the volcano. Video backs this up. The Eagles can be seen rushing into action, disappearing behind the wall of ash. We also let the nation know that the Coast Guard is escorting a Russian freighter out of the Gulf of Alaska and that Kesler was duped."

"What about Terrington?" Makani asked.

"With my input, Knox laid out Russia's attempt at creating a panic in the United States, and he explained the entire UFO scare to the nation, complete with the 'Bigfoot' warm-up last week to set the mood. We are including Terrington as a part of that, a well-paid mole in the CVO guiding the men disguised as Bigfoot so they wouldn't be caught by geologists exploring the volcano. Steinsson was killed because he was suspicious of him, which gives our lie a dash of truth."

Both cats leaped up and ran into the kitchen as they heard

Hanson crack open a can of cat food. After a minute, Hanson walked back into the living room.

"What's being done with Terrington?" Hanson asked.

"He was facing the death penalty for treason. For his life, we swung a deal that just might help turn this entire debacle around. First, he led us to the ship docked in Seattle that was to take him and the Russian agents out of the country. We quietly took the last of them into custody."

On the television, a photograph of Terrington's face was displayed.

"We're telling the world that we are still looking for him. What is really happening is that we are putting together a false file of nuclear secrets. With Terrington's help, we are going to transmit that, and some malware, to the Russians. There's a chance that we can turn the tables on them."

"So that, and the attempted hack on Apex, is off the history books?" Hanson asked.

"Yes. President Hayes is covering her political ass," Fished answered. "If word got out that she put critical national secrets in jeopardy, she would be in a world of trouble." Fisher's phone pinged. He briefly looked at it.

"It's Kesler. His employees are going to be okay," Fisher said, turning away. "That reminds me, I'm going to check on Spiros; he's awake now." Fisher put his hand on the door and gave them one last look. "Steve, thanks for your help. It's been an educational experience." He turned to Makani. "Good luck with your interviews tomorrow, Doctor. And remember, being sworn to secrecy by the President is a serious matter. Don't tell anyone about Apex."

"We won't, though keeping secrets from those closest to you doesn't sound easy," Hanson said. "Has something like this ever happened to you in your line of work?"

"Only once, after that week I spent in Area 51," Fisher answered.

Stunned, Hanson stared at the FBI agent. Fisher's face was a mask of seriousness.

"You're kidding . . . right?" Hanson asked uncertainly.

Fisher's face broke into a grin. "Of course I'm kidding. Geez, Hanson, for a skeptic, you're sure are gullible," Fisher laughed. The cats scampered to the window as he shut the door and walked toward his SUV.

Shaking his head ruefully, Hanson turned toward Makani, taking a step toward her.

"And what's on your slate?" he asked.

"The volcano's quiet now," she answered. "It stopped erupting in the early evening. I have about a week left here, then it's back to Hawaii." Her eyes were distant as she paused for a moment. "I need to see my sons," she added.

"Are you ready for your interviews tomorrow?"

"With all of the morning shows? No. But they want more details now on the crater rescue, and I can't hide forever. I'm just wondering what to say. How do I start?"

They were both drifting toward each other in the living room. At the window, the cats watched Fisher drive away.

"At the beginning, I guess," Hanson answered. "You have a compelling story. A young girl already set on being a geologist at six years of age . . ." Hanson thought about it for a moment. "What happened back then, did you have an epiphany?"

They were side by side now. She looked a little embarrassed.

"I didn't tell you at first because I knew how you feel about these things."

Hanson tilted his head quizzically.

"When I was six, my father took me out to see Kilauea at night. As we approached volcano, I could see the lava fountains in the distance.

"We got a flat a mile out, the front left. My dad pulled over to work on it. I hung out by the right rear bumper to watch the volcano.

"And that's when I saw Pele.

"She was walking up the road behind us. I knew it was her. I had heard stories of people occasionally seeing the Goddess of Fire and Volcanoes on that very highway.

"She looked thirsty from her walk, so I offered her my juice box. She drank it down with a smile of gratitude. I reached into the car to get another, but when I turned back—"

"She was gone," Hanson filled in.

"I didn't tell you because I thought you wouldn't believe me," she finished.

She was right. Hanson knew her story as a version of an urban legend. One of the oldest and most common.

The Vanishing Hitchhiker. People all over the world had tales of seeing someone walking along the road late at night, briefly caught in their car's headlights. When the driver looks to their rearview mirror, the apparition is gone. Some stories go even further. The hitchhiker is picked up and has a conversation with the driver, only to disappear from the back seat a few moments later.

Makani was still standing close to him. She had a look of trepidation on her face as she waited for Hanson to explain that what she saw was simply her imagination.

Now was not the time. He thought of a question to ask her instead.

"And what does the Goddess of Volcanoes look like?" he asked with a smile.

"She appears as an old woman with long white hair. She wears a red muumuu, and she is always accompanied by a white dog."

The smile on Hanson's face was gone, replaced with one of shocked amazement.

She saw his expression.

"Please, tell me what you are thinking."

He reached out and pulled her close.

"I'm thinking that sometimes, it's best to leave some things in the 'unexplained' column."

He kissed her. Her arms wrapped around his waist and held him tight, her body pressing onto his. The cats protested at being ignored by winding between their legs.

Her hands slipped underneath his shirt and up his back. She kicked off her sandals and began backing up, pulling him with her towards the couch.

"I'm hoping you can stay here until you fly back to Hawaii," Hanson said, stepping out of his own shoes.

"Oh, I will," she answered, now tugging his belt off. "I have to make sure you're safe."

"From what, Doctor?"

"There are hundreds of active volcanoes in the world. I need to make sure no one tosses you in one as a sacrifice."

"I'm not a virgin!"

"So you say," she said, now dragging him down with her. "All I know is that I will never rest easy until I'm absolutely sure."

Epilogue

Six weeks later

Moscow

General Baranov dropped a large bundle of papers on Tonkov's desk.

"A list of my failures, *tovarisch?*" Tonkov asked.

"They are many this time, Tonkov," Baranov stated.

General Baranov was Tonkov's superior. As head of the Second Directorate, Tonkov only answered to the military's highest officer, the Chief of the General Staff.

And he didn't look happy.

Tonkov wasn't worried. He had been playing this game for decades now. He carried many secrets, aces up his sleeve should he need to put pressure on the right people to cover his ass.

He had used one of those aces in the late 1990s when Baranov's own son was tasked to investigate Tonkov for corruption. Tonkov had him killed, and had made it look like the bomb used was set by

Chechenian rebels. The ruse was so complete that Baranov never even suspected that Tonkov had been behind it.

"I admit Project Rod, my plan to draw the two F-35B Lightnings to us, didn't work. But Project Front Door did! They never caught Terrington, and he was able to connect with Chernov and transmit the nuclear secrets to us. Think of the advantages that gives us. Surely it tempers the loss of the F-35s."

Baranov looked at the papers. "The Americans fooled you, Tonkov. The nuclear data was all a lie."

Tonkov felt anger rising in him.

"What makes you think that?"

"The Americans themselves told me. I received a message from them. They moved against your operatives in the states last night, capturing most of them. The rest are compromised, and trying to make their way back home."

Tonkov was stunned. "How did they know who to target?"

"Terrington. He didn't escape. The FBI had him in their custody. Their computer specialists were the ones who transmitted the data to us."

Baranov moved over to a window and looked out.

"When Chernov downloaded the data that was sent, malware came along with it. As usual, Chernov saved that data for us. But I've come to learn that he had a habit of routing information to his own storage disks. He did that regularly, so that he could sell our hard-won secrets on the side. The American's program copied all of the data that Chernov had been gathering. That information was sent then sent back to America."

Tonkov couldn't believe it. Everything was in ruins. But something didn't make sense.

"Why would the Americans tip their hand to you? If they had kept quiet, they could have done much more damage to us."

"There's a loose end the Americans want to take care of."

Tonkov's heart went cold. He could guess what that loose end was. He looked to his top desk drawer. He had a gun in it.

"I realize this has been a disaster," Tonkov said, turning his chair so that he had a better angle to the drawer. "But not one worthy of execution for someone of my stature."

Now Baranov was moving away from the window. He stopped on the far side of the desk.

"Normally, no," Baranov said. "But the Americans told me something else. They let me know how you had my son killed."

"A lie! How would they even know such a thing?"

"You should not have trusted Chernov. All this time that you have been working with him, he has also been in your own computer, General. You had many secrets. He saved them all."

Tonkov realized there was no way out of this. He lunged for his drawer.

Baranov already had his gun out. It was an OTs-38 sound-suppressed revolver. Its silencer was integrally built-in, so one didn't have to screw a cumbersome suppressor to it. It was compact and easily hidden.

It also had a laser sight. A small red dot was on Tonkov's chest.

"Baranov! *Nyet!* The Americans, they want you to do this. You're being used by them!"

"I know, *tovarisch.* I'm just going to have to live with that."

Baranov squeezed the trigger, and a bullet quietly pierced Tonkov's chest.

Vladivostok

Chernov grunted when he hit the floor.

The fall was painful. His hands were cuffed behind his back, and he had a dark hood over his head. His face smashed into the ground.

Judging by the sound of jet engines nearby, he guessed he was in the belly of a large cargo transport.

He wondered why. Just an hour ago, he had been in a Vladivostok casino, gambling with the money he had gained from crypto-mining Europe's supercomputers. He had planned to use more of that money to hire prostitutes to keep him company later in the evening.

But then he had been grabbed in broad daylight and taken to an airport. None of his captors had spoken to him on the way over.

The cuff on his right hand was undone while he was on the ground. Then he was roughly picked up and made to sit in a chair, and the cuff was attached to it.

Footsteps retreated. The sound of a large door being closed filled the air. Chernov removed his hood with his free hand.

As he guessed, he was sitting in a fold-out seat against the fuselage of a large cargo plane. What surprised him was the man sitting across from him.

"Gontarev! What is happening?"

The Russian troll was in the same state he was, though, of course, less well dressed. He looked forlorn as he addressed Chernov.

"Siberia! I am being punished for my failures."

"But what about me? I delivered the nuclear files as promised."

"It was a trap. One of the soldiers here told me. The Americans knew what we were doing. Terrington must have been aiding them. They used a program to get into your files, Siberia. They took everything."

Chernov blanched. He was planning on selling those files in the near future. The things he knew . . . .

The engines were being revved up. The plane was moving.

"Do you know where they're taking us?

The Russian troll gave the hacker known as Siberia a mirthless smile.

"You're going to find this ironic . . . ."

* * *

Washington DC, Andrews Joint Base

"Where are you taking me?" Terrington asked.

He was handcuffed to a seat on the side of a large military cargo plane. It was the middle of the night. Activity was minimal where the aircraft was parked.

"You have been declared a traitor and a terrorist, Donald. We have places overseas for people like you," Chief of Staff Elaina Prichard answered.

Terrington was glad to be alive, but he didn't like the sound of that.

"What if the American public asks questions? Even someone like me has rights."

"The public thinks you are still at large. We can hold you indefinitely, and no one will know."

Terrington looked her over. Prichard was a tall and attractive woman with long blonde hair. He wondered if the President had chosen her because she looked good on camera. A crafty look came over his face.

"Maybe you should rethink my accommodations. You know, somewhere more comfortable," Terrington said. "Guards can talk. What would happen if I passed along what the President did with the Apex supercomputer?"

Prichard glared at Terrington. She brought out a phone and held it to the geologist.

"Russian secrets weren't the only things in Siberia's files," she said.

The phone was running a video. It was one of Terrington's own, a recording of him with a child. He recalled it was one of his favorites.

Prichard stopped the video. Her voice was ice. "I wonder what would happen if this recording ever wound up in the hands of your cellmates."

Fear gripped Terrington. "They torture and kill people like me in prison!" he said.

"That would be an unfortunate development," Prichard said. "Do we have an understanding, Donald?"

Outside, the plane's engines were starting up. Terrington weakly nodded his head.

* * *

Highway 26, halfway between the Oregon Coast and Portland

The blue sign in his headlights spelled out *View Point*. Hanson slowed down and turned left onto the graveled patch of ground.

His daughter, Elanor, looked up from her phone.

"Why are you stopping?" she asked.

"It's a lookout for Mount St. Helens. We're on the eastern slope of the Coast Range Mountains," Hanson answered. "This spot has a clear view of the volcano. Your grandmother and I used to stop here every time we made the trip to Portland."

She held up both hands, a dramatic emphasis to her next point.

"But it's dark out," she said.

"It'll be worth it. Come on," Hanson said, exiting the *Galileo 7*.

They stood at the hood of the van, facing northeast. She was already almost as tall as him. Her hair was long and the same color as his, as were her eyes. She had his ex-wife's beautiful face. She was one of the few things they had gotten right in their marriage.

They were returning from a weekend trip to his mother's place. After his several close calls with death, Hanson appreciated the time with his loved ones.

The landscape was dark. Mount St. Helens, now dormant, couldn't be seen in the gloom.

"Told you," his daughter said.

"Look up."

Above them, the stars were brilliant, and countless.

"Wow, I didn't know there were so many."

"That's because we can't see them when we're in the city," Hanson said. "When our eyes adjust to the darkness a bit more, maybe we will be able to see the Milky Way."

They stood there together, and Hanson glanced back to where Mount St. Helens rested under the night sky.

He remembered past stops here, forcing his mother to pull aside. He wasn't interested in the mountain itself, but what it represented.

It was the home of Bigfoot. He had stared at the then peaked mountain top, and dreamt of going there and finding the gentle giants himself.

Then the mountain erupted, and he grew up. He began to disbelieve the strange and unusual, and the people who promoted them.

But there were a few notable exceptions, and Kenneth Arnold was one of them.

Hanson still believed the pilot from Idaho had seen something that bright summer day. He had been meticulous in his observation, taking time to study and notice important details. And since the encounter was one of the first, his sighting had been uncluttered by prejudice.

He had reported the event not for fame, but out of civic duty. The Cold War had just started. The threat of the enemy in America's skies was real. Arnold had felt someone should know.

He had gained nothing and only earned hardship for his family as people constantly hounded them for answers they could not give. Despite that, he had stuck with his story to the end.

Hanson looked at the dark forest around him. He used to gaze deep into the woods as he made this trip in his youth, hopeful to catch a glimpse of Bigfoot. He didn't anymore.

He turned his face up, as his daughter was doing next to him.

But he still looked to the night sky whenever he had a chance.

And wondered.

Afterword

Write what you love.

That's a piece of advice I found online, replacing the limiting phrase 'write what you know.' I took it to heart, realizing writing would be easier if I focused on something I was passionate about.

And I do love the strange and unusual.

I was born in 1964, and thus a child of the seventies. It was a weird decade, and I'm not talking about disco and flared pants.

Bigfoot's popularity was exploding on television. With him he brought along the Loch Ness Monster, Easter Island, the Nazca Lines of Peru, The Bermuda Triangle, and Stonehenge. The unexplained was being paraded in front of my young eyes.

I ate it up. Who drew those huge figures in Peruvian deserts? What did a Scottish plesiosaur eat? And sailing the waters east of Florida? Worst idea ever.

Like Hanson, I had my watershed moment in belief of the paranormal. It was the infamous 'surgeon's photograph' of the Loch Ness Monster that did me in. The fact that a surgeon had taken the photo lent an air of respectability to the grainy black and white image. A surgeon wouldn't lie about such things.

Well, guess what?

He lied.

The photo was taken by an acquaintance of his who had a beef with the local newspaper and wanted to make them look like fools. Forty years later, that same photo suckered me in also.

The revelation of that hoax started my transition into skepticism. I still went to the library to check out books from the *Time Life; Mysteries of the Unknown*, a 33-volume set, but I was now tempering that with reading various skeptic publications. The journey to rational thought was a slow process.

But I still find the paranormal fascinating, so now we are back to writing what you love. I had a broad range of subjects to write about, (as noted above, 33-volume set). What would be both interesting and timely?

It was around this time that the 'Storm Area 51' raid was coming to a head. Someone online had posted the idea of overwhelming the security of Area 51, a secretive military base in the Nevada desert, and finding and revealing to the world the corpses of the alien bodies stored there.

The idea took a life of its own, and the media reported that the government and locals were worried about the strain on local resources if thousands arrived at the gates of the base.

Their worries were unwarranted. Only a hundred fifty people, and a handful of media, showed up. As I watched a reporter broadcast the event to his studio with a patch of empty desert behind him, I felt disappointment. Storm Area 51 was turning out to be a nonevent.

Then a kid, his arms held out behind him, raced across the screen in the background.

He was emulating the 'Naruto Run,' a style of sprinting in which characters from the anime series *Naruto* can outrace even bullets. Earlier postings on the web had foreshadowed that the alien liberators were going to employ this style of running to confound Area 51's guards.

I laughed out loud when I saw it.

And then wondered how we all came to this moment in history.

I grew up in the Pendleton, Oregon area, and my dad worked at the *East Oregonian*. He informed me of the Kenneth Arnold incident and the local connection in 1997, the event's fiftieth anniversary. I was living in the epicenter of flying saucers. I decided to set my story around them.

Bigfoot is also a fixture of the Pacific Northwest lore, so I included the creature. And since it laired on Mount St. Helens, memories of an erupting volcano loomed large in my mind also.

But are these subjects relevant today? I thought so. Nearly seventy years ago, due to hysteria around Washington DC, the nation reacted to false information, and saw flying saucers where there were none. Our government worried that foreign influences could jeopardize our nation.

And their predictions are becoming real now. The web, though full of information, is rife with misinformation. The CIA was right; an opposing nation's misdirection can cause us to harm ourselves. Though instead of panic due to alien invasion, our population struggles over the merits of vaccinations and medical advice while foreign powers fan the flames.

But that said, it is not my intention to stomp on paranormal fans' fun. There are festivals, parades, and conventions in honor of aliens and Bigfoot. And when I watch video of these events, all I see is a group of people having a good time in the pursuit of what they love doing.

That's cool.

But while I don't want to squash another person's dreams and pursuits, I do want people to understand how we got here (while reading a thrilling story). Like I did, go back to the beginning. Read the articles and the newspaper clippings. Understand how it all truly began.

As for me, there will always be a small part that hopes to witness the paranormal, the extraordinary. A lot of it is gone for me, but, like

Hanson's wall in his study, aliens are still a question mark. Does intelligent life outside our world exist? Due to sheer probability I believe it does. Are they flying spacecraft in our atmosphere?

Doubtful.

I could have said no. But, nearly seventy-five years ago, on a bright and clear June afternoon, I believe Kenneth Arnold saw something that will always remain in the unexplained column.

And for that, I am grateful.

Acknowledgments

I would like to thank my parents, Bill and Barb Andrus.

When I announced the improbable goal of writing and publishing a book, their faith in my ability to do so never wavered, though I sometimes did. It kept me going through the trying times when producing a book seemed like a pipe dream.

Mom passed away a few months before this book was printed, but memories of her confidence in me still kept me going. That, and my dad's continuing support.

More family has helped me along the way. My daughter, Maggie, and my brother and sister, Mark and Stephanie. Their confidence in me also never wavered.

Four friends have stood by me since the early eighties. Craig, Mac, Ron, and Tim have endured almost four decades of *Dungeons & Dragons* fan fiction written by me. They are the best, and I am thankful for their support during my writing.

And special thanks to Joyce. Her encouragement meant everything to me.

This being a self-published book, I searched the internet to put together a small team to assist me in releasing my story to the world.

I would like to thank Amanda Nicole Ryan, a beta-reader I found on Fiverr. Her enthusiasm and input on the novel were invaluable.

Beth Hale of Magnolia Author Services, and Lauren of Ebook Launch, helped with the editing. Thanks for cleaning up after me! Not an easy job with a debut writer.

For the interior layout and formatting I turned to Brady Moller at Fiverr. The inside of the book looks amazing because of him.

For the awesome cover on the book I want to thank Jeff Brown, of Jeff Brown Graphics. Are there people out there who judge a book by its cover? I'm hoping so.

Thanks to Kathryn B. Brown, owner of the *East Oregonian*, for her help in obtaining and letting me use the original Kenneth Arnold article, an important moment in UFO history. I appreciate her for allowing me to reprint it.

And finally, I have gratitude to you, reader. I hope you enjoyed the story.

About the Author

Matt Andrus is a native to the Pacific Northwest and is currently residing in Olympia, Washington. Whenever he gets the chance, he is at his desk writing his next story, while the family cat naps nearby.

And though he is a skeptic, he is still a fan of the paranormal, and is always vigilant for the weird and unusual when exploring the area

To Follow this author on his website:
https://www.mattandrus.com

Made in the USA
Middletown, DE
22 October 2020

22552840R10215